"MAYBE THE WOMEN OF YOUR CIRCLE ENJOY THESE GAMES, BUT I DON'T BECAUSE I DON'T KNOW THE RULES."

Galen straightened slowly. "You are really telling me no, aren't you?"

"Yes, Galen. No more gowns or anything else. Are we agreed?"

"No," he replied. "Call it the selfish desire of a wealthy man, but I refuse to give you up without a proper fight." He took her hands and gently urged her to her feet. "And what I want is this . . ."

Hester could have stopped what came next, but when he leaned down and softly brushed his lips across her own it was already too late.

"Feel what you do to me . . ." he murmured thickly. "This is no game . . ."

Other AVON ROMANCES

A MAN'S TOUCH *by Rosalyn West*
MINX *by Julia Quinn*
SCANDALOUS SUZANNE *by Glenda Sanders*
SOMEONE LIKE YOU *by Susan Sawyer*
SPRING RAIN *by Susan Weldon*
WICKED AT HEART *by Danelle Harmon*
WINTERBURN'S ROSE *by Kate Moore*

Coming Soon

LOVE ME NOT *by Eve Byron*
THE MACKENZIES: FLINT *by Ana Leigh*

And Don't Miss These
ROMANTIC TREASURES
from Avon Books

LADY OF WINTER *by Emma Merritt*
WILD ROSES *by Miriam Minger*
YOU AND NO OTHER *by Cathy Maxwell*

INDIGO

BEVERLY JENKINS

AVON BOOKS ◆ NEW YORK

INDIGO is an original publication of Avon Books. This work has never before appeared in book form. This work is a novel. Any similarity to actual persons or events is purely coincidental.

AVON BOOKS
A division of
The Hearst Corporation
1350 Avenue of the Americas
New York, New York 10019

Copyright © 1996 by Beverly E. Jenkins
Inside cover author photo © 1995 Glamour Shots
Published by arrangement with the author
Library of Congress Catalog Card Number: 96-96432
ISBN: 0-380-78658-3

First Avon Books Printing: November 1996

AVON TRADEMARK REG. U.S. PAT. OFF. AND IN OTHER COUNTRIES, MARCA REGISTRADA, HECHO EN U.S.A.

Printed in the U.S.A.

RA 10 9 8 7 6 5 4 3 2 1

The art of creative writing is in and of itself a solitary endeavor, but you can't be successful without guidance and input. It's a bit like trying to build a house with a single brick.

So, thanks to the following individuals for their support.

My agent, Nancy Yost. When I threw a "Hail Mary" into the end zone with no time left, she caught it and scored! Great hands!

My editor, Christine Zika, who always makes me dig deeper.

Jill Hipple and Nancy Kuzniar, two of the best keyboard goddesses I know.

My mother, Delores, who has made it her mission to put my books in the hands of everyone on the planet.

My children.

Rochelle Hardy, aka the First Fan, for her love, laughs, and plot help.

And, as always, a special thanks to Alex for being the consummate hero.

It is to be regretted that effectual efforts were not made at an early date to furnish a history of the services of men (and women) of color.

—William Butler Yeats, 1838

Prologue

September 7, 1831

Dearest Katherine,

I hope my letter finds you well. I am aware it has been over a year since my last correspondence, but circumstances have prevented me from writing before now. Dearest sister, all my life you have cautioned me against making rash decisions. Had I taken your wise counsel to heart maybe I would not be paying so dearly for that flaw now, but the die is cast. For the love of a woman named Frances Greaton, I have forsaken all I am and given my freedom over to her master. I am a slave now, Katherine. My worth is no longer measured by how well I can steer a ship or the languages I've mastered or the lands I own, but rather by my strength, my weight, and the health of my teeth. According to Master Greaton I am very valuable— much like a prized steer.

To her credit, Frances was furious upon learning what I'd done and refused to speak to me for days. But Katherine, to be near her I would carry water in hell. This is a hard life, especially for those in the fields. Master Greaton has for the present put me to work in his clerk's office where I help with ledgers and accounts. I realize now, after much raging from Frances, that I could have arranged to be with her in a less dramatic fashion, but at the time the captain of my ship refused to delay leaving port until a more rational solution could be found. So I chose love over freedom—possibly the last free choice I will ever make in this life.

Frances will give birth to our first child around the new year. Master Greaton has agreed to keep our family together in exchange for my lifelong servitude, but Frances doubts the pledge will be honored by his heir should Master Greaton pass on, especially if the child is male. So, she and I have made a pact to somehow send our child north to you. No child should be made to suffer the repercussions of my decision. Slavery is truly an abomination against God. It is against the law to post this letter to you and I am risking much by doing so, but I cannot let you think I have died at sea. Pray for me.

> *Your loving brother,*
> *David Wyatt*

December 12, 1833

My dearest Katherine,

My worst fears have come true. Old Master Greaton was killed in a carriage accident and, as Frances predicted, Greaton the Younger has not honored his father's pledge. My Frances has been sold Deep South. The anguish and rage I feel over our forced parting pales in the face of the horror of watching the child of our love sold also. Her name is Hester. Greaton's ledgers say she has been sold to the Sea Islands of the Carolinas to a man named Weston. Find her, Katherine. Move heaven and earth, but find her. If you must, offer the owner everything I possess in both land and monies to secure her freedom. Alas, it is too late for me. I have contracted a wasting disease that will not let me see the New Year. My Frances is gone from me forever and I grieve for her every day. However, I will go to my grave less haunted if I know Hester is safe in your

*loving care. To help you in identifying Hester, Frances
severed the tip of the little finger of her left hand the day
she was born in anticipation of this tragedy. Both Hester
and Frances cried for days after the severing, but the cut
healed clean. I hereby relinquish all my accumulated
Michigan properties, possessions, and monies to you in
Hester's name. Goodbye, dear sister. My love for you will
live on in my sweet daughter.*

*Your brother,
David Wyatt*

Chapter 1

Whittaker, Missouri
October 1858

Three loud thumps echoed through the floor beneath
Hester's feet—a signal that her guests had finally
arrived. She quickly moved aside the rocker, positioned
as always in front of the big bay window, then the heavy
rug underneath which hid the trapdoor. The visitors were
late by more than two hours and she wholeheartedly
hoped the delay resulted from the fiercely raging storm
outside and not some unforseen trouble.

Mr. Wood, an old Quaker friend of her late Aunt
Katherine's, appeared first on the steps leading up out of
the tunnel that ran beneath the house. He acknowledged
Hester with a terse nod and handed her a drenched and
shivering tarp-wrapped child of no more than five years.
Hester carried the boy to the fire and set him down as
close as safety would allow, then quickly returned to
offer assistance to the others in Mr. Wood's party.

In all, he'd transported six on this trip: one man, and a
couple with their three children.

The small family had fared well considering the dangers of the journey. Hester knew from her own experience what they must have experienced escaping north.
Along with having to place their lives in the hands of
strangers, even such dedicated conductors as Mr. Wood,

4

fleeing slavery—and the only life they ever knew—had probably been a very difficult decision to make. However, they'd ridden the "train" together, and unlike some of the other guests who'd passed through Hester's station on the Underground Railroad, this family had arrived north intact.

The sixth visitor had not fared as well, Mr. Wood explained as he and Hester hurriedly made their way down the length of the lamp-lit earthen tunnel. "I wanted to take him on down to Harsen's Island, but he's hurt pretty bad."

The tunnel emptied out onto the banks of the Huron River, and outside the wind and rain swirled ferociously. Hester, fighting the force of the storm, pulled her shawl closer around her shoulders. She had to squint against the deluge in order to help Mr. Wood undo the false bottom of the wagon. The man inside lay motionless. To Hester's surprise, he was dressed and rouged as a woman. The injuries had drained the color from his mulatto-gold complexion, but the angry red swelling and dark bruises associated with a severe beating stood out brilliant against the pallor of his skin. With the rain pouring over his face, he looked like a corpse.

"There's a price on his head!" Mr. Wood shouted to be heard in the storm. "You sure you want to do this?"

"I don't care," Hester screamed back. "Bring him in."

Between them, Hester and Mr. Wood managed to drag the unconscious man back through the tunnel and into the room built behind the wall of the house's underground cellar and finally settle him atop a cot.

"Who is he?" Hester asked softly. Kneeling beside the unconscious man, she listened to his shallow breathing while she hastily shrugged out of the wet shawl. One side of his face had borne the brunt of the beating. The eye was swollen shut, the skin around it had turned a vivid violet and black.

"The Black Daniel."

With a shocked expression, Hester turned his way. "Are you certain?"

Mr. Wood nodded a grim confirmation. "It'll be very dangerous hiding him, Hester."

She agreed. His exploits were legendary; slave catchers had been hunting the elusive Black Daniel for years for leading slaves north. His condition left her few options, however. He didn't look up to going on to the next station, a thirty-mile trip, especially not in the bottom of a storm-jostled wagon. He'd have to stay.

Hester gently opened his heavy woolen coat. Her stomach lurched at the deep red stain saturating the right side of the old dress he wore. "Are you going on tonight?" she asked Mr. Wood.

"Not with this storm," he responded while she ran her hands lightly over Daniel's upper torso and shoulder blades in search of less visible injuries. A soft touch over the surface of his ribs made him moan and his battered face twisted with pain.

"I believe he has some broken ribs," Hester said, looking up into Mr. Wood's concerned blue eyes. "He needs more help than I can give. If you're not going on, I need you to fetch Bea Meldrum and bring her here."

Bea lived about a half mile up the road and did most of the doctoring for their community, and right now Hester prayed she was home. "Help me get him out of this coat, then go get Bea."

At fifty-six years old, Mr. Wood was still a formidable-sized man, but the strain of raising the Daniel so Hester could slip the coat off showed plainly in the old man's face. The Daniel was big. He towered over Mr. Wood's six feet by more than a few inches. He also looked to outweigh him by a good fifty pounds. Mr. Wood described it as trying to raise a mountain.

When she freed him of the coat, Hester tried not to dwell upon the blood staining the sheet where the Daniel had lain, and silently signaled Mr. Wood to ease him back down to the cot.

Hester placed a hand on his damp forehead; fever had set in. He was beginning to shiver and shake. Because he'd been concealed in the false bottom of the wagon, his clothing, except for the blood staining it, felt relatively dry, so Hester left the dress, and the trousers he wore beneath, on him for now. After she and Mr. Wood removed the Daniel's boots, another maneuver which seemed to cause him much pain, she drew three large quilts from the old chest in the corner of the room and covered him gently.

Mr. Wood left to fetch Bea, and Hester went back up to the house to check on her other guests. The children were sleeping soundly in one of the bedrooms on the second floor of the big old house. Their parents were seated and talking quietly in front of the fire in the dining room. At her entrance, both looked up with tired smiles. After assuring Hester they'd had enough to eat, she directed them to the room they would have for their time here. In another few days, after they'd regained their strength and adequate clothing had been acquired for them and their children, they would decide whether to go on into Canada or try to carve out a new life somewhere else.

There was still a bit of hot water left in the kettle from the tea Hester had made earlier in the evening so she poured what was left into a small basin. Then she refilled the kettle and put it to boil just in case Bea needed the hot water. After covering the basin with a clean towel, she went in search of some clean rags that could be used for bandages. Ready, she extinguished the lights in the front rooms and went back to the man in the cellar.

Hester placed a hand on the Black Daniel's forehead and felt fever-driven heat scorch her skin. In the short time she'd been away, he'd grown hot as a flatiron. Dampening one of the rags in the warm water, she gently began to clean up the cuts and abrasions on his swollen face. She hoped she wasn't causing him any pain, but there was no other way to tend the superficial wounds.

Mr. Wood returned with Bea a short time later. Hester considered Bea one of the oldest and wisest people around and was glad she had arrived to help with this situation.

Bea declared that the wound in his side had come from a knife. She treated the ugly gash and stitched it closed, along with the wicked slashes across the backs of his hands. Three ribs were indeed broken and she bandaged him gingerly, though tightly, to give them support.

Bea also discovered why the removal of his boots had seemed to cause such pain; the left ankle was injured and very badly swollen. She wrapped it to keep it still.

When she was finished, Bea looked up and pronounced, "He'll live, although it's apparent someone wanted it otherwise." She gathered up her supplies and slowly got to her feet, saying with mock severity, "Lord, I hate getting old."

Bea had celebrated her sixty-seventh birthday last August First. She was a valuable member of the community, and Hester knew that when she inevitably passed on, there would be a hole left in everyone's hearts.

Bea shrugged back into the old olive-colored slicker she'd discarded earlier and said, "You know, Hester, beneath all that bruising is probably a very good-looking man."

Hester could see nothing of the man's true features beneath the injuries. "Why do you say that?"

With all seriousness, Bea replied, "Because the Good Lord would not put a mule's face on a man as finely made as that."

Hester, accustomed to Bea's frankness, simply shook her head and chuckled. The old woman could always be counted upon to bring a smile. Hester looked down upon the sleeping man. Earlier, Bea had cut away the old dress he'd been wearing to facilitate her work. He lay now on the cot, chest bare but for the white bandages encircling his ribs. Hester had seen a man's bare chest only two or three times in her adult life, but even she knew Bea spoke truth; he was indeed handsomely made. The chest appeared sculpted, the arms and shoulders powerful.

Bea's voice broke her reverie when she asked, "Hester, who is he?"

Hester looked quickly to Mr. Wood, who gave an

almost imperceptible nod of "no" in response. Hester wholeheartedly agreed. Bea was a long-standing conductor on the road and could be trusted, but for now, the less people knew of the Daniel's presence, the safer it was for everyone. "He's simply a friend in need."

Bea nodded understandingly and did not press. "Keep him warm, Hester. The needlework may be damp for a time, but should hold. He'll have to stay off that leg for a while, though."

Before she left, Bea gave a few more instructions and told Hester she'd be by in the morning to check on him again when she dropped off her weekly basket of eggs. Mr. Wood also promised to stop by in the morning before making the long trek back to Ann Arbor.

After their leaving, a quiet settled over the small hidden room, broken only by the man's labored breathing. Hester looked around wondering where she might be able to sleep since Bea had suggested Hester keep an eye on him at least for tonight. The draught he'd been given would ease some of the pain and more importantly, help him sleep. It was doubtful he'd awaken before morning, but if he needed someone in the middle of the night, Hester had to stay close at hand.

However, the cot he lay upon offered the only real bed. Hester was left with a choice of the old hardback rocker in the corner, or the packed dirt floor. Deciding on the chair, she pulled it closer to the cot and unearthed another few quilts from the chest. She'd gotten a good soaking transferring Daniel from the wagon. In her haste to see to his well-being she'd forgotten her own. Only now did she notice the cold dampness clinging to her dress and the slips beneath. Shivering, she cocooned herself in the chair. Common sense told her to go to the house and change into dry clothing. The arrival of tonight's guests and their need for a safe haven meant she would need all her faculties. She would be of little help to anyone if she became sick. But she didn't want to leave her patient.

She searched through the big chest again and brought

out a long-tailed flannel shirt and a pair of long drawers.
Both articles were sized for a much larger man, but they
would have to do.

Shirt and leggings in hand, she moved over to the old
black-belly stove. Despite the stoking she'd given it earlier
while awaiting Bea's arrival, the underground room had
only now begun to echo any heat. Hester shot her guest a
quick glance. The draught seemed to be working. Comfortable that he wouldn't awaken, she stripped down to
her well-worn muslin shift and drawers. The cold air in
the room felt even brisker against her bare skin, motivat-
ing her to dry herself as swiftly as possible with the driest
of her slips. That done, she quickly donned the long-
sleeve shirt and ankle-length underdrawers. The damp
dress and slips were laid out on a small bench near the
stove so they'd be dry by morning.

Hester turned back to the chair and froze. The Black
Daniel had been watching her. His one good eye made
him appear kin to Cyclops. He was obviously fighting
the draught and its effects because the lid refused to stay
open. Again he opened it and again it slid closed. When
the lid fluttered down for what seemed the last time,
Hester gratefully thought he'd given up. But again he
proved her wrong. To her amazement he tried to get up
off the cot. When he tried to speak, Hester hastened to
his side, telling him, "You must lie still."

When she began to bathe his fever-hot forehead and
cheeks with the now-tepid water, he grabbed her wrist
with such force she cried out. The eye opened and for a
space of time she looked down into the gaze of a lucid
man. She could see the questions and confusion there as
he peered at her face. His attention shifted to her
captured hand and she saw his surprise. She stiffened,
damning herself for not remembering the gloves. He
studied her for a moment. Then, as if he were somehow
satisfied, he relaxed, released her wrist, and went back
into the arms of the draught.

Hester exhaled the breath she was holding and rubbed
her sore wrist while her heartbeat slowed to a normal

pace. Under her assessing palm, his face still felt unnaturally warm. Remembering what Bea said about keeping him cooled down as much as possible, Hester resumed bathing his face. She just hoped he didn't grab her again.

While she worked to bring his temperature down, she sang softly: hymns, lullabies, popular tunes, songs she'd heard at rallies. All the while he continued to fight against Bea's medicine and seemingly his own demons; tossing and turning, murmuring fitfully in what sounded to Hester like French.

"Lie still," she cautioned softly. "You're safe here."

She had no idea if he understood, but she kept up the soft coaxing voice and her whispery crooning while continuing to soothe the heat in his skin with the cool cloth. At last, his breathing dropped to a more even pace and he quieted. Hester sighed in relief. When she was certain he would not reawaken, she placed the cloth beside the pan. She flexed her wrist, thinking that despite his condition, he did not lack strength.

After repositioning his quilts, she tossed more wood into the belly of the stove, and settled into the rocker as best she could. She wearily swathed herself in her own two quilts and closed her eyes.

Noises awakened Hester only a few hours later. For a moment she had trouble comprehending her whereabouts. A loud crashing sound rendered her wholly awake and alert. Her first glance swept the cot and found it empty. Alarmed, she looked around the small space and came face to face with the man called the Black Daniel. He stood by the shelf-lined wall which concealed the entrance to the room. The crashes she heard had been made by the falling of some jars of stored vegetables and fruit. In the dark he loomed like a giant, evaluating her silently.

She could tell he was in pain, but he didn't speak. A tremor passed through her under his scrutiny and she swallowed unconsciously.

She also saw that his strength did not equal his will. He was grudgingly using the edge of the shelf to support his weakened body. His shirt was unbuttoned and the bandages Bea had wrapped around his ribs glowed white against his golden skin in the shadows thrown off by the turned-down lamp on the floor. "You shouldn't be up," she stammered.

He didn't move. His gaze held her like a fist and she couldn't ease her racing heart nor the shivers rippling her skin. She began to wonder if she'd made a rash decision letting him stay.

"Who are you?" he finally asked in a voice thick with strain.

She hesitated for a second, then replied, "Hester Wyatt."

"Am I still in Michigan?"

She nodded, then said, "A town called Whittaker—"

"Whittaker?!"

"Yes. This cellar is beneath my home. You've been here since a few hours past midnight."

He thought a moment more, then asked, "You do the doctoring?"

"No."

Hester wondered if he'd demand to know Bea's name, but he didn't. Instead he asked, "Is there some place a man can relieve himself?"

Hester turned away. "There's a pot over there," she said in a small voice.

"Outside," he clarified.

"You can't make it outside."

"If I can't, you'll be the only one embarrassed, I assure you."

Telling herself his attitude likely stemmed from his injuries, Hester bit back a retort, and threw aside her quilts. Clad in the long-tailed shirt and red underdrawers, she walked barefoot over to the wall where he stood. It took her practiced hands only a few seconds to release the latch. When it slid free, she pushed at the shelves and they swung out into the cellar. "Up those stairs and around to the back."

She waited smugly for him to fall on his face because

of the injured ankle, but he didn't. He struggled, yes, and every step he took reinforced how weak one could become after being severely beaten and stabbed. However, he made it to the top of the stairs.

However, the big plank door above his head proved him mortal. That door was heavy and a man with broken ribs could not raise it. He did try though, making Hester worry about Bea's needlework and his sanity. Looking defeated and not liking it, breathing hard from the exertion, he turned and scowled at her.

Without a word, she joined him at the top of the stairs and pushed up on the cellar's door. He grumbled something which might have been a thank you, but she couldn't be sure.

Fifteen minutes later he hadn't returned, and Hester, still standing at the foot of the stairs, cold in the early dawn air, debated what she should do. Going out and making sure he hadn't fallen head first into the privy seemed to be the appropriate choice, however she didn't want to barge in only to find nothing amiss and wholly embarrass them both. She finally decided to give him a bit more time.

He returned a few minutes later and Hester noted that although his innards probably felt a lot better, on the outside he looked nearly as pale as he had in the wagon.

"I'm going to need your assistance, Hester Wyatt," he stated from above.

Hester went to his side. She groaned when his weight came down on her shoulder. This time she heard the thank you quite clearly.

The cords in Hester's neck were tight as bow strings from the strain when they finally made it back into the small room. He eased himself back down onto the cot and she stood beside it breathing hard.

Hester left him a moment to go back and close the cellar's big door, and when she returned she found him asleep. She felt his forehead; he was warm, but not as hot as he'd been at the beginning of his stay.

Chapter 2

The Black Daniel slept on through the morning and into the afternoon, thus giving Hester time to see to the welfare of the small family. Bea came by as promised and pronounced her sleeping patient healing, but not fully recovered by any means. When Hester related the privy incident, Bea simply shook her head. "Men," she replied, as if that explained everything. Bea left soon after, warning Hester to keep him in bed. Hester thought pigs would fly first.

Mr. Wood came by after lunch. He was heading back to Ann Arbor now that the storm had passed, but he wanted to take a last look at the Daniel. As he and Hester stood talking quietly in the cellar room, Mr. Wood asked, "Are you sure you want him here?"

Hester glanced over at the man in question, lying asleep on the cot. The Black Daniel was one of the most successful conductors on the line. He needed the refuge she provided so he could recover and resume his work. "Bea says he should be well enough to travel in a week or so. I think he'll be safe enough here until then." She sensed her old friend had his doubts, but he offered no further arguments.

"Don't worry," she told him, draping an arm around his waist and giving him an affectionate squeeze. "If anything happens, I'll let Hubble know. Now you get on back to your family and I'll see you on the next trip."

He kissed her cheek, gave her a hug of his own, and was gone.

"Can he be trusted?"

Hester whirled at the unexpected question from the man on the cot. How long had he been awake and listening? "I see you're awake."

She came over and placed a palm against his forehead. His skin still felt too warm. "Yes, he can be trusted." She thought the question absolutely ridiculous considering all Mr. Wood had done for him last night. "In fact, were I you, I'd say a prayer for him."

"If you were me, you'd know I never pray."

His words struck her like a slap. He had not a whit of apology for his battered face and again Hester wondered if she'd been wise to take this man in. Surely he believed in a higher being.

"Do you think you can eat something?" she asked frostily.

"Long as I don't have to pray to get it."

Hester left without a word.

For the next two days Hester gave the Daniel a fairly wide berth; she saw to his medical needs and brought him meals, but his surly mood kept her at arm's length. She spent most of her time getting the guest family ready to move on. She procured winter clothing from the pastor at the church, along with a small donation of cash from the congregation. The family had decided to settle in Ontario so Hester sent word to contacts there to expect their arrival. Hester also made discreet inquiries about strangers in the area. Most of her immediate neighbors knew about Hester's conducting, either because of their friendship with her late aunt or because they had traveled on the Road themselves. They all knew whom Hester meant as strangers—slave catchers. And yes, some men had been seen as recently as yesterday in Detroit, less than thirty miles away. By the questions the strangers were asking, their dress and speech, slave catchers were all they could be. Word had it they were hunting the Black Daniel.

Hester thought about the news as she drove her two-horse team home from church service. The very idea that the Black Daniel could possibly be in the area filled the congregation with excitement. Many speculated on his whereabouts while a few publicly stated they didn't believe the Black Daniel actually existed. Hester, of course, knew differently. He existed all right, and she had yet to meet a more sullen or rude individual in all her twenty-four years.

Giving credence to her point, he lit into Hester the moment she entered the room. "Where have you been?"

Having just come from church, Hester was determined not to be provoked by his temper. She set down the tray holding his evening meal on the edge of the cot. "I'm pleased you missed my company. I was at church. Today is Sunday."

He made a rude noise in reply and Hester skewered him with a look that dared him to comment further. He didn't, though she doubted his silence had anything to do with him being intimidated by her glare. He didn't impress her as the type easily intimidated by anyone—male, female, Black, or White.

He told her, "I'd appreciate knowing when I'm going to be left here alone."

He was right, she knew, so she nodded in agreement.

"Folks were talking about you at church today," she related, figuring he should know about the speculating going on.

"Why?"

"There are some slave catchers in Detroit asking if there is anyone in the area harboring runaways, and does anyone know a man called the Black Daniel?"

"And how did your church-going neighbors reply?"

"No, and no, despite the five-hundred-dollar reward."

"That much? That's an awful lot of silver for some Judas."

"There are no traitors in this community."

"There has to be, otherwise I wouldn't be here."

"What do you mean?"

"The catchers who ambushed me boasted of a snake being in Whittaker's garden."

Hester stared in shock. "In Whittaker's garden?! You must be mistaken. This part of the Road has operated since after the War of Independence. Everyone is highly trusted."

"Which means nothing," he pointed out. "Had it not been for a timely rescue by the Wesleyites, I'd be dead."

Hester knew of the Wesleyites. They were conductors—sons of a Kentucky slave holder and as fervently against slavery as the most dedicated abolitionist. Despite their Bible-quoting ways, they were also as unpredictable as cannons rolling loose upon the deck of a ship. They'd been known to sell their passengers then resteal them many times before bringing them on the trip north. They were also known to leave dead slave catchers in their wake. Once when Hester asked why the Road even employed the Wesleyites, her Aunt Katherine explained that the cause accepted all warriors, even those as questionable as the Wesleyites.

Putting the Wesleyites out of her mind, Hester still found it hard to believe Whittaker harbored a Judas. She knew there were individuals on the Road who would harbor a fugitive at night, then accept a bribe to betray that same fugitive when the sun rose; but not in Whittaker!

She told him, "I'm afraid the local Vigilance Committee is going to need more than the word of a boasting slave catcher to take your charge seriously."

"I take it you don't believe me."

"I believe you may have been betrayed. The injuries you sustained speak for themselves, but it wasn't done by someone from Whittaker."

"Are you saying that to protect someone, or are you truly that naive?"

After putting up with his temper and surliness for the past few days, Hester held onto what was left of her patience and said, "I am risking prison sheltering you. How dare you call me naive. Your lack of manners and

gratitude could make me turn you in just to get you out
of my home. Have a pleasant meal. I'll return in the
morning for the tray." She spun on her heel and left.

Picking up his fork the Daniel shook his head at her
stubborn refusal to entertain his theory. He wondered if
she lived alone. He hadn't seen anyone else on the
premises, but that meant little. If her man were a part of
the Road, he could be anywhere. He had noticed her
hands, however. Indigo. He'd only seen hands stained
like hers a few times. He'd be willing to bet she'd been a
slave in the Sea Islands of South Carolina where he knew
the few existing indigo plantations operated. Working
the plants to extract the dye turned the palms and backs
of the hands of the slaves permanently indigo.

Judging by the way she spoke and carried herself,
she'd been free some time, though; either that or she'd
been educated down south, a scenario he found unlikely
due to the deep rich darkness of her skin. Educated
slaves had a tendency to be mulatto like himself.

She was feeding him well, though: hominy, eggs, and
fat biscuits rolling in butter had been the morning meal.
Plump roast chicken anchored tonight's tray and the
honeyed yams accompanying it all but melted in his
mouth. He hadn't tasted such well-prepared fare since
his last stint in New Orleans, but attempting to chew
solid food around his loosened teeth made for very slow
going. He forced himself to keep eating, knowing he'd
recover much faster if he could manage to get it all
down.

He finished his meal and lay back drained. He cursed
his lack of strength. He wanted to question Hester about
the area, but all his body craved was slumber. He fought
it off as long as he could, then surrendered. A few
seconds later, he slid into sleep.

The local women of the Detroit Ladies Abolition
Circle met every third Sunday of the month. The sites of
the local meeting usually rotated between the homes of

those on the board and tonight would be Hester's turn. The group, founded ten years ago by Hester's aunt, had grown to almost one hundred and fifty members; some women from as far away as Toledo and Amherstburg, Ontario, attended the annual summer convention.

The rumors of slave catchers in the area resulted in a smaller than usual turnout—only nine of the twenty local women ventured out, but the meeting went well. Reports were given on the upcoming Christmas bazaar to be held in conjunction with the church, the state of the organization's financial needs, and the neverending search for shelter and clothing for runaways.

The meeting lasted a little over an hour, and when it was over nobody wanted to stay for dessert and tea. With slave catchers rumored to be in the area, all felt it best not to tarry. A few of the women had risked the wrath of their husbands by attending the circle's meeting and had promised to return home as soon as it ended. No one wanted to be stopped on the way home tonight.

But as they moved to adjourn, a deafening blast of knocks pounded against the front door. Everyone froze. The thundering continued. Hester moved quickly to the lace curtains, and she saw that outside were eight mounted men. "It appears we have guests."

They'd rehearsed for emergency circumstances many times and all knew their roles. They quickly gathered up the ledgers and all other incriminating materials concerning their circle, placed them in the designated strongbox, and shoved it into the hidey-hole built into the fireplace. Others hurriedly retrieved and distributed the sewing always positioned nearby. Hester put on her gloves.

The pounding continued as Hester looked back. Her friends nodded that they were ready and she opened the door.

"Bout damn time!"

Hester did not know the short, black-toothed man glaring angrily at her. Beneath the light cast onto the porch he appeared ghoulish. He wore a long coat stained with dirt that appeared age old. The filth in the coat matched the dirt on his skin and the stench of him in the night's breeze blew strongly.

She did know the man at his side. "Good evening, Sheriff Lawson."

"Evening, Miss Hester. Sorry to disturb you. This here is Ezra Shoe."

"Mr. Shoe."

Shoe looked her up and down like a buyer would a woman on the block, then smiled a smile so vile, Hester had to force herself to hold his gaze.

"You got a man, gal?" he asked, showing the blackened teeth and gums once again. "Cos if you don't, me and my friends been riding a long time, we could sure use a little bit of comfort, if you take my meanin'."

Hester took his meaning and wished him taken straight to hell. She turned to the sheriff and felt salved by his obvious anger. "Hester, this *man* wants to search your house."

"Why?"

"Thinks somebody around here is transporting runaways."

"Slaves?"

"Slaves. He's got a writ from some court down south for a man called the Black Daniel."

Hester hid the sudden rise in her heartbeat. She asked quizzically, "The Black Daniel? And he is?"

"A slave-stealing bastard is what he is," Shoe interjected, spitting a stream of nastiness on her porch. The dark eyes taunted her ferally. "And I plan on searching every nigger house in this state until I find him."

The slur slid from his lips easily and without apology. Hester stood in her doorway tight-lipped beneath her outward mask of calm. By law, she could not challenge the writ. She stepped back and let them enter.

Shoe wanted to bring in the other riders and their baying dogs to help with the search, but the sheriff refused. "They're not tracking mud all over this woman's home."

Shoe protested, but Lawson, a lifelong friend of Hester's Aunt Katherine, remained firm.

The women seated around the front parlor were offered a sincere apology from the lawman for the interruption of their evening, but he explained it was his duty. They nodded their understanding and went back to their needles.

Shoe looked around at the fine furnishings, then whistled appreciatively before asking, "Some white man give you this house, gal?"

Hester answered calmly, "No. My great uncles built this house."

The thunderstruck look on his face almost compensated her for having to endure his noxious presence in her home.

He looked to the sheriff. Lawson's answering nod confirmed her story. Shoe then turned back to Hester and stared as if she possessed three heads.

She explained, "My great-grandfather received this land as payment for fighting in the War for Independence, Mr. Shoe."

"Gal, you been drinkin'?! They didn't let no niggers fight in that war." He began to laugh. "You hear that, Sheriff? This gal claims she got relatives fought in the war. I heard being up North sometimes makes their kind go crazy in the head cos of the cold, but this the first time I known it to be true." He guffawed again.

Lawson had had enough. "Let's get this search over with, Shoe."

Shoe nodded his agreement and Hester shepherded the two men through every room in the house: upstairs, downstairs, even outside to the barn where she kept her team. Shoe poked in closets, kitchen cupboards, and even the stove. All the time he chuckled to himself. "Niggers fighting in the war," he kept saying.

Hester bore his slander without emotion. His prejudiced ignorance made it certain he'd never conceive of Black people being intelligent enough to design and build a house specifically to accommodate the Road, so

Hester didn't even flinch when he demanded to be shown the cellar.

While Hester and the sheriff looked on, Shoe waved a lantern into the dark corners of the cellar. She thought of her guest on the other side of the wall. Hester just hoped the Daniel didn't suddenly begin bellowing her name. Shoe might not be able to sense the room behind the wall, but he would for certain investigate any strange sounds.

As Hester predicted, Shoe never looked at anything but the surface during the whole investigation. He found no clues of the Black Daniel or the small family sent on their way after the sunrise service at the church that morning. They were making the journey to Amherstburg in the company of a visiting pastor and some of his parishioners. The runaways, complete with letters of introduction and a small amount of cash, were posing as part of the returning flock.

"Well he ain't here," Shoe declared angrily.

"I told you that," the sheriff answered, "now let's let the ladies finish their visiting."

Shoe looked around once more at the fine carpets, the lace-draped windows, and the women sewing quietly. His face seemed to show a resentment at the fine things the Wyatt family had accumulated over the years.

Hester ignored his sneer but as she showed them to the door, she had a question. "What makes you think this Black Daniel is hiding around here, Mr. Shoe?"

"I got my ways of knowin'," he said smoothly. "I also heard he had a knife stuck in his gut, so he couldn't've gotten far. He's here somewhere."

"What does he look like?" she asked.

"Mulatto and tall, according to my source."

A chill went up her spine at his words. Was the Daniel correct? Did her community indeed harbor a traitor?

"Oh, and gal?"

Hester turned to Shoe.

"When I find the bastard, and I will, I hope you're involved. I'd love to put you on the block."

"Let's go, Shoe," Sheriff Lawson barked.

Shoe gave Hester one last soul-chilling leer then followed the sheriff back out into the night.

Hester watched until they'd ridden away. Only after she closed the door did she notice that her hands were shaking.

Her friends rushed to her side, all eager to get her to a seat where she could calm herself. Hester waved them away, sat down, and took a deep breath. After a few moments, her shaking subsided. Pulling off her gloves, she asked, "Lord, could you smell that man?"

"You could smell that man in Ohio," one of the women offered. The dry tone first drew snickers, then gales of laughter. It broke the tension and for the next few minutes they took turns giving their reactions to his odor and his stupidity. The hilarity ended when Hester summed up what they all knew. "Any man that ignorant is very dangerous. Let's hope he gives up and goes back south."

"He's probably not smart enough for that," someone remarked seriously. Although Hester could still hear Shoe's promise in her mind, none of her friends voiced reactions to Shoe's threats to put Hester on the block.

The women left soon after, promising to alert their husbands and neighbors to Shoe's presence, and Hester hurried down to the cellar. Her fears of the Daniel bellowing and bringing Shoe and his men down on their heads proved unfounded. She found him asleep, and so quietly withdrew.

When Hester first came north, the sounds of the house at night always frightened her until her grandfather explained the creakings were just her ancestors tipping around making sure everyone was having good dreams. As she grew older, she knew her grandfather's tale had been just that; a tale to soothe the fears of a scared child. However, she clung to that memory now, lying in her bed, listening to the house settle in for the night. She wondered if her aunt would now join the corps of tipping ancestors? The mental picture of Aunt Katherine tipping around brought a smile to Hester's face; Katherine Wyatt never tipped anywhere. When she entered a room, people knew immediately, either by her full-bodied laugh or by the knot of people surrounding her and arguing over her stand on some issue of the day. She loved to argue, or as she always termed it, debate. The day the town buried Katherine Wyatt, the weather had been glorious up until the moment the bearers set the coffin in the ground. A thunderstorm came up out of nowhere to pelt the mourners with rain, wind, thunder, lightning, and hail the size of crabapples. As they all ran for cover to await the storm's passing, one of her aunt's friends swore Katherine was up in heaven arguing with the Lord.

Katherine, for all her unorthodox ways, would not have argued with Ezra Shoe tonight. She would've handled the situation just as Hester had done—seen Shoe for an ignorant wastrel and held her tongue until he exited. Katherine would not have jeopardized years of work for an unwashed slave catcher. However, Hester did not know how her aunt would have handled the Black Daniel. The man was a walking mystery, but she supposed one needed to be to steal slaves.

Chapter 3

The next morning when Hester entered the cellar room with his breakfast tray, he was gone. She assumed he'd gone to the privy, so she set the tray on the table beside the bed and took a seat on the rocker to await his return. She tried not to be upset by his disappearance. After all, everyone had needs, especially first thing in the morning, but thinking of slave catchers searching for him made her nervous. She felt as if he were deliberately placing the entire community in the path of danger simply because he had an aversion to using the pot in the corner. She calmed herself and decided it wouldn't do to get upset. In less than a week's time he would be recovered enough to travel, and thus be out of her hair.

He came hobbling in a few moments later, aided by the cane Bea had loaned him. He took one glance at her stern face and said, "You look like a disapproving school teacher rocking in that chair, Miss Wyatt."

He eased himself down to the cot, the strain on his face showing plainly.

Hester chose not to reply to his unflattering description. Instead she said, "Slave catchers stopped by for tea last evening."

He turned and stared. She was pleased to see she'd finally gained his undivided attention.

25

He assessed her a moment, then said, "Start from the beginning."

Hester related the story of Shoe's visit. The only detail she didn't divulge was Shoe's vow to place her on the block. When she finished, Hester asked, "Do you see now why I'm rocking like a disappointed school teacher? By venturing outside, you're jeopardizing everything we've worked for to keep this route safe. I don't mind emptying the pot, I do it for passengers all the time."

"Where I prefer to relieve my needs is none of your concern, Miss Wyatt."

"It is when slave catchers are on my front porch, Mr.—" She had no idea what to call him. "How do you prefer to be addressed?"

He smiled inwardly. She was a virago one moment then primly polite the next. The beating he'd received from the slave catchers had left him with a pounding head. The throbbing had lessened considerably since last night, but having her in here menacing him seemed to be making the ache worse. At full strength he'd be able to handle Hester Wyatt and her bossy nature, but right now he was at her mercy.

"How long have I been here?" he asked.

"This is the fourth day." Hester was still waiting to hear the name he wanted her to use.

"Name's Galen."

Hester was certain he'd plucked the name from the air. He would hardly reveal his true identity to her, a stranger, but for his remaining stay, she'd address him as Galen.

Galen wished he had two sound eyes; it hurt to try and keep her in focus. Because of the swelling, he had only a hazy picture of what she actually looked like: small, dark-skinned, passable looks, a full head of thick, ebony hair worn coiled on her nape like a spinster.

His growling stomach interrupted his thoughts. He glanced over at the tray that presumably held his breakfast. "Are you punishing me for going outdoors by letting my meal get cold?"

Hester looked at the tray and wondered if he had any manners at all. Silently, she brought the tray to the bed and set it beside him. Up close she could see the perspiration beaded on his face. She placed her palm on his forehead and was not pleased to discover he'd worked himself into a rise in temperature again by going outdoors. She felt his shirt front. The blue flannel was damp with sweat. "You," she said to him, "need a keeper."

She strode over to the old chest and extracted another worn shirt which appeared large enough to fit his muscular build. She returned and thrust it at him. In an even voice she made a request. "Put this on, please."

She thought he smiled for a moment, but with the damaged face, she couldn't be sure.

He took the shirt from her hand and she waited while he struggled out of the old and into the new. Because of his bound ribs, she made a move to help him at one point, but one flash from that coal-black eye made her keep her distance.

When he finished, he asked, "How cold is my meal now?"

Hester replied, "Not nearly as cold as I'd like, I'm sure."

He did smile then. "You always this combative, Miss Wyatt?"

"Not as a rule, no."

"That's too bad. A combative woman is usually a passionate woman," he added.

Something in the low tone of his voice touched her like the faintest brush of a breeze, then was gone. "I thought you stole slaves. I didn't realize you were also an authority on women."

"Women are no great study. They are either passionate or they're not."

Hester knew women to be a bit more complex than he

espoused. She thought to herself how convenient it must be to be male and confident enough in that maleness to give such short shrift to the supposed weaker sex. She simply shook her head and said, "I would love to debate the merits of your argument but there are none, so I will take my leave."

"I thought you were combative."

His soft voice stopped her. She replied, "Not with an injured opponent. Trouncing you in a debate seems hardly fair, considering your condition, sir."

That softly spoken barb struck bone. Galen eyed her in a new light. "You've very sharp claws, Indigo. Are you one of those women who has no use for men?"

Hester almost missed the question because her brain stuck on hearing him name her Indigo. "No. Some of the men I'm acquainted with are stellar individuals."

Galen thought the name Indigo fit her well. Her hands were the only parts of her he could see without real difficulty. However, it did occur to him that she might find the appellation offensive, so he said, "I didn't mean to offend you by pegging you Indigo, Miss Wyatt. Code names are *de rigeur* in my line of work. Since your hands are so distinctive—" He shrugged. "I apologize."

"The name does not offend me," she replied truthfully. She found his gentle regard for her feelings surprising, though. "I was once told my hands would brand me a slave for the remainder of my years."

"They were correct, but as long as it doesn't brand who you are in your heart, the color of your hands, like the color of your skin, is of no consequence."

She gave him a kind smile. "You sound very much like my Aunt Katherine. She raised me to be proud of the life I've led."

"Where is she now?"

"She passed away a few months ago. I still miss her dearly."

Galen waited while she paused a moment to linger over her grief. She said then, "This was her house. She and my father grew up under this roof."

Galen asked, "Is your father out on the Road some-where?"

"No. He died before my third birthday."

"And your mother?"

"I've no idea. She and I were sold to separate places after I was born. My aunt was never able to learn her whereabouts."

Galen thought how similar their lives were. Even though he'd been born free, he, too, had grown to adulthood not knowing his parents. "Surely you have a husband, you don't live here alone, do you?"

"Yes, I live alone. I have a fiancé but he's in England until spring."

Galen wondered for a moment if the fiancé was an abolitionist, then asked, "When did your family escape and come north?"

Hester shook her head at his faulty assumption. "Only I escaped. My aunt and the rest of the Wyatts have been free since my great-grandfather was given freedom in exchange for enlisting during the War for Indepen-dence."

Galen's aching head began to pound as he tried to make some sense of her tale. If her aunt and father were free, how had Hester and her mother wound up being sold? By law, children born of free women could not be placed on the block. He cast around for an answer to the riddle. "Then your mother was a slave?"

"Yes. My father sold himself into slavery to marry her."

Galen stared in shock. He'd never heard of such a thing!

Hester saw his look and responded with a bitter chuckle. "Yes. He was a free merchant seaman. Accord-ing to one of my father's mates, my mother and her master came onto the ship one morning to look over the hold's manifest, and my father fell in love."

"Why didn't he offer to buy her?"

Hester shrugged. "The mate said my father tried, but the owner wouldn't agree. In the letter my father wrote to Aunt Katherine, he said selling himself seemed to be the only solution available at the time." After a quiet moment, Hester added, "Love must be a terrible thing." She shook herself free of the melancholy threatening to claim her over the tragic plight of her parents, then picked up his tray. "I'll rewarm your breakfast."

Galen nodded and watched her depart.

She returned with his breakfast a few minutes later, then left him to eat. When she came back to fetch his tray, she found he'd eaten all of the soft-cooked eggs and potatoes, but the draught he was supposed to drink for the pain in his ribs and ankle stood untouched in the small tin cup. "You didn't drink your medicine," she stated.

"It puts me to sleep. I can't think if I'm asleep."

"You won't be able to think at all if you don't recover fully."

He still bore a startling resemblance to Homer's Cyclops. The one eye, so riveting, stared out of a face less swollen but more distinctively colored in bruises of violet, yellow, and blue. "You must drink this draught."

He answered by asking, "How long have you lived in this house?"

"Since my ninth year, but I am not the person under discussion here. Drink this."

She thrust the cup at him. He looked up at her, and although she could feel herself begin to shake, she neither flinched nor backed down.

He asked, sounding a bit amused. "If I drink it, will you go away?"

"Hastily," she replied.

To her surprise he took the cup from her hand, but he didn't drink. Instead he placed it firmly upon the small table beside the bed. "We need to talk about this traitor."

Hester could not believe this man. "We have nothing to discuss until you are in a better condition. Look at you, a simple meal makes you break out in a fit of sweat."

Hester reached down and picked up the cup. In a calm voice she said, "Fine. Don't drink it. I shall simply put it in your food like one would for a stubborn child."

As she headed to the concealed door he growled, "You wouldn't dare."

She turned back. "If only that were true."

"Hester Wyatt!"

"I'll be back later."

Galen was still bellowing her name when the wall swung closed.

Hester entered with his dinner later that evening. He viewed the plate of yams and chicken suspiciously. "Is the draught in here somewhere?"

Hester did not lie. "Yes, it's in the yams if you must know."

"You're truthful, if nothing else," he stated grudgingly. He set the plate aside.

Hester wanted to rail at him when he set the plate aside, but she held her tongue. He'd eat eventually—not even the mighty Black Daniel could survive without sustenance, and with the volume of food he'd been consuming lately, she doubted he'd hold out for long. His appetite had improved markedly in the last day and a half, shockingly so to a woman who'd never had to feed a grown man of his size. He'd eaten everything she'd put before him, two helpings in most cases. She thought it too bad his personality hadn't improved as well.

"Will you be needing anything else?" Hester asked.

There would be no passengers arriving tonight, not with Shoe sniffing around. She planned on using the free evening to catch up on her correspondence with Foster, her fiancé.

"You can get me some shears and get this needlework out of my side." Since this morning the stitching had been itching something awful.

"The threads will come out when it's time, not before."

"Shears, Hester Wyatt."

"Has it ever occurred to you to say please?"

"It has."

Hester thought him to be the most exasperating individual she'd ever had the misfortune to meet, and so she told him calmly, "I've seen children who've taken to the sick bed with better manners than you. Haven't you ever been laid low before?"

"No."

"Surely when you were a child?"

"I've never been sick or injured a day in my life. I've led a very charmed existence up until now, but thanks to one of your neighbors, that appears to have changed."

Hester still found his accusations offensive. "You malign us without reason, sir."

"Near death is reason enough."

She had no desire to prolong this discussion. "I will leave you to your meal."

"Running from the truth won't change matters. There's a traitor here, and the longer you deny the possibility, the more lives you place in jeopardy. Sleep well, Miss Wyatt."

Hester did not sleep well. She spent a restless night dreaming of slave catchers, dogs, and the one-eyed Black Daniel.

Chapter 4

❧ ⌒~⌒ ❧

After returning from his predawn trek to the privy, Galen, mindful of the previous fit his hostess had thrown upon finding his shirt wet with sweat, donned a clean dry shirt from the big chest by the wall. He was now seated on the cot, breathing heavily from the exertion. He'd awakened this morning determined that today would be his last full day in bed, but his body didn't seem to cooperate. He could move around a bit better, but the ankle was still too tender to bear his full weight. The swelling in his face seemed to have lessened and he could see more clearly than he had in days. However, the threads in his side itched so fiercely he was tempted to go out and rub the spot against a tree as a bear would. Admittedly, the forced confinement had him surly as a bear. He'd been there six days. Six days too many. Snow would arrive soon, effectively shutting down his runs south until spring. If Ezra Shoe hung around for the winter, the chance to leave might never come.

Galen looked up as his hostess came into the room carrying the tray which held his breakfast.

"Good morning, Galen," she said cheerily.

He nodded, not sure if he were up to such animation so early in the day. "Good morning," he murmured.

Breakfast this morning consisted of piping hot hominy, a mound of eggs, cooked maple sugar apples spiced

33

with cinnamon, and three fat biscuits running with melted butter. He surveyed it all and knew that when he did leave he'd sorely miss her cooking.

Hester saw him eyeing the mound of food and said, "I hope I didn't give you too much." She had awakened this morning determined not to let his dark moods sully her day. She would be pleasant no matter what.

"No, the portion is fine."

"Good, then I will return later."

"What about the shears?" he asked, looking up at her.

Hester did not want to begin the day with an argument. She said calmly, "We've already discussed that. The stitching stays until Bea says differently. If it's uncomfortable, it means you're healing."

"I know that," he replied testily, "but the damn itching is driving me mad."

Hester fished around in the pocket of her black skirt. "Bea sent this unguent. She says it will help."

He took the small silver tin from her hand, pried off the top, then sniffed at the stuff inside. "Smells female."

"Cures all," Hester replied, thinking of how he would try a saint. "Bea said to rub the salve into the skin by the stitches. Can you do it alone or do you need assistance?"

He handed her the tin without a word.

"Are you always so rude?" Hester asked.

His one good eye bore into her, but she didn't flinch. He said, "Normally, no."

"That's something," she stated, though she tended to believe he was lying.

After he unbuttoned his shirt, she put a bit of Bea's unguent on her fingertips, then sat beside him on the small cot. Forcing herself to concentrate on the wound and not on the nearness of their bodies, Hester very gently rubbed the ointment into the long line of stitches that ran below his ribs. His skin was warm, and as she added more ointment to her fingertips and continued, it became next to impossible to ignore the soft heat rising from his golden chest. That heat, in tandem with the feel of her hands gliding slowly over his firm flesh, made her acutely aware that she'd never touched a man's body with such intimacy before. She hazarded a glance up to his face and found herself being watched. She quickly lowered her eyes back to the job at hand.

Galen thought her hands held magic; her every touch brought soothing relief. He closed his eyes at one point, unable to do anything other than savor the balm flowing from her indigo hands. He knew most of the relief could be attributed to Bea's unguent, but Hester's touch seemed to have a healing effect all its own. "You're very good at this, Hester Wyatt . . ."

Hester continued to gently work the unguent into his skin, telling herself she was not affected by his soft pronouncement.

"I'm done now, Galen."

He'd been lying back with his eyes closed. In response to her words, the one good eye opened and held her. Her heart began to beat so fast, she felt compelled to say something, anything. "Bea says the ointment should be put on three times a day."

"Good, because I was wondering how I might bribe you into agreeing to do it again . . . later . . ." His voice was thick; the air filled with tension. Hester could feel herself becoming warm also. "I have apples to pick in the yard—"

He nodded.

She pocketed the tin of ointment and fled.

Outside, Hester ventured into the wild apple orchard behind the house.

At one time, the orchard had been her father's pride and joy and encompassed nearly two hundred well-manicured trees. When he sold himself, Katherine had no choice but to let the orchard go wild because she was unable to afford the expense of hiring a caretaker. Over the years, the branches had been pruned and nurtured only by nature. In the late fall, like now, the one hundred or so trees which remained continued to bear tart, red fruit.

Hester had picked nearly a basketful of the apples downed by the last rain, but she halted upon seeing Galen, aided by Bea's cane, come slowly hobbling in her direction. Her first instinct was to quickly scan the countryside for possible witnesses. It was not uncommon for slave catchers to be lurking amongst the trees outside houses on the Road. However, she saw nothing but the open fields of her land and the brilliant leaves of the autumn-kissed trees off in the distance. She wondered what Galen found so pressing he could not wait for her to return to the house? At least he'd had sense enough to put on the old fisherman's sweater from the chest, she noted approvingly. The air of the sunny mid-October day held the chilly warning of the winter soon to come.

He was breathing harshly when he came abreast of where she stood amongst the trees. The short walk from the house had cost him much in the way of strength.

Wondering if he had any sense at all, she told him, "I'm going to assume there's a sound reason for you to be out?"

He found a cleared stump and eased himself down. "Yes. If I stay locked in that room for one more minute, I'll go insane."

Their eyes held and Hester found herself remembering how warm his skin had felt under her fingertips. She looked away.

"Is it time for a second helping of that ointment?"

She chuckled inwardly and wondered if he possessed mind-reading capabilities. "No," she answered. "After luncheon. Then again after supper."

"Pity," he stated, looking up at her.

When he spoke again his voice was serious. "Hester, I'd like to apologize for my behavior since my arrival. You've been patient and gracious. I was raised better, even if I haven't shown it."

Hester studied his bruised face, sensing his sincerity. "Apology accepted," she replied more softly than she'd

intended. Pulling herself away from the dangerous un-
dertow she sensed in him, she busied herself with
looking for more of the downed apples littering the
ground. She was only interested in the ones still in
relatively good shape. Most of the best fruit had been
shaken down by hired hands less than two weeks ago,
then taken to market to be sold, or, sold by the barrel to
her neighbors who put them up for winter, turned them
into pies or cooked them down to apple sauce. Hester
had her own supply stashed away in barrels in her cellar,
but she checked every day anyway in hopes of rescuing
any fruit which might be salvageable.

As she walked around, stooping here and there to add
an apple to her basket, she was very conscious of Galen.
She knew he was watching her, and because he did she
felt the return of that heart-racing nervousness. She told
herself she was being silly, why in the world should she
be as skittish as a young girl with her first beau? At
twenty-four years of age, she was past the days of being
rendered breathless by a man, even one as intriguing and
mercurial as Galen. Yes, he was the Black Daniel, the
most famous conductor on the Road, but he could also
be rude, foul-tempered, and arrogant to a fault, not to
mention his face, which still looked as if it had been run
over by a wagon wheel. She couldn't possibly be affected
by such a man.

Galen's voice interrupted her thoughts when he asked,
"Who's the biggest land owner around here?"

"Jacob Aray. He settled here in '28 and has about one
hundred and eighty acres." She came back and took a
seat on a nearby stump then looked out over the land.
"In my great-grandparents' day, the biggest land owners
in the area were the Montgomery families. According to
my aunt Katherine, they owned over a thousand acres on
this end of the county."

"Do they still have descendants in the area?"

"No, the Montgomerys were Tories. When the Crown
lost the war, the Montgomerys lost everything. They

eventually emigrated to Canada with the other fleeing Tory supporters and my great-grandfather purchased some of the land."

Galen looked out over the unplowed fields and asked, "How many acres do you own?"

"About one hundred and ten."

"You don't farm?"

"No, but Mr. Hubble does on the land I lease him. At harvest time he gives me a portion of the profit. He lives about five miles east."

"Anyone nearby selling land?"

"Why? Are you looking to live amongst us traitors?"

"Maybe."

"You're jesting, surely?"

"Maybe."

He struggled up off the stump. Aided by the cane, he stood, then said, "I think I've had enough outdoors for one day."

Hester was still stunned by the possibility of him buying land somewhere nearby. She wanted to badger him with questions.

Galen sensed this, and unable to resist teasing her, asked, "Have I piqued your curiosity, Miss Wyatt?"

Hester was surprised by the smile on his battered face. "Yes, Galen, you have."

"Good," he said, chuckling softly. "Good."

Hester watched him hobble away back to the house, her questions unanswered.

Later in the day, Hester pondered his startling revelation. Did he really intend to purchase land in the area, and if so to what purpose? She'd never heard any stories about where the Black Daniel resided when he was not on the Road, nor had she heard anything about his having a family. All she knew was that the Black Daniel helped slaves escape and guided them north, and that he, like the Wesleyites, had never lost a passenger. Did he have a wife somewhere who was right now worried sick over his absence? Having a spouse on the Road had to be harrowing. With all the dangers to be faced—the catchers and dogs to be avoided—the very real threat of betrayal looming everywhere, it made Hester a bit thankful her fiancé, Foster Quint, had no official ties to the Road. Her own involvement was dangerous enough. Foster, a Canadian by birth, was presently in England finishing up his studies at Oxford. He would be returning to America's shores in the spring. Foster's dark face formed in her mind, and she realized she'd written him only once since Galen's arrival. She added one more disparaging mark to the Black Daniel's slate, then stopped herself—Galen had apologized this morning for being such a thorn in her side. He'd even smiled. She'd no idea how long this behavior would last but she hoped it continued for the remainder of his stay.

Hester entered the cellar room and found him feeding wood to the belly of the old stove. The chill in the air down there was perfect for wintering vegetables and other staples, but being below ground with the damp and the cold was not an ideal location for humans. She might have to consider moving him up into the house if he stayed much longer.

"Here's your luncheon," she called.

He turned from the stove, acknowledged her with a nod, and made his way back to the cot. He sat, propped the cane against the thin mattress, and took the tray.

"Is there draught in here?"

Hester shook her head. "No. When Bea stopped by this morning, I told her how you were progressing and she said you can probably do without it."

Once again he surprised her with his smile.

Hester smiled shyly in reply. "I told her you would be pleased. She'd like to come by and see about removing some of the stitching in the next few days."

"Good. The sooner these threads come out of my side the better."

Luncheon consisted of stewed tomatoes, succotash, and the sweetest fish he'd ever tasted. "You're a damned fine cook, Hester Wyatt."

"Thank you."

He held her eyes and she felt the pull of him, tugging at her again. In an attempt to ignore those sensations, she asked, "After your meal, will you tell me about the ambush? We have a Vigilance Committee meeting this evening, and the members will want to know about the traitor."

"So you believe me?"

"Your injuries speak for themselves, but whether the Judas is from Whittaker has not been proven."

"I was bringing some passengers in by wagon—a man named Ephraim, his wife, Liza, and their six-year-old son, Jake. I had rigged myself up earlier to look like an elderly white widow, complete with hat and veil because we'd ridden part of the way to Michigan by train. Ephraim and his small family were posing as my servants."

Using the trains to come north was a bit more common than slave owners and catchers realized, Hester knew. Light-skinned Blacks in particular often utilized their skin color to pose as white and then ride the rails to freedom. One of the most celebrated escapes of the era had been undertaken in 1846 by the very fair skinned Ellen Craft and her husband, William, both slaves from Georgia. Ellen, after transforming herself into a young male planter, had, with her darker-skinned husband posing as her manservant, ridden trains and steamers on the journey from Georgia to the free soil of Philadelphia.

Galen's voice recaptured Hester's attention. "We entered the state over by Cass County. I knew a family in Ann Arbor who would shelter us so we journeyed there. It took us three days, but when we approached the house I saw no light in the windows and no light in the jockey's hand."

Many of the houses on the Road had on their porches or in their front yards a small statue of a black-skinned, red-coated jockey holding a lantern from its extended arm. If the lantern was lit, runaways knew it was safe to approach the house and ask for refuge. If the lantern was dark, travelers knew to move on because the area was not safe. Hester's home had sported such a jockey for many decades. It stood out by the road, ostensibly to light the way to the back of the house. Due to the lurking presence of Shoe and his men, it hadn't been lit for days.

Galen continued. "One of the reasons we needed to find a hidey-hole was due to the full moon that night. If we could see for miles under the light of that moon, so could any slave catchers."

"So where'd you head?"

"To another safe house I knew outside town. Only we never made it. We crossed a small stream and had driven about a mile when six mounted men showed themselves on the banks above."

Galen's voice softened. "They rode slowly down the bank like apparitions from a nightmare. Their presence took us so much by surprise, we could do nothing but hold our ground and wait."

"What happened next?"

"They wanted to know who we were and why we were out so late. I still had on the garb, but I was seated in the bed of the wagon swathed in blankets supposedly to keep away the chill. I immediately closed my eyes and pretended to be just a doddering, but sleeping old woman. We'd rehearsed a story for just such an occasion, so Ephraim pointed me out as his sleeping mistress. He further explained that I was mute and that we were on our way home from a burial in Cassopolis."

"Did they believe him?"

"They asked to see the family's papers."

Hester stilled. "Did you have papers prepared?"

"I'd prepared them before coming north."

Fraudulent papers of freedom were common on the road. Hester's own free papers had been copied many times for others to use. Her neighbor, Branton Hubble, did most of the document forging in her area.

"The man who acted as the leader took the papers from Ephraim and looked at them under the light of the moon. I was afraid he'd keep them or burn them, but after a moment he seemed satisfied and gave the papers back. He then asked if we'd seen any runaways. Ephraim told him no. The man slowly leaned down into Ephraim's face and said he and his men were slave catchers and he hoped Ephraim wasn't lying because he hated liars. Ephraim repeated, he'd seen no one."

"Did that satisfy him?"

"It appeared so, however, they weren't content to simply let us pass. The leader said he and his men had been on the road for a long time. He thought it would be real neighborly if Ephraim would let him take Liza back in the woods."

"Whatever for?"

Galen looked over at her and said softly, "Surely *petite*, you are not that innocent?"

Suddenly getting his meaning, Hester stared aghast.

He continued, "Before any of us could react, one of the riders snatched up the child, Jake, and took him up on his mount. He put a gun to his head and offered Ephraim a choice."

"They didn't harm them did they?"

"In the end, no, because I offered up myself instead."

"What do you mean?"

"I stood up in the wagon, threw off the shawl and wig and identified myself. I told them the bounty they'd receive in exchange for turning me in would buy all the whores they'd ever need. I took the chance their greed would override their lust."

"You also took the chance they'd capture you and harm the woman anyway."

"I know. However I had no other option. There were six of them, they could have just as easily taken what they'd wanted and killed us where we stood. At least this way, Ephraim's family might be allowed to leave with their lives. They were my main concern."

"But your life?"

"Meant less than theirs. They hadn't come all the way from Georgia just to be terrorized by a gang of illiterate kidnappers. Their son was only six. He'd been stoic and helpful the entire trip. He deserved to have a life. I was not going to allow him to watch his mama brutalized and see his father killed trying to defend her—not while I drew breath."

"So what happened?" she whispered.

"The leader seemed a bit stunned by the good fortune that had just fallen into his lap because it took him a moment to figure out what to do. In the end, greed won out. He had me get down from the wagon, then told the family to go on. Ephraim didn't want to leave me, but I assured them this was for the best."

"When did the Wesleyites make their appearance?"

"Not soon enough, believe me. After the family departed, the catchers decided to have a little fun with me. Teach me never to steal anyone's property again, they said."

Hester could hear the bitterness in his voice.

"I've no idea how long the beating lasted, but sometime towards the end I heard gunshots. By then, the pain was so great I'd lost all sense so I didn't care if it were Gabriel and his angels or the hounds of hell. I came to—I'm not sure when or even where—but I looked up and there was old Jeb Wesley's bearded face leaning over me. I heard him say, 'Just lie still, Daniel. Once me and the boys exterminate this vermin with the righteous wrath, we'll get you to a place of safety.'"

Galen added, "I don't remember much else until I woke up here."

"Do you remember waking up and grabbing my wrist?"

He seemed surprised. "No. Did I hurt you?"

She shook her head, but said truthfully, "Frightened me, though."

He searched her face. "Again, my apology."

She nodded her acceptance.

Galen said then, "I do remember hearing someone singing. It sounded like an angel. I wondered if somehow I'd been allowed into heaven?"

"You, in heaven?" she said teasingly.

He smiled. "Those were my thoughts exactly, but the singing was beautiful. Maybe I was simply dreaming."

Hester had never been one to call attention to herself, so she didn't tell him the voice had been hers.

"Well?" he asked.

His question brought her back to the moment. "Well—what?"

"Did I dream the singing?"

Hester hesitated a moment, then said quietly, "No. The voice was mine. I thought to calm you—you were speaking French and being so fitful. It was all I could think to do."

He searched her face a moment, then said, "Thank you for keeping me alive. I might have died had you not agreed to harbor me."

"You're welcome. The Road needs you." Hester then asked, "So when did the catchers mention Whittaker?"

"Some time after all six of them had taken turns teaching me the error of my ways. I remember lying on the ground and being in such pain I would've welcomed death. The leader leaned down and cackled there were catchers all over the state massed on the Ohio border waiting for me, but he'd been the one to find me. Said you people, meaning we on the Road, had a snake in our garden over in Whittaker. He considered it only fitting I know I'd been betrayed by one of my own before he sent me to hell."

"Do you know anyone in Whittaker?" Hester asked.

Galen shook his head. "No."

"Then I don't understand. Who here would have known you were coming? Surely you didn't announce your intent to travel here ahead of time?"

"Unfortunately I did, in a way. Do you know anything about the men who put together the Order?"

Hester did. The Order originated with the Black conductors in Detroit. The men of the Order were known by various names, one being the African-American Mysteries: Order of the Men of Oppression.

Their secret passwords, handshakes, and coded identification system had been modified for use by many of the agents and conductors on the Road. Among the founders of the Order were two of the most successful conductors in Detroit—William Lambert, the leader of Michigan's Black Road network, and George De Baptiste, a Detroit tailor. De Baptiste was so hated in areas of the South, a reward of one thousand dollars awaited any slave catcher who could capture him. Hester said, "Galen, I can't believe any of those men betrayed you. You said yourself you were in a lot of pain after the beating. Are you certain of what you heard?"

"I'd stake my life on it."

Hester could see he had faith in what he believed. She didn't know what to say.

Instead she asked, "Why did you let them know you were coming here? Do you do that often?"

"Usually my plans are known only to myself and my passengers. However, I had some information I was bringing north—information the Order had requested. They knew the approximate dates of my arrival so it would have been fairly simple for someone to pass that knowledge on to the slave catchers."

Hester found this all very stunning. "Let's say for the sake of argument there is a traitor, how do you propose to find him or her?"

"That's a question I can't answer yet."

"Can't or won't?"

He smiled. "Both."

Hester didn't press. She stood and asked, "Do you want to meet the member of the local Vigilance Committee?"

"No. The fewer people who know I'm in the area, the better."

"I agree, but the conductors deserve to be alerted if there's a traitor in our midst. They'll certainly want to know where I received such incriminating information."

"I understand, and that's a risk I'll have to take."

Hester then asked the question that had been weighing on her mind. "Galen, why are you divulging all of this to me? How do you know I'm not the traitor?"

"Are you?"

"Of course not."

"Then the point is moot, *petite*."

He spoke the diminutive so softly she felt as if he'd stroked her with more than just his voice. She managed to ask, "Are you ready for more of Bea's salve?"

He nodded.

She sat on the edge of the cot while he undid his shirt. When his chest was exposed she tamped down the tingling he seemed to inspire and began a slow repeat of this morning's application of the salve. The heat rising from his chest seemed to be even more distracting than it had been earlier. While she worked, she couldn't help but peek up at his flat brown nipples, then ordered herself to pay attention to what she was supposed to be doing.

With his eyes closed, Galen could feel her warm fingers slowly working him into a lazy state of arousal. It had been quite some time since he'd felt the soft caress of a woman's touch; he usually remained celibate while on the Road, however, her indigo hands reminded him just how long it had been. Rather than embarrass her with the soon-to-be-evident proof of his growing desire, Galen placed his hand over hers to stay it.

Hester looked up in surprise. Her hand caught beneath his own felt as if it were on fire. "Have I hurt you?"

He chuckled and slowly opened his eyes, "No, Indigo, you haven't hurt me. I just think I've had enough salve for today."

Galen thought about how it might feel to have her touch him without inhibition. He realized such images would not help quiet his awakened arousal, so he lifted her hand and peered at it.

Hester tried to remain calm and unmoved, but she could not still the shaking of her hand.

"You have beautiful hands, Hester Wyatt. They're like exotic indigo orchids."

Hester could only swallow.

"You're shaking," he stated.

For the first time Galen could see that the smallest finger on her hand had no nail. It appeared to have been severed. He gently moved his own finger over the shortened digit and asked softly, "What happened here?"

"My mother did this a few days after I was born. She and my father hoped it would make me distinctive enough to be found by my aunt."

"You'll have to tell me the story one day."

Galen experienced the overwhelming urge to bring the finger to his lips, but he didn't want to frighten her so he ignored the urge, then slowly released her hand.

"What is that scent you're wearing?" he asked softly.

It took her a moment to pull herself away from his eyes. "I—don't wear a scent."

He leaned over and inhaled the sweet fragrance lingering against her trembling neck. "That isn't a scent?"

Hester fought to speak in a calm tone. "It is vanilla."

"Vanilla?"

"Vanilla."

"Vanilla that is placed in sweets?"

"Yes. I don't see the value in wasting coin on real scents, but I am a woman and I do like to smell nice. So, I use vanilla, just as my aunt did."

Hester had no idea what this interlude meant or where it might lead, but she was still shaking. He was a powerful presence and she could feel that power arching around the room like captured lightning. She stood in order to put distance between herself and the man on the cot.

"I'll—bring you your supper later and go on to the meeting."

He nodded, then watched her go.

Chapter 5

~~~⌒⌒⌒~~~

As Hester drove her small buggy to the church for the meeting, she, like all other abolitionists, looked forward to the day when slavery would be abolished, thereby making the oft times secret work of the vigilance committees no longer necessary. Until then, committees like the one in Whittaker were desperately needed to provide the runaways with lodging, food, clothing, and medicine. Members also informed the former slaves of their legal rights, saw to the fugitives' establishment of a new life, gave direction, guidance, and in many instances secured small amounts of money and letters of introduction to potential employers.

Vigilance groups existed from Maine to California. Some were large, others small. Some boasted members from a variety of races, while others, like the committee in Detroit, were all Black. Regardless of a committee's size or makeup, all fashioned themselves after one of the most dedicated committees of the abolitionist era, the New York Committee of Vigilance, founded in 1835 by a Black man named David Ruggles. Ruggles personally assisted the secret passage of hundreds of runaways to the quasi-free areas of the segregated north, one of the most prominent runaways being the great Frederick Douglass.

To further the cause, Ruggles often visited the docks of New York to make certain slaves weren't being smuggled in on arriving ships. He went door to door in some of the city's wealthiest neighborhoods to inform domestic workers that under the laws of New York imported slaves were free after residing in the state for ninety days. Under his leadership runaways were invited to address the audiences at some of the New York committee meetings and relate their struggles for freedom.

Mr. Ruggles eventually severed his ties to the New York group due to a problem with his eyesight, but continued to offer his personal assistance to those seeking freedom.

Yet over twenty years later, slavery still fouled the land. Like the passage of the Fugitive Slave Law, the Supreme Court decision denying Mr. Dred Scott's petition for freedom had been a blow to the cause of abolition. The court stated in part that because the men and women of the race had always been considered inferior, the race had no rights a White man was bound to respect. Slaves continued to escape however, despite the court's outrageous decree. Their refusal to remain chattel made the continued existence of the Vigilance Committees imperative.

Like many of the other committees in the country, Whittaker's Vigilance Committee used a modified version of the Order's coded methods to communicate secretly. Bea Meldrum served as the area's messenger because her egg deliveries and doctoring took her all over the county. Hester had been alerted to this evening's emergency meeting, not by anything Bea had said, but by the color of the cloth in the egg basket Bea had left on the porch that morning. The cloth had been red, the standard color for a committee summons. The number written with paraffin on the shell of one of the eggs told the meeting's time.

Hester could hear the voices of the choir rehearsing as she entered Whittaker's A.M.E. church. While the choir rehearsed in the small sanctuary on the church's main floor, below ground, in the church cellar, the Reverend

Joseph Adams called the meeting of the Vigilance Committee to order. There were twenty members on the official roll, but only four had shown up tonight— Hester, Bea, Branton Hubble, and William Lovejoy. Lovejoy owned a very successful barbering business and was the wealthiest man in Whittaker.

"First of all," the Reverend Adams began, "I'd like to thank Bea for contacting everyone. There are fifteen choir members at the rehearsal upstairs, a good turnout for such short notice."

Bea accepted the thanks with a nod of her gray head. The rehearsing choir would serve as a mask for the meeting.

"Now, the reason we are here. There's been much speculation over the whereabouts of the Black Daniel. Rumors have him gone to ground from here to Ontario, and back. The Order has asked all chief conductors to ask their local agents if anyone knows where he really is."

Hester hesitated to reveal Galen's location upon hearing of the Order's interest, but Galen had given her permission to reveal his presence so she said, "He's in my cellar, Reverend."

Suddenly she was the center of attention. "Bea patched up his injuries, but I never told her his true identity."

Bea smiled. "So that's who he is."

Bea then swung around on her chair to get a good look at William Lovejoy, and said, "Guess a woman can keep a secret, eh Lovejoy?"

Bea's cackle of amusement seemed to further sour Lovejoy's petulant features. William Lovejoy was a stooped, balding little man of about fifty years of age. He had made it clear for many years how he felt about women being members of the Vigilance Committee: he was opposed. His prejudices had caused many arguments among the members, especially in light of all the work done by women on behalf of similar committees throughout the country.

Lovejoy turned to Hester and asked sharply, "Why haven't you told anyone before now?"

Before Hester could answer, Branton Hubble, Hester's neighbor and good friend, asked Lovejoy coolly, "Do you ever announce who you are harboring in your loft, Lovejoy?"

Lovejoy knew the answer. He did not respond.

Hester smiled her thanks at Branton for his support, saying. "I didn't want to reveal his whereabouts without his permission."

Bea cracked, "Secretive *and* smart."

The reverend then asked, "Do you think the Daniel will agree to meet with us?"

Hester could see the enthusiasm in the reverend's eyes as he voiced the question. The Black Daniel was a legend; few if any had ever seen him. Hester understood the reverend's desire to be one of those few. "I'm not certain he will agree. He's convinced we have a traitor in our midst."

Everyone stared. Branton Hubble asked, "What do you mean?"

Hester told them Galen's story. When she finished, the room was silent.

"That's impossible," Branton barked.

"I agree, Branton," Hester replied. "However he is convinced the slave hunter was telling the truth."

"There are no traitors here," Lovejoy stated.

"Suppose it's true. How do we proceed?" Bea asked.

"The Daniel says he has a plan," Hester stated.

"What sort of plan?" the reverend asked.

Hester shrugged. "I've no idea." She thought about revealing Galen's questions concerning local land for sale, but she'd not asked him if he wanted that information revealed, so she did not.

The group spent a few more minutes discussing the faults and possible merits of Galen's theory. In the midst of this, Lovejoy said, "Reverend, I seriously think we should discuss Hester's continuing role in the harboring of such an important man."

"Why?" the reverend asked skeptically. "Hester seems to have everything well in hand."

"Because if he needs protection, a man should be there."

Bea asked, "Are you offering to be that man?"

"I don't see why not," Lovejoy stated proudly. "My home is large, and—"

"And," Hubble broke in, "you're the worst shot in three counties. If the Daniel finds Hester's care lacking, I'm sure he'll let someone know. Until then he stays where he is. Agreed?"

The reverend and Bea shook their heads in mutual agreement.

Lovejoy sat back in angry silence. Hester knew the wealthy barber did not like having his lack of firearms skill aired, but the truth was that Whittaker had schoolchildren who could shoot better.

Reverend Adams then asked Bea about the movements of Shoe and his men. Bea's answer was disheartening. "Unfortunately, it looks as if he may be here for the winter. He's holed up over at Porter Greer's."

Everyone acknowledged that to be a distressing turn of events. Porter Greer lived about twenty-five miles south of Whittaker and made his living kidnapping runaways. He posed enough of a menace alone; in tandem with Shoe and his brigands, he would be even more of a threat to the Road's operation.

Branton Hubble remarked dryly, "It's too bad the both of them can't meet with an arranged accident."

The reverend admonished Branton with a disapproving look. Branton Hubble, and a growing percentage of abolitionists were of the opinion only a violent confrontation would push the government to outlaw the holding of men and women as slaves. Until 1840, many abolitionists, both Black and White, viewed abolitionism as a pacifistic endeavor. With the passage of the 1850 Fugitive Slave Law and the resulting kidnappers spreading terror across the North, many vigilance committee members were meeting slave catchers' writs with guns drawn. Even Frederick Douglass, long a supporter of the nonviolent approach to abolition, had publicly voiced support for those who would take up arms to end slavery.

Reverend Adams said, "Branton, I ask that you not intercede with violence."

"Are you going to tell that to Greer and Shoe too, Reverend Adams?" Branton asked in return.

The two men had argued before over their differing approaches. The reverend still believed prayer more valuable than arms. Branton did not agree.

Hester sensed the rising tension in the room. "Gentlemen, can we postpone this discussion until the next time, please? We have more tangible issues to discuss now."

Both men gave imperceptible nods and the meeting's talk returned to the Daniel's betrayal. Hester asked, "Branton, could there be a traitor in the Order?"

"It is possible I suppose. For now, I suggest we not answer the Order's summons about the Daniel's whereabouts. If the Daniel decides he wants his presence revealed, he will tell us."

Everyone agreed.

It was dark outside when the meeting and the choir rehearsal came to a close. Branton Hubble walked with Hester to her buggy, which was parked beside the church. They'd always been special friends. He'd loved her Aunt Katherine from afar for most of Hester's life, yet he'd never acted upon his feelings out of respect for his wife, still in bondage in Kentucky.

"Hester, is the Daniel giving you any problems?"

"He did in the beginning, snarled at me the whole time. We're progressing a bit better now that's he healing."

"What type of man is he?"

"Stubborn."

Branton smiled. "Well, if you need anything, let me know."

"I will."

She picked up the reins, but Branton's voice stopped her. "Oh and Hester, be very careful if you're going to continue to move passengers. Shoe and his men seem to be particularly nasty."

"Don't worry. I doubt I'll do anything while the Daniel's here."

Hester slapped the reins and drove away.

Hester looked in on Galen when she returned. She'd expected him to be sleeping but was surprised to see him lying atop the cot, awake. He turned his face her way and smiled. "Good evening, Miss Wyatt."

"Good evening, Galen. I thought you'd be sleeping."

"I hoped you'd stop in to tell me about the meeting."

Hester noticed the chill in the room. "Aren't you cold in here?" She walked over to the stove and tossed in more wood.

"I've slept in colder places," he replied.

"We should move you up into the house. You will heal faster in warmer surroundings."

He smiled. "Are you trying to rush my recovery so I'll be out of your hair, Miss Wyatt?"

His teasing made her lower her eyes, then say, innocently, "I simply thought you might be more comfortable."

He laughed, the first time she'd heard him do so so robustly, and she liked the sound.

Galen said, "I'm fine here. In the house I may be seen."

"No one will see you. There isn't a house for miles. Besides, Shoe is holed up south of here, down in Monroe."

"It isn't Shoe I'm worried about—it's the good citizens of this town."

Hester shook her head at his continued harping on the trustworthiness of her neighbors. "The few good citizens who are aware of your presence here have vowed to keep you safe. Trust us."

When he didn't reply, Hester added, "Galen, I know

we are strangers to you, but aren't you a stranger to the people you bring north?"

He nodded.

"So, if they can trust you, you should trust also. Believe me, you will heal better up in the house."

"And your reputation? Won't there be some old church biddies quacking about you being compromised?"

"I don't know where you're from originally Galen, but on the Road here, we women don't always have the luxury of worrying about our reputations when there's work to be done." She paused, then added, "Besides, the reverend from the church knows you're here, and even if he didn't, I'm of the opinion that slavery's reputation is far more sullied than mine will ever be."

Galen could see the flash of determination in her eyes. He sighed visibly in surrender. "All right, Miss Wyatt. You win."

Hester's smiled triumphantly.

The next day, Hester showed Galen up to the attic room. "This room was originally built by my great-grandfather Ellis," she explained. She crossed the portal and opened up the drapes and windows to let in fresh air and light. The morning sun revealed fine dark wood paneling the walls from floor to ceiling.

Galen looked around. There were large windows all the way around the big bedroom. The wood floors and walls gleamed with the care they'd been given. There was a big canopied four-poster bed. The four-poster, the largest bed Galen had seen in quite some time, would surely give him a more restful sleep than the thin pallet on the cot in the cellar room. There was a desk, a beautifully polished wardrobe, and a screened area that he assumed disguised the chamber facilities. "All this wood reminds me of a ship."

Hester agreed. "He apprenticed on a whaler as a young man. After the war, he came to Michigan and sailed the lakes on a merchant vessel. He loved the sea."

Galen's eyes swept over a big black bathing tub inlaid

with mother of pearl. Its exotic beauty captured his attention. "Where did you acquire this?" he asked, walking over to view it more closely. The work was exquisite and the tub's circumference appeared large enough to accommodate a man his size quite comfortably.

"My grandfather brought it back from Arabia on one of his last sea voyages."

"Looks like it might have belonged to a sheik's harem."

"It certainly appears lavish enough," Hester said with a smile. "But I wouldn't know. Once you're healed, feel free to use it if you like. There's a drain beneath it, and a pipe which takes the water out of the house. You still have to haul the water up here however, so it hasn't been used on a regular basis in many years, though Aunt Katherine did use it occasionally."

Galen looked around the room again, then walked over to gaze out of the small, lead-paned windows at the world spread below. On the window seat he saw an eyeglass. He picked it up and, after lengthening it, held it to his eye. He was treated to a commanding view of the countryside. "That's quite a view," he told her. He swept the area a moment longer, then set the glass back on the window seat.

"It's one of the reasons I want to put you up here. You can see the approach from any direction."

"The other reason?"

Hester walked over to the wall behind the big four poster bed. "This."

He watched as she touched the wall. A portion of it swung open without a sound. He came over to the opening and peered into the darkness.

Hester explained. "There's a wooden incline leading down to the tunnel below the house. Great-grandfather Ellis said one can run faster down an incline than a flight of stairs."

Galen agreed. He'd known many a man to break a limb running hell bent down a flight of stairs.

Hester then said, "Close your eyes."

He raised an eyebrow.

"Please?"

To her surprise he complied without argument. "Now, give me your hand." When he did, she gently moved his strong, warm hand over the grain of the panel. "Can you feel the slight roughness of the wood here, as opposed to here?"

He nodded yes.

"Now open your eyes." She then had him inspect the area, after which she showed him the place on the wood which sprung the opening. To the casual observer it appeared as just another whorl in the highly polished oak. "I have a similar panel in my room. My aunt Katherine made me practice until I could find the spring in the dark. You should probably do the same."

"How many other escapes in the house?"

"Not many more, but enough where we can always get a head start, hopefully," she added in a serious tone. "I can show them to you whenever you care to view them."

"How about now?"

Hester nodded, then led him from the room.

She showed him the secret panels in the three bedrooms which were oft times occupied by her passengers, and the tunnel entrance beneath the rocker in the study. He'd already seen the passage behind the kitchen leading to the room in the cellar.

When she finished the tour Galen asked, "Is that all of them?"

"Except for the one in my bedroom, yes."

"I need to see it also."

Hester blinked. She'd never had a man in her bedroom. "Why?"

"So I will know where it is."

She supposed the logic of the request made sense, however, she doubted he would ever need to escape from her bedroom, but rather than argue over the matter, Hester led him back upstairs.

Inside her room, Hester walked over to the paneled

wall to the right of her wardrobe, and showed Galen what he wanted to see. As in the other rooms, the whorls of the wood camouflaged the spring. Her fingers pressed the spot and the panel swung open. Her expression asked, Are you satisfied?

He nodded like a tall monarch pleased with a royal subject.

A touch and the opening was concealed again.

Galen took the opportunity to glance around her room. He no longer had to imagine where she slept at night. His gaze slid over her bed. Atop the mussed quilt and exposed sheet lay a nightgown which could have belonged to a Quaker woman. There were no ribbons or geegaws for a man to linger over. To his practiced eye the fabric appeared rough and uncomfortable.

Seeing his interest in her gown, Hester hastily retrieved it. His face held nothing that could be construed as lustful, but an embarrassed Hester opened a drawer on the wardrobe and threw the gown inside.

His eyebrow raised but he didn't speak. For a few seconds, they stood silent, observing one another. Hester couldn't imagine why her heart was racing so. As she'd reminded herself before, she was far past the age of being so affected by a man. Hester asked over her pounding heart, "I—have you seen all you need to see?"

Galen thought she looked far too innocent to be in this business. In his mind, she should be married to a good man having his babies, not risking her life every day for a cause which appeared to have no end. "No, Hester Wyatt, I have not, but we can leave now."

Hester blinked, put her heart back inside her ribs, and led the way.

Galen chastised himself for playing with her in such a fashion. He'd be willing to bet she did not possess the experience to do anything but flee in the face of his teasing, yet he found the play disturbingly stimulating.

Hester prepared his lunch and joined him at the dining room table. He asked, "Aren't you going to eat?"

"I'll eat later."

He studied her face a moment.

Hester added, "I ate a big breakfast, I'm not really hungry."

He nodded, then began to eat. Between bites, he said, "Tell me about the area. How many families are there?"

"About fifty. Most have moved here in the past six or seven years."

"Are most runaways?"

"Yes. After the passage of the Fugitive Slave Law, many families fled to Ontario and are just returning."

Galen knew that many thousands fled to Canada immediately after the passage of the 1850 law. Major cities all over the North lost great percentages of their Black populations as a result of the terror evoked amongst all who'd escaped slavery.

Like its 1793 predecessor, the law forbade the escaping of slaves from one state to another. It also denied arrested fugitives the right to trial by jury and the right to take the stand in their own defense. Instead, Congress appointed special commissioners to try the cases.

If the commissioner decided in favor of the slave owner, the commissioner received ten dollars, but only five if the fugitive won. Abolitionists called the payments nothing more than glorified bribes, but Congress justified the discrepancy by saying the commissioners deserved the payments for the time spent processing all the documents needed to send a slave south.

The penalties for assisting or harboring an escaped slave were stiffened by the law, and any U.S. marshall or federal deputy who refused to help a slave owner reclaim his property faced a stiff thousand-dollar fine.

Given such carte blanche, slave owners and their slave hunters repeatedly abused the edict. They felt free to bring before the federal commissioners any individual of color, whether they'd legally owned them previously or not. In some cases they bypassed the law altogether and simply kidnapped the alleged fugitive and took them south.

"This kidnapper you spoke of last night after the meeting, Greer, how active is he?"

"Very."

"Does he know you're a station?"

"Yes. He had my aunt arrested several times. He was never able to produce the runaways in court though, so she was never tried."

"And have you ever been arrested?"

"At rallies, but never for station work. At least not yet." She paused, then asked, "What about you?"

"I spent three years in a Carolina prison."

His voice was so cold she didn't dare ask the particulars of his imprisonment. She could only assume it had to do with slave stealing.

After lunch he asked her, "Do you keep any weapons in the house?"

He expected her to have a pistol at best, not the small, well-stocked arsenal she showed him hidden in the false back of the kitchen sideboard. He took down a rifle and inspected it. He was pleased that the guns were well maintained. "Can you use any of these?"

"My aunt trained me on them all. I don't like firearms, but I know my life may depend upon my ability to use one, so I tolerate them."

"Are you any good?" he asked.

"With my aunt Katherine as a teacher, of course. With her you either did your very best, or listened to her lectures on doing your very best."

Galen rehung the rifle in its spot, then spent the next few moments inventorying the arms available. He took down an excellently weighted pistol.

"That one belonged to my father," Hester explained.

"I'd like to keep it in my room, if that is agreeable."

"Whatever you need, Galen."

She showed him where she kept the cartridges, and he placed the small wooden box of ammunition on the kitchen table beside the pistol. He'd take them up to the room later. Having a firearm gave him some measure of assurance. At least now he'd be able to defend himself should the circumstance arise.

Hester's voice interrupted his thoughts. "I have some errands in town tomorrow. Will you be wanting anything?"

Galen had met women all over the world but none drew him like this woman with her diamond-black eyes and indigo hands. She could become a distraction if he weren't careful. "Do you think you could manage some barber supplies, without attracting too much attention?" The hair on his face had begun to grow, shadowing his face like a pirate. He decided he'd let the beard grow as a way to mask his real features, but it would need grooming regardless.

"Not necessary. There are supplies here which I keep around for my passengers. I'll get them for you."

She left the kitchen but returned a few moments later and handed him a small canvas bag. Inside he found a razor, a soap brush, and scissors. "Thank you," he said. "Now I want to inspect those inclines and the tunnel."

"Today?"

"Today."

By the time they were done, Hester could see weariness restaking its claim on his body. He'd made her lead him up and down the secret inclines, after which he looked over every inch of the earthen tunnel beneath the house and its branch-covered entrance from the river bank.

Afterward, Hester said, "Galen, maybe you should go on upstairs to bed. I'll clean up down here."

Galen didn't argue. He climbed the stairs with the sound of her whispered, "Sleep well" caressing his ears.

Chapter 6

The next morning, as Hester was preparing breakfast, Bea Meldrum stopped by to remove the
stitching from Galen's side. When Hester informed her
Galen hadn't awakened yet, Bea promised to return later
in the day.

After Bea's departure, Hester cracked three large eggs
into the sizzling skillet which had just fried five hardy
slabs of back bacon. When the eggs were done, she
removed them from the hot skillet and gently set them
on a plate beside the bacon. Also on the plate sat a
mound of steamed, seasoned potatoes, and two large
wedges of the bread she'd baked last night after Galen
retired to bed. She couldn't help marvelling at the size of
the portions and wonder who fed him on a regular basis.
She couldn't believe how much he ate.

She set the plate on a tray, added a large steaming cup
of coffee, silver, and a clean linen napkin. Because she
and the women of her circle practiced Free Produce,
Hester didn't keep sugar in the house. Free Produce
supporters hoped to strike at slavery by affecting the
slave owner's profits. Supporters did not use or consume
any products made by slave labor, and so did without
items such as sugar, rice, and American-raised cotton.
The women who could afford them purchased the
higher-priced English or Egyptian cotton fabrics, even
though they were in some instances coarser and not as

finely woven as their American counterparts. Those women unable to afford the imported fabrics made do with their old gowns, choosing principle over fashion.

To sweeten tea and coffee, Hester used either honey or maple syrup. Galen preferred the syrup, so she poured a bit into a china demi-cup. She picked up the tray, turned, and was so startled by the sight of him standing in the doorway she almost dropped the tray. "You frightened me to death!" she gasped. How long had he been standing there observing?

He simply smiled. "Good morning. That tray for me?"

Looking at his smile, Hester noted that in spite of his still healing face, he had a presence about him which made her believe women found him hard to resist. He exuded a masculinity that flowed around her like fading tendrils of smoke. "Um, yes—I was just on my way up."

Still smiling, he gently took the tray from her shaking hands.

Galen was well accustomed to flustering women, but Hester made him feel differently about his prowess. Unlike the calculating women he sometimes attracted, Hester's show was no act. She drew him to explore what else that innocence might encompass. Had she ever been kissed?

They left the kitchen to go into the dining room where Galen set down the tray and took a seat. She sat also, but he noticed she had no plate in front of her. "Aren't you going to join me?" he asked.

She shook her head no, then said, "I ate earlier."

For some reason, Galen didn't believe her, probably because she looked so guilty. She'd never make a convincing liar, he thought to himself. He made a point to remember that for the future. He said softly, "Tell me the truth. Have you eaten this morning?"

Hester knew if he'd seen through the initial lie he would undoubtedly see through another one. She wouldn't meet his eyes. "No," she confessed.

Galen wondered why on earth she would lie about something as mundane as eating? As the possible answer came to mind, a chill ran over him. He slowly got up from the table and went back into the kitchen. In the small sink he spied one lone coffee cup. He walked over to her cupboards.

Hester came into the kitchen and found him opening up drawers and bins. "What are you doing?"

"Seeing how much food you have, Indigo."

That name again. He spoke it as if she were someone he cherished. But she immediately let that thought slide away. "Why?"

"Because you haven't eaten. You didn't eat much last night either."

His inspection now complete, he took down a clean plate and went back out to the dining room. Hester followed, then watched him spoon portions of everything on his plate onto the second plate, then he pushed the plate in her direction. "Sit. And eat," he ordered.

Hester sat. He looked so upset, she didn't dare argue. She supposed he'd discovered the true state of her larder.

He asked, "Why have you let me eat you out of house and home?"

"You needed the food."

"Never go without for my benefit again."

She didn't like being dictated to, not even by someone who thought they had her best interests at heart. "You wouldn't have recovered as quickly if I hadn't gone without. You were certainly in no position to write me a bank draft."

"But I am now."

"That's hardly the issue, is it?"

"It is as far as I'm concerned. How do you support yourself?"

"I do, that's all you need be concerned with."

"Obviously it isn't. You don't have enough food in this house to keep crawdads alive!"

"I can hardly do the work I do without some sacrifice."

"I understand that, but never sacrifice yourself. You're no good to anyone half starved."

She took immediate offense. "I am not half starved."

"When was the last time you had a full meal?"

She didn't answer. He hadn't raised his voice during any part of the confrontation, but Hester felt as if they were shouting loud enough to be heard in Ohio.

"Well?" he asked, still waiting for her to answer. From her continued silence, he knew it had probably been some days ago. "Get a fork and eat all of that."

A tight-lipped Hester complied, then came back and took her seat.

Galen observed the mutinous set of her jaw. She was eating, grudgingly, but he didn't pay her manner much mind. Instead he found himself lingering over the features of her face. God she was beautiful. Even with his limited vision, he had no difficulty discerning that fact. Her skin looked like the gift of an African night goddess. Dark with the true colors of her ancestry, the sable highlights beneath added to the luster of a face as clear as precious obsidian. The jet-diamond eyes sat beneath lashes so long they brushed her cheeks. He knew it would only be a matter of time before he succumbed to the urge to touch her. He shook himself. For all his musing, he had no business thinking along those lines; he would be leaving Whittaker as soon as it could be arranged, and once gone would probably never see her again. He was surprised at how disturbing those thoughts left him feeling. "When you're in town today, do you think you can send a wire for me?"

"Yes." Hester was still smarting from his lecturing. "Bea may stop in later, she wants to remove those threads."

He nodded, then asked very seriously, "Hester, how do you support yourself?"

Hester would have preferred her finances, or lack

thereof, not be a topic for discussion, but she knew he would not let the subject rest until he received a satisfactory answer. "I write antislavery tracts for an English publisher. I offer piano lessons to the children in the area. I have a bit of a pension from my aunt and father. And I sell apples," she explained.

"That's it?"

Hester cut him a look which instantly made him contrite. "I'm sorry," he said genuinely. "I'm prying I know, but it's only because I'm concerned."

"I'm doing fine, Galen. Foster has some income. Should the purse become truly empty, I can always sell some of the land. I'd hate to, but even I know I must eat."

Her frank eyes held his own. Galen experienced the overwhelming urge to protect her, but knew the prideful little Indigo would toss him out on his ear should he even propose to help her escape the pinch of poverty. He didn't know why he hadn't figured out her strained position sooner; her clothing stated her need quite plainly. Her garments were always clean and pressed, but the cuffs at her wrists and the hems of her skirts were frayed with age. He knew she practiced Free Produce and he thought the vow she'd taken to be a noble one, however, the women of his circle back home would have reduced such clothing to polishing rags long ago; Hester carried herself as if the old gowns were made of woven gold.

"Galen."

He shook himself free of his musings. "I'm sorry Indigo, did you ask something?"

Once again the name rolled over Hester like the brushing of a cloud. She struggled a moment to remember what she'd been about to say. "Yes. My plate is clean, may I be excused now?"

He raised an eyebrow at her sarcastic little dig and the light shining in her dark eyes. He decided her wit was just one more of her attractive attributes. He smiled. "Yes, *petite,* you may be excused."

Hester spent most of the day in Ann Arbor, the town situated only a few miles west. She stopped off at the post office only to be told the draft she'd hoped to receive from her English publisher had not arrived. She swallowed her disappointment, then crossed the street to post Galen's wire. His note seemed innocent enough—a message alluded to the ordering of lumber and nails— but Hester assumed it was a code. Afterwards, Hester stopped by Kate Bell's boarding house for lunch, after which she sat a spell to gossip with the women in Kate's back room parlor. Most of the gossip centered around Bethany Ann Lovejoy, the seventeen-year-old daughter of Vigilance Committee member William Lovejoy. Bethany Ann had run away from home rather than marry her father's hand-picked groom, a middle-aged business associate named John Royce. That she had disappeared on the night before the wedding had tongues wagging as far east as Detroit. No one had heard a word from her since. Lovejoy had spent a fortune on the construction of one of the largest and grandest homes in the county for the newlyweds to reside in, but with Bethany Ann's flight, it sat empty.

The dusk of late afternoon had already fallen by the time Hester completed the trek home. She put the buggy in the barn, then went into the house. On the kitchen table she found a note left by Bea indicating the threads had been removed from Galen's side. Beside the note lay a smoked ham Bea had dropped off courtesy of Branton Hubble, along with two rashes of bacon. Hester silently offered thanks for the generosity of her neighbors, then went to call up the stairs after Galen. When she received no reply, she assumed he was sleeping. She decided to start dinner, then go up and check on him.

* * *

Carefully balancing the tray holding Galen's meal, Hester knocked lightly upon the attic room's door and entered when he called. She found him lounging in her grandfather's big black porcelain bathing tub. The sight of his bare chest rising golden above the water threw her into such an embarrassed disarray, she instantly spun her back on him. "I thought you said come in!" she gasped.

Galen couldn't help smiling at her scandalized manner, but said truthfully, "I'm the one who should apologize. This warm water had me so lulled I forgot where I was. I answered your knock without thought."

"Are you saying you commonly invite females into your bath?"

"At one time in my life, it was not uncommon for me to invite females to share my bath."

Hester's eyes widened.

Galen chuckled inwardly, wishing he could see the look on her face. He guessed he'd shocked her silly with his truthful revelation, even if that had not been his intent. He told himself he should remember just how sheltered a life she probably led.

Hester was indeed shocked—both by finding him in the tub, and by the startling admission. She knew men were allowed to conduct their lives in ways far outside the strict boundaries governing female behavior, but would a woman of good reputation cavort with a man in a tub? She wondered what kind of man Galen really was and what social circles he traveled in when he was not the Black Daniel. Still standing with her back to him, she said, "I'll just leave the tray here by the door and return for it later."

His soft voice stayed her. "Was it my imagination or did I see two settings on that tray?"

The room seemed to grow very warm, and Hester looked down guiltily at the two plates and two sets of silver, then said, "I—thought you might enjoy some company. You've been here all alone today and—"

"I would enjoy that," he replied in a tone so gentle it set her pulses to beating.

Hester stammered. "Then I'll—step out—so you may—"

"No need for you to leave. If you'll just stand as you are—"

The sound of sloshing water filled the room. Hester momentarily forgot his caution and instinctively turned to the sounds. Seeing him about to emerge from the tub she gasped again, and spun back.

His soft laugh behind her only increased her dismay. He chuckled, "I told you to stand still."

She countered in her own defense, "I'd no idea you were—"

The sloshing began again and she froze, rooted like a tree. It ceased only a moment later, followed by the sounds of him quietly moving around behind her. A big, standing oak mirror stood to Hester's right. She unsuccessfully fought the unladylike urge to peek at what it might reflect across the room. In the glass he stood with his back to her, drying himself with a flannel drying sheet. Her eyes roamed slowly over the golden muscles rippling across his back and shoulders, then lower over the powerful thighs, hips, and legs. Shocking herself at this brazen breach of good manners, she raised her eyes and her breathing stopped upon finding him watching her in turn. Scandalized, she hastily looked away.

Galen said amusedly, "The curiosity is only natural, Indigo," though he wondered what to do with the natural rise in his manhood brought on by her innocent voyeurism. "Maybe someday, you'll offer me the opportunity to indulge my own curiosity . . ."

His voice was filled with heat, causing Hester to sway. She lacked the experience to even begin forming a reply to such an intimate request.

She felt relieved when he finally said, "You may turn around now."

He'd donned a simple shirt and trousers, but the image of him standing nude had burned itself into

Hester's memory. "Maybe we should eat downstairs," she offered.

"Wherever you feel most comfortable."

She broke contact with his potent gaze, and drew a calming breath. Hester wondered why it suddenly felt like July in there, and why looking at him made the tingling start up again. She knew why. In spite of her previous denials, she found herself attracted to Galen.

Downstairs at the table, Hester told herself that she did not feel the heat of his body warming her own as she went about setting the plates, but knew she lied. The heat was as rattling as the memories of his boldly expressed desire to see her nude.

Galen looked down at her hands as she placed his plate before him, and fought down the urge to stroke the indigo-colored backs and the small severed finger. He knew he shouldn't be indulging himself with the imagined touch and feel of her, for he would be out of her life very soon, but the more he denied himself, the stronger the urge became. To her credit, she'd chosen to eat at the table. The atmosphere in the room upstairs had been sultry and charged. He'd felt it and was fairly certain she had also. Propriety dictated she not be alone in his room. Propriety also dictated that he do nothing to undermine her relationship with her fiancé, though Galen wished it sorely.

In her seat across the table from him, Hester fought to keep herself on an even keel. By all rights she should be viewing Galen as just another passenger seeking a safe harbor, but he'd become more than that and she'd no idea how to proceed. She thought to neutralize the intensity by asking, "Where'd you learn to speak French?"

"Louisiana. Where'd you learn to cook?"

Hester smiled. "My aunt Katherine."

"She taught you well."

Before Hester could stop herself she asked, "Is Galen your true name?"

He observed her over his plate for a few, long moments, so long in fact, Hester said contritely, "You don't have to answer. I'm sorry. That's really none of my business."

"No apologies are necessary. My true name is Galeno. It's Spanish, and means 'the light one.' Galen is the English version."

"I see," she said, still shocked at her serious breach of Road manners. She knew better.

"Any other questions?" he asked softly.

She shook her head, no.

"Then I've one for you. Is your fiancé real or just a ploy to keep strange men from intruding into your life?"

Hester looked over at him, and into his heated gaze. "Which would you prefer?"

He gave her that smile again. "The latter, truthfully."

"Are you always so blunt?"

"With you, always."

"Surely if there are women in your life who will willingly enter your tub, what use would an inexperienced, purple-handed, ex-slave girl be, but for amusement?"

"You devalue yourself for no reason, Indigo."

Hester felt herself blossom again under the name. She told herself to remember her fiancé Foster. "I prefer you call me Hester."

"But you're not a Hester. You're an Indigo. Hesters are joyless, pruny old women who look down their noses at sinners like me. Take the word of an authority on women. Indigo is what you are, Indigo is who you will be." Then in a voice which further constricted her breathing, he added, "At least to me, you will be Indigo."

She didn't argue.

He then asked, "Who told you your hands would always brand you a slave?"

Hester was so relieved by the change in topics she answered gladly. "A woman who took care of me on the place in Carolina where I grew up. Her name was Dot.

"Dot's daughter, Ella, was my best friend back in

Carolina. We were about eight or nine, and had just been allowed to work the vats with the older women in the yard . . ."

"You think our hands will ever be dark as my mama's?" Ella asked Hester. The two young girls stood over the big steaming vat of blue-black indigo, their small hands immersed to the wrists, twisting and squeezing the smelly dye through the cotton cloth.

Hester pulled her hands out and surveyed the palms and backs. "Don't know. They're pretty dark now, but no way near dark as your mama's or Aunt Kay's."

"Well, pretty soon, don't you think? I mean it didn't take long for our toes. Hands shouldn't take that much longer." Like all the other children on the place, the girls' first job had been to help macerate the indigo plants by using their feet, in much the same way European workers processed grapes for wine.

The young Hester shrugged at Ella's assessment. Ever since they'd been allowed to work the vats, all Ella could talk about was getting her hands as dark as her mama's. Ella's day began and ended with her mama, Dot. To hear Ella tell it, Dot was the smartest woman on the place. Hester had to agree; Dot knew everything from where to find the herbs Aunt Kay used to keep everybody on the place healthy, to the position of the Freedom Star. She could even read, a skill Hester found absolutely amazing since she didn't know anyone else who could. Ella had confided this surprising information to Hester one night the summer before while they lay side by side on their pallets in the small cabin Dot's family called home. Ella made Hester swear not to tell another soul because if the owner Master Dill ever found out he'd sell Dot deep south for sure.

"Ella!" came Dot's warning voice. Both girls looked across the yard.

"You and Hester stop that dawdling and get to work. Lot of dyeing to do before Dudley blows that horn tonight."

Dudley was the overseer. His horn called them to the vats at dawn and sent them all back to the cabins at dusk.

Ella's mother and the other older women stood barefoot in the ankle-deep, mud-filled yard, hands immersed in steaming, smelly vats of their own. Ella held up her stained hands, then boasted proudly, "See mama. Pretty soon my hands will be just as dark as yours."

The sounds in the yard were usually a mixture of voices, soft humming, and the rhythmic slap of the cloth being dipped in and out of the vats. On the heels of Ella's boast the yard became very silent. Some of the women lowered their eyes, others shook their head as if saddened.

Hester, having no idea why Ella's comments had drawn such a strange reaction, looked over to her friend and saw Ella's confusion mirrored her own.

Dot said gently, "Ella, Hester, hands like these are nothing to be proud of. They're slave hands. Marked hands. Until the day you die your hands will say slave. Now, you two get on back to work."

Hester looked over at Galen. "We were children and until that moment Ella and I had never been ashamed of our life, because it was the only life we'd known. That night, Dot sat us both down and told us the truth about our lives and how the world viewed us. I never forgot it."

"How long after that did you escape?"

"Ironically it was only a few days later. A speculator showed up on the place."

Galen had posed as a speculator on more than a few ocassions. Speculators were itinerant slave salesmen who traveled from plantation to plantation, purchasing any slaves a master might want to sell—usually the unruly, lame, or aged slaves no longer able to pull their weight. The speculator then sold them wherever he could.

Galen asked, "So what happened?"

Once again, Hester's voice spirited them both away and back to the past.

* * *

News of the speculator's arrival had everyone on the place tense and afraid. As a result, the yard was thick with silence. The master hadn't had much trouble with his slaves, but no one claimed to know the master's mind; for all they knew someone might have committed an infraction, and whether the infraction be real or imagined, any slave could be sold in a whip's flick.

As the speculator, accompanied by Master Dill, slowly made his way towards the women in the yard, Ella cautioned Hester, "Don't look at him. Look at him and he'll buy you for sure."

Hester definitely didn't want to be bought so she dropped her head and focused her attention on the dyeing, but when she heard, "How about this one?" she tightened with fear.

Hester forced herself to concentrate on her task, praying with all her might they were speculating on someone else.

"How much?" the master asked.

"How old is she?" the speculator countered.

"I've had her for . . . let's see . . ."

Hester heard the rustle of paper as the master looked through his ledger. He then said, "Six years. So that makes her about eight, nine."

"She a good worker?"

"Far as I know." The master turned to Dot. "Dot?"

Dot looked up, her eyes brushing Hester's own for a breath of a second. "Yes, Master Dill."

"This here girl a good worker?"

Dot held Hester's eyes. "Yes, sir, she is."

"Good. Just like I thought. Turn around here girl, let's get a good look at you."

Hester felt a tap on her shoulder. It confirmed her worst fears. Shaking so badly she could hardly move, she turned.

The speculator had the coldest blue eyes she'd ever seen. They were like chips from the sky. She knew her fear showed itself plainly on her face.

He asked her, "What's your name, girl?"

"Hester," she whispered.

"Hold out your hands. Man I know wants a girl your age to train in his loom house."

Hester complied, hoping her cut-off pinky would somehow make her unfit.

"What happened to your finger?" the speculator asked then.

"I don't know. Dot says it was this way when I came here."

He looked to Dot. She nodded verification.

When he brought his attention back to Hester, she shook under his piercing, blue gaze.

He said, "Go on back to work, Hester."

The men moved on.

That next morning, Hester was amongst a group of four slaves purchased by the speculator. Mistress Dill allowed Hester only enough time to gather up her meager belongings and to share a quick, tear-filled goodbye with Dot and Ella. Tears streaming down her cheeks, Hester went and stood with the others, two women and a man, sold because they kept running away. The man was shackled at the ankle to a long chain attached to the back of the wagon. Hester and the women were allowed to ride in the wagon bed behind the cold-eyed speculator.

They departed at dawn. As they rolled away, Hester saw Dot standing outside the cabin, holding a quietly sobbing Ella to her side. A tearful Hester held Dot's stoic eyes until the wagon took her from sight.

As Hester ended her story, Galen could see the tears standing in her eyes. He wanted to hold her in his arms until the pain of that day vanished from her memory forever. "Were Dot and Ella the only family you'd ever known?"

She nodded yes, then said softly, "I never saw either of them again. I pray for them every night."

"How long after that did you escape? You said earlier you came north when you were nine."

"About two weeks later. The speculator left the others at various houses in and around Charleston. He took me across town to the home of a man named Hancock, gave me over to his care, then departed. I remember being terrified. I stayed there only a night or two before embarking on a train trip to Philadelphia with Mr. Hancock and his young daughter, Julia. It was the first time I'd ever worn a pair of real shoes. I'd never even seen a train before." She turned to Galen and gave him a bittersweet smile. "Everything was new."

Her unashamed offering of her past touched yet another cord in Galen. What else hadn't she seen, he wondered. Had she seen the fabled wall of China, the great pyramids of Egypt? Had she ever walked through the vibrant marketplaces of Havana, or had her fortune told in Madrid? He realized he wanted to make up for all she'd lacked in the past, drape her in silks, and gift her with pearls to match her eyes.

Her voice returned him to her tale. "When we got to Philadelphia, the Hancocks took me to a man in Philadelphia named Robert Purvis."

"Robert Purvis of the Philadelphia Antislavery Society?"

"I didn't know it at the time, but yes, the very same."

Robert Purvis stood as a giant amongst abolitionists. Although he was fair-skinned enough to be considered White due to his English and Jewish ancestry, he'd chosen to be true to his heritage and lived life as a Black man. The inherited wealth of his family had always been used to promote freedom.

"Mr. Purvis took my hand, and led me into his home. I never saw the Hancocks again. Only later did I learn that my aunt Katherine had arranged my escape. The speculator had been hired by her and her friends to find me. It took him almost six years. Aunt Katherine said that in the last letter from my father, he'd mentioned I'd been sold to a man named Weston. Evidently the search for me became complicated because Weston lost his slaves and land to foreclosure. Her sources said every slave he owned, including six baby girls, had gone on the block. The records of the sale did not list the children by name, only age. The records also indicated each baby had been purchased by different owners. Her friends spent those six years trying to determine the whereabouts of those six babies in an effort to find me. Aunt Katherine said she'd just about given up hope when I showed up on her doorstep, courtesy of friends of Mr. Purvis."

"So are you legally free?"

"As legally free as a Black woman can be in these times. The speculator sold me to Mr. Hancock and then he, in turn, freed me. He gave me and my free papers over to Mr. Purvis. I have copies on file at the sheriff's office, and one hidden here in the house."

Galen knew that one's free papers were the most valuable documents a freed slave could own. Without them, a person could be subject to kidnapping by vermin like Shoe and sent south, all without benefit of a hearing due to the mandates of the Fugitive Slave Law.

Hester had never described her past in such detail to anyone other than her aunt; not even her fiancé Foster knew all she'd revealed to Galen just now. Even though she'd only known him for a short time, she sensed that her tale would not shame Galen's sensibilities. Since he made his life assisting people in the transition from slave to free, he would understand how strange everything had seemed to the little purple-handed girl from Carolina.

Hester glanced over at the candles and realized by their shortened size that she and Galen had been talking for some time. She stood and began to clear the table. "Does your side feel better now that the threads are gone?"

"Immeasurably. Soaking in the tub helped also. I owe Bea for assisting me with the water."

She looked at him and their eyes held, his gaze wrapped around her again like smoke. She finally tore herself away and began taking their plates to the kitchen.

A few moments later, Galen came in asking, "May I help with the dishes?"

"It isn't necessary, there are only a few."

"I'd like to earn my keep."

Hester tossed him a drying towel.

It soon became apparent that Galen had never dried a dish in his life. The first plate he touched, he dropped and broke.

Hester waved away his sincere apologies with a smile and grabbed the broom. As she swept up the shards, she asked playfully, "Not much call for dish drying where you come from or did you have servants for that kind of thing?"

When he didn't answer, Hester searched his eyes. He looked guilty as a child caught pilfering cookies. "Does your family know you do the Work?"

Again silence.

Hester said, "I'm sorry. I didn't mean to pry. Why don't you go on up. I'll finish up down here."

He left without a word.

That night as Galen finally gained sleep, his last thoughts were of a purple-handed little slave girl.

Down the hall, in her own bed, Hester dreamt of the man who whispered, "Indigo . . ."

Chapter 7

When Galen approached Hester after breakfast with the idea of taking a walk as a way to strengthen his injured ankle, she agreed to accompany him. Standing high on the bluff behind her house, they looked down at the river stretched out below. It was a gloriously warm autumn day. The sky held the brilliant blue of a Michigan October and the clouds were as ripe as cotton. Hester spotted a flock of geese flying south in their signature vee, their honking faint against the gentle wind.

She'd suggested coming here mainly because she doubted they would be seen, and because standing on the bluff and gazing out over the river had always been one of her favorite pastimes. For her, no other place equaled the peace and tranquility found there.

"Who owns that house?" Galen asked, pointing off in the distance at the very large house sitting like a sentinel on the bluff's point.

"William Lovejoy. He had it built last year as a wedding gift to his daughter, Bethany Ann."

"Very generous man," Galen replied, sounding impressed.

"Apparently not generous enough. She ran off the night before the wedding."

Galen raised a dark eyebrow in response, then turned

back to the house. "How long has the daughter been gone?"

"Almost three months now. Folks are starting to call the place Lovejoy's Folly. He'll probably sell the house whether Bethany Ann returns or not. He's a man of some importance in Whittaker, not the type to stomach folks whispering about the scandal behind his back."

Galen stared at the house until Hester called his name.

Her voice apparently broke the spell because he glanced down at her and said, "I apologize, my thoughts were elsewhere for a moment. Did I miss something?"

Hester glanced over at Lovejoy's Folly as if it might provide a clue to what Galen had been thinking, but of course it could not. "Nothing. You missed nothing. Shall we continue our walk?"

"Lead the way."

They walked along the bluff in silence, each harboring their own thoughts, until Galen said, "Tell me about your fiancé."

Hester's steps slowed. She searched his face, trying to glean the reason behind the request. "What do you wish to know?"

Galen shrugged. "Oh, the usual, his name, what he does for a living, does he love you . . . ?"

His last words were spoken so softly, it made it hard to remember what she wanted to say. "His name is Foster Quint. He's Canadian free born, and our local teacher."

"And?"

"And, what?"

"Does he love you?"

"You're an awfully curious man," she pointed out with a smile.

"It's the only way to get one's curiosity satisfied."

His tone and vivid eyes made her think back three days ago to the night he caught her peeking at him in the mirror. That night, he'd boldly voiced a desire to satisfy a different type of curiosity. She wondered if he were slyly referring to that. The amusement she saw on his face seemed to be all the verification she needed. "I believe you are accustomed to a more spirited level of conversation than I, Galen."

"It is indeed possible, *petite,* but I believe you will learn to hold your own soon enough. Now, I'm still waiting for an answer to my question. Does he love you?"

Hester smiled up at him and shook her head, no.

He raised the eyebrow again, a signature quirk she'd come to realize, then he said quizzically, "No?"

"No. We aren't marrying for love. We are marrying for something far more lasting."

"That being?"

"Companionship."

"Companionship," Galen echoed skeptically, doubtfully.

"Yes. Many couples marry for love only to find they have nothing in common. They pledge eternal devotion but reap years of misery instead. I don't wish to live that way. Foster and I share common interests—we both love to read, we both love the theater, the intellectual stimulation of debating another person of equal intelligence. He is educated, kind, and highly regarded here."

"Sounds like a virtual pargon, this Frederick."

"Foster. His name is Foster."

Galen nodded, then turned to look out over the panoramic view of trees, and water. "Why would a vibrant, beautiful woman like yourself want to marry for anything beside love?"

Hester ignored his reference to her supposed beauty. "Have you ever been in love, Galen?"

"Once when I was about nineteen. Her name was Yvette. She was—" He stopped himself from speaking further. He doubted the prim Indigo would appreciate tales of one of Paris's highly celebrated courtesans. "Let's just say, I thought I was in love at the time."

Hester said, "Well, I've never been in love either, but when I see what it has done to people who have—it brings only sadness. Take the circumstances love forced upon my father. Take my neighbor, Branton Hubble. He loved my aunt Katherine all of his free life, and she loved him. They spent nearly thirty years pining for one another because he chose to be an honorable man and remain loyal to the wife he had to leave behind when he escaped Kentucky. Then there's poor Bethany Ann Lovejoy. Do you know why she ran away? She made the mistake of falling in love with Sheriff Lawson's son David, and David loves her, but in some parts of the country their love is a jailable offense. She couldn't bear to marry another. If I need more examples I have only to sit in Kate Bell's house and listen to the woeful tales of love her patrons tell. So, no, Galen. I don't wish to marry for love. I don't need misery in my life."

Galen realized she believed every word. "It isn't always that way, *petite*. I know of love matches that have spanned a lifetime."

"It doesn't matter, Galen. I'm past the age of a love match anyway. Foster and I will suit fine."

"So if I may be so bold to ask, are you planning on babies?"

Hester laughed. "Of course not. Foster and I absolutely agree that bringing children into a society such as this is nearly as great a sin as slavery itself. If a miracle occurs and slavery ceases, we will revisit the issue."

Galen did not find their decision on children to be out of the ordinary; many members of the race were vowing not to have children until freedom could be assured, but Galen did wonder about this Frederick. Did this mean there would be no shared marriage bed, and if so, what man in his right mind would consent to do nothing more intimate with Hester than debate the issues of the day? She deserved to be both loved and cherished, especially in the face of her past. In spite of her intellectual theorizing, the plain truth was that she was afraid of love, he realized. "So does this fiancé of yours have any faults?"

She shrugged. "He can be a bit long-winded at times, but it's a result of his advanced education. He believes society should be more aware of the many erudite and articulate members of the race, so he tends to talk on and on to the point of boring one to tears at times, but that's part and parcel of who he is."

"Yet you're willing to marry him."

"Yes, Galen, I am. No man is perfect. Not even you."

"Touché, madam, I forgot about your claws."

She smiled up at him. "You'd do good to remember. One would think you were my maiden aunt with all these questions."

"Curiosity, *petite,* nothing more. Forgive me."

"You're forgiven," she said. The beard shrouding his face had grown in thicker over the past week. It all but covered the remains of his beating and gave him the look of a pirate. Bea had been correct. He'd healed up quite handsomely. She then asked, "How's your ankle faring? Shall we take a slow tour back towards the house?"

Galen didn't want to relinquish her company just yet, so he said, "How about we sit a moment? My ankle is a bit tired."

"There's a bench up here a little ways, we can sit there."

Galen knew his ankle was in much better shape than he'd let on, but decided the small untruth justifiable if it kept her dark beauty at his side.

Just as Hester had promised, they came upon an old, weatherbeaten stone bench and they each took a seat. Hester leaned her head back and looked up at the beautiful sky. "When I was young, I would sit on this bench for what seemed hours, staring up at the clouds. I'd see unicorns, and eagles, huge mansions. Once I even saw the Great Mr. Douglass himself. Bold as day it was."

"What else did you do when you were young?"

"For fun, not much more. My aunt thought I'd be better served by mastering my studies, and I agreed. After all, I was totally ignorant when I came to live with her. I had to learn to read, write. I still recall how proud I was the day I learned to write Hester Wyatt without assistance." She turned his way. "I wanted so much to please her. She would come up to my room at night and there I'd be, asleep at my desk, head atop some book or another, because I wanted to learn all there was. I suppose, I'm still that way in many respects, even though I know some men find intellect in a woman quite disconcerting. Do you?"

Galen searched her frank eyes, and replied truthfully, "No, Indigo, I don't . . ." The urge to raise his fingers and trace the sweet blackberry curve of her lips roared through Galen with such force it almost blazed past his defenses. To distract himself he asked, "Surely, you did girl things for fun—played with dolls, made mud pies?"

She laughed. "Mud pies?! Have you any idea what my aunt would've done had I come home covered with river mud? No Galen, I had a few dollies, but I've never played in mud in my life."

"Then let's go make mud pies!" he yelled, snatching her by the hand. Before Hester could protest she found herself being pulled down the bluff in his wake.

Laughing, she yelled, "But I don't want to make mud pies!"

He didn't ease his pace, or his hold on her captured hand.

"Galen?!" she called over her giggles. "You can't make me make mud pies against my—will!"

The last word was a laugh-filled scream as Hester reacted to being scooped up into Galen's arms. She came to rest cradled against his broad chest, her hands around his neck. He stared down into her startled face and said, "Now, you were saying?"

Hester blinked and wondered if she would ever breathe again. Because of her scrambled brains, all she could think to say was, "You're going to reinjure your ankle . . ."

"I've carried birds that weigh more than you."

He was so near and so overpowering, Hester could feel herself on the verge of fainting for the very first time in her life. His hot nearness seemed to have burned away the fabric of her blouse. "You must put me down," she told him in a voice far softer and more strangled than she'd intended.

"Are you going to come make mud pies with me or not?"

For the life of her, Hester couldn't speak. She couldn't believe how hard her heart was pounding. She knew agreeing would undoubtedly alter her life forever, but she said, "Yes."

He eased her to her feet, took her indigo hand again, and said, "Let's go."

Disagreement flared as soon as they reached the river's edge. Hester refused to take off her shoes. Galen, in the process of removing his own boots and socks, stopped and said, "Hester, you have to take off your shoes."

"Galen, I am not removing my shoes. I don't know where you were raised, but that's a bit risqué for me."

"I'm not asking you to remove your chemise, *petite,* just those brogans on your feet." The boots were scuffed and old. He doubted he'd ever seen an uglier pair of shoes on a woman in his life.

In her mind, Hester formed a brazen image of herself willingly removing her chemise in response to his imagined heated request. She shook herself free. "My shoes stay on."

Galen said, "You are the contrariest woman I have ever met."

Hester snorted. "Contrariest. What kind of word is contrariest. French?"

He grinned. "Be careful baby girl, I bite. I'll give you more French than you'll know what to do with."

The heat in his eyes made her heart race even faster than before. "What on earth does that mean?"

"You're the one laughing at my vocabulary, you tell me."

Hester felt as if she'd just walked into a wolf's den, and it was the most tantalizing and forbidding place she'd ever entered.

"Now," he said coaxingly, "take off your shoes please, or so help me, I will come over there and kiss you so long and deep, those ugly little brogans will melt from your feet."

Hester swayed on legs suddenly turned to sand. "You are incorrigible . . ."

"And this is only the beginning . . ." he promised her.

Hester removed her shoes and once she was barefoot, she felt so out of her element, she hesitated to join him at the river's edge. The years of stomping raw indigo plants had stained her feet far more heavily than her hands. Her feet were purple all the way past her ankles. "Galen, this is very embarrassing for me."

"I won't let it be. There's not a portion of your body that isn't beautiful, Hester Wyatt."

It was the second time today he'd referred to her as beautiful. She had no idea how to react to such a comment; no one had ever described her in those terms before.

Encouraged by his patience though, Hester stood, and as she did, the sweeping movement of her skirt's hem revealed her bare feet. No man had seen her feet bare since she'd come north and began wearing shoes.

Galen smiled. "Now, is that so bad? You have lovely little purple toes."

Hester glanced down at her feet. "A real gentleman would not make mention of a lady's bare feet," she said with mock rebuke.

"A real lady wouldn't be out in her bare feet."

Her reaction, an offended-sounding gasp, made him laugh aloud. He told her, "I'm sorry, but you're so prim sometimes it's hard not to tease you. You need more fun in your life, *petite* Indigo, and I'm here at your service. Now come on over here and play with me."

In spite of Hester's initial misgivings, she did have fun. She and Galen sat on the river's edge and made mud pies and castles complete with bridges and moats. He taught her how to skip stones and call to the ducks on the river. They looked at clouds, dug for pirate gold, and fed on one another's smiles. When the sun began its slow slide below the horizon, they both knew the time had come to head back. They'd been at the river all day.

Hester couldn't decide who was the filthiest; they were both covered with mud. "This is all your fault, you know," she scolded him with mock severity.

"Guilty as charged," he replied. Galen regretted he would not be able to invite her into his bath and slide a bar of scented soap over her ebony body until she was clean. He felt his arousal awaken in response to the imagined scenario and decided they should probably head back to the house before he broke his vow to leave her untouched. It was the hardest vow he'd undertaken in quite some time; he only hoped he didn't break it in the few days he had remaining.

Back at the house, while Galen hauled in water for hot baths, Hester set about getting them something to eat. The lateness of the day made a real dinner impossible, but she did have the remains of Branton Hubble's ham and plenty of bread. They ate sandwiches and drank coffee while the water heated.

Hester looked across the table and said truthfully, "I had fun today, Galen. Thank you."

"Just a way of showing my appreciation for all you've done for me."

"Do you really think I need more fun in my life?" she asked with all seriousness.

"Yes, I believe you do. Life is too short to be so serious."

Hester thought about the political upheaval gripping the country and said, "These are serious times."

"Yes, they are, which is why it's important to seek out humor and beauty whenever possible. If we don't, we'll all be buried beneath the weight of the misery."

"Philosophy, Galen?"

"No, *petite*. Truth."

After the large cauldrons of water heated, Galen hauled them up to the attic room to fill the big tub. When he returned downstairs, he pumped more water for Hester's bath and set it back atop the stove to heat.

Hester was reluctant to end the day. Her eyes settled on his firm, full mouth a moment. How would it be to be kissed by him, she wondered. She could still recall the dizzying sensations of being held against his strong chest, and how his arm supporting her thighs burned her flesh. Her gaze rose to meet his.

He told her, "You shouldn't look at me that way."

"Which way?" she asked.

"Like you want to be kissed . . ."

She reeled inwardly, then fought off the desire to succumb to the temptation in his frank eyes. She said instead, "You should go on up to your bath before the water cools. I'll read while my water heats."

Galen was just as reluctant to leave. He wanted to stay with her and relish these last few days. He'd said nothing to her about his departure, but he knew he did not have much time left to bask his weary soul in the healing pleasure of her company. "Will you need help carrying the water? I can come back down when I'm done."

Shaken by all this, she shook her head. "No, that won't be necessary, I've hauled water all my life. I'll be fine."

"Then I will say goodnight."

"Goodnight, Galen. I'll see you in the morning."

Hester very rarely bathed in her bedroom. Her aunt Katherine always considered it far more sensible to bathe in the kitchen, where one could take advantage of the warmth generated by the cauldrons of water heating atop the stove. Hester found the idea practical as well, so when the water finally became hot enough to use, she set aside her reading, the latest issue of William Lloyd Garrison's *Liberator,* and began the preparations. She took a moment to douse all the candles on the main floor, then tipped upstairs to get her toiletries and a clean gown to sleep in. She retrieved the hip tub from the storeroom connected to the warm, steam-filled kitchen. After filling the tub, she turned down the lamps in the kitchen to their lowest wicks and removed her clothes. The small hip tub was not large enough to lounge in as Galen had undoubtedly done in the tub upstairs; this one, white, and decorated with fat red roses, was only high enough to reach one's thighs when standing, and only deep enough and wide enough for the bather to master the stooping position needed to rinse clean.

Hester had never known the luxury of dawdling over her personal habits, so after scrubbing herself clean with the serviceable unscented soap, she stooped to rinse, then stepped out.

The kitchen door swung open.

Her startled eyes widened at the sight of Galen. It took her only a flash of a second to snatch up her drying sheet and haphazardly shield herself, but it was too late. He'd seen more than enough.

She gasped, heart pounding, "What are you doing in here?!"

"Well, I came down here for a few more slices of that ham—"

"You're supposed to be sleep!"

"And you're supposed to be in your bedroom, not down here . . . nude . . ."

His voice instantaneously brought her scrambled thoughts back to her barely covered state. "Turn around, dammit," she scolded.

She didn't know which infuriated her more, the eyebrow he raised in response or the smoky, spellbinding grin.

"Dammit?" he asked questioningly. "When did you start using words like, dammit?"

"When I'm as angry as I am now. Turn around!"

Galen chuckled, but turned his back. "You're very beautiful you know."

Hester hastily began to dry herself. "I don't wish to hear that from you, Galen."

"Why not?"

"Because I think you probably say those words quite easily, and far too often."

He chuckled again. "You're wrong. I'm actually very discriminating."

She snorted and bent to dry her still-damp legs and feet, keeping a pointed eye on his back the whole while. "If you turn around, I swear, I will never feed you again."

His responding laugh filled the shadows. "Now that is a very serious threat, *petite,* so I solemnly promise to remain still as marble." Galen had come downstairs for something to eat and instead stumbled upon the sweetest treat of all. The sight of her, nude against the soft light, her body wet from her bath, stunned him. His arousal had been instantaneous. Who would have thought she would be even more beautiful than he'd ever imagined? Not even his most vivid fantasies could have conjured up such dark sable breasts, or the succulent curve of her ebony bottom. His hands ached to slowly bring those silken breasts to his lips and pleasure them until the nipples hardened like jewels. He wanted to taste her kiss, brush his caresses over the flare of her hips, and teach her things she'd never dreamed possible. He shook himself and forced himself to entertain more calming thoughts; his passionate musings were taking him down a path with no end.

Meanwhile, Hester struggled into her gown. After doing up the line of hooks and fat ribbons which ran neck to waist down the front of the rough muslin garment, she said to Galen, "You may turn around now."

Galen turned, took one look at her trussed up like a Sunday chicken in that ugly, high-necked gown, and laughed and laughed until he cried.

Hester stood there with her hand on her hip, wondering if he had truly lost his mind. "What is so funny?"

When Galen could catch his breath, he wiped at his eyes and said, "You, my *petite* Indigo. Where did you get that awful gown? I've seen meal in better sacks than that."

The smart of humiliated tears stung Hester's eyes. The barb hurt, especially in light of the good time they'd shared that day. She could feel her chin tighten, and swore she would pluck her eyes out before letting him see her cry. The gown was not fashionable, but it served her well.

Galen's smile died as he watched her whole manner go cold. He realized he'd hurt her feelings—very badly if her chin were any indication. She looked so devastated he whispered, "Oh darling . . . I'm sorry."

Galen quickly crossed the room and very gently placed his fingers beneath her chin. He raised it so he could look down into her hurt eyes. "Forgive me," he entreated softly. "I have a vicious tongue sometimes, but I never meant to use it on you."

He searched her face. Her manner made him ache in places he never knew existed, until now. He said to her, "Where I'm from, rapier tongues are *de rigeur*. I forget you weren't raised among vipers as I was. Please, *petite* . . ."

He touched his lips to her brow, brushing them against her dark skin slowly, contritely. In a short few days he'd be leaving, and he didn't want to part this way—with sadness and hurt. "I'm sorry . . ." he whispered almost desperately, seeing the tears standing like jewels in her eyes. "I'll never make you sad again . . ."

His mouth brushed her lips, and he gathered her in closer. She came willingly, rising up on her bare toes to meet his lips.

Galen groaned as her arms encircled him. Her luscious mouth was as perfect as he'd dreamed. It had not been his intent to kiss her this way—not this deeply, not this slowly, not this intensely—but he could no more stop himself now than he could halt the pounding in his blood. He teased her lips into opening by slowly sliding the tip of his tongue against the trembling corners. When she moaned in sweet response, he partook fully of the honeyed cove within, pleasuring her at a leisurely pace. He didn't want her to be afraid of this—or of him.

Galen left her mouth, then kissed his way along the ebony line of her jaw, whispering, "Indigo . . ."

Hester's head dropped back. His kisses were devastating, masterful. She had no experience to call upon, and as a result was sent reeling from the bold pressure of his kiss against the small stripe of skin above her high-neck gown. She had no name for what he was making her feel, but she didn't want it to end.

"I want to touch you, Hester," he breathed against her ear, her lips. "You're beautiful everywhere. Let me show you . . ."

She had no idea what he meant, but if the touches he promised were as achingly potent as his kisses, she knew she wouldn't protest.

He recaptured her lips and his hands slid over her back. The rough muslin rustled in the silence of the shadowy-filled kitchen, the only sound more soft than the echoes of their passionate breathing.

When he began to untie the top ribbon of her gown, Hester knew she shouldn't be allowing such liberties, but her virgin's curiosity had been made brazen by this interlude. She let him undo the top ribbon, then the one beneath, and then, when she felt his mouth flirting with the hollow of her throat, she trembled in response. She found it hard to remain coherent; his lips were warm, his tongue flicking against her skin, hot as a stove. She couldn't speak, she couldn't think; when she felt the touch of his hand cupping her breast, she couldn't breathe. To her surprise he bent his head to taste her nipple through the rough fabric of her gown and she swore his mouth set the skin aflame. He gave the same caress to her other nipple. She moaned and dropped her head back, her body wanting more.

Galen gave her more. He opened another two ribbons and slid the halves aside so he could pleasure her without restraint. Her nipples were hard as polished points of onyx, and as succulent as the rarest of fruits. He kissed first one, then the other, savoring each.

As he slid his hands into her gown to sample the soft skin of her waist and hips, Galen swore she'd been created from the finest of silk. She was warm and her hushed sighs rose in tandem with his own burgeoning desires. He knew it would not take much more to coax her virgin's body into surrendering all; he sensed it in the fervent way she returned his kisses, and in the uninhibited way she trembled and rose under the intimate movements of his hands. She was ripe, lush and open to all the pleasure he could bestow, but he could not take her, she was not his. The right to love her fully and sample the dark sweetness flowing from within her silken thighs belonged to another man. He had to stop at that moment or risk compromising her.

When Galen gently and reluctantly eased himself away, Hester stood there feeling a shimmer from the heat still pulsing within. "Proper women aren't supposed to enjoy this are they?"

He gave a low chuckle and slid a finger over one tight nipple. "You're pretty proper, you tell me . . ."

She felt boneless, limp, yet on fire. He placed a kiss upon her lips and then began to redo the ties on her gown.

She asked softly, "What are you doing?"

"Helping you remain innocent, though lord knows I don't want to."

When the last tie was done, he kissed her again, this time so warmly it sent the flames soaring once more.

He whispered against her mouth, "Go up to your room, *petite,* before I strip this gown from you and never give it back."

Hester's senses spiralled. Parts of her wanted to throw caution to the wind and let him have his way, but she knew he was correct. She raised herself up on her toes to give him a smoldering kiss of her own, then whispered, "I did enjoy it. Goodnight, Galen."

He grinned. "Goodnight, *petite*."

Despite the tumultuously sensuous events that day, Hester went right to sleep, only to be gently shaken awake by Galen a few hours later. A lamp had been lit but its low glow barely pierced the room's shadows. Seeing him seated on the bed beside her made her smile. "Did you change your mind about letting me keep my gown?" she asked sleepily.

Before he could answer, her bedroom door opened and a man she'd never seen before stuck his head in. "We must go, Galeno."

Hester sat up in surprise, defensively dragging her quilts to her chin.

Galen placed a calming hand against her cheek. "He's a friend, Indigo."

Galen then turned to the man. "Raymond, meet Hester Wyatt. Hester, my good friend, Raymond LeVeq."

Raymond, who equaled Galen in both handsomeness and size, replied in a French-accented voice, "*Enchanté,* Madmoiselle Wyatt."

"I'm—pleased to meet you, Mr. LeVeq," Hester responded confusedly.

"Give us a moment, Raymond."

Before leaving though, Raymond reverted to his native French and asked, "Is she as innocent as she appears, my brother?"

Galen replied in English, "Yes, now go away. I'll be there in just a moment."

Hester saw Raymond smile as he bowed gracefully in her direction, then he departed and closed the door.

"What is he doing here?" she asked.

"He and his brothers are here to take me home. I've awakened you to say goodbye."

"Goodbye?" she whispered.

The sadness in his eyes told all. Her heart broke, but she stoically buried her emotions and asked quietly, "How soon?"

"Moments."

Her eyes closed for the briefest of moments. When she opened them, the pain had not lessened.

Galen wanted to curse, to howl, do whatever possible to make this parting occur at some other time. He didn't want to leave her like this, but he had no choice. Raymond had received the coded message Galen asked Hester to wire the other day. He knew his old friend would waste little time in coming to his rescue, but Galen had not expected him so soon. "*Petite,* I—"

Hester placed a tender hand against his lips to stop whatever he'd been about to say. "Just go, Galen, please . . ."

He placed her indigo palm against his cheek, then pressed it to his lips, wishing for more time, wishing he could remain. His dark eyes were bleak as he whispered, "I promised I'd never make you sad again. I lied . . ."

He pulled her into his embrace and kissed her—a sweet, poignant goodbye. In an emotion-thickened voice he vowed, "This is only *adieu.* I'll be back soon."

He pulled back so he could see into her face. "When I return you must pretend we've never met. Can you do that?"

Hester had no idea why he would make such a request, but she nodded.

Galen also wanted to ask her not to marry Foster before his return but knew he had no right, at least not yet. Instead he asked, "Promise me you won't make mud pies with anyone else while I'm gone."

Hester couldn't suppress her watery smile. "I promise."

"At least I got you to smile," he replied wistfully, gently tracing her full mouth. "That's something."

From outside the door, Raymond bellowed, "We must go, Galeno!"

Galen yelled back angrily. "I'm coming, keep your damn pants on!"

Raymond yelled back in French, "It's *your* pants I'm worried about!"

Galen whispered a soft but vivid curse. Time had run out. "I must go."

He reached out and ran a finger down her soft cheek. "Make sure you eat enough while I'm gone."

She nodded. "Godspeed, Galen."

Galen walked slowly to the door. He took one last look at her sitting there, her beautiful eyes holding his own, and he forced himself to leave.

Alone now, Hester could hear movements in the house at first, then only silence. She left her bed and ran down the stairs, hoping they were leaving by coach and not by the tunnel because she wanted one last look. She ran outside and got in position just in time to see a big black coach traveling away from the house at a furious pace, heading east. Flanking the coach were five mounted riders dressed in black. As the coach and riders faded into the night, Hester whispered, "Goodbye, Galen . . ." because in reality it was goodbye. She doubted she would ever see him again.

She stood outside for a few moments longer, then, feeling the wind against her tears, she went back inside the silent house.

Chapter 8

As the month of October waned, and the November winds gave way to the snow and cold of December, Hester heard no more from Galen. Although the mystery surrounding the phantom traitor remained unsolved, she doubted she'd ever see him again. He was the Black Daniel after all. The abolitionist cause would be better served by his being on the Road tweaking the nose of slavery rather than here in Whittaker. At last week's meeting of the Vigilance Committee, the members decided that the exposure of the informant could very well be handled without outside assistance, and Hester was certain Galen had come to the same conclusion. As she'd stated on the night he departed, goodbye had been just that, goodbye. She'd convinced herself that never seeing him again was for the best.

She stood looking out of her bedroom window at the snow covering the open fields like a white, velvet blanket. The passionate memories of Galen had plagued her dreams for weeks following his leaving. He'd come to her nightly, his voice whispering, "Indigo . . .", his caressing hands as potent as they'd been in reality.

Mercifully, time had passed. By the fifteenth day of the new year 1859, her bearded, nocturnal lover visited her less frequently—and that, too, was for the best. An unknown side of herself had been brought to life by

Galen's spell, and Hester had no desire to free that
woman ever again. The real Hester had no time for mud
pies and men who whispered passion in steamy, shadow-
filled kitchens. Looking back on that night she was
shocked by the shameless, wanton creature she'd become in Galen's arms, especially in light of the vow
she'd made to Foster. As penance, she wrote to her fiancé
every evening before going to bed.

Hester planned on going into town that morning to see
if the still unreceived draft from her English publisher
had arrived, but six inches of new snow had fallen
overnight. The snow with its accompanying winds and
blowing drifts negated any thoughts she might have had
about leaving the house. Instead she poured herself a cup
of tea and settled in to review the newspapers she'd
borrowed from Bea at church last Sunday. The slavery
question had turned the country into a powder keg.
Congress was in turmoil, the chasm between the north
and the south seemed unbreachable, and now, there
were slave owners seeking to strike down the ban on
importing new African slaves. The U.S. ban instituted in
1807 was being challenged because the price of slaves
had risen sharply during the past decade. In some parts
of the south, prices were approaching an additional
seventy percent of what they'd been in previous years.
Both pro and antislavery forces were aware that illicit
trafficking in imported slaves had continued on a small
scale despite the law, and one of the most celebrated
cases occurred only last year. A southern syndicate
headed by the very .wealthy Charles A. L. Lamarr
contracted for a cargo of five hundred Africans and
brought them to Georgia aboard a fast schooner named
Wanderer. The four hundred Africans who survived the
middle passage were sold at a great profit. The U.S.
government indicted Lamarr and some of the crew, but
all charged were acquitted. Northern abolitionists were
furious at the grand jury's verdict, but the South viewed
the North's stance as so much hypocrisy. A southern
newspaper asked, "What is the difference between a

Yankee violating the fugitive slave law in the North and a southern man . . . violating the law against the African slave trade in the South?"

The North knew the difference, which is why the renewed call to end the ban had northern abolitionists so worried. In years past, slave holders challenging the ban had done so under the banner of economics, but now, the South viewed the ban as not only a threat to their economic survival, but to their honor and way of life as well.

They were vowing to extend their agricultural empires beyond the U.S. borders, thus placing themselves and their slaves outside the reach of American law. The idea had surfaced before back in 1848 when the South wanted Cuba for expansionism. Senator Jefferson Davis echoed the mood of his fellows when hc vowed, "Cuba must be ours . . . in order to increase the number of slaveholding constituencies."

The beginning of February brought the publisher's bank draft she'd been anxiously awaiting but its sum was not as large as she'd anticipated. There was enough to buy the supplies and food needed to supplement her meager stores, enabling her to stay above water for another few weeks, but nothing more. If the situation became truly serious, she knew she could apply to her neighbors for help, but they'd seen her and her aunt through last winter's lean months. Pride prevented Hester from asking for charity yet again.

Her only recourse would be to sell some land, something she'd vowed not to even consider until she reached the last knot on the rope.

Well, by early March, the time had come.

William Lovejoy found a buyer for Lovejoy's Folly, and according to Lovejoy the new owner was in the market to purchase some additional land. Since Hester's land bordered the Folly on the south near the river, Lovejoy had given the man Hester's name. She was due to meet the man that day.

At precisely two o' clock, Hester heard the rap at the door. Dressed in one of her better gowns, and wearing her gloves to hide her hands, she answered the summons.

He was tall, tall as Galen and with a sparkle in his eye which only added to his handsome brown features. He was a young man and very richly dressed. His expensive black boots were so highly polished a person could see his reflection. Over his shoulder, Hester spied the fine coach waiting for him out on the road. He inclined his head politely as she faced him, then asked, "Are you Miss Wyatt?"

Hester nodded.

"I'm Andre Renaud. I represent the new owner of Mr. Lovejoy's house on the bluff. Mr. Lovejoy led me to believe you might be interested in selling some of your land?"

"Yes. Please come in."

He followed her into the small parlor and at Hester's request, took a seat, though he declined the tea she offered.

Hester sat opposite him.

He began, "As you've undoubtedly heard, my employer is very interested in purchasing some of the land surrounding his new home. He is willing to offer you . . ."

While Hester waited, Renaud extracted a pen and paper from his small valise and wrote something on the paper. He handed the paper to her. Her eyes widened at the number written down. "Mr. Renaud, this is entirely too much."

He stared as if confused. "Too much?"

"Mr. Renaud, I know what my land is worth. Were I the greediest woman in the world, I would not have asked for such an outrageous sum."

He stared at her as if she'd grown two heads.

She said, "Surely your employer is not so wealthy he can afford to pay three times the value?"

"Truth be told, he is, but—?" His confusion seemed to be growing because he slowly surveyed her from head to toe. "Do you not want to sell?"

"In reality, I do not, but circumstances force me to."

"But you won't accept my employer's offer."

"I will accept a reasonable offer. Yes."

Renaud observed her a moment longer then seemed to shake himself. "Well, Miss Wyatt, what about this?"

Once again he scribbled a figure on the paper and handed it to her.

It was less than the original offer but still more than Hester would have dreamed of asking, however, she thought about all the good she could do with the boon. Even if she gave a good portion to the Cause, she would still have ample funds to see to her own needs for quite some time. She looked over at Mr. Renaud, who seemed to be very perplexed, and said, "I accept."

He sighed with what sounded like relief, then politely bowed his head. "My employer will be pleased."

They spent a few more moments signing documents, and Hester gave Renaud the name of a trusted White barrister friend in Ann Arbor who could be trusted to handle the necessary transactions on her behalf.

Before leaving Andre Renaud said, "Miss Wyatt, I have a note here from my employer expressing his thanks."

Hester took the note from his hand, then closed the door after his coach pulled away. The wax seal had a dragon pressed into the expensive vellum. Hester gently peeled it open and read: "My dear Indigo. Thank you for the land. Galen."

Hester's hands were shaking so badly she almost dropped the note.

She read it again. The wording had not changed. Good lord, he did plan to return!

Hester didn't know how to react, one side of her, the side she wished to keep buried, was overjoyed by the prospects of Galen's return. The thinking, rational side of herself was fairly miserable, because she knew her life would be altered beyond recognition when she met Galen again.

And they would meet again; he'd purchased the Folly, and that would make them neighbors. Good Lord. What type of ruse was he spinning, she wondered. His man, Renaud, alluded to Galen's vast wealth. Could it possibly be true? Could he really be wealthy enough to afford to pay her three times her asking price for the land, and if so, where did all this wealth originate? During his stay with her, she'd had the feeling there was much more to him than he let on—the fact that he spoke French set him far above any one of her circle, but she'd no idea what to believe now. Was the show of wealth simply that, a show? Maybe the bank draft his man had just handed her was really worthless, maybe it was nothing more than part of his plan to catch the traitor. Hester didn't know what to believe. She spent the rest of the day mulling over the possibilities, then decided that speculating was useless. She'd have her answers when Galen returned and not until then.

That night, Hester lay sleeping in her bed unaware that Galen sat in a chair in the shadows watching her sleep. He'd entered her room nearly an hour ago, by way of the secret panel in the wall, and during that hour he'd been waging an inner battle to stay seated. He wanted to awaken her to see if her kisses were really as lush as he remembered, but knew he had no right to be there at all. Yet he stayed, daring not to disturb her, but unable to leave. He asked himself again, why he'd come here tonight? Why would he willingly waste valuable time and money trying to track a traitor in a place like Whittaker when there were far more important issues in need of his attention in other parts of the country? He knew the answer—Hester. He began missing her the moment the coach pulled away that October night. He spent the months after leaving recuperating further at a

leased house on the Detroit River, and had been unable
to get her out of his mind. The whys were boggling. That
Hester was beautiful was undeniable, but he had his pick
of beautiful women wherever and whenever he chose, so
the desire for her had to be rooted in something far less
obvious.

His *grandmère,* the venerable Vada Rousseau, would
be appalled to know he was being haunted by a young
woman who lacked the family and wealth she prized so
highly; not that Galen cared about Vada or her snobbish
ways. The women Vada preferred he spend time with
were usually vapid, perfumed bits of fluff, or calculating
predators masquerading as virgins. Hester fit neither
category and maybe that was part of her appeal; she was
nothing at all like the jaded women who traveled in his
social circles. He found her to be dedicated, fervent, and
educated; she read, had opinions, and was not afraid to
voice them.

He was pleased she'd accepted his offer for her land,
and he'd laughed at the confusion on Andre's face as
he'd related the encounter. It didn't surprise Galen that
she'd turned down the initial offer because she'd deemed
it too high. Galen had expected her to be contrary, which
is why he sent Andre in his stead. Had she known Galen
to be the "employer" behind the sale, her pride might
have prevented her from selling altogether, even though
she dearly needed the money according to Andre's
discreet enquiries around the community on Galen's
behalf. Her dire straits were the reason Galen offered for
the land in the first place. He didn't really need to
acquire the surrounding land, but he couldn't stomach
the idea of her not having enough to eat. Upon Andre's
return to the Folly, Andre assured Galen that Hester
appeared well, but Galen wanted to see for himself.

Her soft breathing barely ruffled the silence in the
room. He lingered over the fantasy of kissing her into
wakefulness and running his hands over her. He imagined brushing his lips over the sleep-dampened throat,

and then the valley between her breasts. He could feel himself becoming aroused and the need to awaken her roared through him, but he buried the desire lest he act upon it, then stood.

He moved as silently as a shadow and approached the bed. He stood there a moment looking down upon her sleeping so unaware, and he wondered where this would all lead. He had no answers. He reached into the inside pocket of his black, velvet-collared Chesterfield coat and withdrew a red rose. He brought it to his lips, then gently placed it beside her on the pillow. He gave her one last look, then departed as silently as he'd come.

Hester awakened in the morning filled with the vague sense of having dreamt of Galen. Shaking off the lingering sensation, she got up and quickly dressed in the chill of the room. After taking quick care of her personal needs, she came back to right the sheets and quilts on the bed. When she pulled back the sheets, she went still as she spotted a small rosebud. "Where in heaven did this come from?" she asked quietly in the silence. The color of the bud was such a deep dark red it almost appeared black. She'd never seen one quite this shade before. She brought the soft petals to her nose and savored the faint fragrance. Her fingers inadvertently brushed against something on the outside of the rose. She peered at it and for the first time saw the small circle of wax on the base of the bud. It was a seal, and pressed into it was Galen's signature dragon. Her eyes closed from the implications and she swayed on unsteady legs a moment. He had been in her room while she slept. *Did this mean he was still in the house?* Hester hastily left her room and hurried down the hall. She found the attic room empty, and the rest of the house too. She tried to convince herself that she was not disappointed at not finding him, but in reality knew it was a lie. Hester looked at the small rose once again. Since Galen had been in her bedroom last night, why hadn't he awakened her? And why did he leave the rose? Her feelings were in a jumble over the whole episode, because she too had no idea where this would lead.

At church the next Sunday, everyone was all abuzz over the new owner of Lovejoy's Folly. No one had seen him yet, but it didn't keep folks from speculating. Word had it that he was a rich French-Canadian and that he'd made his fortune in shipping. Hester told no one that the rich French-Canadian also went by the name of the Black Daniel or that he left roses on her bed.

One evening during the last week of March, Hester answered a knock and was surprised to see Andre Renaud on her porch.

"Good evening, Miss Wyatt, may I come in?"

Hester could see a wagon filled with crates waiting out by the road and a man atop the wagon waiting for Renaud. She invited Andre in and he took a seat. "My employer wonders if you will accept a small gift?"

"What type of gift?"

"I'm not certain what it is."

Hester wondered what Galen was up to now. "Tell your employer further gifts are unnecessary."

In response to her words, Andre suddenly appeared quite uncomfortable. "He won't be pleased if I return with the items."

"Is your employer such an ogre?" she asked with a small smile on her face.

Andre stammered, "Well, no. It's just that—"

"What, Mr. Renaud?"

Renaud searched her eyes for a moment as if trying to evaluate how to respond. "You see he's concerned that you haven't drawn on but a small portion of the funds from the land sale."

"Ah. Your employer has been poking around in my affairs, Mr. Renaud."

Andre Renaud seemed damned uncomfortable under Hester's amused scrutiny. She finally took pity upon him and said, "Don't worry, Mr. Renaud, an answer is not necessary. Tell your employer I've only drawn out a small portion because I've no idea if the funds are legitimate."

"Didn't the draft clear?"

"Oh, yes it did, but I wonder if I sold my land to a legitimate buyer or to someone who expects to reclaim the funds once he's accomplished his goal and moves on."

Andre Renaud stared a moment. "He would never seek to reclaim an investment, Miss Wyatt. Never."

In spite of Renaud's staunch denial Hester chose to reserve final judgment on the funds until she could speak with Galen.

"So, what gifts are you bearing, Mr. Renaud?"

"As I stated, I've no idea."

"Then bring it in. Lord help us if your employer doesn't get his way."

The "it" turned out to be all the crates Hester had seen on the wagon outside. When Andre and the other man finished stacking them in her parlor, she had hardly any room to turn around. "What is all this, Mr. Renaud?"

"Well, some of it is corded wood as you can see. That crate over there holds hams from—"

Hester held up a hand to silence him. "Let me rephrase myself. Why did he send all this?"

"Well, he's concerned that—"

She interrupted, "He's concerned that I'm going hungry."

Renaud hesitated.

Hester sighed. "Tell him I appreciate his concern but I do not need all of this. If he doesn't want to take the bulk of it back, I'll donate it to the church first thing tomorrow. Is he always this extravagant, Mr. Renaud?"

Andre nodded his head yes. "Especially with women—" He cut his comment short with a look of panic in his eyes.

Hester simply shook her head. The revelation did not surprise her. "I'm old enough to hear the truth, Mr. Renaud. Please, don't be embarrassed. I doubt your employer considers me one of his women."

If Renaud had an opinion he kept it to himself. "If you won't be needing us any further, we'll leave you, Miss Wyatt."

Hester thanked both men, then watched as they drove away.

She spent close to an hour opening crates and conducting an inventory. When she was done, she found she had enough food to feed an army of runaways. There were the hams Renaud remarked upon earlier, along with smoked salmon, dried beef, and smoked turkeys. She found rashes of bacon, flour, cheeses, lard, salt. One box held only spices, many of which Hester had never seen before, and another was filled with candles. There were jars of put-up vegetables and jams. She even found a cache of oranges, of all things. She'd only had an orange once in her life. She found the whole exercise so overwhelming, she had no idea where to begin culling what she wanted to keep. Were Galen here she would have boxed his ears for such extravagance. She picked up one of the oranges, and, unable to resist, broke the skin and extracted one of the juice-filled sections. She ate it slowly, savoring the sweet coldness. She decided maybe she would keep a few of the oranges after all.

By evening she'd put away most of the items and decided that the rest could wait until morning. As she turned to douse the parlor's lights, she spied one thing she didn't remember Renaud or his helper carry into the house. It was a large wooden chest. She snaked her way through the crates, pushed aside the ones on either side of the chest, then knelt beside it. Hester thought it looked as if it had been in someone's family for quite some time. Its gleaming dark wood showed off years of polishing. The front panel on the outside was beautifully carved all over with garlands of flowers. The workings were delicately exquisite. Hester was curious about the contents and so opened the hinged top slowly. Inside she found nightgowns, dozens of them in a variety of styles and lengths. Some were made of the finest Egyptian cotton and others appeared to have been fashioned from only a handful of silk. There were also some so daringly sheer, she could see right through them. They were all beautiful, even though none would keep her warm on a Michigan night. She smiled at this gift, because she remembered Galen's comments about her ugly, service-able gowns. Should he ever see her in these, she'd willingly bet he'd whistle a different tune. The idea of wearing them for his eyes alone was as thrilling as it was inappropriate.

With a sigh, she closed the chest and headed upstairs, forcing herself to think of Foster, hoping he would return soon. Without his presence she doubted her ability to brook Galen's pull on her imagination.

Chapter 9

T he warmth of early April signaled winter's eventual demise, but everyone knew spring wouldn't come to stay for good until later in the month. For now, the folks around Whittaker had to contend with thawing roads, axle-deep with mud, and weather so changeable it sometimes went from rain to sunshine to blowing snow all within a day's span. There'd been no word of the slave catcher Shoe and his men all winter. Rumor had it he'd been shot in a fight with members of a Toledo-area Vigilance Committee, and had fled south to lick his wounds. Hester didn't care why Shoe had gone south, only that he was gone. With one less menace hanging over their heads, the conductors on Hester's section of the Road began transporting their freedom-seeking passengers once again.

Hester hid a group of fugitives in her cellar for three days during the first week of April. She fed them well from Galen's storehouse of goods, then drove them into Ann Arbor hidden in the false bottom of her wagon. The going was muddy and therefore slow, but she reached the next station without mishap.

Most of the conductors on Hester's line were women, even though some men, like William Lovejoy, disapproved. The circle of female conductors took root during her grandmother's day. The daughters and granddaughters of these founding families continued to do their part.

Hester pulled back on the reins and halted the mule and the wagon in the back of the house owned by her good friend Abigail Grayson. Hester stepped down into the slushy mud. Shivering beneath her well-worn cape, she slogged her way around to the back of the wagon. She took a moment to glance around the countryside to determine if Abigail's house was being watched. When she saw no one, she undid the false bottom and helped her passengers out. Abigail met them at the back door and quickly ushered everyone inside. She and Hester shared a brief welcoming hug, then Abigail took the others into the kitchen for some hot soup and something warm to drink. Only after seeing that all the fugitives' needs had been met did Abigail invite Hester into the parlor for talk and tea.

Abigail eased herself into a soft chair then set her cane beside her. She had walked with the aid of a cane for as long as Hester had known her, close to ten years now. Gail was a full decade older than Hester but it had not stopped them from being fast friends.

Hester savored the warmth of the cup in her hand and asked, "How's Jake faring in Niles?" Jake was Abigail's ten-year-old son, and the apple of her eye.

Abigail smiled. "He's hunting and fishing with my brother, Absalom, and his son, Nate. They're having a grand time. It's certain he won't want to come home any time soon. Absalom keeps asking if Jake can stay for the rest of the year."

Abigail's brother resided in a small town outside of Niles, Michigan, a place known as Grayson's Grove. According to Gail, as Abigail preferred to be addressed, the Grayson family owned the grove and everything in it.

"Are you going to let him stay?" Hester asked.

Gail shrugged. "I'm leaning towards it. I'll miss him greatly but Jake needs to be around men. He's growing up."

Hester had never been told the story regarding Jake's father, only that there'd been some type of scandal many years ago.

Hester turned the conversation to the runaways in the kitchen. Gail had already made arrangements for them to go on to the next station that night as the five people had decided to exercise their dearly earned freedom on Canadian soil.

The conductors who'd carry them on to the next station were a married couple named Martha and Reginald Travis and they knocked on Abigail's back door just past midnight. They were Quakers and had been conductors for as long as Hester had been alive.

Hester and Abigail waited outside in the cold night air while the passengers fitted themselves beneath the mound of hay filling the bed of the Travis wagon. The hay would serve as cover for their passage and more importantly keep them warm on the long trek to Detroit.

When the wagon rolled away, Hester and Abigail quickly ran back into the house.

"Hester, are there any houses for sale in Whittaker?" Gail asked as she showed Hester into Jake's bedroom.

Hester had decided to spend the night rather than brave the cold, lonely trip back home. She set her worn valise on Jake's bed and opened it to remove her night clothes. "Not that I'm aware of. Why, are you thinking to move?"

"I am. This house has become cloying. It contains too many terrible memories."

"You can always come and stay with me for a while if you'd like," Hester said. "I've more than enough room."

"It wouldn't be a bother?"

"Oh, Gail, no. I'd love to have you."

"Maybe I'll take you up on the offer. Lord knows I don't wish to reside within these walls any longer. Did Katherine ever tell you the story of Jake's father?"

Hester shook her head. "I was too young, I suppose."

"Well, you're old enough now, and if I'm to stay with you, you should at least know the sordid details." Gail offered a bittersweet smile, then added, "We'll talk in the morning. Right now, we both need to get some sleep."

Over breakfast the next morning, Gail told Hester of the betrayals and falsehoods which undermined Gail's short marriage to Roland Grinell.

"He was a bigamist?!" Hester asked.

"Yes, there were at least two other wives. The one in Kalamazoo had borne him three children. He also had a wife in Windsor."

According to Gail, Grinell married her to grab her share of the Grayson lands. He assumed the land would be put under his control once he became her husband, as was customary. Evidently he'd run the flim flam successfully on spinsters and widows many times before. He'd marry, gain control of whatever properties or funds the women possessed, sell the assets, pocket the profits, and disappear. But the terms of the Grayson will forbade any sale or transfer of the land without the approval of any other living Grayson family members.

Gail's twin brother, Absalom, refused to give his permission.

"Why?"

"Absalom took an instant dislike to Roland. The day Roland Grinell first rode into the grove, supposedly seeking information on a recently escaped family member, Absalom said he smelled like trouble. Unfortunately, I had a less acute sense of smell than my dear brother. I smelled only his Bay Rum cologne." She added, "However, he stank like week-old fish by the time he vanished."

"How was he exposed?"

"Absalom hired a man to check on Roland's past. The wife in Kalamazoo was posing as a hairdresser. Absalom's man said she preyed on lonely old men and widowers in much the same way as her husband. The pair were wanted by authorities in Michigan, Ohio, and southern Ontario."

She paused a moment and her eyes became distant.

"You have to remember, I thought I loved him very much. When he came courting, I'd never had a suitor before. He was handsome, well educated. He brought me flowers and candy. He described all the exotic places we'd visit after we married. I was overwhelmed by it all, and defied my family to marry him. When my brother confronted me with the information about his trail of misdeeds, I refused to believe any of it. I was convinced Absalom didn't want to see me happy, so I took the train to Kalamazoo to confront this woman myself. I just knew she was lying about being married to Roland and I planned on proving it. I went to her house, and when I told her who I was she laughed and said, 'So you're my husband's little country pigeon. Welcome to the big city, Miss Grayson Grove.' Then she slammed the door in my face."

Hester was speechless.

"When I returned to Detroit, he was already packing to leave. Absalom had just departed and had threatened to have him jailed if he did not leave town. Roland swore he'd done nothing to deserve such treatment, and that if I truly loved him, Jake and I would leave, too. When I told him who I'd visited while in Kalamazoo, and that the jig was up, he flew into a rage. He said yes, he was married to another. Then he began to taunt me. He told me my land had been the only reason he'd stooped to marry a woman as ugly as me. Told me I'd never find a man to love me without my land as a bribe.

"He cursed my brother and cursed me. He became so enraged, he began striking me. Hester, I am six feet tall in my stocking feet, I was raised around men, and I can pretty much handle anything that comes my way, but I have never had a man raise his hand against me in violence. When he struck me we were at the top of the stairs. The blow was so unexpected and so filled with anger it knocked me backwards. I remember losing my balance and falling. When I came to, I was lying at the bottom of the stairs. One of my neighbors, Mrs. Neal, was kneeling beside me and holding my squalling Jake in her arms. He was still an infant at that time and he must have been bawling for some time because she said his constant crying made her fear something had happened to me, so she came over to take a look."

"Where was your husband? Surely he didn't simply leave you lying there after what he'd done."

"Oh, but he did. Mrs. Neal lived directly across the road. She said she saw him leave long before she heard Jake's crying begin."

Hester was appalled by the man's behavior. "And all this happened here, in this house? Is that why you need the cane?"

"Yes. The doctors said I'd walk with a cane for the rest of my life because of the damage done to my hip in the fall. After Roland left, I had all the rooms repainted, changed all the furniture, and told myself I would not let those memories win. I loved this house when we first moved here, hell, I loved him back then, but I fought the good fight almost ten years by staying here. I'm ready to move on."

They spent the next hour or so discussing the logistics of Gail's move to Whittaker. It would be nearly a month before Gail could make the move, but Hester told her she'd be welcome whenever the time came.

Hester thought about Gail's story as she drove the wagon back to Whittaker later that day. In Hester's mind, it was just one more tragic example of the painful side of love. Marrying Foster for companionship seemed to be a much better choice.

Like a god send, she heard from Foster the very next day. Branton Hubble dropped off the letter he'd picked up for her in town and Hester hastily broke the seal. According to the date on the top of the missive it had been posted in England nearly three months ago. She knew how long the mail took at times but her eyes widened when she saw the date of his expected arrival in Detroit. "That's tomorrow!" she said aloud. He would certainly expect to be met at the train in Ann Arbor. She could hardly wait to see him again, but she did not relish another slow trek through the mud-filled roads.

The trip was even worse than Hester could have imagined. The previous night's torrential rains turned the roads into slush. The thick liquid concoction of rain, mud, and melting snow sloshed high up on the wheels as they rolled, intermittently splattering Hester as she guided the reins of the mule. The mule didn't appear to enjoy the slop anymore than Hester. The animal stopped time and time again, refusing to take another step. After much yelling and pleading she finally made it to the depot, but mentally threatened to sell the mule at her first opportunity.

Hester spotted Foster over by the pile of luggage stacked trackside. She took a moment to observe him. The slightly balding Foster with his plain brown face and short rounded figure would never be considered handsome, but he was dependable and true. She didn't need to be in love to pledge her life to him.

He must have sensed her presence because he looked up and upon seeing her in the crowd, he smiled widely and hurried to her side. He squeezed her hands affectionately, then greeted her with a quick peck on the cheek. She found herself comparing his welcome to Galen's sultry kisses before burying the unfair thoughts. Foster would never be the lover Galen was, but she didn't care.

"Welcome back. How was the passage?"

"Tedious. The purser refused cabins to all the Blacks on board. We were forced to either sleep in the hold or stay on the deck. However, something wonderful happened as a result."

Still holding her hands he looked her in the face and smiled. "Hester, I've taken a wife."

Hester's eyes widened.

"Her name is Jenine, and Hester she is the most beautiful and gracious creature I've ever had the opportunity to meet."

He paused a moment to chuckle, "She's not smart like

you. I'll never be able to debate anything of substance with her, but I don't care—"

Hester could not believe her ears. "Foster—"

"Hester, I know you and I were to be wed, but I'm in love. For the first time in my life I've been impaled by Cupid's arrow and I am not ashamed to admit it."

Hester wondered if he had contracted a mind fever. Foster in love?! Foster waxing over being impaled by Cupid's arrow?! If she weren't so stunned she might be able to see the humor in this, however right now, all she could see was a Foster she admittedly had never met. The Foster she knew had never pursued anything other than the serious sides of life. He debated the issues of the day, read the *Liberator,* and taught school. What had happened to him?

Foster said, "I know I should have wired you, but my mind's been so muddled since meeting Jenine, I sometimes have trouble deciding whether I'm coming or going. She's like sunshine, Hester, pure sunshine."

She wanted to ask him where that description left her but she held her tongue. It wasn't as if she and Foster had been in love; their marriage would have been built upon mutual respect and admiration. That said, why did she feel angry? Because she had been replaced by a woman who fit the description of sunshine, she told herself.

Foster's voice brought her back to the matter at hand. "I want very much for you and Jenine to be friends, Hester. She can be very shy."

"Where is Jenine now?"

"Right over here. Come and meet her."

Hester had no desire to meet anyone but she told herself that no matter how she felt personally, Foster was still a good friend and she should be happy for him.

Jenine was seated on one of the benches. She was fashionably dressed and greeted their approach with a sunny little smile. She was indeed as beautiful as described. In a sweet little voice she asked, "Is this your friend Hester?"

Foster beamed under her loving looks. "Jenine Quint, this is indeed Hester Wyatt. Hester, Jenine."

Hester nodded. "Pleased to meet you, Jenine. Welcome."

She sighed, "Oh, thank you. I just knew you'd hate me for taking Foster from you. Fostie kept telling me not to worry, that you wouldn't mind, but I did worry."

Hester kept the smile pasted on her face as she turned to Fostie. He had the decency to duck away from her pointed look. Hester tried to reassure the new bride. "There is no need to worry. *Foster* is correct."

"I'm so relieved to hear you say so. I've been dreading this moment since he told me about you. He thinks the world of you. Did you know?"

Not enough to wire me and prepare me for this humiliating event, she thought to herself. Aloud she said, "Foster and I hold each other in high esteem. I'm sure your marriage won't alter my opinion of him."

Jenine looked to Foster and said, "She's as understanding as you said she'd be."

"I told you. Hester is the most practical person I know."

In the past, Hester would have taken Foster's assessment as a compliment, today she did not.

She pulled her emotions together and said cheerily, "I came to the depot to give Foster a lift home. Do you still require one, or are you heading elsewhere?"

Foster seemed unable to tear his eyes away from Jenine's lovely face. "A lift would be in order, Hester, thank you. Come, Jenine, help me fetch our trunks, and we'll let Hester drive us over to Whittaker."

The first part of the journey proceeded fine, albeit slowly. The mule kept balking and Hester kept threatening to turn the animal into hide. She got the animal to move for almost a mile, but a few steps later the mule stopped once more, this time apparently for good.

Nothing Hester or Foster tried could get the animal to move. While Jenine looked on, they finally stepped down into the mud and attempted to pull the mule forward by the reins, but the mule simply dug in its heels. Hester even tempted it with an apple from her coat, a ploy which always worked in the past, but the mule simply turned up its nose. Hester didn't know what else to do outside of taking a crop to its stubborn back, however she'd never struck an animal in her life, and she would not begin now. "I give up, Foster," Hester confessed. She didn't even want to think about how muddy her clothes had become as a result of this frustrating situation. Both she and Foster resembled mud pies.

Foster began to walk back the way they'd come.

"Where are you going?" Jenine called.

"We passed a farm house a ways back, maybe they have an animal we can rent. I'll return as soon as I can."

Hester called, "Tell them they can have this mule for free in exchange."

Foster laughed and gave her a wave goodbye.

This was not a very good homecoming, she thought with irritation as she watched him round the bend. She cast a malevolent eye at the four-legged beast responsible, but then she thought that if she were a mule, she probably wouldn't want to pull a wagon in this muck either. Luckily it was a beautiful day; the sunshine felt good on her face, even though it was still cold enough for a winter bonnet and mittens.

She was dressed warmly. Fashion would probably frown on the old flannel long drawers she always wore beneath her woolen skirts, but fashion obviously never spent winter in Michigan, she thought dryly. On the other hand, the fashionably dressed Jenine appeared to be freezing in her lightweight coat and thin-soled shoes.

Hester took two quilts from beneath the seat. She handed one to the very grateful Jenine, then wrapped the other around her own legs and mud-soaked boots. Frostbite continued to be a real danger this time of year. She hoped Foster would find help quickly because in spite of her warm clothing, the longer she sat, the colder she would become.

About thirty minutes later, Hester could hear the rumble of an oncoming coach on the road behind her. She turned and saw a big black coach pulled by a team of powerful horses come barreling around the bend. The mud thrown up by the pounding hooves and the wheels cascaded high in every direction. As the coach drew closer, she could see its lines and structure more clearly. Hester realized she'd seen the coach before, and it caused her heart to pound. Recognition hit her like a lightning bolt. The coach bearing down on her was the same coach that had spirited Galen away.

The driver drew the coach to a halt. Hester tried to compose herself but a voice inside herself wailed that now was not the time for this meeting, not here, not this way. The day had already been disconcerting enough. She consoled herself with the fact that maybe she was wrong, and even if the coach did belong to Galen there was no guarantee he would be inside.

The driver's head and face were hidden beneath a burnoose he'd wrapped around himself to ward off the spraying mud. He removed it, revealing the darkly handsome and bearded face of Raymond LeVeq. He greeted her with a brilliant smile. "Good afternoon, mademoiselles. We hear you are in need of assistance."

Hester swayed and wondered if the day could become any worse.

Before Hester could think of something to say to LeVeq, the door of the coach swung open and out stepped Foster. On his heels, Galen made his slow, smooth exit. Hester watched him straighten his tall, lean body up to his full height and found herself nearly blinded by his handsomeness. He bore no resemblance to the beaten, one-eyed man she'd first met. Instead she saw the face of the Galen who invited women in to share his bath, the Galen who spent extravagant amounts of money, and the Galen who left rosebuds in her bed. He was dressed richly and he wore the look of understated wealth well, almost as if he had been born to it. Hester took a deep steadying breath as he and Foster slogged over to where she and Jenine sat atop the wagon. She hazarded a quick look back up at the driver. He smiled at her, winked, then placed his finger across his lips in the age-old gesture conveying silence. His prompting made her remember her vow to pretend as if she and Galen had never met. She just hoped she could hold onto herself long enough to support the charade. She also hoped Galen knew what he was doing.

A smiling Foster said, "Ladies, we are in luck, this gentleman has kindly offered to share his coach with us."

"We are in your debt, sir," Hester offered softly, bowing her head politely so she could momentarily escape the power in Galen's vibrant black eyes.

The shivering Jenine added, "We certainly are. Fostie, you never said Michigan was so cold."

He replied, "The weather will warm soon, I promise."

Foster then made the introductions. "This is Galen Vachon. Vachon, my wife, Jenine, and my neighbor, Hester Wyatt."

Galen paused a moment and met Hester's eyes, but she kept them void of all emotion.

Galen bowed first over Jenine's hand, then took Hester's mitten-covered hand in his. His eyes burned her as he brought it to his lips. *"Enchante,* mademoiselle, I am privileged to be at your service."

He released his hold without incident, unless one counted the faint pressure of the gentle squeeze he gave her fingers in parting. She forced her attention back to Foster.

"Mr. Vachon is going to be residing in Whittaker of all places."

"Where in Whittaker?" Hester asked. She found it hard not to stare at Galen's new face. The bruises and swelling had disappeared. He had skin the color of pale butter. The moustache above his lips added an air of danger to his uncommon handsomeness. He'd not worn a moustache during his stay with her, but the effects of it here today, coupled with his aristocratic bearing, seemed to rattle her senses even more.

His rich voice brought her back to the present as he replied, "I've purchased Lovejoy's Folly as I believe it was once named."

Hester met his deep gaze fully. "Then you must be Mr. Renaud's employer, and the purchaser of my land."

A smiling Galen inclined his head in acknowledgment. "So, you are that Hester Wyatt. Thank you for being so open to my proposal."

"It was very generous."

Foster interrupted to ask, "Hester sold you some of her land?"

"Yes," Hester said.

Foster's face turned serious. "The situation must have been dire for you to sell, Hester. Why didn't you write me?"

"I didn't want to worry you, and besides, thanks to Mr. Vachon, the crisis is now remedied."

Foster observed Galen for a moment as if seeking some answer.

Galen slowly raised an imperial eyebrow at the silent questions on Foster's face before saying, "Mr. Quint, your wife appears to be freezing, why don't we adjourn to the warmth of my coach?"

Foster blustered, "I'm sorry. You're quite correct. Jenine, love, are you ready?"

Foster offered her a hand down from the wagon. She accepted his help, and he escorted her over to the waiting coach. Exasperated, Hester watched him go. It was not as if she really needed help stepping down, but politeness dictated he at least offer her his hand, too.

Galen offered instead. "Your beautiful eyes are flashing like an August thunderstorm. Did you know your Frederick had taken a wife?"

Hester warned him. "If you so much as smile I will sock you."

"I'd rather have a kiss."

She shook her head at his outrageous request. "Just help me down, incorrigible Frenchman."

He did and she tried not to wince as the cold mud seeped into her brogans.

He asked, "Are you still wearing those godawful shoes?"

She couldn't suppress her humor. "Stop being blasphemous, and tell me what I should do about the mule. I can't just leave her here."

Galen grinned. It felt so good to have her near again. "Frederick and I made arrangements with a farmer at a house back up the road. He promised to hold the animal and the wagon until I send a man for it tomorrow."

LeVeq had already draped tarps over a portion of the bench like seats inside the coach to protect the fine velvet covering from the mud clinging to the new passengers. While he transferred the trunks from the wagon to the boot of the coach, Hester took a seat across from Foster and Jenine, who were whispering and nestling like lovebirds. Hester tried to ignore them, prefering to concentrate instead upon the interior's gleaming wooden panels carved with dragons. Galen entered shortly thereafter, and settled onto the undraped portion of the seat beside her.

Hester could not get over his elegant attire. The voluminous great coat appeared expensive and well made. Beneath it she glimpsed a gray silk waistcoat and a cravat the color of snow. On the seat between them lay an elegant black walking stick. He used the golden crown to tap the roof, and the coach pulled away.

"I apologize for the tarp, but I recently had the interior redone."

For the first time, Hester noted that the seats were the color of indigo. Her startled eyes flew to Galen's. He met her gaze with a slight smile. "I had a difficult time finding the exact shade I had in mind. What do you think of my choice, Miss Wyatt? I'd appreciate your opinion as a woman."

Hester surveyed the plush indigo fabric and replied, "I think you chose well, Mr. Vachon."

Hester sensed herself being drawn into Galen's spell. She was glad to hear Foster ask, "Why did you decide to settle in Whittaker, Vachon? Surely a man of your class could afford to live elsewhere."

"True, but I've recently relocated some of my business to Detroit. It would be simpler to live there but I enjoy the solitude Whittaker offers. How long have you lived in Whittaker, Mr. Quint?"

"Just a few years. I'm Canadian by birth."

"How long have you and Mrs. Quint been married?"

Jenine replied shyly, "Less than two weeks."

Galen said, "Ah, newlyweds."

Foster gazed into Jenine's long-lashed eyes. "Yes, Jenine and I met on a steamer crossing the Atlantic nearly a month ago."

She took up the tale. "The purser wouldn't let anyone of color have a cabin, so most of us slept in the hold. It was awful and damp and filled with large rats. Fostie offered to sit with me when he saw how afraid I was. He was so gallant, I couldn't help falling in love with him."

"She is the best thing to ever come into my life. Are you married, Mr. Vachon?"

Galen shook his head. "No, and frankly, I never had a desire to be, but after viewing how happy you two seem, I may be inspired to change my mind."

While Foster and Jenine shared a long, loving look, Hester glanced Galen's way and gave him a tiny roll of her eyes. He raised a covert eyebrow in response. She hid her grin by looking out of the small portal at the passing landscape.

The three made small talk to pass the time. Hester was still amazed by Foster and his bride Jenine. She wanted Foster to be happy, but she harbored reservations over his choice. How could he find happiness with a woman who professed no interest in the things that interested her husband? Hester couldn't believe her ears when

Jenine sunnily confessed she had never attended a lecture of any kind, nor had she a desire to do so. Hester and Foster had attended many lectures and conventions over the past few years and the experiences were always uplifting. But in response to Jenine's declaration, he'd done nothing but smile indulgently, as if her stance hadn't mattered.

She sat that conundrum aside for a moment to concentrate on a riddle of another sort. Galen. So far, he had treated her with the distance one would afford a stranger, but even so she still found it difficult to relax. Every time their eyes met the memories resurfaced. How could she look at him and not remember the night in her kitchen? His kisses had been magical; they left her breathless. Even now, as she thought of the way he'd opened her gown then feasted so lustily, her nipples tightened in heady anticipation. She willed herself to direct her thoughts elsewhere.

Galen asked Foster, "Where were you returning from when you and your wife made your fateful meeting?"

"I was returning home from Oxford. I am pleased to report I am now a certified graduate."

Jenine clapped heartily.

Hester joined in. She could not help but be proud of his accomplishment. He'd worked hard. The children of the area would benefit greatly from having such a learned teacher.

Galen appeared properly impressed. "What was your discipline?"

"Philosophy," Foster replied importantly. "The race needs more men like myself wouldn't you agree? Men able to debate the opposition on an equal plane. Men able to strike back with the words of Plato and Aristotle."

Galen gave Foster a slow, assessing perusal. "The race has enough philosophers, Mr. Quint. What we need are more men with guns."

Foster stared. "Surely you are making sport of me."

"Unfortunately, I am not. Philosophers can debate until the Second Coming but only bloodshed will resolve the issue once and for all."

"I agree that is a possibility but—"

Jenine tugged on his arm. "You promised no politics. Remember?"

Foster smiled. "I'm sorry love. Mr. Vachon, maybe you and I will have an opportunity to discuss this at length in the near future."

Galen inclined his head. "I'd be pleased."

Jenine asked, "Where are you from originally, Mr. Vachon?"

"Louisiana."

"Ah," she said. "I knew a man from Louisiana. Creole, just like you. He used to get in fights all the time."

Hester asked, "Why?"

"Folks kept telling him he wasn't Black. You ever have that problem, Mr. Vachon?"

"Occasionally, and I find it is always a pleasure to meet someone from the Race Inclusion Board. After all, where would the race be without them telling us who may be in the race and who may not?"

Everyone chuckled.

Jenine asked, "So you consider yourself a member of the race?"

It was an odd question, Hester thought. Galen's eyes met Hester's for a fleeting second before he turned his attention back to Jenine.

"Yes, Mrs. Quint. I consider myself a member of the race, why would I not?"

She shrugged. "Because some mulattoes choose not to. They use their skin and their well-connected families to escape the hardships we darker souls must endure."

Hester looked over at Foster with surprise.

He in turn stared at Jenine.

"Did I say something wrong?" she asked.

She raised her eyes to Galen's and must have seen the

coolness there because she gasped quickly, "Oh, Mr. Vachon, I'm sorry. I didn't mean to offend you. It was just an observation. I meant nothing by it."

Galen offered just the trace of a smile, then inclined his head, "Apology accepted."

The tension in the coach eased somewhat after that, and the small talk continued. Hester thought about Jenine's observation. There were those who believed men and women with mixed blood could not be trusted on matters concerning the race because they were perceived as having divided loyalties. On the other side there were mulattoes who would never let Hester enter their circle because of the darkness of her skin. She thought the prejudices of both sides ridiculous. The fight against slavery consisted of soldiers representing the full spectrum of the race, just because one had a light-toned skin, did not mean that person could vote, or testify in a court of law, or avail themselves of any of the other rights denied their darker brethren.

Hester had never condoned the attitudes of those who took it upon themselves to declare one segment of the race superior to another. It was a divisive and destructive practice, especially in light of all they had to face.

Galen tried his best to appear interested as Foster droned on about the peers he'd been introduced to during his stay in England. He remembered Hester mentioning how Foster tended towards pompousness and she'd been absolutely correct. Galen was certain the man had many positive attributes, but he hadn't been giving a good first impression; the man was a bore, a blowhard reminiscent of a German burgher Galen once knew. Out of respect for Hester, Galen made all the appropriate responses, but even as Foster rambled on, Galen preferred to silently bask in the joy of having Hester seated at his side.

The beauty of Hester's dark face made one overlook the awful bonnet and the well-worn cape with its frayed edges. Instead he found his eyes lingering over the curves of her lushly perfect mouth. He could have been knocked over by a feather when he first saw her sitting atop the wagon back there. He'd no idea his very own Indigo would be one of the stranded women Quint wanted him to assist. He could've kissed the burgher for bringing about this meeting, but now, Galen just wanted him strangled and tossed from the coach. On second thought, Galen decided his presence may indeed be a blessing. Were Foster and his lovely bride not present, Galen would, without a doubt, be seeking ways to cajole sweet kisses from Hester's lips. He wanted to undo the buttons of her shirt and trace the heated scents of vanilla he knew awaited him at the base of her throat and in the valley between her breasts. He could feel himself hardening to the thoughts and so forced himself to concentrate on whatever Foster was saying now.

Hester, too, tried to concentrate on Foster's words but could not because of Galen's disturbing presence. She'd avoided looking directly at him for most of the journey because she'd found out early on that she did not have the ability to remain unaffected by Galen's eyes telling her everything he could not say.

They made it back to Whittaker later that afternoon. LeVeq brought the coach to a stop at Hester's house first. Jenine and Foster were going on to the boarding house where Foster lived. As she prepared to depart, Foster said, "Hester, why don't you come and have dinner with Jenine and me, say in a few days?"

Hester opened her mouth to politely decline.

Galen interrupted smoothly, "I've a better idea, why don't the three of you join me for dinner? It will be my way of showing my appreciation for such a pleasant afternoon."

"Thank you, Mr. Vachon. I'm going to wear my best dress," Jenine said happily.

Hester simply shook her head.

Foster asked Jenine, "Darling, do you mind if I walk Hester to the door?"

Jenine placed her hand against his brown cheek. "Of course not. Just as long as you don't let Hester steal you back."

"Rest assured, Jenine. Foster has eyes only for you," Hester replied.

She turned to Galen. "Mr. Vachon, thank you for the rescue, I hope we didn't put you out too much."

"Not at all, Miss Wyatt. You will join me for dinner, won't you?"

Hester's senses shimmered in response to the heat she sensed veiled behind his eyes. "I wouldn't miss it for the world." She bade him and Jenine farewell, then let Foster escort her up the walk.

When they reached her door, he said, "You've taken this well, Hester. I deserve to be flogged for treating you so shabbily, but you can see how wonderful she is, can't you?"

Hester had to look away a moment before saying, "Yes, Foster. I can."

He smiled. "She has made me very happy."

"Then that is all that matters. But are you certain you wish to pledge your life to someone you've known only a month?"

"A month, a year, it wouldn't alter my feelings. I love her, Hester."

She didn't press, but instead said genuinely, "Then I'm sure I shall also."

"Are you angry with me?"

She looked him in the eye. "I'd be a liar if I said I weren't, but we didn't have a love match, so my heart isn't broken. I wish you happiness."

"Do you mean that?"

"Yes, I do."

He took her hands and kissed them. "You're a very special woman, Hester. Very special."

But not special enough to be your wife, she thought. "You shouldn't keep Jenine waiting, Foster. I'll see you at Vachon's dinner."

"Thank you, Hester. For everything."

"You're welcome."

Later, after donning clean, dry clothes, and warming up her shivering innards with some hot tea, Hester answered a knock at her door.

She opened it and was surprised to find Galen standing on her porch. Waves of emotion washed over her in that moment. "Why did you come back?"

She could see his coach waiting down by the road. "Is Foster still inside?"

"Interesting man, your Frederick. May I come in?"

She backed up and let him enter.

"How are you *petite?*"

"As well as any other woman who suddenly finds herself replaced."

"She did you a favor."

"How so?"

"You didn't really want to marry him."

"Yes, I did."

"I wouldn't have allowed it. Not after meeting him. I'd have married you myself to keep you from wasting your life with that burgher."

She knew he was only teasing but the declaration set her heart to racing anyway. "He's not a burgher, Galen, and you could not have stopped me from marrying him."

"I'd have stopped it if I had to make love to you in the center of town."

Hester swayed. She observed him a moment, saw the seriousness in his eyes and said, "You wouldn't have dared."

"If you knew me better, you wouldn't say that. Has he ever left roses in your bed?"

Hester shook her head.

"Another reason you didn't need to marry him."

She wondered how many hearts he'd broken over his lifetime. He was more handsome than a June day. "Did you come here for a reason?"

"I wanted to see you alone."

She had to look away from the heat in his eyes or be singed. "Well, you've accomplished your goal. I think you should go home."

He was as potent as he'd been the night LeVeq and his brothers came to fetch him home, and she was just as vulnerable.

"I'm trying to leave, believe me, but I'm having trouble."

"Why?"

"Your mouth, mostly."

"My—mouth?"

"I lay awake at night wondering if your kisses are still as sweet as I remember . . ."

Hester's eyes closed a moment and her knees felt like water. "You are audacious," she whispered.

"Not as audacious as I'd like to be, Indigo, believe me."

"Hester. My name is Hester."

"Maybe for Frederick—not for me. For me you are *ma petite* Indigo . . ."

Hester was having trouble breathing. "You'll have to go now."

His smile reflected in his eyes. "One kiss."

"No!" she gasped.

He inclined his head. "For you, I can be patient. *Au revoir, ma petite.*"

Hester closed the door and stood with her back against it. Her heart was pounding, her senses throbbing and she could not deny it.

That night, as she prepared for bed, she knew that above all else she was going to have to avoid Galen; if she didn't she'd be in love with him before her summer flowers bloomed.

Chapter 10

Early the next morning, Hester's recalcitrant mule and the wagon were returned to her by one of Galen's workers. Thankfully, Galen had not chosen to accompany the man. After last night's parting she needed time to recover before facing him again.

Once the worker departed she drove the wagon around to the barn, then spent the remaining morning hours readying her late aunt's room for Gail's anticipated arrival.

Later that evening as Hester sat reading in the study, she heard a knock on the door. A peek out of the curtain showed Galen's big black coach. She went weak in reaction, then let the curtain drop. What could he possibly want from her now? She drew in a deep breath to steady herself. She walked to the door, bracing herself for Galen's lean handsomeness, but instead found Foster on the other side. Confusion colored her voice. "Foster?" she exclaimed as she looked over his shoulder at the waiting coach.

"Hester, yesterday Vachon and I were discussing some of the improvements I'd like to see in Whittaker, and he wishes to take the conversation further. He's leaving tomorrow on business so he's suggested we have our dinner this evening. Would you mind?"

Hester did not think she had it in her to fight off Galen's spell two evenings in a row and she wanted to offer an excuse, any excuse to avoid this, but she could not come up anything plausible.

Foster seemed so intent upon the meeting he did not notice her distress. "Hurry and dress, Hester. We shouldn't keep him waiting."

Hester vowed to throttle Galen for this, but she told Foster politely, "Give me a few moments, and I'll be right out."

Hester had no idea what to wear to dinner with someone as rich as Galen. Everything she owned shouted its true age. She decided she didn't have time to bemoan a wardrobe whose contents had never distressed her until now, so she dressed quickly, then peered critically at her reflection in the big standing oval mirror by her bed. The green shirtwaist dress still fit; she wondered if Galen would know it was six years old. She hastily brushed the edges of her hair, grabbed her gloves and cloak, then rushed from the house.

Inside the coach Galen greeted her with a nod as she took her seat beside him. "Good evening, Miss Wyatt. I'm pleased you could join us. I hope my sudden disruption of your plans caused you no distress."

His low-toned voice slid through her defenses. She nodded a greeting to the well-dressed Jenine, then replied, "No distress at all, Mr. Vachon. Thank you for the invitation."

He smiled, tapped his cane's gold head against the ceiling of the coach, and they were off.

Even as Hester wished they were alone so she could box his ears and tell him how she felt about playing his cat and mouse game, she was glad for the presence of Foster and his wife. She needed them as a buffer because Galen affected her like no other man before. He made her senses bloom with just a glance, made her long to feel his lips tracing the edges of her throat simply by being near her in a shadowy coach. Only he could wield such heady power, and as a result threatened the safe, sedate life she'd envisioned for her future.

The coach halted a while later at a small boarding

house well known in the area for its excellent food and service. Because it was an expensive place Hester had eaten at the establishment on only a few special occasions. She was quite surprised to find the dining room unoccupied upon their arrival; usually all the tables were full.

When she expressed her confusion, Galen replied, "I've leased the room for the evening, I didn't want us to be disturbed."

Foster and Jenine both looked astonished. Hester simply shook her head, thinking he was far too extravagant.

"Shall we take that table over there?" Galen asked smoothly, and from then on he proceeded to be an excellent host. He made certain they were comfortable, then had them order to their liking. Foster chose the squab—the price of which widened Hester's eyes, but his wife followed his lead. Galen chose lamb. Hester settled for the least expensive choice on the menu, the whitefish. As she handed over her menu, she noticed Galen's eyes on the black crocheted gloves she always wore in public, but he said nothing.

Instead his eyes swept her face. "Are you certain you want nothing else?" he asked after the waiter left.

"I'm certain, Mr. Vachon. Thank you."

The waiter brought tea and coffee and Hester asked for honey. Galen's request for maple syrup brought Hester's eyes to his. His answering gaze made her remember their time together in October.

Foster said to Galen, "I see you take syrup in your coffee. Are you a Free Producer, Mr. Vachon?"

Galen stirred his cup, and replied easily, "I fell victim to an accident this past fall. The woman who nursed me was a Free Producer. I developed a fondness for the syrup, and for her."

Hester choked on her tea and began to cough.

Everyone looked to her with concern. She waved them away and grabbed up a napkin. "I'm sorry," she gasped. "It went down the wrong pipe."

When she could breathe again, she saw Galen observing her with just the faintest hint of amusement. She added one more mark to his list of sins.

Foster picked up the thread of Galen's conversation and said, "Women can be quite remarkable, can't they? Take Hester for example—she's no beauty, but her mind is first rate."

"What about me, Fostie?" Jenine asked with a childish pout.

"You, my darling, are as beautiful as Sheba."

Jenine preened happily.

Galen decided Quint must be as blind as he was pompous. Though Hester seemed to be covering her feelings well, Galen could see the slight tightness in her chin. She'd been hurt by the flip remark, and he wanted to take her into his arms and passionately show her just how wrong he thought Quint to be. She was as beautiful as a black velvet sky; beautiful as a sunrise. If Quint couldn't appreciate her dark loveliness, it was just one more reason why Foster would have made her an unsuitable mate.

The conversation flowed on to other topics. Hester kept telling herself there'd really been nothing offensive about Foster's assessment of her comeliness; she wasn't a beauty, so why did she feel thunderous towards him?

The waiter brought their meals moments later and Hester found it necessary to look Galen's way in order to pass condiments and bread. His eyes had taken on a distinct coolness that appeared to be directed at Foster. She sensed it sprang from Foster's remark about her beauty or lack thereof. She wanted to assure him that Foster had meant no harm, but she dearly appreciated Galen's desire to be her champion.

They began to eat and Foster, seemingly oblivious to the currents flowing around the table, spent the meal sharing his view of Whittaker's future. He had some sound ideas about the school he wanted to establish and the potential for investment in the area.

Hester spent the meal alternately contributing to the

conversation and fighting off Galen's spell. He neither said nor did anything forward or ungentlemanly; his manners were impeccable as his dress, but the heat from his eyes touched her vividly each time their gazes met, making her remember the passionate touch of his hands, and the sweet thrill of his kisses.

As the meal progressed, she forgot all about Foster's remarks. Galen's presence across the table pulled her in and held her. She tried to ignore her attraction and focus her attention on the conversation only to find herself compelled to meet Galen's gaze again, and again. She grew warm, found herself wanting to succumb to this man who'd taught her to make passion and mud pies, but knowing she should be running for her life. Foster chattered on—about what Hester had no idea.

She saw only Galen.

She felt relief when the evening drew to a close, so much so she tripped over her chair as she stood. Only the quick grasp of Galen's strong hand upon her arm saved her from falling to the floor. As she stared up at him, she decided falling may have been better; her arm beneath his hand's hold burned from the contact.

He asked, "Are you all right, Miss Wyatt?"

Hester realized that everything about him made her dizzy: his height, his gaze, his touch. "No. I—mean yes. I—wasn't looking where I was going." She nervously backed out of his hold and turned a smiling face to the waiting Foster and Jenine. "Are we ready?"

The coach took them home, stopping first at Hester's door. As she rose to depart, Galen said, "Thank you for joining us, Miss Wyatt. I hope to see you again."

Hester found she had no defense for his soft, French-inflected words. Forcing herself to once again brave his waiting eyes, she replied with all the calm she could muster, "Thank you, Mr. Vachon."

She nodded goodnight to Foster and Jenine.

"Let me escort you to the door, Miss Wyatt," Galen said, rising to follow her from the coach.

"That won't be necessary."

"As a gentleman, I insist." He took her by the elbow and walked with her up the dark walk.

She asked, "When are you leaving town?"

"I'm not."

Hester stopped and looked up into his handsome face. "I thought you extended tonight's invitation because you were going away on business."

"I lied," he replied without a hint of guilt. "I simply wanted to see you."

"Galen?!"

He shrugged. "What can I say, *petite*. I've developed a craving for you."

Could any woman alive resist such a man? "How many bedroom doors have you conquered with that silver tongue?"

"Frankly, many, but the one I wish to conquer most seems stuck."

"And it shall remain stuck if I have to put chairs in front of it."

He grinned. "You are more of a match for me than I thought."

She smiled even as his words made her senses flare. "Go home. You have guests in your coach, remember?"

"A pity that. Had I a choice, I'd let Raymond drive them on home without me."

"And undoubtedly give the gossips plenty to talk about."

"Undoubtedly," he replied with blazing eyes.

In order to lower the heat rising between them, she asked, "So are you going to invest in Foster's school?"

"I'm not certain as of yet, but I'm sure I will. Though I must confess I have my doubts about a man who would throw you over for a woman with the brain of a plant."

Hester laughed, "Go home."

"I'm going, but I'm still waiting for that kiss."

Admittedly, Hester wanted to grant the request, but now was not the time or place, so she said nothing.

"Good night, *petite*. Oh by the way, if you really want

me to fund that school, come by the Folly later on and
we'll discuss it."

"Tonight?"

"Yes, tonight."

"That sounds suspiciously like blackmail."

He bowed. "And a black male is what I am. See you
later tonight."

She couldn't suppress her humor. "Galen?!"

She watched him walk away and almost yelled for him
to come back. However, she swore she'd get even with
the teasing Creole.

Establishing a school in Whittaker was everyone's
dream. By law the schools in Michigan were segregated
by race. Foster presently taught in an abandoned cabin.
The community had restored it as well as it could, but
when it rained the roof leaked, supplies were minimal,
and for now, only children with parents able to afford
the tuition were allowed to attend. The tuition was the
only salary Foster received for his services. To supplement his income he clerked for some of the businesses in
the area, but Hester knew teaching to be his true
vocation.

She also knew that without Galen's generosity, it
might be years before the community could scrape
together the funds necessary to build a good school, and
even longer to pay Foster a fair and decent salary. It was
also certain that Galen's offer tonight had more to do
with his so-called craving than anything else, and therein
lay the rub. What were Galen's true intentions? Had he
come back to Whittaker to expose the traitor or just to
throw her well-ordered life into a spin? It would be a lie
to say she didn't find him exciting. He was very exciting,
easily the most exciting man she'd ever encountered, but
she wasn't so naive as to believe he actually had more in
mind than just a dalliance. Even though they were of the
same race, socially they were of different classes and
very rarely were the boundaries crossed. Admittedly, she

enjoyed the sparks that flowed between them, but she did not plan on succumbing to his charms and being left with a broken heart.

However, the woman he'd brought to life that October night, did want to see him alone, if only for a short while. Tonight, as he sat across the table from her, all she could think about was how wonderful it would have been had they dined alone, just the two of them. And when he made reference to his fondness for maple syrup, and for her, she was certain she would choke to death.

Yes, secret parts of her basked in the knowledge that Galen cared for her, desired her, but in spite of Galen's declared fondess, she was certain that she was nothing more than a diversion, something to ease the boredom until he returned to his wealthy station in life. That she was highly attracted to him made no difference.

She waited until the clock on the fireplace mantel struck ten, then she shrugged back into her cloak and went out to hitch up the mule and wagon.

Hester had no trouble driving the relatively short distance to the Folly in the dark. She'd been conducting passengers for over a decade now and knew the country roads like the back of her hand, even at night. As she neared the big house though, she began to question the soundess of her decision. Had he been simply teasing? Had she read more into his speech than he'd intended? She wanted to think not, but she didn't see his coach as she approached. What if he weren't home? She'd been raised very conventionally by her aunt, and Katherine was undoubtedly flipping in her grave knowing Hester was out visiting a man in the middle of the night. Hester also hadn't considered the fact that his hired help might turn her away from the door, but she did now. Lights could be seen burning behind some of the curtained windows, and there were a few coaches and buggies in the drive. What if he were entertaining? She doubted he'd want to be pulled away from his guests.

She sat a moment and tried to figure out what she should do. In the end she drove up into the yard and set the brake. She hadn't ventured out on such a cold night just to turn tail and run all because of a few "what ifs."

She tied the reins to the hitching post then confronted her next dilemma: which door to use, front or back? She didn't want anyone to know about her nocturnal visit, so she chose the back door.

Once there, Hester gathered her courage and knocked. No response.

She knocked again, this time a bit harder. In April the night air was cold. She'd dressed warmly as always, but had begun to notice the air's sharp bite penetrating her clothing. She knocked once more. Nothing. Telling herself she had no intentions of standing out there all night, she turned to head back to her wagon. The sound of the door opening made her halt. Light streamed out into the night, framing a dark-skinned woman of about fifty years. She wore the black dress and white apron of a servant. Her expression was curious as she took in Hester standing on the bottom step. Her voice was musical and sounded foreign as she asked, "May I help you?"

Hester fought down her nervousness. "Um—yes—I wish to see Mr. Vachon."

The woman surveyed Hester intently. "Is he expecting you?"

Hester gave a tiny nod. "I believe so."

The servant assessed Hester a moment longer, taking in the worn bonnet and the cloak that had seen better days, then said, "Well, Mr. Vachon is engaged at the moment and I've no idea when he'll be done. But you may wait."

Hester could just about imagine what the woman thought of her, so she replied, "No, I'll return another time. Thank you."

"Just a moment," the woman called gently.

Hester stopped and looked back.

"What is your name?"

"Hester Wyatt."

The woman's face registered surprise. "Hester

Wyatt?" The woman smiled and opened the door wide, "Come in Hester Wyatt. My name is Maximilia, but call me Maxi. I've been very anxious to meet you."

The remark so surprised Hester that a myriad of questions in her head all shouted to be asked at once, but rather than stand out in the cold trying to make sense of it she let herself be ushered inside by the smiling Maxi.

The back door led into a large, well-equipped kitchen filled with the scents of brewing coffee and baking bread.

"You know of me?" a puzzled Hester asked as she followed the servant through the kitchen and down a long breezeway that led to the main portion of the house.

"Everyone knows of '*la petite* Indigo.' You're all Galeno has talked about for months."

Hester stopped in mid step. The revelation was unnerving. "Months?" she croaked.

Maxi nodded yes, then laughed softly. "You, my chiquita, have done what no other woman in this whole, wide world has accomplished, though scores have tried."

"And that is?"

"Bring the dragon to his knees." Then she laughed again and resumed their journey, proclaiming loudly, "I love it!"

Maxi ushered Hester into a beautifully furnished sitting room, then left Hester seated while she went to fetch Galen. Hester stared around at the delicate statuary, the fine prints gracing the walls, and the chandelier hanging from the ceiling sparkling like winter ice. Being in such elegant surroundings reminded her of the one time she'd been summoned up to the big house in Carolina. Of course being a slave, she hadn't been allowed to sit while she waited for the mistress to appear and put her to work, but Hester remembered standing stock still in the middle of the room, afraid to move lest she accidently bump something and break it. She felt the same way now. She was glad when Maxi returned.

"He will be with you in just a moment. Let me take your cloak and your bonnet. Would you care for some tea?"

Hester shook her head as she handed over the garments and the mittens she'd worn over the black crocheted gloves. "I don't want to make more work for you, I simply wish to speak with Mr. Vachon and return home."

"It is no trouble, chiquita. It's cold outside, I'll bring tea and honey."

Maxi departed and a short while later, Galen walked into the room.

"I'm sorry to keep you waiting, *petite.*"

"No apology needed. I haven't been waiting long."

She seemed unable to move and so did he.

He broke the thick silence. "There are some friends I'd like you to meet."

She didn't really want tonight's visit to be the subject of tomorrow's gossip. "Galen, I'm not certain that's a sound idea."

"They will guard your secrets like the Sphinx. I promise." He then held out his hand. "Please?"

She knew without having known him very long that he did not say please often, if at all. She asked, "Can we talk afterwards?"

"We'll do whatever you desire afterwards."

She ignored his golden spell and those smiling eyes, saying, "Then yes, I'll meet your friends."

His "friends" turned out to be some of the most important and wanted men on the Road. She found herself introduced to William Lambert and George De Baptiste, two highly placed individuals in the Michigan Underground, and founding members of the Order of the African-American Mysteries. She'd seen both men from afar at rallies and lectures but had never been formally introduced. She found their presence in Galen's smoky study to be absolutely amazing.

She looked up at Galen, hoping her astonishment did not show too much but he simply smiled and continued introducing her around. The names of some of the others belonged to men known only to her through Mr. Garrison's *Liberator* and the competing *Frederick Doug-*

lass's Weekly, men like Alan Pinkerton from Chicago, and the Virginian, John Fairfield, whose reputation for slave stealing was surpassed only by Galen's. Each of the eight men in Galen's low-lit study held a unique prominence in abolitionist circles and all were worth their weight in bounty gold for "crimes against the South." Were a slave catcher like Shoe to stumble upon the gathering he'd be rich overnight.

When the introductions were concluded, another man stepped out of the shadows and made his presence known to Hester for the first time. He came forward, but did not offer his identity. He was an older man, tall, thin. His blue eyes seemed to have a fire burning in them as they met Hester's. Recognition flared through her with such force she felt her knees weaken.

He looked down at her and said, "I'm sorry about the passing of your aunt. Katherine Wyatt was a good Christian woman. The Cause lost a valiant soldier; she will be missed."

Hester was so nearly overcome by the sincerity in the man's eyes, she could only whisper, "Thank you. I miss her also."

Galen said softly. "Come *petite,* let's let them finish their business."

Afterwards, Galen led her back to the sitting room and Hester immediately took a seat on one of the embroidered back chairs. Her hands were still shaking. She asked, "The man with the blue eyes, who was he?"

"John Brown."

The reply rendered her speechless for a second. "Not the John Brown—of Osawatomie?"

"Yes, one and the same."

"Galen, he's the speculator who stole me out of Carolina."

"Then I am forever in his debt . . ."

The softness of his words slid over her senses. She had to force herself to remain focused. "Why is he here?" Then, remembering her manners, said, "I apologize, that's really none of my business."

"He's traveling around garnering support for war."

Hester's face showed her surprise. "War? When?"

"Later this year. He wants to attack a government arsenal in Virginia and arm the slaves in hopes of plunging the nation into war."

"Can he succeed?"

Galen shrugged. "Who really knows. I'm not convinced, neither are Lambert, De Baptiste, or Douglass for that matter. The Old Man says he has recruits, but no one is certain of their true numbers."

Hester thought about the startling revelation. Could John Brown really bring down the house of slavery? Brown's raid into Missouri last December to liberate eleven slaves had been hailed as one of the most daring events in antislavery history. Brown and his small regiment took the fugitives on a 2,500-mile dash across the country to Canada in spite of the dogged pursuit by state and federal authorities. Slave catchers had also joined the chase, motivated by the three-thousand-dollar reward offered for Brown's arrest by Missouri Governor Stewart. The journey spanned three grueling weeks, but with the help of Quaker Road agents in Iowa, Alan Pinkerton's railroad friends in Chicago, and the men of the Detroit Order, the fugitives safely reached Queen Victoria's Canada.

"Will you help him?" Hester asked.

"As much as I am able," Galen replied.

"Why did you introduce me to them? Their being here is not the type of information one should bandy about."

"I am aware of that, but I wanted you to meet them so they would know you. Should anything ever happen to me and you find yourself in danger, feel free to call upon them."

"Galen, I don't need looking after."

"We all need looking after at some point in our lives."

"But they know nothing of me. Why should they take me under their protection?"

"Because I've asked them to, as a favor to me."

"They owe you that much?"

"We all owe each other that much."

Hester scanned his eyes and saw the seriousness reflected there. She realized he'd meant every word.

"Promise me you will seek them out should the need arise."

He was so compelling, she had no other choice but to agree.

She asked, "Will your friends be spending the night? I—don't wish to keep you from them."

He shook his head no. "In fact, more than likely they have all disappeared back into the night even as we speak, so you have me entirely to yourself for as long as you desire."

Maxi interrupted them momentarily to bring in the tea and Hester sighed with relief. At home she'd been fairly certain of her abilities to handle Galen, but with him sitting across the room viewing her so boldly, she could hardly keep her breathing even. Her nerves rattled even more under his lazy scrutiny, and to hide her nervousness she picked up the pot and poured. "Would you like some?"

He unfolded his lean frame from the chair and crossed the room to where she stood. She handed him a delicately made cup and matching saucer. He took it from her hand, but set the offering on a nearby table. Then, to her surprise, he relieved her of her own cup. He set it next to his own. "Give me your hand," he commanded softly.

Hester had no idea what he was about and so she hesitated. Undaunted, he gently raised her hand, then holding her gaze captive, very slowly removed the glove. He nodded to her other hand. She held it out and he repeated the move, saying softly, "You don't need the gloves when we're alone."

Hester trembled under the force of his gaze and had a hard time focusing her thoughts on anything else.

He placed her gloves in the inner pocket of his black velvet dinner coat. He politely handed her her cup and Hester took her seat.

To focus on something besides succumbing to the desire arcing thickly through the room, Hester asked, "Why did you tell me about John Brown's plans? I would think you'd want only those directly involved to know."

"Because talking with you is an easy and relaxing way to spend an evening. And I wanted you to be aware of the prevailing winds. Now, did you come here tonight to give me the kiss I asked for yesterday?"

She laughed. "No, I came to talk about Foster's school."

"How about afterwards?"

She smiled at him over her cup. "We'll see."

"Ah, hope. It can keep a man alive."

"The school, Galen."

So for the next hour they discussed the educational needs of the area's children. Hester also brought up the subject of Foster's salary. Galen seemed amenable to it all.

She asked, "Are you certain this is within your means? Funding the school won't be a strain?"

"Not at all."

"Foster will be pleased."

"I find your acceptance of Frederick's marriage quite admirable."

"What choice have I really. He says he is happy. He and I weren't in love, so—" She shrugged as if no further explanation was needed.

"But it has to be uncomfortable for you. Shall I kill him for you?"

Her eyes widened. "No!"

He grinned. "What did you think of the gowns I sent you?"

"I think they should be returned to you."

"Why?"

"Because they are made for—"

"A mistress? A lover?"

"Both, and I am neither."

"You may take a lover some day, one never knows."

She ignored his velvet voice. "Then he will have to be content with the gowns I already own."

"Indigo, I've seen the gowns you own, they inspire warmth, not the passion a lover expects."

"And you are an expert on this also?"

"In some corners, yes."

Hester shook her head. "Galen, have you ever had a woman tell you no?"

"Fortunately, or unfortunately, no."

"Never?"

"Never."

"No wonder you play this game so well."

"This isn't a game."

"Of course it is. The players are an ex–slave woman and a man who may or may not be the wealthy Galen Vachon."

She swung her eyes to him. He neither refuted nor gave credence to her remark, so she continued. "To pass the time on his rustic adventure, this man who may or may not be Galen Vachon dallies with the ex–slave woman. He seems to believe that because she was foolish and naive enough to fall prey to his expert kisses, she is his for the taking. Does this sound familiar?"

"Vaguely," he replied distantly. "But continue."

"He sends her gifts of gowns, money, and even oranges, of all things. She is as impressed as he hopes, but she is not sure of his intentions."

"Did you enjoy the oranges?"

She nodded.

"Good. I'll send you more."

"No, Galen. You are not to send me anything else. And no more entering my room while I'm sleeping."

"Would you rather I awakened you? I did toy with the idea."

"You are incorrigible."

"So you keep reminding me."

He set aside his cup then came over to where she sat and hunkered down before her. His eyes were serious as he spoke. "*Petite,* look, I understand your misgivings and if I could put a stop to all this I would, but I can't."

Hester eyed him warily. "What do you mean, you can't?"

He shrugged. "I can't. Ever since I left you back in October I've thought of nothing but returning. Whether you care to believe me or not, not a day went by that I didn't wonder how you were or what you were doing."

She could not help but be moved by his impassioned confession.

"And now that you can't bar the door with a fiancé, I want us to enjoy one another."

"But for how long, Galen? A few weeks, a few months. What happens when you become bored? Who will pick up the shards you leave behind?"

"I've no answer, other than to say I will do my best to leave you whole."

"But you *will* leave."

"You're twisting my words."

She looked into his eyes and said softly. "No. Maybe the women of your circle enjoy open-ended games, but I don't, because I don't know the rules."

He straightened slowly. "You really are telling me no, aren't you?"

He had such a surprised look on his face, Hester could only smile. "Yes, Galen, I am. No. No more gowns, oranges, or anything else."

Hester wondered what he was thinking. "Are we agreed, Galen?"

He ran his eyes over her ripe mouth, remembering how sweetly they'd parted under his kiss and said, "No." To watch her black-diamond eyes close with passion was well worth the price of the campaign he planned on waging to have her. "No," he replied again. "Call it the selfish desire of a wealthy man, but I refuse to give you up without a proper fight."

She thought back on what he'd mentioned earlier. "You wouldn't really kill Foster would you?"

He laughed at the serious look on her face. "Only if you want me to, so don't fret." He took her hands and gently urged her to her feet. "And what I want is this . . ."

Hester supposed she could have stopped what came next, but when he leaned down and softly brushed his lips across her own it was already too late. He repeated the gesture, cajoling, tempting, promising, and her eyes fluttered closed. The sharp sweetness filled her, drawing her in much the same way he slowly eased her into the warm circle of his arms and pulled her close.

Galen could feel himself begin to shake. He touched her lips faintly, magically, whispering, "Deny this and you deny yourself . . ."

He kissed her fully and Hester was unable to deny him anything.

Chapter 11

❦

The sensations brought on by his splendid kisses set off flares of need. Her virgin's body bloomed and blossomed, embracing the thrill of the moment, casting aside the misgivings in favor of the pleasure he could bring.

Galen wanted to carry her off to his private wing and make slow, sweet love to her. He wanted to bare her breasts, rising so lushly against his palms, and bring them to his lips, wanted to slide his hands over her full, ripe hips and touch her in places that would bring shock and then delight. He filled his hands with her tempting bottom then boldly brought her in fully against the rock-hard length of his desire.

"Feel what you do to me . . ." he murmured thickly. "This is no game . . ."

The brazen possession made Hester tremble in response. She felt swept up in a firestorm, unable to stop this though she knew she should. Instead she let him suckle her nipples through the thin worn silk of her shirtwaist, let him slide her dress over her hips with a lazy sensuality. Not a word of protest passed her lips as his hands raised her skirt then began to wantonly explore. She allowed him liberties that were plunging her into a dementia. How else could she explain her muteness as he caressed her in places that seemed to blaze

149

under his touch, caressed her until her silence gave over to soft, hushed cries.

"This is what you would have missed in a loveless marriage, Indigo . . ."

He wantonly increased the intensity of his teasing. His boldness made her body arch and her head drop back. Galen pleasured her with an expertise born of many years of sensual practice and his eyes blazed as he watched her dark eyes close and her lips part in response. Unable to resist, he touched his mouth to her lips, enjoying the kiss, the seductive rhythm his bold touch drew from her hips, and the sweetness flowing from her core.

Suddenly, Hester's body soared to crescendo and her world exploded. She became a shooting star streaking across the night sky. The intensity of the feeling flung her into realms never before known and she clutched at his arm as she rode the buffeting wave.

Later, as he helped her back to earth with soft kisses and even softer touches, she shook and trembled. Something told her she would never be the same, but she didn't care, at least for now.

A knock on the door, however, brought her back to her senses. Hester hastily removed Galen's hand and jerked down her skirts. It was Maxi. She'd come to retrieve the tray. Hester tried her best to appear nonchalant, but as Maxi took in her mussed hair and twisted clothing, Hester wanted to hide beneath the furniture.

To Hester's surprise Maxi said to her, "I don't blame you, *chiquita*. You are the innocent. He is the wolf. Women have been falling in love with him since the day he was born. I was there, I know."

She then turned to Galen and said, "Consequently he should know better and do his best to preserve an innocent's reputation."

Hester looked over to Galen to see how he was taking the upbraiding. He had a decided frown on his golden face.

Maxi appeared to ignore his mood. "Galeno, it is time

for the *chiquita* to return home. Raymond will drive her."

Galen echoed, "Raymond?!"

"Yes, Raymond. I don't trust you." That said, she marched from the room presumably to fetch Raymond.

Hester, who stood there still pulsing from his magnificent tutoring, met Galen's glittering eyes. He said coolly, "She's correct, I should know better, but I'm finding it hard to maintain the proper decorum when you stand there with my passion lingering in your eyes and the taste of your kisses still fresh upon my lips. I want you Indigo, in all the ways a man wants a woman."

Hester fought down the swooning feeling that rushed over her in response to his heated eyes and words. Never in her life had she imagined herself in such a situation. His kisses were still fresh upon her lips also and one would have to be blind not to see the desire blazing like flame in his eyes. He was far more dangerous than she feared, even now after the embarrassment of Maxi's entrance, Hester continued to want more.

Luckily for Hester, Maxi returned, bringing with her the handsome Raymond LeVeq. He grinned at the brooding Galen, then crossed the room to where Hester stood. He bowed low. "*Enchanté* Miss Wyatt, Maxi says you are in need of a drive home?"

Hester nodded, wondering how much he knew. This was the second time she'd met LeVeq under questionable circumstances. She could only imagine what type of loose woman he thought her to be. But his smile was kind, open. She sensed that he too played a role in Galen's game, for Raymond LeVeq was dressed as richly as Galen and appeared far more cultured than any ordinary coachman she'd ever met.

Maxi handed Hester her cloak and bonnet and she quickly put them on. She hazarded a look Galen's way and found him still viewing her with heated intensity. "Good night, *petite*." Then he turned and strode smoothly from the room.

* * *

Later, after Raymond drove Hester home, Maxi found Galen sitting in the study staring into the roaring fire. She stood there in the doorway a moment trying to gauge his mood, then asked, "You're not terribly angry with me, are you?"

His voice was void of emotion. "Angry yes, terribly angry, no."

He looked over at the woman who had taken him into her vast kitchen at the age of seven and taught him more about the world and the people in it than all his fancy private tutors combined.

"Wait until you meet this Frederick she was going to marry. Tonight he sat at dinner and boasted about her lack of beauty. I could see the remark pained her while he thought he'd given her a compliment."

For a moment the room held only the crackle of the fire as Galen tried to seek a solution from the flames. When he finally spoke it sounded as if he were speaking more to himself than to Maxi. "I don't believe I've ever had a woman turn me so inside out. I can't place my finger on what it is about her that has me so obssessed, but I am. After she left with Raymond, I actually sat here and plotted ways to seduce her so she'd have no other choice but to be mine. Never in my life have I ever done anything that remotely outrageous. I want to take care of her, buy her jewels. It's the oddest and damndest experience I've ever had."

Maxi's smile reflected how much she cared for him. "Sounds as if the dragon has finally found love."

A small smile lifted his thin moustache. "I detest it when you're so wise."

She replied sagely, "That's why I keep you near me, so I can dispense this detested wisdom whenever it is needed most."

"And your recommendation?"

"From all you've told me of her past, and after seeing her here tonight, I say either offer to marry her or leave her be. This isn't New Orleans, she knows nothing of dragon games. You'll ruin her if you don't pick one or the other."

When Galen didn't answer, Maxi said softly, "Goodnight, Galeno," and she quietly exited from the room, leaving him to his thoughts.

He was in Detroit by the next evening, deciding perhaps he needed some distance from Whittaker. Galen did not recognize the manservant who opened the old mansion's door. It made no matter because over Galen's lifetime most of the servants had been strangers. His grandmother Vada rarely kept servants more than a season because her bitter spirit usually drove them to seek employment elsewhere.

Galen passed his hat and coat to the unsmiling man, then made his way to the drawing room.

As usual the room was filled with hangers on. Most were family; penniless, destitute relatives who depended on Vada for their very existence. In return, she treated them as badly as the servants, caring nothing for their opinions, feelings, or desires. Galen thought her treatment of them no better than they deserved for putting up with the tyrannical old harpy in exchange for free lodging and meals. He'd moved out and into his own home the day he gained his majority. Forty years ago, Vada had fled to this ancestral Michigan home in order to escape the gossip that roared through New Orleans in the wake of her husband's desertion. He'd tossed her aside for his dark-skinned mistress only two generations removed from the Mother Continent.

The others in the room, men both young and old, competed with the family to be treated like the dirt beneath Vada's feet. Their motives centered around the young wealthy daughters of Vada's friends.

His entry into the room brought silence. Vada, seated on a chair surrounded by her court, drawled in a loud voice, "Well, if it isn't my prodigal grandson. Back from your annual sojourn with your whore?"

Galen had learned long ago not to let her vicious
tongue bother him and it did not now. Knowing how
much it infuriated her to have to wait, he took his time,
nodding coolly at the assemblage before acknowledging
Vada or her words. "I came to visit Racine, *grandmère.*"
He winked at his aunt Racine and she smiled in reply.
"As usual, where I've been is none of your concern."

The silence of the others made the confrontation that
much more charged. His grandmother's mulatto-blue
eyes flashed anger. "Then I trust you will not sully my
house with your presence for very long." She then called
to her eldest son, "Reginald! Take me to my chambers. I
can't stand the stench of him."

Galen's uncle Reggie hastened to her side. Vada stood
and slapped her cane to the floor. Bouyed by Reginald's
solicitous hand, she strode with stiff majesty from the
room.

As soon as Vada retired, her daughter Racine hurried
to her nephew to give him the welcoming embrace he
deserved. He returned the greeting, swinging her around
until she giggled like a young girl. "Put me down you
wretch."

He smiled and eased her to her feet. Of the ten people
in the room, only Racine had the spirit to defy Vada and
approach Galen with love. Racine and Galen's late
mother Ruth had been sisters. Ruth had been only a bit
over a year older and the sisters grew up very close to
one another. Galen always believed the loving parts of
his mother continued to live on in Racine.

Racine looked up at her tall, handsome nephew, and
said teasingly, "That whore must be feeding you well;
you've put on a little weight since I saw you last."

Galen laughed. His grandmother believed Galen's
annual April to October disappearances were tied to a
whore he had sequestered away. Only Racine knew the
truth. "I came to offer you dinner, Tante. Will you join
me?"

"Why of course, just let me get my cloak."

Although it would soon be the dinner hour at his grandmother's table, Galen had no intentions of joining them. He'd been forbidden to attend these dinners since the day he moved to his own quarters more than a decade ago. He hadn't protested his grandmother's edict. Seeing Racine was the only reason he'd come this evening.

While Galen waited for his aunt's return, he ignored the others' scrutiny. In his eyes they did not exist in much the same way he hadn't existed in theirs while growing up. Not one of the uncles, great-aunts, or distant cousins had come to the defense of a little boy whose only crime lay in his mother's desire to be with the man she loved. Only Racine had sheltered the hurt and bewildered orphan child he'd once been. He would never forget her kindness.

Galen and his beloved aunt had dinner at the river house he'd leased last autumn. Most of the servants had been in his service for many years and they loved Racine as much as their employer. Having been notified earlier in the day of Galen's plan to invite her to the evening meal, they'd practically outdone themselves in providing her favorite dishes.

When the last of the dessert dishes were cleared, Racine groaned and pushed back her chair. "I'm stuffed," she confessed. "Go and tell Little Reba to pack her bags because she'll be coming to cook for me. You already employ Maxi, and no bachelor should be allowed two great cooks in one lifetime."

Galen chuckled. "Maxi says the little one is not learned enough to call herself a cook yet."

"Well, Maxi's wrong. That woman your grandmere has masquerading as a cook could take lessons from Maxi's little niece Reba."

They removed themselves to Galen's small study and Racine viewed her golden nephew over her glass of after-dinner wine.

"So, Galeno, what do you hear on the wind?"

"There are rumblings of secession in the South, and talk of a war to preserve the Union should it occur. How it will affect slavery, no one's certain."

"How much longer do you propose to stay on the Road?"

"I've no idea, but until the situation changes I'll continue tweaking their noses."

Galen could not ignore the concern in her face. He knew she respected his work as the Black Daniel and would never ask that he discontinue the role, but like the mother she considered herself to be, she worried constantly about his safety.

"I heard you were injured last autumn."

He nodded.

"I also hear you've taken to having maple syrup in your coffee."

Galen surveyed her slowly.

Her eyes, so dark blue they appeared black sometimes, were unreadable. She said, "I have my own ears to the wind."

He smiled. "The woman who hid me was a Free Producer. I suppose I've grown accustomed to it."

Galen got up and poured himself more wine from the crystal decanter atop the desk.

"Raymond says she's very beautiful."

Galen lifted his glass and took a small swallow. "Raymond talks too much, as usual."

"He's only concerned."

"He's only concerned because he hopes to have her for himself."

"The two of you have shared women over the years, so why the possessiveness now?"

Galen smiled his surprise at his aunt's question. "I'm getting too old to share."

Racine held his eyes a moment. "Then she really is as innocent as Raymond described?"

"Yes."

"She's not of our class though?"

Galen shook his head no. "She's slave born, *Tante.*"

"We all were at one time, but your *grandmère* will suffer a death spasm for sure."

"The thought has crossed my mind."

They both smiled, then Racine asked, "Do you love this innocent?"

He shrugged. "Maxi is all but convinced. Me. I'm not certain."

"Vada and the others will not treat her well."

"I will kill the first one to offend her."

Racine raised her glass to him in toast. "I knew I raised you well." Then she asked, "When do I meet this beauty?"

"Soon, *Tante.* Soon. In fact that's why I wanted to have dinner with you. I need a favor."

Racine laughed. "And here I thought you just wanted your old *tante's* company."

Galen grinned.

She waved him on. "Well, go ahead, now that you've dulled my mind with good food and drink, ask away."

"Will you come and hostess my household for a few months?"

Racine stared confused. "You've never needed a hostess before, why now?"

"Maxi insists Hester needs a duenna."

Racine stared in surprise. "Maxi has never cared one fig about the vast numbers of women you've entertained over the years."

"I know—"

Racine peered at him. "Galeno, how serious are you about this woman?"

"So serious I actually plotted her seduction. I've never done that with an innocent before."

"But she has a fiancé according to Raymond. You've never gone out of your way to pursue someone belonging to another. Well, I take that back, there was that countess in Madrid. I—"

"She is no longer engaged, but *Tante,* promise me you won't tell Hester any of those stories."

Racine stared. "Are you certain this is you, Galeno?

You, who never gave cat's tail about society or rules or—"

"*Tante* Racine."

"I'm sorry, *neveu,* it's just—" Racine paused, taking in his serious eyes. "This young woman has really affected you, hasn't she?"

Galen didn't answer.

"Then I will come and stay, just so I may meet this remarkable woman."

"Thank you, *Tante.*" Then he added softly, "I think."

Hester saw nothing of Galen during the week following her visit to the Folly. Gail moved in during that time and Hester was elated because she now had someone to share her house with and something to do besides muse upon Galen's next kisses.

A few days after Gail settled in, she and Hester decided to take a trip to Detroit. Bea Meldrum's son, Lemuel, made his living by driving an old refurbished carriage there three days a week. Anyone not wanting to drive the thirty-mile trip themselves could make arrangements with Lemuel to convey them for a small price. He'd started the taxi service soon after his arrival a year ago in Whittaker. Like his mother, he too was a fugitive. It had taken him nearly a decade to learn Bea's whereabouts after his own escape, but once they were reunited, Bea cried with happiness for days.

Hester and Abigail had Lemuel stop by for them a little after dawn as Gail had an appointment with her doctor in Detroit. Hester went along to keep her company, and also to do some shopping. She'd finally decided to draw out some of the funds she'd received from the sale of her land.

Once they reached their destination, Lemuel let everyone out. They would meet him for the return ride later in the afternoon. Abigail hired a hack to take her to her doctor's home while Hester made her way to the Free Produce store.

Free Produce began as a Quaker movement in the

1820's. By the 1830's many Blacks had embraced the concept, especially those residing in Philadelphia. At the city's Bethel Church, five hundred Blacks formed the Colored Free Produce Society of Pennsylvania. They stocked their store with goods made from free labor, and made it into a booming business. They were so successful that in January of 1831 the women of Bethel Church founded the Colored Female Free Produce Society.

Hester supported the ban on slave-produced products whenever she could. The store in Detroit founded by members of Detroit's historic Second Baptist Church was always a pleasure to shop in. They stocked everything from antislavery pamphlets and books, to ten- and twenty-five-pound bags of free sugar. The items in the store were a bit higher priced than the nonfree stores, but unlike the free stores in the Northeast, Detroit's prices were slightly lower due to the ready access to goods brought in by the lake freighters. Detroit Free Producers also had the convenience of shopping in Canada right across the Detroit River.

Hester went into the store looking for dress fabrics. She hadn't purchased any in quite some time. Before she sold the land to Galen, her funds had been designated for essentials only. Now, however, she had the urge and the means to splurge a bit. Her friend Kate Bell was an excellent seamstress and could whip up a dress in no time.

As Hester looked over the selection of dress goods the store had on display, she spied a bolt of ivory silk. The card above it said the silk had come from the Asian continent and had been imported by way of Canada.

Hester thought the silk the most beautiful material she'd ever seen, but the price was far too steep. She dearly wanted to own the silk, but the practical Hester Wyatt raised her head. She knew if she went with cheaper fabrics she could purchase twice as much. Besides, where in Whittaker would she wear a gown so fine? She most certainly couldn't have Kate fashion the gown for Hester to plant in. The practical Hester won

out. Giving the silk one last wistful caress of her hand,
she turned and stumbled right into the solid wall of
Galen Vachon's chest. His steadying hands kept her
upright.

"I'm sorry," she gasped. "I—wasn't watching."
Where on earth had he come from? He seemed to have
sprouted from underneath the floorboards.

He apologized smoothly, "It was my fault. I didn't see
you down there."

She cut a look up to his sparkling eyes and asked with
mock offense, "Are you mocking my height, sir?"

"One cannot mock what isn't there, *petite*."

His habit of addressing her by that diminutive always
made her head spin and she'd yet to find a way to
counteract the effects. "What are you doing here?"

"I came in to pick up some sugar Maxi ordered. And
you?"

"I had some time on my hands until I meet Gail
Grayson, so I thought I'd look at dress material."

He reached past her and picked up the bolt of silk. "I
noticed you admiring this silk."

"Yes, it's quite beautiful."

"Are you going to purchase it?"

"No."

"Why not?"

"Look at the price."

He paused to read the amount written on the card
above the bolt's space. "And?"

She chuckled, "Maybe for you the price means nothing, but to me it is quite steep."

"I'll purchase it for you."

Hester could see the clerk behind the counter observing them. Hester smiled over at her and the woman
smiled in return. Hester turned back to Galen and
whispered warningly, "No, you will not."

"Why not? Consider it my way of saying thanks for
taking such good care of me back in October."

"You've already given me enough gifts."

"Then let me buy you some gowns. Shall we go shopping?"

"No!"

"Then let me treat you to luncheon."

"Galen?!"

He enjoyed her attempts to keep him at arm's length. It made the kisses he received from her all the more thrilling. "Either luncheon, or I kiss you right here and now. You don't want to be responsible for making that poor woman fall off her stool do you?"

She couldn't keep her smile from her face. "You are outrageous, incorrigible, and—"

"And the man who taught you how to make mud pies, don't forget to mention that."

She surrendered just as they both knew she would. "All right, where are we going?"

"This way, please."

They had luncheon at a small establishment not too far from the store.

Afterward, he suggested, "Come and take a drive with me."

"Galen, I must meet Abigail in an hour."

"I'll have you back on time. Don't fret."

"Promise?"

"Promise."

She agreed.

It was the first time they'd been alone in the coach together and Hester felt very reckless when he got in and sat on the velvet seat across from her. His presence was a constant reminder of her growing attraction, an attraction becoming harder and harder to ignore.

Once the coach got underway, she asked, "Did you come to Detroit just for Maxi's sugar?"

"That and business. I had to look over a manifest from one of my ships before it sailed this morning."

"How many boats do you own?"

"Last count about fifteen."

"And what area of business are you in?"

"Imports, exports, lumber. My ships travel all over the world."

"It sounds very exciting."

Although the conversation revolved around a fairly mundane subject, Hester could sense the temperature rising in the coach. He'd been on his best behavior throughout the day, but looking over at him now, she felt certain it wouldn't last much longer.

He asked, "What are you thinking?"

"That you've been a perfect gentleman."

"I'll take that as a compliment, but I must admit, my present thoughts are less than pure."

When he held out his hand to her and said, "Come, I can't kiss you if you're way over here . . ." Hester's heart began to pound.

The temperature rose as she took her seat beside him. He looked into her eyes. "All day I've had this craving for vanilla . . ."

Hester drew in a ragged breath. They were so close she could feel the warmth of his body shimmering around her like heat on an August day. When he drew his finger very slowly over the outline of her bottom lip, her eyes closed from the flaring intensity.

He leaned down and gave her a soft, sweet kiss, then eased back. "Your kisses are like wine, Indigo. If I have too much, I'll forget my promise to have you back on time . . ."

He kissed her again, more passionately, and she savored him with equal measure.

"I mustn't be late . . ." she managed to whisper, but all other thoughts concerning time and place were lost in the burgeoning heat.

Gifting her lips with short, magnificent kisses, Galen eased her atop his lap and drew her closer. He could feel the heat of her thighs and hips burning through the expensive gray wool of his trousers, and his manhood rose in sensual response. He kissed her lips, her jaw, the shell of her ears while his hands moved possessively over her spine. He fought to remember that they only had a short while. The lavish, prolonged loving she so richly deserved would have to wait, but he was content; there would be other times and other stolen moments.

The practical Hester had been left behind the moment she stumbled into him in the store; atop his lap now, melting under his knowing hands, sat the woman who refused to be buried any longer. She thrilled to the kiss of his lips against her throat and the slide of his golden hands over her thighs. This Hester wanted to be touched everywhere and to touch him in return. She let his passion fire her own. His arms and shoulders were strong and firm beneath her slowly wandering hands. When he began to undo the buttons on her high-necked collar, she didn't protest. But when more buttons were undone and his lips began to brush fleetingly over the exposed skin of her throat, she dropped her head back against the strong pillar of his supporting arm and moaned.

Heat filled her and made her tremble. He slid a worshipping finger over the twin crowns of her breasts, then placed his lips against both silken tops. Her nipples were already pleading, anticipating his bold caresses and he didn't make her wait. He eased down her plain, muslim camisole, then slowly pleasured each dark bud. A moan rose from her throat. Her body arched in response. His hands roaming languidly beneath her hips and thighs were hot as fire.

Galen took his time. The taste of her fueled an arousal that demanded he have all she had to offer. Her breasts were so ripe, so lush, it would take an army to make him relinquish the dark sweetness. The smell of the vanilla scenting her warm skin filled his nostrils and befuddled his senses like fine cognac. To hell with time constraints; she was too lovely to turn loose.

But he knew he had to take her back and the person with most experience, he had to be the one to stop.

He raised his mouth to her lips and said reluctantly, "You're going to miss your coach, *ma coeur* . . ."

She slipped the tip of her tongue over the edge of his parted lips and whispered, "I don't care . . ."

He chuckled softly. Kissing her again, he replied, "You will when you have to walk the thirty miles home."

She brushed her lips over his ear. "You'd take me home."

"I'd take you, but it might not be home . . ."

The provocative word play set her spinning. "You're very tempting . . . and too damn handsome for your own good, Galen Vachon."

"And you are too beautiful and lush for yours, Hester Wyatt . . ."

He ran a slow finger over her kiss-dampened nipples and her eyelids slowly lowered. "Marry me and we can make beautiful children."

She wanted to giggle but the heat rising from his expert touch overrode all.

He leaned down and gave both nipples a gentle bite. "You're never going to get out of this coach, if you don't close your dress . . ."

The intensity of his play increased and she groaned her pleasure. "You must stop, Galen . . ."

"I know . . ."

But he didn't, and for Hester time stood still as his hands slid beneath her dress.

She arched to the heat of his cupping hands. He kissed her mouth. "This is so you'll dream of us tonight . . ."

It took him only a few moments to bring her to a peak, and when he did she muffled her shuddering scream into the comforting solidness of his shoulder.

In the silence that followed, Hester opened her eyes and looked up into his amused gaze. He asked, "Now, are you ready?"

She replied softly, saucily, "I am, but for what, is the question?"

He grinned. "Temptress. Let's put you back together, otherwise you will be late."

Hester let him right her clothing, but the kisses continued.

When she was all done up and respectably clothed once more, Galen instructed the coachman to turn around and head back downtown. A few blocks away from the rendezvous point with Gail, the coach drew to a halt. Inside, Hester and Galen shared a short but passionate kiss of goodbye, then she left him to meet Gail.

When Gail asked Hester about her lack of packages, Hester waved her away saying she'd found nothing to buy.

That evening, alone in her room, Hester sighed with the memories of the afternoon. She realized by succumbing to his kisses she was only opening herself to the heartbreak sure to come. Galen made her body sing like a bird and made her forget all about who she was and who he was. But here in the quiet of her room, she had to face reality. There was no future in a relationship with him and she had no desire to fall in love with him. It was too late to remedy the latter because she knew deep in her heart that she did love him. Her fears of the emotion made her remember her father. She didn't want to be at the mercy of love. She didn't want to be so tied up in love's knots that she'd do something irrational. Her feelings for Galen were as elating as they were terrifying.

As the weather warmed and the first week of May breezed in, everyone received an invitation to Galen's first party. He was giving it to formally introduce himself to the community and to honor the recent nuptials of Foster and Jenine. At church that Sunday, the party was all folks could talk about. Word had gotten around that the wealthy Mr. Vachon had no wife. Every mamma with an eligible daughter, every widow, and every other unattached female over the age of sixteen threw their bonnets into the ring. Hester kept her bonnet on.

Abigail was very curious about the invitation, written in ornate gold script, which was sent with a runner Galen had hired. "What on earth is Galen Vachon doing here in Whittaker of all places?"

Hester looked up from her sewing and asked, "Do you know Mr. Vachon?"

"I met him about a decade ago or so by way of his aunt Racine."

Hester spent a few moments telling Gail about Vachon's recent arrival in town and that he'd purchased some of her land, then asked, "Is he as wealthy as everyone is speculating?"

"Wealthier. His shipping interests reach all the way to the Orient. He could live anywhere in the world. Why would he choose to settle here?"

Hester forced herself to push the needle in and out with a steady rhythm so as not to alert Gail to her own secret knowledge of the mysterious Mr. Vachon. She held up the cloth to view the evenness of the stitching. The cloth would be an altar linen when finished. "The women here are in a tizzy over him. I heard a few talking as though he were already gutted and trussed."

Gail laughed. "If the predatory beauties of Europe and New Orleans haven't managed to land him, I doubt anyone in Whittaker will."

Hester realized that Gail had inadvertently echoed Hester's own fears. "He's quite the ladies' man then?"

"Quite. For many years Racine despaired over his becoming anything other than that. In his younger days, he was a rake in every sense of the word."

"Then you know his aunt well?"

"Yes, she and I were in the same circle at one time."

"She works on the Road?"

"She did in those days. Her family has been free for nearly a century but she's a staunch abolitionist. Racine used to say she was a product of many races, but it was her African blood which gave her life and it is the African blood which keeps her strong."

"She sounds like a very interesting woman."

"That she is."

The party was only three days away. Hester went over to Kate Bell's boarding house to drop off some new antislavery tracts she'd received in the post but could hardly get inside for all the women waiting for Kate to do their hair. Kate was not only the best seamstress in the area but also the woman everyone paid to do their hair on very special occasions. And Galen's party qualified as the most special occasion in Whittaker's recent history. Hester declined Kate's offer of service on her own hair because Hester did not plan to attend.

Foster stopped by that evening and Hester was glad to see him. Although she'd been sent reeling by his sudden marriage, she found she could not deny him her friendship.

"What brings you here, Foster? Where's Jenine?"

He looked uncomfortable. "Uh—she's over at the room."

Hester peered into his face. "Is something wrong?"

He shook his head in denial. "No. I just stopped by to make certain you are coming to the party. It is good of Vachon to fête us this way."

"Yes, it is nice, but no, I wasn't planning on attending."

"Why not?"

"Because this is for you and Jenine."

"But I would like for you to attend. Jenine knows so few people and she's so shy. She considers you a friend. I realize I've caused you a bit of embarrassment leaving you high and dry the way I did, but if you could see past it and help Jenine fit in, I'd be grateful."

Hester wanted to tell him no. Her dilemma with Galen took precedence over any problems Jenine may be experiencing in adjusting to life in Whittaker. Jenine was one of the reasons Hester had decided to stay at home in the first place. Hester had so far avoided hearing whatever the gossips were saying about Foster returning with a bride, and she had no desire to spend the evening being the subject of whispers or pitying stares. That she was also avoiding Galen sealed the decision.

"Foster, I'm certain everyone will love Jenine just as much as you. She shouldn't have any problems winning them over."

"I want so much for her to settle in and be liked. If Vachon builds the school, she and I are going to be prominent members of the community. I can't have her hiding away everytime someone approaches her."

"Is she truly that shy?"

"She's so shy she won't even let me—" He stopped.

Hester waited in the silence for him to continue, but when he did not, she ran her gaze over his seemingly frustrated manner. "Foster?"

He shook his head. "Nothing. It's nothing."

Hester had the impression that he was hiding something, but she didn't press.

He asked her again to attend.

She replied, "You don't need me there, but I will think about it."

He took her hands and held them lightly in his own. "That is all I ask. Thank you, Hester."

Hester saw him out, then watched him drive his old buggy down the road.

Chapter 12

⟨～⟩⟨⟩⟨～⟩

The only time Hester would admit wanting to see Galen again was at night when she lay in her bed alone. In the light of day, the wanting made little sense; Galen was turning her world on its head, she had no idea of his true identity, and he was far too wealthy for his own good.

But at night, when darkness protected her secrets, she confessed. Being with Galen opened her emotions to new and volatile sensations, sensations her virgin body craved to explore even while the no-nonsense Hester inside shook her head in serious disappointment. She wanted to see him again, if for no other reason than the way he made her feel. He treated her as if she were precious, touched her as if she were treasured. She'd never been called beautiful until Galen entered her life, and indeed his kiss and his touch made her feel so. The memories of the night at the Folly were still as sensually vivid as the afternoon in the carriage. Alone in the dark, she wished Galen were there to ease the flames he'd left simmering inside, wished he were there to bestow his magical touch on her throbbing nipples and the damp, pulsing places that shocked her to think about. Both interludes had been a revelation. Who knew passion could wrack a woman's body with such blinding force? He'd made her body ache in places she'd never known could ache, but she'd loved every bold stroke of his golden hands and she wanted more.

The day before the party, Hester came to a decision. In spite of Foster's plea, she would not attend. When Abigail enquired as to her reason, Hester gave the excuse that she didn't feel well and blamed it on an oncoming bout of the spring sniffles. Gail offered to skip the event and keep Hester company, but Hester insisted that there was no need for Gail to miss the good time.

Bea stopped by later that afternoon to fetch Gail. They both had appointments with Kate to have their hair done.

On the heels of their departure, a knock sounded on the door. Hester opened it to find Andre Renaud. He held a large box wrapped in gold paper in his hands. Atop the box sat a beautiful gold lace bow.

"Good afternoon, Mr. Renaud."

He cleared his throat. "Um, Miss Wyatt—"

His uncomfortable face told all.

"More gifts from your employer?" Hester asked.

"I'm afraid so."

Hester stepped back so he could enter. "What is it this time?"

"I don't know."

She shook her head and took the box from his hands.

He headed back to the door, explaining, "I'm supposed to leave before you open it."

"I'll wager it is because he doesn't want me to make you return whatever is in here."

Renaud swallowed. "I believe so."

Hester chuckled and thought to herself, *Galen, Galen, Galen. Whatever am I going to do with you?* She looked over at Andre's distressed face and said, "Thank you, Mr. Renaud. If it has to be returned, I will beard the dragon personally. You may tell him you accomplished your mission."

Renaud appeared genuinely relieved. He bowed. "Then I will take my leave. *Adieu,* Miss Wyatt."

"*Adieu,* Mr. Renaud."

He departed and Hester spent a few moments musing over this latest show of Galen's affection. Whatever it contained would be extravagant. Galen did nothing by half, so she was also fairly certain that the contents would have to be returned.

She removed the delicate bow, then the beautiful gold paper. The top of the beige box inside bore the scrolling stamp of one of Windsor's finest dressmakers. Hester's hands shook as she lifted the lid, and then her eyes widened at the sight of the dress inside. The beauty of it took her breath away. It was made from the ivory silk she'd coveted at the Free Produce store in Detroit. Marveling, she lifted the dress fully free, and a small card spilled out. It read: *Your wishes are mine to make true.* He'd signed it with an elaborate letter G, and below it had placed his familiar dragon seal.

Hester could not deny the happiness that filled her heart. He had indeed made her wishes come true, but she could not accept such a costly gift no matter how beautiful. It was far more elegant than anything she'd ever owned and the handwork was magnificent. There would be no stares of pity were she to wear this gown. No one would point her out as the woman Foster threw over; everyone's eyes would pop. Hester's aging wardrobe had figured in her decision to stay at home, but now lord knew she wanted to wear the dress if only to rock Foster back on his heels and show him once and for all that she was indeed a desirable woman. She also wanted to wear it for Galen, to show him that she did appreciate his gifts, but deep inside she was afraid of where it might lead. She was afraid she would be drawn in even further by his immeasurable charms, thus making it even more difficult on herself when he returned to his world.

She debated with herself for the rest of the day and into the evening. By the time she sought her bed, she'd made up her mind. Galen had given her a gown dreams were made of; she'd be a fool to not wear it at least once. If the gossips were going to whisper, let them have something substantial to say. And as for her fear, she told herself that during her years on the Road she'd faced numerous real dangers: slave catchers, dogs; being afraid of her feelings was silly. She was a full-grown woman, and if Galen broke her heart, she'd undoubtedly survive.

The evening of the party, Hester stood before her mirror. The ivory gown floated around her like a cloud. The neckline was daring and the puffed sleeves left the crowns of her brown shoulders bare. In the box along with the dress had been a pair of soft kid slippers, lisle stockings, a lightweight silk wrap, and ivory gloves. She picked up the wrap and gloves, gave one last pat to her shiny hair, and joined Abigail.

Abigail was speechless.

Hester grinned at the stunned look on her friend's face. "How do I look?"

"My goodness, Hester. Is that really you?"

Hester giggled and turned, making the hem flare. "I clean up rather well, don't you think?"

"Indeed you do. Where did you get that gown?"

Hester told her about seeing the silk in the Free Produce store and then gave her the name of the Windsor dressmaker.

"It must have cost a pretty penny."

"I thought I deserved a gift."

"Yes you do, dear."

Hester felt a small twinge of guilt for not being fully truthful with Gail, but she hadn't lied. The dress had come from Windsor and Hester did deserve a gift.

Gail said, "When Foster sees you he may have second thoughts about picking that child bride."

Hester let the remark go as Abigail added, "I admire Foster very much, but his wife seems so empty-headed. What does he discuss with her?"

"I've no idea, Gail, but he says he's happy."

Gail snorted. "Well, I can't begin to see what the attraction is—outside of her formidable bosom of course."

"Abigail!" Hester laughed with astonishment.

"It's the truth."

"Get your wrap," Hester scolded with a smile. "Foster and Jenine will be here any moment. And you behave tonight."

Gail pointed to herself. "Me? You're the one in the dress. What type of trouble are you anticipating this evening?"

Hester simply grinned and arched an eyebrow.

Abigail's eyes narrowed at Hester's smugness. "Hester Wyatt, what are you about?"

"Nothing."

"Lightning will strike you for lying."

"I've nothing to say."

Gail did not appear satisfied. "Are you going to inform me eventually?"

Silence.

"Okay, Miss Sphinx, keep your secrets, but I will find out."

With Foster guiding the reins, Hester, Jenine, and Gail made the trip over to the Folly. Dusk had fallen by the time they arrived and they drove through the open wrought iron gates. They found themselves at the rear of a long line of vehicles, all slowly inching their way up the horseshoe-shaped gravel drive to the house. Along the drive sat beautiful multicolored lanterns to illuminate the way. The effect of the lanterns shining softly against the imposing house gave the surroundings a magical air.

The house sat at the apex of the horseshoe and they were still a few feet away. Behind their wagon, Hester could see that many other vehicles had joined the slow-moving line. Some held occupants she recognized while others were driven by strangers. She wondered just how many people had been invited.

When they finally reached the door, two men in black and gold livery approached the wagon and helped the ladies down. Another came and held the reins while

Foster joined them. Hester's eyes swept over the magnificent, forest-green structure. It was quite obvious William Lovejoy had spared little expense in building the corniced, gabled beauty Galen now owned.

One of the men then took Foster's seat and drove the wagon off around the drive. His remaining liveried companion explained, "We'll bring the wagon back around when you are ready to depart. Enjoy yourselves."

Inside, the hum of the well-dressed crowd filled the air. Although the room with its high ceilings and beautiful chandelier was huge by Whittaker standards, there didn't appear to be an inch of unoccupied space within its cream-colored walls.

A man with a deep, loud voice announced the entrance of Hester's party as if they were royalty. Foster appeared so impressed, Hester thought he'd burst out of his waistcoat. She found the whole thing a bit silly, but she followed her party into the room as if she made announced entrances as a matter of course.

The room was so packed Hester doubted anyone had even heard their names. She saw many of her neighbors. Their friendly smiles of greeting helped Hester feel more at home. As she tried to hear what Abigail was shouting about over the din, Hester's eyes took a discreet tour around the room in search of Galen. His height made him easy to spot on the far side of the room. He was dressed in a coat of indigo velvet. The shirt beneath was snow white and the black silk pants were matched by his black silk waistcoat. He stood next to an elegantly gowned older woman with skin the color of ivory, and hair the color of night. When he looked up and found Hester's eyes, she felt his silent greeting as surely as if he'd kissed her mouth.

Foster said, "Ah, there's Vachon over there. We should pay our respects."

Gail chimed in excitedly, "Why, if I'm not mistaken, that's his aunt Racine at his side."

Gail grabbed hold of Hester's wrist and said, "Come Hester, I want you to meet her."

They made their way through the crowd. Hester saw Bea Meldrum and Branton Hubble standing with a knot of people. Their eyes widened at the sight of her in the elegant gown and she smiled. Since her arrival, many of her neighbors had greeted her appearance with similar reactions. Not even Foster seemed immune. During the ride over in the wagon he'd spent the whole time staring at her as if he'd never lain eyes on her before.

As Galen watched Hester making her approach, he felt as if he were surrounded by silence in spite of the din around him. The gown graced her to perfection. He was pleased she'd worn it; he'd half expected to find her on his doorstep last night demanding he take back the dress; that she hadn't gave him hope that she'd willingly accept more gifts in the future.

His aunt Racine interrupted his thoughts. "Galeno, did you hear a word I just said?"

When he didn't answer she peered up into his face and turned her eyes to see what had him so totally enraptured. She saw the dark-skinned beauty in the ivory gown. "Is that her?"

"Yes."

"You've chosen well, *neveu*. She is lovely." Then Racine gasped, "Oh, my, is that Gail Grayson also?"

Before Galen could reply, Racine bounded gracefully off into the crowd. He smiled as the two women embraced, but his eyes were on Hester. He took in the soft brown grace of her throat and shoulders, the lush curve of her mouth. He thought about the last time they'd been together and his blood rushed as if he were an untried youth. He sensed his heart pounding, felt his arousal awaken. He wasn't certain how he felt about being so singularly attracted to the lovely Indigo Wyatt, but he was certain he was up to the challenge.

Gail and Racine were arm in arm as they returned to where Galen stood. Questions, laughs, and tears filled the next few moments as they renewed their friendship. While they continued talking excitedly, Galen greeted the Quints.

Foster said genuinely, "Mr. Vachon, Jenine and I want to thank you for including us in this wonderful affair."

Jenine added, "We didn't have the chance to celebrate our wedding so I'm real grateful."

Galen replied smoothly, "No need to thank me. You're doing me a favor by giving me the chance to formally meet my neighbors. It is I who am in your debt."

Galen then turned to Hester. "Miss Wyatt, you look stunning." He raised her hand to his lips. "How are you this evening?"

"I'm fine, Mr. Vachon, and you?"

He answered, "Now, I'm fine as well."

Hester ignored his devilish gaze even as it warmed her senses. She had no intentions of letting herself be swept away by him so soon into the evening.

Gail motioned Hester closer. "Racine, I want you to meet Hester Wyatt. Hester, Racine Rousseau."

Racine's dark eyes were smiling. "I'm very glad to meet you, Hester Wyatt."

"I'm pleased to meet you also."

Galen made the rest of the introductions. "And *Tante,* this is Foster Quint and his wife, Jenine. Our newly-weds."

"Congratulations," Racine replied. "I hope the two of you will be in love for many years to come."

Jenine cuddled up close to Foster's arm and he gave her a tight squeeze. "Fostie and I are going to be married a long time, aren't we, sweetheart?"

"For eternity, darling."

Hester saw Abigail roll her eyes, then she quickly looked away from her friend.

"I've heard so much about your house, Mr. Vachon," Jenine said. "It really is beautiful."

"Thank you, but Mr. Lovejoy is due the credit. He commissioned the design."

They spent a few more moments exchanging small talk, then Galen said, "If you are hungry, there are refreshments out on the veranda and a well-stocked buffet. Feel free to sample whatever you wish."

The Quints left to explore the offerings on the verandah, while Racine and Gail announced they were off to find a quiet spot to catch up on their friendship, and promised to return later.

Hester felt herself jostled by the crowd, but the spell woven over her by Galen's dark eyes made her barely notice.

"Will you let me show you the grounds?"

"No," she said softly, drowning in his eyes.

"Why not?"

"Everyone in the room is already staring at us."

Galen had to admit she was correct. Although his guests were engrossed in conversations and in the trays of fine food and drink circulating around the room by the liveried staff, they were also scrutinizing the two of them closely, especially the women.

Galen asked, "Am I correct in assuming there aren't many available men in the area?"

"Yes, you are," Hester replied. "Have the local mamas been thrusting their daughters at you?"

He nodded.

Hester smiled and cooed sympathetically, "You poor soul," adding, "I hope they give you fits all evening. It's no less than you deserve for all this extravagance. You'd think you were royalty the way folks have been carrying on since you moved in here."

"But I am royalty, Indigo. My title—"

"I don't want to know," she said firmly, even though she was reeling from this latest revelation.

He asked softly, "Then what do you want?"

"To get through this evening without bringing the gossips down on my head," she quoted. "But you probably don't care about gossips, do you?"

"I'm afraid I don't."

"You really should be meeting your neighbors. It isn't

polite to spend all your time with one guest. If you'd like I'll introduce you."

"For you, anything. Lead the way."

So Hester spent the next hour or so helping Galen get acquainted. Many of the people were uncomfortable at first; after all, few had met anyone this wealthy or cultured. But Galen charmed them all. The men were impressed by his knowledge of farming, hunting, and his easygoing manner. The women were dazzled by his smiles.

Through it all Hester felt his eyes, his presence. Though difficult, she was still able to maintain a neighborly politeness. Every time she looked his way, she remembered their last meeting. Those stolen moments in his carriage still had the power to make her breathless. Even now as they stood talking to Branton Hubble about the local price of feed, she had no trouble recalling the intensity of his touch.

After she introduced him around and she felt confident he could now move about the gathering more comfortably, Hester politely excused herself from his side. For the remainder of the evening he stayed a respectable distance away. Yet, each and every time she glanced up, she found him watching her. By the time the evening came to a close, she was finding it harder and harder to ignore his dark-eyed pull upon her will.

But when it became time to leave, Gail and Racine were far too excited over their renewed friendship to be parted; one evening had not been enough time to talk about all they wished to share, so Gail accepted Racine's invitation to spend a few days at the Folly as Racine's guest. Hester thought it was a grand idea and gave them both her blessing. Hester found Foster and Jenine out in front of the house. They too opted out of departing. It seemed Raymond LeVeq had invited some of the men to stay on after the gathering to enjoy a game of billiards. Foster had been included in the invitation. He did not want to stay, but Jenine thought differently. In fact, he did not appear very happy with his wife's idea since he had always deemed billiards to be one of those idle pastimes detrimental to the forward movement of the race.

Hester asked, "Foster, have you ever played billiards?"

He shook his head no.

Jenine countered, "But it hardly matters, this revolves around wealth and class, the billiards mean nothing. Only the men of influence like Hubble and Lovejoy have been asked to stay. LeVeq says Vachon especially wants Foster to attend."

"But why?"

Jenine smiled up at her husband, "Maybe he realizes he was wrong the day we all met, and that men like my Foster are valuable. I certainly believe he is. He's the schoolteacher here, that alone entitles him to rub elbows with the others."

Hester wondered what Gail would think of Jenine's tiny show of ambition on Foster's behalf. Maybe the young woman wasn't as empty-headed as some folks believed.

Foster asked, "But darling, how will you get home?"

Jenine said, "I can ride with Lemuel Meldrum. He and Bea can take me when they leave. I'm sure Mr. Vachon will see Hester gets home safely. Don't you think Hester?"

Hester didn't want to become embroiled in their discussion. "I'll be fine. Don't worry about me."

She bid them farewell and walked back over to the porch. Hester found the night air relaxing compared with the noise of the party inside. The cool silence of the breeze was lulling, making her reluctant to return. She was certain she would be able to find a ride home with someone, but she didn't want to go asking just yet. Hester pulled in a few breaths of fresh air. She was tired. Many of the people had already departed. Most folks in Whittaker farmed, and the daily chores began with the cock's crow. They weren't accustomed to fancy parties thrown by men who may or may not be counts, and neither was Hester.

"Good evening, Miss Wyatt."

His all too familiar voice blended seamlessly into the
hush of the night. She tried to control her breathing as he
came and stood beside her. "Good evening, Mr.
Vachon."

"Are you heading out for home?"

"Yes, but I seem to be without a ride at the moment."

"My carriage is right over there. I can see you home."

Hester had no intentions of walking off into the dark
with Galen Vachon, not with some of her neighbors still
milling about the vast grounds. "I'm enjoying the night
air. I'm content to wait for someone heading my way."

He didn't move.

"There's no need for you to neglect your guests. I
doubt I'll be kidnapped from your front door."

"You look very beautiful tonight . . ."

Hester continued to stare ahead lest someone like
Viola Welsh, who happened to step outside at that very
moment, think to start gossip. Viola was one of the
largest women Hester knew. Her zest for food was
surpassed only by her appetite for nosing around in
other folks' affairs.

"Well Hester, how are you?"

"I'm well, Viola, and you?"

"Well as can be expected when one has an unmarried
daughter." She laughed.

Hester could almost sense Galen stiffening.

Viola said, "Mr. Vachon, such a lovely party. Have
you met my daughter, April?"

April was as thin as her mother was large. The girl had
never been known to smile, though her mother was
forever going on about April's sense of humor and the
magnificence of April's mincemeat pies.

Galen bowed politely to the sad-faced April.

Hester couldn't resist, and so asked, "Viola, have you
told Mr. Vachon about April's prize-winning pies?"

For the next few moments, Hester stood smiling
serenely while Viola touted her daughter's mastery of
mincemeat. Viola was just getting warmed up when
Galen suddenly remembered a guest he needed to speak

with. He bowed politely to the ladies and practically ran back into the house.

Viola did not take Galen's hasty retreat well, saying, "The rich can be terribly rude."

April said, "Mother has it ever occurred to you that he might not like mincemeat. Why do you do that? Must you try and throw me at every unmarried man as if I were fish bait?"

Hester was impressed by April's show of spirit. She was a nice enough young woman, but many people thought she'd stand a better chance of landing a husband if she could somehow barter for a new mama.

April's voice reeked with frustration when she proclaimed, "I'll never get married."

Viola's voice was filled with shock. "April!"

"Oh, let's just go home, Mother."

Neither of them bothered to bid Hester goodbye as they left the porch and walked out into the night.

Hester was not surprised when Galen's coach drove up a few moments later. Galen set the brake and hopped down. "Your chariot awaits, madam, although you should be made to walk home for that stunt with Viola and her daughter. I've never liked mincemeat or women with pushy mamas."

Hester smiled at his words. "I'll remember that for the next time. But you know I can't let you see me home."

"I know. I'll have my driver take you."

"That isn't necessary. I'm certain Mr. LeVeq has no desire to be taken away from the festivities. I'll find someone else."

"Raymond drove only for me as a favor until I found someone suitable. He doesn't have the temperament to be hired help."

The driver appeared. As he nodded at Hester she noted that he was the same man who'd driven the coach in Detroit.

Galen asked, "I suppose I can't have a kiss either."

She shook her head and got into the coach.

He stood on the ground looking up at her and Hester

could feel her body answering the desire's call in his eyes.

"I do wish you'd stay so we could talk."

"I can't."

"Ah, yes, reputation is everything."

She ignored his slight sarcasm. "I have to live here, Galen."

He eyed her in the darkness. "I'm sorry. I'm being selfish. You're very humbling for a man, Indigo."

She was succumbing to the memories of their times together. "That isn't my intent."

"You're humbling just the same."

Galen didn't want her to leave, but could not conjure up a plan that would convince her to stay. Were she a more worldly woman, he knew any number of ways to woo her, but Indigo had him in a complete flux. "May I come and see you later?"

Hester's first instinct was to see if they were being overheard. Her next was to try and slow her thumping heart. She'd never known a man of such directness. "I—no."

"I think I might anyway," he replied smiling.

"No," Hester gasped softly. "Promise me you won't."

"I can't give my word when there's a good chance I may not keep it."

"Galen?!"

"Don't fret."

She took that to mean he would not visit and she sighed with relief.

"I—must go," she stammered.

He stepped back. *Au revoir, petite.*

The driver slapped the reins and the coach rolled forward.

Back at home, Hester made sure the jockey's light was lit, then went up for bed. Galen's request to visit still stirred her peace. She wondered what would happen if she had agreed? Would she have done something terribly forward like donning one of the gowns in the chest? She glanced at the chest sitting against the wall. It hadn't been opened again since the day it arrived. She walked over to it. Kneeling, she ran her hand over the fine wood carvings, once again caught by its beauty, then undid the small lock. As she slowly lifted the lid, the smells of the fine scents packed in the bottom of the chest wafted out and filled her nose with a fragrant aroma. What gown would she have worn for him, she asked herself. This one? She held up a dark, emerald-green gown. The seams had been left unsewn. The edges were beautifully scalloped and overlaid with an even darker emerald lace. The only closures were a delicate little ribbon at the base of the bodice and one on each hip. The lace-edged decolletage was far more daring than Hester would have liked, but she supposed men appreciated such things. She held it against herself imagining how it would feel to wear something so provocative. She decided she wanted to know, so she took it over to the bed and began to undress.

Hester stood in the mirror and surveyed a woman she didn't recognize as herself. The emerald gown flowed sensually to her feet. Her breasts were barely covered by the brief lace-edged bodice. Her shoulders and upper arms were draped by the fine, thin silk, but the sides of her waist and the line of her hips and thighs would have been bare above and below the small strategically placed ribbons had Hester removed her coarse, muslin drawers. Modesty had compelled her to keep them on—Hester had never gone naked beneath her clothing, ever. She realized the bulky drawers looked silly peeking from beneath the thin silk, and she doubted a lover would be pleased by the sight. Lifting the gown, she undid the drawer's strings, then stepped out of them. With a high kick she propelled the drawers towards the bed.

With the removal of the drawers, Hester could feel the slide of the silk on her bare hips and thighs. Would her mythical lover find her enticing, she mused, turning to look at the back view. A sound in the room froze her and she stared aghast as the secret wall panel opened. A

heartbeat later, Galen Vachon stepped smoothly through
the portal and into her room.

"Good even—"

Galen's voice died as he took in the vision of sensuality standing across the room. His manhood hardened
instantaneously. He didn't know where to settle his eyes
first. Her beautiful breasts, her bare throat and the sultry
hips all fought for his attention. "I do hope this is for
me, Indigo, because I will surely die if you've dressed
this way for another . . ."

His husky voice caressed her like a hand. The heated
look on his face made her ask almost shyly, "Do you like
it?"

Galen nodded. "Very much so. Turn for me."

Hester complied slowly. "What are you doing here?"
she asked over her pounding heart.

Galen could feel himself become more and more
aroused at the lusty picture she made. "You haven't
answered my question."

His desire for her made her bold. "I was imagining
what I would wear had I said yes to you tonight . . ."

Galen had to force himself to remain where he stood.
He knew if he took even one step in her direction, the
next steps would lead to her bed. "I came to talk, but
seeing you like this makes talking seem a true waste of
the moment."

Hester's voice came out a lot less firm than she'd
intended, "You're going to get us both in serious trouble,
sneaking in and out of my room this way."

"Only if I touch you, *petite* . . ."

Hester's eyes closed for a moment in reaction, and she
fought to stay unaffected by the heat in the air.

Galen wanted to place her atop the bed and slide the
thin emerald silk up and down every inch of her firm,
lithe body. During the party, the sight of her in the ivory
gown had kept him in a state of high arousal all evening.
All he could think about was slowly removing it. Now
however, she had on something far more provocative.
He wanted to slowly strip it from her too. He said then,

"Do me a favor. For now, would you put on a robe? Preferably one of those ugly ones."

Hand on hip, she took mock offense.

He grinned at her reaction. "Please? Let me talk business a moment and then you can torture me."

"If you insist, but only because you said please."

She crossed to her wardrobe, shucked on a muslin wrapper, then firmly tied closed the fat beige ribbons that ran from prim high collar to her waist.

When she turned back, Galen's face held a decidedly disappointed look. "I take it this is ugly enough for you?"

"More than enough."

But Hester noted that not even the ugly robe kept away the heat of his eyes. "I thought we agreed you wouldn't come here tonight . . ." she said, walking over to where he stood.

"You agreed."

"You told me not to fret."

"Yes, I did."

He reached out a finger and traced her cheek.

Her eyes slid closed and she asked, "Why can't you use the front door like everyone else?"

Unable to resist the lure of her, Galen leaned down and placed a warm kiss upon her mouth. "You expressed a concern about gossip. I didn't think you wanted anyone passing on the road to know I was visiting you at night."

"This talk couldn't wait until morning?"

His lips brushed her jaw as he shook his head no.

"Then let's go down to the table."

"No, I don't think it's wise for your lights to be lit again. Let everyone think you've gone to bed." He pulled away.

"Aren't you supposed to be playing billiards with LeVeq?"

Galen liked the way she looked after being kissed. "I pleaded fatigue and retired to my quarters a bit after your departure."

"And your guests, are they still at the Folly?"

"Undoubtedly. The game was a ruse, really. LeVeq wants to study some of the men around here. We're evaluating their potential as traitors." Galen couldn't take his eyes off her. The memory of the beauty hiding beneath the gown kept his arousal high.

Hester knew she was fighting a losing battle. His eyes were hotter than she'd ever seen them. She struggled to keep up her end of the conversation. "I doubt you'll find a traitor amongst the men you invited tonight."

"I was once as optimistic as you, *petite,* but after my naivete landed me in a South Carolina prison for three years, I was cured. Traitors can be anyone: mothers, fathers, individuals you may know and love. I went to prison because I was betrayed by the husband of a woman I tried to help escape."

"He didn't want to join her?"

"No. He thought his first loyalty was to his master and it outweighed all else. He found his wife's desire for freedom dishonorable."

" 'Tis slavery that's dishonorable."

"Well, he didn't view it that way."

"How did you get out of the prison?"

"LeVeq. My punishment for slave stealing was three years of hard labor, after which I was to be sold deep south. The day I was put on the block, I was purchased by a ringer Raymond bribed to pose as a legitimate planter."

"When was this?"

"Over a decade and a half ago. I was twenty."

"You've been on the Road quite some time."

"As have you," he softly said. "So, may I stay?"

"Do I have a choice?"

He grinned in the shadows. "Of course you do. You will always have a choice."

Hester motioned him to the rocker positioned next to her small room stove. He took a seat then patted his lap. She nervously took her seat atop his hard thighs.

He whispered, "Lean back."

When she did she felt the solidness of his chest and

shoulders warm against her back and the encircling strength of his strong arm.

"That's better. You and Foster didn't do much cuddling, I take it."

"We never cuddled."

"The man's a fool, but the fool's loss is the dragon's gain."

He kissed her brow. "Now, the real reason I needed to see you—"

Hester looked up into his face.

He corrected himself, "Well, one of the reasons."

He withdrew a sheaf of paper from inside his coat. "I have a list of all the people invited tonight. If you would, I'd like you to tell me which ones are associated with the Road."

"Let me take it over to the light."

As she crossed the floor she could feel the silk tempting her skin beneath the muslin wrapper. Each move of her legs made the fabric caress her like the soft hand of a lover. The no-nonsense Hester scolded her mightily for being so brazen, even as the other Hester wanted to kiss him until dawn.

She walked over to her desk where the room's only light sat and withdrew a pen from the stand. With her back to him, she made a small mark adjacent to the names she knew. She looked over at him. "I don't recognize all the names here."

He came and leaned near as he looked at the names she'd marked. His faint cologne and his nearness washed over her.

"You've narrowed the names down a bit. That's a help."

His eyes were so filled with desire, Hester began to tremble and she could not stop. He was so tall and so beautiful any woman in her right mind would probably jump at the chance to be with him this way. Hester had apparently lost her right mind the moment she met him, because she wanted to be with him, too.

Galen lifted a finger and slowly traced the outline of

her mouth. He was mesmerized. He delicately drew his finger across her soft cheek and then the curve of her jaw. She had skin like silk, he noted, dark indigo silk that drew his touch like a powerful magnet. He could spend a lifetime just touching her. Unable to resist, he leaned down, gave her one fleeting kiss, and prayed she wouldn't deny him more.

The passion exploded in Hester with a power that was as buffeting as it was tender. She responded to his coaxing lips. She saw nothing wrong in sharing his kisses for just the tiniest while, after all he thought her beautiful.

And she felt beautiful as his hands began to move over her back and up and down her waist. The kiss stoked the embers still red from their last encounter, but this time there would be no interruptions. She gave no protest when he undid the ribbons of the coarse cocoon to free the emerald-green butterfly inside. She shuddered in reaction as his hot lips slowly devoured her bare throat, her ear, her jaw. He worked her free of the muslin gown and tossed it aside. Hester felt disembodied yet she was very conscious of the gentle bite on the underside of her jaw; conscious of the heat of his kiss against the vee of her breasts. His hands cupped her, caressed her. He placed kisses against the dark satin tops, then pulled aside the lace to set one breast free. She moaned when his lips found her nipple. He suckled gently, his tongue circling expertly. Hester stood with her head back and her mouth passionately wide, unable to corral her vibrant response. He pulled down the other side of her gown, then ran his firm palm over the berried points.

She heard him whisper, "This is how I envisioned you when I first saw this gown . . . bared for me so I could pleasure you in just this way . . ."

He dropped his head and tasted the breast he'd just freed. She found it harder and harder to stand, especially as his hands were mapping her hips and sliding through the gown to journey over her thigh. He raised his head to recapture her lips in a kiss that was possessive and fervent. She was so enraptured, she didn't even know the ribbons at her side had been undone until she felt the gown's seams lift and the heat of his hands cup her intimately.

He pulled her in against him, solidly, boldly. They both seemed to have caught a shared fire because he couldn't seem to get enough of her or she of him. She moved her hands over the strength of his back, kissing him, flicking her tongue against the edges of his lips, experimenting with the boldness his passion had planted within her, while his hands beneath her gown toured lustily.

Hester could feel the sweetness pouring wantonly in response to his intimate teasing. No man had ever touched her this way. Her legs were so shaky, she knew she was going to fall, but he didn't stop. Truth be told, she didn't want him to stop. "I'm going to shatter, Galen . . ."

"No, you're not . . . I won't let you . . ."

Hester shuddered as his fingers took up a dallying, lazy rhythm so potent her hips began to sway. "You're very good at this . . ." she heard herself say.

"I knew you'd like it." He grinned.

Eyes closed, she whispered, "Audacious man, ohhh . . ."

He bit her gently on her breasts, then suckled softly, his fingers still moving. "I have a treat for you . . ."

He kissed his way back up to her mouth, after which she felt herself lifted effortlessly into his arms and taken over to her small canopied bed. As he laid her on the thin mattress a small voice inside Hester's head shook her sanity awake and made her think about the dangers of what she was doing. "Galen I—"

He was seated on the edge of the bed. "Don't worry, *petite,* there will be no harm in this. You will remain as chaste as you are now. After we marry, it will be different."

Hester sat up and blinked. "Galen, I'm not marrying you!"

"Yes," he said, "you probably are."

"No, I'm not."

"Do you want your treat or not?"

"I'm not marrying you. Why would you want to marry me?"

"It certainly won't be for your obedience, *ma coeur*. Now lie back."

"Galen?"

He leaned over and kissed her with such magnificent passion she nearly swooned. He slowly backed away. As she sat there, eyes closed, he clouded things further by gently feasting on her breasts until she moaned softly.

"Now lie back . . ." he commanded.

Hester melted back onto the mattress without a further word.

Words continued to fail her as he once again set her on fire from the roots of her hair to the tips of her indigo toes. When he leaned down to circle his tongue around the whirl of her navel, Hester moaned in response to it and to his hand moving lazily over her thighs. The gown lay in scandalous disarray, it no longer covered very much of her body at all, but it provided his hands tender access to all that made her woman.

With kisses he slid down her navel and flirted with the edges of the hair crowning her thighs. She instinctively stiffened. She was just about to protest when his fingers parted her, his kiss wantonly branded her, and then, the only word she could find to say was, "Glory . . ."

It was the most shocking and delicious experience of Hester's life. His mouth set off a heat stoked higher by the intimate accompaniment of his dallying fingers. A passion-induced dementia gripped her, tossed her. Her thighs parted in wanton invitation and he rewarded her with an erotic thanks that lifted her hips off the bed. The crescendo shattered her with the force of a lightning bolt, racking her as she screamed out his name.

Chapter 13

Galen eased her back to earth with sweet tenderness. When she finally opened her eyes, she stared up at him with such wonder, he smiled smugly. "Well?" he asked.

"Is that one of the reasons women rarely tell you no?" she asked in a voice that mirrored her half-dazed state.

"Partially. Did you enjoy the treat?"

"Partially? You mean there's more?"

He chuckled softly. "Much more."

Hester shook her head. She couldn't imagine what "much more" entailed, but being a woman of the 1850's she did know properly raised women weren't supposed to enjoy this, yet she had. So much so, just looking up at him made her want to be shown "much more." "Well, treats or no, I won't be marrying you."

Galen sat beside her, ignored her statement for a moment, concentrating instead on her mattress. Using the flat of his hand he pressed down upon it. It had all the resiliency of wood. He'd slept on open ground that was softer.

"I'll have Raymond order you a new mattress. This one feels as if it's filled with rocks."

Hester sat up. "You are not sending me a mattress or anything else. Haven't you been listening these past few weeks? No more gifts. None."

Her face was not very far from his own. He ran his eyes over the lush curve of her mouth and her gorgeously half clad frame. "It's a wonder you don't wake up bruised every morning. It shouldn't take long to acquire a new one."

Hester dragged the gown over her nakedness as best she could. She wanted to shake him, even as she responded to the heat emanating from his eyes. "Is it the wealth, or were you born with this arrogance?"

He shrugged his magnificent shoulders. "It's a bit of both I suppose, but it is of no consequence, *petite*. Before the leaves turn, you will be mine."

Hester shook her head at his presumption.

Galen had no doubt she would be his. Yes, his manner was rooted in years of wealth and privilege but his desire for her was true. He would have her or die trying. He told her softly, "I should go so you can sleep. Give me a kiss."

Hester wanted to box his ears. Did he think she'd be able to sleep?

He raised an eyebrow at her mutinous manner. "Ah, the contrary woman has returned."

Hester's lips lifted into a tiny smile. She found it impossible to stay angry with him. He was a rascal wrapped in charm and she had no defense against him. "If I kiss you, will you promise to go?"

"Kiss me and we'll see . . ."

He left an hour later.

Abigail returned later in the morning as Hester sat eating breakfast.

"You look as if you didn't get much sleep," Abigail remarked.

"I—was up for a while catching up on a few things."

Gail peered at Hester's face and the faint rings beneath her eyes. Hester sought to distract her by asking, "I thought you and Racine were going to spend a few days together."

Gail smiled. "We are. I came back here to get some

clothing. There's a coach outside waiting. We didn't get much sleep either."

Hester sipped her tea.

After Gail departed, Hester sat and brooded over her life. She didn't believe for a minute Galen's professed desire to make her his wife. Just because she lived in the country didn't mean she had turnips for brains. Surely he didn't believe her to be that naive. She and Galen were from two different worlds. She knew from her school lessons a bit about the Louisiana Creoles. They were known as the *gens de couleur libres,* free people of color. Their ancestry embraced most of the European races that came to America's shores but it was the African blood in their veins which tied them to the rest of the Blacks in America. That common thread made them subject to all the restrictions and dangers facing the race as a whole. Having lived in Louisiana under both Spanish and French rule many of the Blacks there were free before America was born. Over time they amassed enough wealth to establish successful businesses and found their own schools and newspapers. Many families sent their sons to France to be educated, thereby circumventing America's segregation. During the War of 1812, Free Black brigades played a pivotal role in Andrew Jackson's victory at Chalmette. In December of 1814, Jackson issued a proclamation thanking them for their service to the nation during its time of need. His words on that day were now a treasured part of the race's history. During Hester's school years Jackson's proclamation had been routinely assigned as a memorization piece.

Admittedly she did not know much more about the Creoles of New Orleans, but it was more than enough to know Galen could not have been serious about marrying. The mulattoes of Louisiana did not present purplehanded former slaves as their intended. Their social circles would not stand for such a breach in etiquette.

But Hester soon had other more pressing worries as the days passed. The slave catcher Ezra Shoe and his

band of ruffians rode back into the area during the last
week of May. All movement of passengers either came to
a complete halt or were moved with the utmost of care.
Jockey lights were dimmed all over the county and
conductors held their breaths, hoping he would leave
again soon.

But he didn't leave. In fact the Road went into alarm
as word spread of the writ Shoe had served on Bea's
neighbors, Fanny and James Blackburn. They were being
held in Sheriff Lawson's jail until they could be shipped
south. The community was outraged.

At the Vigilance Committee meeting that night, the
members strove to devise a plan. According to Sheriff
Lawson, the writ from the federal magistrate was vague
at best. It stated only that a married couple was wanted
by a planter in Tennessee. There were no specific names
on any of the documents Shoe presented to Lawson. If
the Blackburns weren't freed somehow, they could be
sent south without a trial or the right to testify on their
own behalf due to the mandates set forth in the Fugitive
Slave Law.

"Will the owner take money in exchange for their
freedom?" Hester asked.

Hubble shook his head no. "According to Shoe, the
master has already been wired and is on his way here to
reclaim them."

"Could he really be their owner?" William Lovejoy
asked.

Bea Meldrum shrugged. "Shoe says he is, but—we
really don't know."

"We must get them to Canada." Branton Hubble
stated.

Everyone agreed.

Hester and Bea recruited four other women to help
with the plan. All the ladies were well known to one
another and all had placed themselves in jeopardy many
times before for the cause of freedom.

The six women went to the jail the next day, carrying
baskets of food and clothing for the incarcerated Fanny

Blackburn. Fanny's husband had already been taken to Detroit because of the fear of violence. Since the passage of the Fugitive Slave Law many recaptured slaves had been freed not by the law, but through "rescue." Most of the nation's rescue attempts were patterned after the celebrated "Abolition Riot" which took place in a Boston courtroom in 1836. On that July day, Eliza Small and Polly Ann Bates were charged with being the runaway slaves of a Mr. John B. Morris, a resident of Baltimore. As Morris's attorney addressed the judge, the spectators rushed the bench. In the ensuing chaos some of the Black women in the crowd whisked Eliza and Polly out of the courthouse. There were reports that one of the women involved, a Black laundress of "great size," immobilized one of the court's officers by throwing her arm around his neck. The subjects of the rescue, Eliza and Polly were never found, and much to the South's chagrin, none of the individuals involved in the melee were ever charged.

Hester supposed Sheriff Lawson wanted to avoid a similar incident and so sent Fanny's husband off to Detroit where the security could be better maintained. Yet, there was a large mixed-race crowd gathered outside the building to protest Fanny's jailing. Hester nodded to those she knew, Branton Hubble in particular, then she and the ladies made their way to the door.

The slave catcher Shoe stood in the entrance. "Where do you think you're going?"

Bea said, "To visit Mrs. Blackburn. We have the sheriff's permission."

Sheriff Lawson appeared in the doorway behind Shoe and the crowd let out a hail of catcalls and derisive words as he stepped out. Most of the people in the county respected Martin Lawson. Hester had never known him to be unfair to anyone, but in this instance folks were incensed at the role the hated Fugitive Slave Law forced him to play. Lawson seemingly ignored the angry calls and slurs as he turned his wintry visage on Shoe. "Back out of the way, and let the ladies inside."

Shoe looked as if he wanted to protest the order but the stare of the big constable appeared to quell Shoe's dissent.

As they entered the small cell, Fanny Blackburn gave them each a weak smile of greeting. In response, each woman gave her a strong hug.

Lawson had followed them in, so Hester turned to him and asked, "Sheriff, may we have a bit of privacy so Fanny can put on the clean clothing we have for her? We'd also like to visit with her a while, with your permission."

The sheriff looked around at the six women. Everyone met his eyes easily. He finally nodded his approval. He left them and closed the door.

The cell's solid wood door had a small panel at the top which could be slid open so the sheriff could check on his prisoners. Olympia Reed, one of the women in Hester's party, had been especially recruited for this afternoon's visit because of her height and girth. Once Lawson closed the door, Olympia stood in front of the panel, effectively keeping anyone outside from seeing what was about to transpire.

Hester and the others moved quickly. Fanny was made to change clothes with Hester. Both women were dark-skinned and approximately the same size. Hester donned one of the dresses from Bea's basket. Kate Bell, the hairdresser and owner of the boardinghouse, had also been recruited for this visit, and she took out her combs and hastily fashioned Hester's hair into the two thick braids Fanny always wore coiled and pinned behind her ears. While Kate worked on Hester, Bea quickly undid Fanny's braids. When Kate was done, she then gave Fanny Hester's signature knot at the nape. The two women sat side by side on the small cot. The transformation had taken only minutes.

Bea looked between Hester and Fanny, then said, "Close enough, wouldn't you say, ladies?"

All nodded their agreement. They then had Fanny don

Hester's bonnet. No one would know Fanny was not Hester when they made their exit as long as they moved quickly and no one outside got too close.

Kate said, "Now, we have to wait for Hubble's signal. Pray this works."

The signal was heard moments later as rocks and stones began to pelt the walls of the small building. From inside, the ladies could hear the angry roar of the crowd and Shoe's shouts for help. They heard the sheriff shouting and then a rifle shot. Suddenly, there was the sound of a key in the lock and Hester quickly laid down on the cot and turned her back to the door. Bea hastily threw a thin quilt over Hester to further disguise the switch.

The door flew open and Hester heard the sheriff urging the women to leave. Outside the roar had grown meaner, and the rocks and stones pelting the building sounded like hail.

The sheriff yelled, "Let's go ladies! Out the back way, so you won't be hit by the stones!"

The door closed and Hester sighed her relief. She was alone.

The sheriff dispersed the crowd a bit after, but he didn't discover the true identity of his prisoner until supper time. Hester, still feining sleep, felt the sheriff touch her shoulder gently and ask, "Mrs. Blackburn, would you care for some supper?"

It was the moment of truth. Hester slowly rolled over, then sat up. "Good evening, Sheriff. I do believe I am hungry."

Lawson stared for a moment, then said, "Aw, hell, Miss Hester, what are you doing here?"

Hester smiled. "Sheriff, you know we couldn't let Shoe send Fanny Blackburn south."

He shook his head as if he knew the joke was on him. "Shoe's going to bust a gut."

"Maybe it will be fatal."

The sheriff shook his head again and a half smile

appeared. "You know I've always liked you because you remind me so much of your father, David. He would have done something like this."

Then his words and manner softened. "He and I grew up close as brothers. I believe a part of me died when your aunt Katherine told me he was lost to us. I missed him so much, I tried to reclaim a little of him by naming my son after him."

Hester could feel his emotion tug at her own. She replied softly, "Everyone says the same thing—how much he is missed. I'm poorer for never having known him."

"He was a special man. You have his eyes. However, eyes or no, I'm going to have to arrest you."

"I know."

"The trial probably won't be anytime soon, providing the missing property is ever recaptured, so until then, I'm confining you to your home. No more troublemaking until after the trial," he warned. Smiling, he added, "Or at least keep it to a minimum."

Hester smiled in reply.

"You can go home in the morning, but you're going to have to post a bond."

"How much?"

When he quoted the figure, Hester's eyes widened. "So much?"

"I'm afraid so. Otherwise, Shoe will use the escape as an excuse to terrorize families all over the area. All he has to do is accuse. The law says he doesn't need proof."

He was right. Many of the families in the area were fugitives. She didn't want Shoe hammering his fist against their doors in the middle of the night because of her. But the sum of the bond would take all of her funds. She was certain the case would never reach trial unless the Blackburns were recaptured, and if they weren't the bond would be returned. However, what if they were found? The state of Michigan, like many other northern states, had passed personal liberty laws to reinstate some of the rights struck down by the Fugitive Slave Law, but the enforcement of the law and its mandates were as ever changing as the tide. The Cause had seen both victory and stunning defeats in the courts. Who knew what might happen to her as a result of impersonating Fanny Blackburn? She could lose everything, from her funds, to her land, to her own freedom. Hester had weighed the consequences going in and she harbored no regrets. "I will write you a bank draft in the morning."

After supper, she and the sheriff spent a few moments talking and Hester asked about his son, David.

Lawson said sadly, "He's turned into a very angry man. He misses Bethany Ann something fierce. I've had to stop him a couple of times from confronting Lovejoy over sending her to Minnesota."

Hester stared. "Bethany Ann is in Minnesota?"

"Yes. You seem surprised."

"Mr. Lovejoy has been telling folks she ran away."

"No, he sent her to family there to get her away from my son. I—"

The door blew open with such force it slammed into the wall behind it.

Shoe strode in, his face twisted with anger. "We can't find the Blackburn woman, and I just received word that a mob overran the Detroit jail this morning and he's disappeared too."

Hester gave a silent prayer of thanks.

He barked at Hester, "Where are they?!"

"Wherever they are, they are free."

He lunged at Hester only to find himself grabbed by the sheriff, who snarled, "Unless you have further business here I'd advise you and your men to move on."

"She under arrest?"

"Yes."

"Good, because if she wasn't, I know a planter who's looking for a gal that fits her description."

Hester stared back coldly. As the sheriff stated earlier, Shoe didn't need proof to accuse her of being someone's runaway property. If he could find someone to back the claim, her life as a freewoman would be over.

The sheriff wasn't cowed. "She's free, Shoe. I knew her daddy. I knew her grandparents. They were all free. You try and bring her to trial or kidnap her and there'll be hell to pay."

Shoe smiled, showing his black teeth, and said, "We'll see, Sheriff. We'll see." He walked out, leaving a decidedly foul stench behind.

While the sheriff hastened Shoe's departure from town, Hester walked over to the small barred window in the wall of her cell and looked out at the trees and land. She hoped the Blackburns would reach Ontario safely. That they had been targeted by Shoe still did not make sense. Fanny and James never bothered anyone. They didn't participate in the Vigilance Committee activities, and very rarely ventured into town. Were it not for their presence at church every Sunday, no one would even know they lived in Whittaker. So how had Shoe known they were fugitives? Did someone tip his hand? She thought it highly unlikely. They had no enemies that she was aware of and she never heard anyone speak ill of either of them. Chills ran down her spine as a thought took hold. Could their betrayal be the work of the traitor who had also betrayed Galen?

Her thoughts were interrupted as the cell door opened and the sheriff stepped in. "Miss Hester, I need a big favor from you."

"If I can help, I will. What is it?"

"If I left you alone here, would you try and escape?"

Hester was certain her confusion was plain to see, but he continued, "I promised my wife I'd attend tonight's recital at her church. My deputy, Patrick, was supposed to take the evening shift so I could go, but he can't. His mother's taken ill and he's had to go home to see about her."

Hester didn't hesitate. "Keep your pledge to your wife. I promise to be here when you return."

And she would be. Lawson was a fair and decent man. On numerous occasions he'd chosen to look the other way where Road business was concerned, and according to her aunt Katherine, he'd hidden a few fugitives himself before taking on the job as sheriff. That Lawson had also been her father's best friend only increased her respect for him as a human being. Hester would keep her word because at some point in the near future he would have to account to his superiors for the escape of Fanny Blackburn, and she didn't want him to be in more hot water by having to explain two escapes. The Road couldn't afford to have him replaced by someone less humane. "Sheriff, I've given you more than enough grief for one day. You go on. I'll be fine here. All I ask is that you lock me in. I don't want Shoe paying me a visit while you're gone." Even though Lawson had asked Shoe to leave town, Hester doubted the southerner would comply with any haste.

Lawson apparently harbored his own misgivings. "Good thought. Hold on."

He left only to return with a rifle and some cartridges. "Here, hang onto this. If Shoe shows his pug ugly face, shoot him with my blessings."

Hester took the rifle and noted that it was loaded. "Let's hope it won't come to that."

"Are you sure you don't need me to stay and watch over you? If you come to harm, I'll never forgive myself."

"I'll be fine. Now go to the recital."

"Be back in under an hour's time."

"Go."

The sheriff had been gone almost a quarter hour. Hester sat upon the cot reading when she heard a key scratching against the door's lock. Her first thought was the sheriff had returned much sooner than planned, but when the fumbling sounds continued, she began to get a bad feeling because she didn't remember Sheriff Lawson having any difficulty opening the lock before. She knew instinctively that the person on the other side was not the sheriff and the hairs stood upon her neck. She forced herself to move slowly as she very calmly placed the rifle against her thigh and covered it with the edge of her flared skirt.

The door opened and Ezra Shoe entered. Behind him were two of his men, whose filthy clothing and feral eyes matched his own. Hester held his rude gaze without reaction.

He smiled, then said softly, "Well, what have we here?"

Hester neither moved nor took her eyes off him or the men still standing at the door. Fear shook her but she refused to let it have its head. If she showed even a hint of submission they'd attack like the pack savages they were.

Shoe came closer, close enough to smell. He leaned down and his smile was lewd. "I saw the sheriff leaving. Me and the boys thought you might be lonely."

One of the men cackled. Shoe looked over at them and grinned. When he turned back to Hester, the bore of the rifle was staring him in the eye. His eyebrows lifted with such shock and surprise, Hester wanted to smile, but she didn't have time to relish his reaction right now. Now she was too intent upon maintaining the upper hand.

"Back away, Mr. Shoe."

He gave her no argument. As he complied she slowly rose from the cot. Her movement gave his men their first look at her behind the gun and one of them uttered a soft curse of alarm.

Hester demanded softly, "Toss the jail key over in the corner, then leave."

They seemed to have been caught unawares, so no one moved. Then she heard one laugh nervously. "Gal, you ain't gonna shoot nobody. Don't you know it's against the law for you to turn a weapon on us?"

Hester shifted her eyes to the man who'd made the remark. He stood in front of the door grinning. She fired the gun into the wood above his head, scaring the bejesus out of them all as they cursed and scrambled out of the way. As the room quieted once more, they stared at her as if she were demented.

Hester didn't waver. Her anger kept her strong. How dare they quote the law at her knowing what they'd had in mind when they first entered. She detested violence, but she'd shoot them all without hesitation.

Shoe snarled, "If we were in the South—"

"But we're not in the South," Hester interrupted coldly. "You're in the North where cold weather makes free Blacks insane. Isn't that what you were taught? Shall I demonstrate just how crazy I am?" she tossed out bitterly.

The sarcasm wasn't lost upon them, because Shoe told his men. "Let's go, boys."

But to Hester he promised, "Your day is coming, gal. You just wait."

And he stormed out.

Hester held her stance behind the gun until she heard their steps upon the plank walk outside. Only then did she collapse upon the cot and let her emotions surface. Her hands were shaking so fiercely when she laid the shotgun down beside her she had to hold them still. Her entire body trembled as if she were suffering from extreme cold. She tried not to dwell upon what Shoe and his men would have done had she not had the gun but the terrible scenario made her stomach churn. Men like them did not view her as a thinking, feeling person, but only as a vehicle for their insatiable savagery. They were the men who believed the awful myths about the women of the race, myths that left women like herself vulnerable to attack anytime and anywhere, myths that slanderously labeled Black women as voracious in pursuit of the vices of the flesh and willing to accommodate anyone to satisfy their carnal cravings. Hester heard footsteps nearing the door and she snatched up the rifle once again. The thought that Shoe might be returning put a fresh fear in her heart and tears of anger in her eyes. She held the rifle stock firmly against her shoulder and waited.

Chapter 14

But instead of Shoe and his men, Foster entered, followed by Galen and Andre Renaud. Relief flooded over her. She slumped to the cot, set the rifle aside, and wiped her gloved hands over her teary eyes.

Foster rushed over and took her hands. "My God, Hester, someone said they heard gunshots. Are you all right?"

In reality she wanted to be held until the shaking passed, but she stoically replied, "Yes, I'm fine."

"What happened?" Galen asked. The last thing Galen wanted to do was stand there and pretend a neighborly concern. He was dying inside from the need to take her into his arms. He wanted to prove to himself she hadn't been harmed by whatever had frightened her so much she'd taken up a gun in defense of herself.

"It was Shoe," she replied. While they listened she told them the story of the Blackburns, then explained where the sheriff had gone, and of Shoe's foul visit.

When she finished her tale, she found it hard not to be moved by the concern in Galen's eyes.

Galen said, "Andre, go see if you can find the sheriff, I don't want Miss Wyatt to spend the night here. Are we in agreement, Quint?"

"Total agreement," Foster replied. Then he asked Hester, "How could you have placed yourself in such danger by posing as Fanny?"

"I wasn't in any danger, the Blackburns were the ones in real peril. My role was insignificant."

"It won't be insignificant if you are sentenced. Do you know they can confiscate your land and your home?"

"Foster, I knew the consequences, but the Blackburns needed our assistance, and we provided it."

"Hester, I was worried sick when Bea stopped me earlier and told me about the escape. No fugitive is worth you being imprisoned."

Hester couldn't believe her ears. "Foster, do you hear yourself?"

"I do, and I admit it doesn't sound very noble, but it's you I worry over. I don't want you rotting away in some prison."

His sincerity softened Hester's mood. "Foster, I won't place myself in an unnecessary danger ever, but I must do my part to stem slavery."

Hester looked over Foster's head to where Galen stood. He stared back emotionlessly and she suddenly wished they were alone. She turned to Foster and said softly, "I won't give up conducting."

Foster appeared to want to further argue the point but he sighed instead. "I understand. I don't agree, but I understand."

The sheriff's hasty entrance drew everyone's attention. "Miss Hester, are you all right? What happened?"

"I'm all right, but I owe you an apology for the hole in the door."

He spun to the door, viewed the damage done by the blast, then turned back. "Did Shoe come back here?"

She nodded.

Lawson offered a curse that curled Hester's ears. He immediately offered a contrite apology though. "I'm sorry, but that trash!"

Hester waved him off. "No apology is necessary, Sheriff. Were I a cursing woman, I'd offer a few invectives of my own."

"Did he touch you?"

She shook her head. "No."

Galen commanded everyone's attention by declaring, "Sheriff, under the circumstances, I believe Miss Wyatt should be allowed to return to her home."

"I agree, but I can't release her until her bond is secured."

Hester said, "I've made arrangements to post a bond in the morning."

Foster asked, "What type of arrangements?"

"I'll use the funds from the land sale and put up some of my land."

"How much is the bond, Sheriff?" Galen asked.

The sheriff named the amount, but unlike Hester's earlier reaction of alarm, Galen didn't appear to be bothered by the steep figure. He turned to Renaud and said, "Andre, take care of this for Miss Wyatt, please."

"My pleasure." Renaud reached into an inside pocket of his tailored coat and extracted a small velvet bag that jingled as if it held many coins. Renaud handed the bag over to the sheriff. Lawson appeared perplexed at first, but when he peered inside, his eyes widened. "Gold?!"

Galen drawled, "It will do, I hope."

The sheriff sputtered, "Why, yes. I—gold?!"

Foster seemed to be transfixed by the sight of the bag in the sheriff's hand. Hester was certain the surprise was plain on her face. As she met Galen's eyes he said to the sheriff, "I believe there is more than enough there to conclude this transaction."

The sheriff still appeared a bit stunned. He stared over at Galen with something akin to amazement, but Galen, standing there as richly dressed as any lord, met the gaze as if he were accustomed to garnering such looks of wonder.

"May we escort her home now?" Galen asked.

The sheriff sputtered again, "Uh—yes, there's some papers to sign—"

"Renaud can see to them. Shall we go, Quint, Miss Wyatt?"

Hester gathered up her things, then after offering the

sheriff another sincere apology for the damage to his door, she followed the men out into the night.

Outside, the sky up above was studded with stars. Hester drew in deep breaths of the sweet, clear air as they walked over to Galen's waiting coach.

Foster helped her inside and once Renaud joined them, the coach was under way. Foster said, "Mr. Vachon, I want to thank you for posting Hester's bond. I'm sure she will not do anything to jeopardize your gold."

Hester had had a rough day; she was in no mood for Foster's not-so-subtle reprimand. "I thank you too, Mr. Vachon, but it was not necessary for you to be so generous on my behalf. I'd already made my own arrangements."

"But Hester, your land," Foster said.

"What was I to do? You heard the amount. Bea and the others had planned to come in the morning to post my bond, but they couldn't meet that price. Should I have asked them to put up their land instead?"

Foster replied, "Maybe you should have. Weren't they responsible for you being imprisoned in the first place?"

Hester wanted to smack him. "Foster, you make it sound as if I were duped into helping the Blackburns. The plan to impersonate Fanny was mine and mine alone."

Hester looked over to Galen seated within the shadows. "Am I correct in assuming you are angry with me also?"

Foster answered before Galen could reply. "Your assumption is correct. You placed yourself in danger."

"Yes, I did, but it was my decision. I took Shoe's threats seriously the first time I met him, but I'm not going to stop my work just because he wants to see me on the block."

Galen asked, "He's threatened you before?"

"Yes, last fall when he first came to town."

"Why haven't you said anything about this before?" Foster asked.

"There was no need. You are not a member of the Vigilance Committee, nor are you in my Road circle."

She could feel herself spoiling for a fight so she took a deep breath to calm her temper and said, "I really don't wish to discuss this any further."

Hester folded her arms and looked away. She knew arguing with them would only serve to make her angrier, so she sat in silence for the remainder of the ride.

When the coach pulled up in front of her house. Hester maintained her politeness. "Mr. Vachon, thank you for the bond. Please be assured I will do nothing to jeopardize your gold."

Galen said softly, "We are concerned is all."

"And I appreciate that concern, but I've been on the Road most of my life, I can take care of myself. Goodnight, Foster. Thank you for coming to my aid."

That said, she stepped out of the carriage and headed up the walk.

Later, the more Hester thought about Foster and Galen's attitudes, the angrier she became. She didn't know whether to cry out her frustration or hurl a vase against the wall. She was thankful for her agitated state though, because it kept the memories of Shoe at bay. After she'd washed up and donned her night clothes, she crawled beneath the light quilt. There in the dark, the fear came flooding back. The images of how brutalized she would have been made her shake. She could well imagine the terrible outcome had she not fired the rifle. That one timely shot may have saved her life. She felt a wave of reaction roll over her and she trembled in response.

Across the room, the wall panel opened and she sat up. She knew instinctively it would be Galen. She barely noticed the panel close soundlessly again because her heart had begun to sing. He'd come. She felt like crying, because he alone knew that she needed solace. He'd come to hold her as she needed to be held.

He walked further into the room. Without a word, he

opened his arms wide. In silent answer, she slipped from the bed and ran to him, letting him encircle her with his strength, letting him hold her tight, so tightly she hoped he would never let go.

Galen held her for a long time, savoring her, sheltering her. When he could bear to ease her away, he gently lifted her into his arms and carried her over to the rocker. He sat with her atop his lap. Moonlight and the night breeze streamed over them through the open window.

Cradled against his chest, Hester felt safe for the first time in a long while. Since her aunt's death, her life had become so crazy, she'd hardly had time to breathe. She'd had to be strong, dedicated, and stoic in response to all she'd experienced in life, but tonight she didn't want to be strong. For just this little while she wanted to be held as if she were precious to someone, and let that someone be her strength.

Galen kissed the top of her head and basked in a contentment he'd never dreamed possible. He'd held many women in his arms, but could not remember finding such inner peace, such total ease of mind. The memory of her angry stance behind the rifle would haunt him for quite some time. He never wanted to see her so frightened by anything ever again. He'd been so eager to get back here and see about her, he'd practically thrown Quint from the coach when the driver stopped in front of his home. "Are you still angry with me?" he quietly asked.

Without lifting her head from the comfort of his chest she answered, "Yes."

He chuckled softly in the moonlight. "Should I apologize for being so concerned?"

"No, but you can apologize for acting as if I need a keeper."

"Now, I never said that. The burgher is the one you want to flay, not me."

"He'll get his chance, rest assured."

"I was terribly concerned about you however. When Quint came to me to ask my assistance in freeing you, I didn't hesitate."

"But the gold was a bit over the top, don't you think?"

He looked down into her black-diamond eyes and shrugged. "Not really."

"Does Renaud always carry around a sack of gold coins?"

"Only when necessary, and tonight it was. I'd no idea who I'd have to bribe to set you free."

She placed her head back against his heart. "Well, you certainly impressed Sheriff Lawson. Me too, if the truth be known."

"Good. I enjoy impressing you."

Hester drew back and looked up at his handsome face. "I'm not going to marry you."

"So you keep saying. Are you trying to convince me or yourself?"

Hester placed her head back on his chest. "We're not discussing this."

"Then what are we discussing?"

Opting to keep the conversation on neutral ground she told him her thoughts on the betrayal of the Blackburns.

Galen heard her out then said, "You could be right. Someone may have given Shoe the information on the Blackburns, but who?"

Hester didn't know. "How far did you and Raymond get with the list of names you showed me on the night of your party?"

"We've investigated nearly everyone so far, but with no results. We've uncovered no one with debts deep enough to make them succeptible to Shoe's possible blackmail, nor have we discovered any names which match the Order's list of known traitors. All we've unearthed is that the people of Whittaker are fine, upstanding people. Not a potential traitor in the county."

"I told you that back in October, so where does that leave us?"

"I've no idea, maybe your committee members will have some clues. When do you meet again?"

"According to my bond conditions I'm not supposed to be meeting with anyone, but the meeting will be held Sunday after church. I'll see if anyone has a new theory. If Shoe could do this to the Blackburns no one is safe."

Galen agreed.

He then asked, "Are you sure you're all right?"

She thought back on Shoe and his leering, evil presence. "He scared me deeply, but I'm better."

Galen hugged her closer. "When I entered the sheriff's office this evening, and saw you standing so angrily behind that gun—then I saw the tears in your eyes—I think I hate it when you cry."

Hester looked up at him with a questioning face.

"I do," he said. "It makes me want to destroy whomever or whatever has caused you pain."

Hester thought he was joking. "Now, Galen, really, that's a bit much, don't you think?"

"That's what I keep telling myself, but after you explained what had happened with Shoe, I wanted to kill him with my bare hands."

His words were plain, his eyes truthful. "We have a problem here, *petite*. It's fairly certain I'm in love with you."

Hester went still. His eyes were intense enough to drown in, and her heart was pounding.

He went on, saying huskily, "You've no idea how you affect me . . ."

Hester closed her eyes in reaction to his bold declaration. She didn't know how to respond. She did know that she needed to get up from his lap before she gave in to temptation, because she was fairly certain she loved him too. But she doubted their love would ever bear fruit due to their social differences. Their classes rarely mixed, let alone married. She didn't want him to be ostracized from his circle because of her past.

"You—should go back, Galen." She made a move to rise, but his hands gently stayed her hips.

"What's the matter?" he softly enquired. "I tell you of my love and you turn morose. Is the thought so disheartening?"

She smiled a half smile and shook her head. "No, in fact I'm very flattered actually, but you aren't in love—not with me."

"Why can't I be in love with you?"

"Because you can't be. We're from different worlds."

"And that means what exactly?"

"It means people like you and I don't fall in love. We certainly don't marry. Your social circle wouldn't allow it."

"Do you really believe I would care what society thinks about who I love?"

"No, you probably wouldn't, but I do."

He searched her face. "You think I would be ashamed of your past?"

"Maybe not at first—"

"I'm going to pretend you didn't utter such nonsense."

"Galen—"

"We're not going to have this discussion because it is unnecessary. Now kiss me so I don't become any angrier than I already am."

"You are far too arrogant for your own good at times, do you know that?"

"Arrogant, wealthy, and . . ." He used his finger to slowly trace the outline of her tempting mouth. ". . . totally captivated by you . . ."

He kissed her then, a slow sweet kiss filled with passion. Suddenly, she was very glad she and Foster had not been man and wife. She would never experience such sweetness if they had. Foster would never have nibbled her lip so delicately, nor made her lips part so willingly. Only Galen had the power to make her throw caution to the wind and thrill to the slide of his strong hand journeying up and down her arms. Only Galen knew how to kiss her until her lips were swollen with passion. His hands circled her shoulders and the back of her neck. He made her long to feel all he could give and give all in return.

Galen wanted to seduce her into agreeing to be his love. He wanted his kisses on her throat and his hands moving so lazily over her hardening nipples to fog her mind so she'd succumb. He sought to convice her by slipping his tongue past the opened corners of her mouth. He thrilled to the sound of her breathless response. "Be mine . . ." he whispered.

Hester was already his. Her body responded as if he had fashioned it for and from his own hands. Her nipples ached from the sensations of his warm mouth closing over them through the thin, rough muslin of her gown. She arched her back as his play became more heated, and her sighs of pleasure rose softly on the night breeze.

"Be mine . . ."

Expert fingers undid the ribbons on her gown, then worshipping hands parted the open halves. The delicate kisses of tribute he placed on the swell of her dark breasts fired her blood. When he slid the gaping material away from one nipple and lowered his head, the bud hardened like an exotic jewel. Desire made her moan. Her head dropped back uselessly against his strong shoulder. Heat began to spiral through her, touching her in all the places that made her woman. He unveiled her other breast with the same reverence and treated it to its own lingering pleasuring.

Her virgin body, now attuned to the caresses and kisses of the man sometimes known as the Black Daniel, remembered their previous, passionate encounters and so, when his hand slid beneath her twisted gown, she offered no protest. The explorations were warm, knowing, dazzling, and in response she shuddered softly.

"Sweet, sweet Indigo . . ."

He kissed her then with all the possessiveness of a lover. Her responsiveness further fueled his already aching need to explore her lushness to the fullest, here and now, while she flowed like honey. However, he would not. Her virgin defenses would be no match for his skill in the art of lovemaking. He could take her over to the bed, ease his long-starved passion and bind her to him just as he desired. But Galen, who in his life had never turned away a willing female, wanted her decision to be made with a clear head. At this moment, with his fingers dallying so erotically between her thighs, Galen doubted she could recall her own name. He slid his hand over the points of her breasts then back down over the soft dark hair below her navel. He decided he should put a stop to this interlude; not even his legendary discipline would hold forever. But she was so open and so womanly ripe he couldn't stop touching her.

Galen leaned down and brushed his lips across her parted mouth. "I'm going to bring you to pleasure . . . and then we're going to stop . . ."

Hester heard his words through what seemed like a fog. She didn't know if she responded verbally or silently and didn't care. Her whole world was defined by the glowing pleasure.

As the intensity increased, her hips rose under the wanton tutelage of his golden hands. He eased her gown up over her hips and whispered, "Open for me, *petite* . . ."

Because it was Galen, she had no inhibitions. She parted her thighs to give him better access to the damp, moist place he'd primed so well, knowing she would be gifted with a sweet reward for complying—and she was. There in the moonlight, Galen brought her to a searing fulfillment that ended with her gasping his name.

As Galen watched her riding out the ultimate pleasure, lord knew he wanted to proceed to the next logical step, a move seconded by his roaring manhood, but he made a vow not to have her completely until she'd made peace with her own desires. He just hoped he didn't die in the interim.

He leaned down and kissed her warmly. She made such a provocative sight lying so disheveled across his lap under the light of the moon. The sight of her only served to rekindle his flames, so he very firmly stood her up and set her on her feet. He needed to leave her, but he was so hard, it would be a while before he could walk. He closed his eyes and thought about January snow, cold rivers, and freezing rain, hoping the images would rob his body of its Indigo-inspired heat.

"Galen, is something the matter?"

"Yes, I'm trying to rid myself of your sweet heat so I can get up and go home."

Hester blinked. "Oh."

He offered her a half smile.

"Will it take long?"

"Who knows? With you standing there with your breasts bared in the moonlight, I could be sitting here until dawn."

Hester smiled saucily, but didn't close her gown. She'd come to enjoy the glitter of desire she could bring to his eyes.

He grinned at her bold manner. "Now who's being incorrigible?"

"This is all your fault, Galen. I never knew being a shameless woman could be so—enjoyable."

"Then thank me by closing your gown before I pull you back down into my lap."

"That sounds like a very serious threat, Mr. Vachon."

"You're treading on thin ice, Miss Indigo."

Hester slowly did up the ribbons. "Does that meet with your approval?"

"No, I'd much rather have you nude whenever we're together, but I do have to go home. When you marry me, I'll have the luxury of pleasuring you however and whenever you desire."

Hester's knees went weak in reaction to the heated promise in both his words and his eyes.

He finished up by saying, "Now, go over there and tuck yourself in. You've had quite a day."

To his amazement she complied. Behind him he could

hear the groan of her old bed and the soft whisper of the bedding as she settled in. "Goodnight, Galen," she yawned.

"Good night, *petite*."

A few minutes later she was fast asleep. Sitting in the dark, Galen listened to her soft breathing and smiled.

Raymond LeVeq, seated across the breakfast table from his brooding childhood friend asked, "How long is this moping going to continue?"

Galen gave his old friend a stony look, then poured a bit more syrup in his coffee.

Raymond said blandly, "That is probably the fifth or sixth time you've sweetened that one cup."

Galen glanced down at the cup as if seeing it for the first time. The fact that Raymond was correct did not improve his mood. He looked over at Raymond and said, "You're enjoying this, aren't you?"

"Frankly, yes. I haven't seen you this moonsick over a woman since we were twelve and you were in love with—what was her name?"

"Daniella Grimette."

"Yes, you were obsessed with her pigtails if I'm not mistaken."

"This is a bit more serious than pigtails, LeVeq."

"It's still enjoyable."

"Such a friend you are. May you be as moonsick as this someday and may I be around to laugh with the same enjoyment."

LeVeq sipped his coffee.

Galen said, "I can't believe she keeps saying no."

"Not every woman is butter in your mouth, *mon ami*. Considering all the women you have lost to me, you should know this."

Galen ignored the boastful claim. "But I haven't lost her to you." After a moment, Galen vowed firmly, "I will have her."

"How?" LeVeq said smoothly, "We could always

shanghai her. In the morning the two of you could be on your way to Singapore or Cape Horn."

"Don't tempt me."

"Well I wouldn't worry about it, I believe Maxi and Racine are taking matters into their own hands. For some reason they think La Indigo should be with a dragon like you. Have you seen all the candles they've lit in the chapel?"

Galen shook his head no.

"Well, between Maxi's Haitian loas and Racine's Catholic saints, you won't have to worry much longer. Either their combined pleas will be answered or the house is going to burn to the ground."

Word came later that week that the Blackburns had indeed arrived safely in Canada. They'd taken up residence in the town of St. Catherine's, which already had an established fugitive community. They were far out of Shoe's dastardly reach.

Chapter 15

〜⟋⟍⟍⟋⟍〜

Galen dreamed of Hester. When he awakened he could not remember the specifics of the nocturnal visit, but the lingering sweet remnants left his manhood aching and hard with need.

As he lay in bed he willed himself to dwell upon less lusty thoughts but found it an impossible task. She'd become his world and that admission propelled him to leave his bed and go seek her out.

To his delight, she was outside the house hitching her mule to the wagon when his coach rolled up. The sight of her made the beautiful spring day seem even brighter. He tapped the crown of his cane on the carriage roof, signaling the driver to stop.

"Good morning, Miss Wyatt," Galen called, stepping out from the coach.

"Good morning," she replied, watching him walk her way. He had to be the most handsome man she'd ever seen. She forced herself to await his approach and not run to him so he could satisfy her growing hunger. "What brings you out so early?"

"You were in my dreams last night."

Heat flooded her as she looked up into his eyes. She quietly confessed, "I dream of you sometimes, too."

Her admission made his heart soar. "Women don't usually plague my dreams."

"It's usually the other way around, I'd wager."

He smiled. "Truthfully, yes."

"Then turnabout is only fair play. All the broken-hearted women you've left in your wake are probably elated knowing you are being put through your paces."

"You're undoubtedly correct, but my day is coming, *petite,* very soon."

"Is that a threat I hear?" she asked saucily.

"No, baby girl, a promise."

Hester's senses rippled with wanton anticipation as she held his sparkling gaze. He had the ability to make her pulse race with just a few words. "Other than your promises what brings you here?"

"I came to see if you'd make mud pies with me."

"Now?" she asked with a laugh.

"Or later, if you have an appointment."

"Foster is out of town but I was on my way to return some of his books. Yes, I'll make mud pies with you, afterwards."

She could see that her answer pleased him. It pleased her also because she'd decided not to fight the feelings he inspired within. She had no idea how long he would stay in Whittaker, but she planned on enjoying the time they had left.

Hester sat with the books in her lap while Galen sat on the seat opposite hers. They passed the short journey in silence, gazing at one another. No words were expressed because none were needed. They were both well aware of the desire arching between them like lightning.

The shack that doubled as the schoolhouse sat on land not very far from Bea Meldrum's place. Her son, Lemuel, had been working on the roof for the past few weeks, so Hester did not find the sight of his old wagon out front surprising.

"Looks like Lem Meldrum's here."

After the coach came to a halt, she gathered up the books from the dark velvet seat, then she and Galen walked through the weed-lined path to the door. She noticed Foster's wagon out back. She wondered if he'd returned from Detroit a few days early. He'd gone there to process the necessary documents the state required for opening a public school, and to attend a philosophy lecture. She knew he hated to be disturbed when he was working, so she had Galen hold the books. She opened the door quietly and peeked in. Sunlight streamed in, banishing the shadows. Hester stared in disbelief at what she saw: there in the middle of the floor, rutting with Lemuel Meldrum, was Foster's wife, Jenine!

If Hester noticed Galen come up behind her she gave no indication. His height gave him a clear view over her head and into the room. Unlike the stunned Hester, Jenine and her lover were making plenty of noise. Clothes were strewn everywhere.

Jenine and Lemuel were so intent upon their pleasure, a few moments passed before either glanced up. Jenine's eyes widened seeing the watchers at the door. "Hester?!" she croaked.

Hester wanted to run away as fast as her legs would allow, but her hurt and anger on Foster's behalf made her stay. "Hello Jenine. Lem."

Jenine had the decency to look embarrassed as she slid her body from Lem's. She turned her back and covered her nakedness with a thin wrapper she picked up from the floor. "Please, don't tell Foster, this will kill him."

Hester agreed that it probably would.

Lemuel dressed casually, and when he finished, he gave Jenine a smile, then left without a word.

"How could you do this?" Hester asked.

She shrugged. "A woman has needs."

Hester stared. "Isn't that why you take a husband?"

"What do you know about needs? Weren't you the woman willing to accept a celibate marriage?"

Hester felt embarrassment burn her cheeks. "Foster is a decent, caring man."

"Yes, he is, but he knows nothing outside of his philosophy books," she said, and she began to dress.

Hester looked to Galen. He raised an eyebrow but didn't speak.

Jenine glared at them both. "I saw you two the night of

the party. Your eyes followed her everywhere, Vachon, almost like a lover."

"And?" Galen asked coolly.

"Folks here won't be happy when they find out you've turned Saint Hester into your whore."

Hester took a step forward but Galen grabbed hold of her arm and made her stay put. "Are you threatening to start gossip, or intent on blackmail?"

Jenine shrugged. "I simply don't want my business spread around any more than the two of you. Keep my secrets and I'll keep yours."

Galen told Jenine plainly, "I don't care if you cuckold Foster with every man in the state, but lay your whorish tongue on Hester and I will destroy you."

The pure force of Galen's soft voice made Jenine visibly tremble a second before she gathered herself. Chin high, she replied, "As I said, you keep my secrets, and I'll keep yours."

Galen gave her a deadly little smile, then escorted Hester away.

Back in the carriage, Hester was so frustrated she wanted to scream her unvented rage. How dare that empty-headed little slut call her a whore.

Galen looked over at her and smiled. "Still mad?"

Her eyes flashed like a summer storm. "How can you be so calm?"

"I told her what she needed to know. She holds her own fate now."

"I had no idea she was so predatory. Foster will be devastated."

"I'm sure he will, but I would not interfere."

"Galen, he's a friend. He needs to know."

"Not from you, *petite*. Remember, he's in love with her. Who's to say he will believe you, especially when we know she will deny the tryst. If you value Foster's friendship, leave this alone. She'll show her true colors eventually."

"But—"

"Trust me on this."

Hester continued to have doubts, but decided to heed Galen's advice for now.

Before going to make mud pies, Hester wanted to return home and change clothing. Abigail stepped out onto the porch as Hester left the coach and came up the walk. Hester could see Abigail's surprised face. "Good morning, Gail."

"Good morning. Is that Galen Vachon's coach?"

"Yes," Hester answered on her way into the house.

Gail followed her inside. "Where are you going?"

Hester was halfway up the stairs to her room. "To make mud pies," she called back.

After changing and coming back downstairs, Hester faced a very confused Abigail, who asked, "Mud pies?"

"Mud pies."

"What on earth for?"

"Galen likes to make them."

"Galen?"

"Yes, Gail. Galen."

Hester could just about imagine what Gail thought of Hester addressing Vachon by his given name.

Gail asked, "So, are you going to tell me what is going on or will I have to pull it out of you like taffy?"

"There isn't much to tell really. I'm attracted to him and he seems very attracted to me."

Gail looked at her as if she'd grown a new head. "Galen Vachon?"

Hester nodded. "So if you want to take me to task do it quickly because he's waiting."

Gail grinned at the show of temper. "Hester Wyatt, is this really you?"

Hester looked down embarrassed. "Yes, it is. Gail, he makes me feel so—I can't explain it. Do you think I'm in love?"

"It's possible, my dear. But why did you look so glum when you came up the walk?"

Hester hesitated to tell Gail of Jenine's adultery, but she knew Gail could keep a confidence. Unburdening herself would also help her feel better.

Hester gave Gail a quick account of this morning's encounter. Gail was speechless.

Hester added, "Galen says I shouldn't tell Foster because Jenine will surely deny the whole thing and Foster won't believe me."

"He's probably correct. My goodness, what a mess. First you and Galen, and now this. Viola Welsh would probably put April on the block for the chance to pass this gossip around."

"I'm sure she would."

"Well, I'm not Viola. You go on and make your mud pies and have a good time. We'll talk about all this when you return."

Hester gave her friend a strong hug for her support then hurried out to join Galen.

They found a spot on the rock-strewn bank below the Folly. Unlike the last time, the hills surrounding the Huron River were no longer bare, but covered with the emerald-green coat of new spring leaves. In another month's time the foliage of the towering trees would be luxurious.

Hester was sitting and peering at the mud castle she'd just fashioned. "How does this look?"

Galen, who was lying on his back watching the changing patterns of the clouds against the blue sky, turned over and studied her creation. "Not bad for a novice."

"A novice? I suppose you can do better?"

"Raymond and I built better castles than that in our prams."

Feiging outrage, Hester threw a handful of mud his way. He rolled quickly out of the way and sprang to his feet. His playful growl propelled her up and sent her running and laughing down the bank. He caught her in less than three strides and scooped her up into his arms. When he began to tickle her, she screamed with laughter.

Their smiling eyes mirrored their joy.

He told her, "We need to do this more often. I enjoy hearing you laugh."

Hester said, "I enjoy you."

He carried her back to their spot then set out the
hamper of lunch he'd brought along. They rinsed the mud
from their hands in the clear chilly water of the river then
sat down to eat. The chicken sandwiches and pound cake
were more than enough to satisfy Hester's hunger. She
washed it down with cold, clear water, then laid back to
help Galen watch the sky. "Can I ask you a question?"

"Certainly."

"Lem and Jenine—what they were doing—was that
the normal way a man joins with a woman?"

When she turned to look at him, her eyes were so
innocent, Galen could not reply for a moment, then said,
"Yes."

She looked away.

"Why do you ask?"

"Curious, I guess." The images of Jenine and Lemuel
had haunted her all day. Hester could not escape the
memory of Jenine's tortured face as Lem coupled with
her. Did the joining cause that much pain? "Is it
painful?"

Galen looked a bit confused by the question so she
tried to be clearer. "I—well Jenine's face, she looked to
be in pain."

Galen wanted to pull her close. Her innocence amazed
him at times. "There is pain sometimes if it is a woman's
first time, but with the proper lover there is no hurting
after that."

"Are you a proper lover?"

He said gently, "I consider myself that, yes."

"Does a man have pain that first time, too?"

"Not usually, but it does become painful for a man if
he's around a woman who arouses him and there is no
resolution."

"Not during?"

"Not during."

A few moments of silence passed as he watched her
thinking. *"Petite?"*

She met his eyes.

"Was that your first time seeing a man and woman joined?"

"Yes."

He supposed to the uninitiated the face of a person making love could appear to be pain-filled, but it was a sweet pain, and he didn't know if he could explain it in a way that could be understood.

"So Jenine wasn't in pain?"

"No, *ma coeur,* she was not . . ."

The endearment seared her like a flame. She reached out and gently stroked his face. He placed his hand atop hers, savoring its small indigo warmth. He then touched his lips to the palm. "Why the curiosity?"

"Because that is the next step for us, is it not?"

"You aren't supposed to ask that question."

"Why not?"

"Because I will have to answer and I cannot lie."

"Suppose it is what I wish also?"

He stilled a moment and scanned her face. "Under normal circumstances I'd shout hallelujah, but are you certain you know what that means?"

"No, not really, but it is my decision to make."

"Of course, but *petite*—"

She confessed with all honesty, "Galen I have never known a man like you and I probably never will again. After the debacle with Foster, I doubt I will wed anyone. You are my only chance of realizing what it means to throw caution to the wind. I am the woman who almost agreed to a celibate marriage as Jenine so tactfully pointed out, but you made me see how joyless that would have been. You made me see there is more to life. I'll go back to being Saint Hester after you're gone."

"I don't envision life after leaving you, Indigo."

"The sentiment is appreciated, but I simply want to enjoy our time together to the fullest."

"Speaking as a man, no man in his right mind would argue with the logic."

She stroked his face, and said softly, "Then don't."

"I won't," he assured her, "but I'm experienced

enough to say you will probably change your mind later after you return home, and I suppose I can accept that."

He paused a moment to run his gaze over her beautiful features. "I want you like no other woman before, Miss Hester Wyatt, but I'll not force you, nor will I press. You are to let me know if and when you are ready."

"Fair enough."

When the day ended they parted in the carriage with lingering kisses.

Hester shared dinner and talk with Abigail over the cuckolding of poor Foster, and Hester's own relationship with Galen.

"You don't think less of me, do you?" Hester asked.

Abigail pushed aside her plate. "The question should be, do you think less of yourself?"

"No."

"Then my opinion shouldn't matter."

"But do you?"

"Are you happy?"

"More than I've ever been in my life."

"Then I'm happy. He may break your heart though," Abigail added sagely.

"I know."

The next morning, Hester drove Abigail to the train depot in Ann Arbor. Abigail planned on spending the next month or so with her family on the western side of the state. Gail made the trek every spring and this year would be no exception. She and Hester shared a brief, fierce hug, then Gail got on the train.

Hester was just about to turn the mule back out onto the road for the return drive home when she spied a knot of people standing near the far end of the station. One of the men she recognized as Branton Hubble, the others were unknown. She became curious as a few more people drifted over to the gathering. She set the brake and went to investigate.

As Hester walked up she could hear Branton saying, "You don't have to stay with him, miss."

Hester made her way to his side. Upon seeing her, he sighed happily. "I'm real glad to see you. Talk to her, see if you can convince her she's free to leave."

The light-skinned young woman in question was tightly holding the hands of two little girls. The handsome man staring angrily was her master. It seemed the woman had approached Branton after getting off the train and asked him to help her to freedom, but when the master appeared a few moments later, fear and uncertainty were making her doubt the decision.

Hester approached her and said, "My name is Hester, I'm a friend of Branton. Are these your daughters?"

The woman smiled a bit and nodded her head.

Hester smiled down at the little ones. "What are their names?"

"This is Bess, and that's Naomi."

"They're beautiful," Hester replied as she knelt down to stroke each soft brown cheek.

Hester asked the young mother, "What's your name?"

"Mary."

"Does this man own you, Mary?"

The woman nodded her head.

Hester looked to the man. "Do you own them, sir?"

"Yes."

Hester told Mary, "By the laws of the state of Michigan you became free the moment you arrived. If you want to be free, the choice is yours."

The owner interrupted. "She knows all about the law, she doesn't want to be free. Look at her, you can see by her clothing that I treat her well, why would she want to be a destitute and penniless fugitive?"

He came over and stood before Mary and implored her in an emotion-filled voice, "Think of what you're throwing away. How are you going to feed the girls, where are you going to go? I told you I'd free you in a few years, and I'm going to keep my promise."

"No you won't," Mary whispered.

Their eyes held. He slowly placed a finger against her cheek and stroked it with the tenderness of a lover.

Mary's lids closed and a tear slid down to meet the caress. His voice was soft. "But I will, I will. Don't leave me, Mary . . . please . . ."

"You sold my sons," she told him, her voice choked with pain and grief. "The children of my flesh, the children of your flesh, and you sold them like they were nothing more than pigs at the trough."

"Darling, I'm sorry. That was business, I explained that."

"Business?! Will you sell the girls for business?" she demanded through her tears. "Would you sell your daughters too?!"

He wouldn't or couldn't answer.

"I will hate you for the rest of my life for what you've done. May the Lord have mercy upon your soul." She turned to Hester and said firmly. "The girls and I are ready, Miss Hester."

Branton helped with the luggage and Hester led Mary and her girls to the wagon. Hester saw Ezra Shoe leaning against the wall of the depot, watching.

Branton saw him too. "Wait for me and I'll follow you back to Whittaker."

She nodded.

It took only moments for Branton to return with his own wagon. As the two vehicles pulled off, Hester glanced back at Shoe. He smiled at her, then touched his hat.

When they reached Whittaker, Branton thought it wise for Mary and her daughters to move on right away. Hester agreed, especially with Shoe lurking about.

Branton drove them on to Detroit personally. From there he'd make arrangements for the fugitive family to be spirited across the river and into Canada.

Hester entered her house tired but glad she'd been able to win the small skirmish for freedom. She'd heard many poignant tales during her years on the Road, but today's incident pulled at her heart. Had Mary really loved her master? He seemed to harbor very strong feelings for her, yet he evidently lacked the ability to see the world through her eyes. Her sons had been her children, but to him they'd been chattel. How many more lives would slavery destroy before it could be put to death? There were already thousands of casualties, and every day the numbers rose.

After washing up and donning one of Galen's beautiful nightgowns from the chest, Hester sat in her rocker. The windows had been thrown open to let in the early evening breeze and she let the flow rid her of the weariness brought on by the past few days. She thought of Foster and Jenine, and the heartbreak her friend was destined to experience because of his wife's adultery; she thought back on poor Mary and the drama at the depot, but most of Hester's thoughts centered on Galen. Love seemed to have brought only sorrow to those around her, but her love for Galen brought nothing but joy. His kisses had become the balm for all that ailed her, and she realized she could use some of that balm now. She walked to her window and looked out over the night. She wondered if he were at home and what he was doing. She decided to put her newly born recklessness into action and go see. She hadn't seen him all day and she missed him.

She took a moment to run down to the kitchen and dab herself strategically with vanilla, then covered her nightgown with her most voluminous cape and headed out the door.

Maxi answered the Folly's door. "*Chiquita?* What are you doing about so late?"

"Is Mr. Vachon in?"

"He's already turned in for the night."

Hester glanced wistfully up the grand staircase. "I see," then asked quietly, "Would you escort me to him anyway?"

Maxi met Hester's eyes, and then asked, "Shall I take your cape?"

Hester thought about the nightgown underneath the cape and stammered, "Um-no. I'll keep it with me."

"This way then."

Hester followed Maxi up the stairs and through the upper floors of the house. Everywhere Hester looked she saw beautiful paintings, fine furnishings, and expensive statues. Maxi pulled open a set of ornately carved double doors, then stepped aside. "His rooms are through the door to your right."

"Thank you," Hester whispered.

Maxi closed the double doors and left Hester alone. Hester braced herself then slowly walked to Galen's door.

She had to knock twice before she heard him call enter.

Inside, the room was dark. It took her eyes a moment to adjust to the dimness, and then a soft rustling sound at her right drew her attention.

"What is it, Max?" he called sleepily.

Hester answered softly, "It's me, Galen."

For a moment there was only silence and then, "*Petite?* What—"

She heard a match strike, then saw the faint flame of a lamp. A beat later, a soft light bathed the shadows. From beneath the large canopy atop his bed he stared at her with confused eyes. He slowly dragged the bedding across his lap as he sat up. "Has something happened?"

Hester shook her head, no. "No. I—simply wanted to see you."

He stayed silent so long, Hester began to question the soundness of being a reckless woman. She asked, "Should I not have come?"

Galen wondered if he were dreaming, or if this were simply a delusion brought on by all the cognac he consumed this evening in an effort to drown his need for her. It certainly didn't feel like a dream and the sight of her standing in the shadows had rendered him undeniably sober. "No, I'm glad you came," he managed to say.

Hester stood shyly in the center of the room.

Galen asked, "Should I come to you or are you going to come to me?"

She felt very nervous all of a sudden as the uncertainty of why she'd come to see him tonight coupled itself with

her desire for him. "I'll come to you," she quietly
replied.

First though, she had to remove her cape. She did so
slowly, then let it slip soundlessly from her shoulders to
pool at her feet.

The fire that leapt to his eyes made her feel powerful,
sensual.

This damn well better not be a dream, Galen thought
to himself. The sight of her standing there so fetchingly
made his manhood throb like a Yoruban drum. As she
walked slowly toward him, Galen found it harder and
harder to breathe. He cleared his throat. Through the
haze of the thin gown he could see the points of her
sweet dark breasts as the fabric swayed in sultry motion.
His limbs trembled in anticipation. When she stopped
beside the bed, Galen's blood began to pound in his ears.

"Lovely gown, *petite* . . ."

"Thank you, the man who gave it to me has exquisite
taste."

"Are you just going to stand there?" he asked huskily.

"I'm waiting for an invitation." Her eyes were as
heated as her words.

"Then come to me."

As soon as she sat on the bed, he covered her with the
thin blanket and cradled her against his body. She
jumped, startled by the warm press of his nakedness.
"You're not wearing anything."

His hand slid over the satin smoothness of her back,
bared by the gown. "It is how I sleep, *ma coeur*. You'll
get used to it." He placed a kiss on her shoulder and felt
her tremble in soft response. It pleased him to have her
near. He continued to make slow, wide circles over her
back. When she purred in contentment, he smiled. "Do
you like that?"

In response she slid closer. She liked the way he
touched her, as if she were made of silk, as if her arms
were the rarest of black porcelain and her back unburn-
ished gold. She raised up and kissed his mouth. He

placed a gentle hand behind her head and returned her
kiss with a delicious, languid intensity that sent heat
surging through every fiber of her being.

"Thank you for coming. Boldness becomes you,
Indigo . . ."

"And who taught me to be forward?"

They kissed one another passionately for a few silent
moments, then parted reluctantly.

She placed her hand against his handsome face. "I
missed not seeing you today."

Galen felt his desire leap another notch at her confession. He searched her small face, saw the need in her
eyes, and replied softly, "Truth be told, I've been waiting
for you to come to me all day . . ."

He kissed the sweetness of her mouth and felt the tiny
sensations brought on by his ardor. The initial stiffness
of her posture melted as she relaxed against him sighing,
pressing herself closer to his hard chest and the spell
woven by his lips.

His ragged breathing and bright eyes matched her
own. He couldn't ever remember wanting a woman as
much as he did Hester right now. The male in him
wanted to ease himself into her heat and fill her until the
night echoed with her pleasuring, her virginity be
damned. But the man in him had vowed not to pressure
her. "If you don't want all I have to give, you should say
so now . . ."

He spoke the words hotly against her mouth and
she kissed every movement his lips made. "I want it,
Galen . . . all there is."

His big golden hand slid over the silk nightgown
gracing her legs and thighs. "You should always be
gowned in silk," he whispered. "Your gowns should be
soft as your skin . . ."

He kissed the warmth of her neck while opening the
tiny ribbons closing the lace-edged bodice. When it was
fully removed he said, "Gowns as soft as this . . ."

His lips brushed the bare skin below her neck and
Hester sucked in her breath. She trembled as he moved

lower, teasing the tender warmth between her breasts then the smooth plane above. His tongue slid over the inside curve when she arched her back. She'd grown up an untouched woman raised by an untouched, maiden aunt. Until she met Galen, she had no idea being with a man held such power, such majesty. The idea that she'd actually sought him out was unbelievable, but she hadn't come this far to back out now. She would not deny herself this one, beautiful night.

Galen traced her lips and when they parted he kissed her slowly, gently, wanting this moment to last an eternity. His lips teased the warmth of her neck, the shell of her ear. He'd never initiated a virgin before; all the women in his past were experienced in the sensual arts and had lost their virginity long before he entered their lives, but Hester was different. Only he had ever cupped her opulent breasts and thumbed the nipples until they hardened like berries. He was the only man to bring those same nipples to his mouth, and hear her soft intakes of breath. She'd come to him tonight to offer her most precious gift. Galen planned to express his gratitude by paying her prolonged, erotic tribute.

His mouth upon her breasts filled Hester with such soaring emotions she couldn't lie still. Her hips were rising in reaction. His hands, moving so possessively over her thighs, only increased her feverish state.

Galen found her more lushly delicate than he could have ever imagined. Her skin beneath his hands, soft as an angel's, drew him to sample her lingeringly. Her responses, virginal yet uninhibited, added to his own driving need. He touched his lips to her mouth, and when it parted in reply he slid his tongue over the sensitive corners. He bit her lip gently, and felt her damp nipples tighten like pebbles beneath his hand.

Her back arched as she strained for more. Galen lovingly and wantonly answered her silent plea. He ran strong hands down the taut expanse of her ribs and waist. Galen had learned the art of pleasure from the hands of the world's most celebrated courtesans, and he'd learned his lessons well. He knew where to touch her and where to caress. He knew her virgin body had never been explored to the fullest so he played her gently, arousing her with vibrant touches of his hands and lips, coaxing her to let him enjoy her so she would enjoy in return.

When his lips brushed her navel, Hester groaned in the half lit silence. He repeated the delicate gesture against the small whorl, then grazed his hand over the soft, dark garden of her woman's hair. Hester reached out to touch him, wanting to give back some of the fire he'd stoked within her, but he brought her hands to his lips, saying, "Just lie back, *petite*. Tonight, it will all be for you . . ."

And he kept his word. Every caress brought a leap of fire. Every touch made her soar. His hands moving up and down her thighs made them part with erotic innocence. He accepted her invitation and slid his fingers over the damp offering.

"Oh . . ." she whispered.

He leaned down and kissed her mouth. "Oh, what . . . ?"

But she couldn't speak. His hands were too knowing, the licks against her navel too exciting. When he parted her wantonly then kissed her heatedly, her hips came up off the bed.

He gently brought her back. "Don't run away yet *petite* . . . the fun's just beginning . . ."

Her virgin body was no match for his tender expertise. Hester wanted to be touched by his powerful magic. The need for completion tore through her like a white-hot bolt of lightning, until she exploded in the age-old bearing of passion.

He brought her back to herself with kisses and touches which left her shimmering like stars. She finally opened her eyes and looked up at the man smiling down. "You are a very proper lover indeed, Galen Vachon."

"My pleasure, La Indigo. Now . . . are you ready . . . ?"

She nodded. Unable to resist, she ran her hand over

the strength in his golden arm. How would she learn to live without him?

But her thoughts soon faded. It began again, the passionate touches, the dallying kisses, the heat. She moaned and twisted in response as he whispered words of love in French, and promised her pleasure in Cuban Castilian. While the strokes of his long-boned fingers teased her into the rhythm of desire, his lips once again teased her breasts in sweet, fevered counterpoint.

To ready her for his possession, Galen slid a finger into her virgin cove. She tightened around him and he shuddered. His own pleasure was put off a moment so he could enjoy the sight of her. He eased his fingers out once more, touching, circling. Then, while she lay, dazed, pulsing, and keening softly, he eased his manhood into her damp heat.

Hester stiffened.

"We'll go slow," he promised grazing his mouth across her lips. "It will hurt just once."

And it did. So much so, tears filled her eyes. He kissed them away, soothing her, trying not to add more pain. For a moment he held there until he felt her relax a bit around him. When she did, he began to stroke her with the gentlest strokes he could manage, forcing himself to maintain a slow pace. Only after he felt certain she would enjoy their lovemaking did he let himself begin again in earnest.

As the pain began to subside, Hester's body began to respond. Soon his strokes became more rhythmic, more enticing. Soon she was once again being heated from within. The rhythm increased, becoming possessive, deeper. She let her body have its head, let it be taught the ways of man and woman, and when the lesson ended in another bolt of heat, Hester screamed his name.

Galen couldn't hold himself back any longer. He knew he should withdraw so as not to compromise her future, but she felt so good around him, so tight, just the thought hurled him into an uncontrollable, shattering release. The world exploded, his hands gripped her hips, and he filled the silence with the sound of his golden roar.

At dawn, Hester lay in the bed watching the soft light fill the room while Galen slept unawares beside her. Her thoughts drifted back to last night. Never in her life had she dreamed such pleasure possible. She now understood the erotic lure of passion. Under Galen's tender tutelage, she'd fully unleashed the woman inside, but that woman now lay smothered beneath the weight of reality.

She and Galen could never be married. If he were truly a member of the elite he could not publicly claim an ex-slave woman with indigo hands as his wife. Any relationship they shared could not advance beyond the role of protector and mistress, and Hester had too much respect for herself to be relegated to such a life. She didn't regret the moments spent with Galen; the memories would linger to the grave, but now that she'd been gifted with the knowledge of passion and desire, would her work on the Road and with the church be enough to compensate for waking up alone, once he left her life?

She had no idea he was awake until she heard him say quietly, "You know you'll have to marry me now."

Silence.

Galen reached over and stroked her cheek. "No reply?"

Hester's eyes closed from the sweetness flowing from his touch.

"Say, yes, *petite*."

Hester hesitated a moment, then whispered, "I can't, Galen."

Galen Vachon had never been turned down by a woman before in his life, and he didn't know whether to be angry or to laugh. "Why won't you marry me?"

"Your family will not be pleased to have me as your wife."

"My family doesn't matter."

"It does to me," she confessed softly.

He scooted closer so he could pull her into the shelter of his arms. She felt the kiss he placed atop her hair and savored the warmth and safe feelings that flowed from being held close. "Galen, last night I experienced the most powerful emotions I've ever known."

"*Ma coeur,* what you gave me last night was a gift for a husband. I want you to be my wife."

"But for how long? Look at my hands. Are these the hands you want presiding over your household? Are these the hands you want presented to your friends and family?"

"Yes."

"I don't believe you," she said softly.

"Believe that I don't dally with virgins and then turn my back on them."

"See, Galen, for you it's duty."

"That isn't what I meant."

The air had become heated with tension. Hester sought to soothe the waters. "Let's not argue, please?"

She placed her palm against his tightened jaw and he covered her hand with his own. "Agreed."

Her eyes were serious as she met his. "Thank you for last night."

He turned her palm and kissed the center. "It is you who's owed thanks."

She could sense herself succumbing. "I—should get home."

Galen didn't want her to ever leave his side. "You will be marrying me, *petite.*"

Hester slowly slid from the bed and began a search for her cape. She refused to dwell on his last statement because she saw no future in it.

His voice came to her soft as the light in the room. "Did you hear me?"

She slipped back into her blouse. "I heard you."

"What if there's a child?"

She stared, confused.

"What we did last night could result in a child."

The reality of that statement made her pause. Granted, she knew coupling sometimes produced babies, but . . . "Surely, that one time—"

"Sometimes, once is all it takes."

"Are you certain?"

He nodded.

Hester was overwhelmed by this information, but she refused to dwell on it. She finished dressing.

"So what if there is a child?"

She faced him and replied honestly, "I don't know."

"If you wait a moment, I'll see you home."

She shook her head. "No."

Galen wanted to drag her into his arms and soothe her fears and worries, but he knew how proud she was. He also knew that if last night's lovemaking did result in a child, all her excuses for not wanting to marry would be moot. He'd make her marry him, and seek her forgiveness afterwards.

"Will you have dinner here with me tonight?"

Hester could only shake her head no. "I must go."

"Petite—"

"Goodbye, Galen."

She slipped from the room and was gone.

Back home, Hester took the time to wash away the remnants of the night's lovemaking, then changed clothes and headed over to see Bea Meldrum.

Bea met her at the door. "Come on in. What brings you out on such a gray morning?"

Hester took a seat at Bea's kitchen table and said, "Bea, I want to know about woman things."

Bea looked over her coffee cup at Hester. "What type of woman things?"

"Coupling, babies—those kinds of woman things. Aunt Katherine's upbringing has left me dreadfully ignorant."

Bea cocked her head at Hester a moment, but complied. For the balance of the morning, Hester asked questions and Bea answered. Some of Bea's explanations were so blunt, they made heat fan Hester's cheeks, but in the end, Hester had a firmer knowledge of the things she needed to know.

Chapter 16

❧᷂᷂᷂᷂᷂᷂᷂᷂᷂᷂᷂᷂᷂

Hester was surprised to find Foster at her door early the next morning. He appeared to be quite upset.

"Has something happened?" she asked as he came in.

"Where were you last evening?" he asked pointedly.

"Excuse me?"

"I came by last evening to talk to you. You weren't here."

Hester did not feel bound to inform him of her whereabouts so she asked instead, "What did you wish to discuss?"

He asked bluntly, "Did you and Vachon threaten Jenine?"

Hester stilled. "What?"

"She says she caught you two fornicating in the school and you threatened to harm her if she told anyone."

"She said what?!"

"You heard me," he snapped angrily. "Hester, how could you let Vachon turn you into a whore?"

Hester's eyes widened. "Foster—"

"Hester, Janine doesn't have a mean bone in her body. The two of you have her absolutely terrified."

"Did she say why Galen threatened her?"

"I already told you. Because you didn't want anyone to know about your illicit acts."

"That isn't the truth."

"Why would she lie?"

Hester held onto her patience and replied, "I don't know, Foster, why would Jenine lie?"

"So, now you are calling my wife a liar?"

"I haven't called her anything, Foster, at least not yet."

He took offense. "And to think I was going to marry you."

"Makes one shudder, doesn't it?"

"You stand there and mock me? I thought we were friends."

"So did I Foster, but now, I want you to leave."

"Hester, I will not let you slander my Jenine."

"Out of my house, Foster. Now!"

He stormed to the door. "This is not the end, Hester Wyatt."

"I'm sure you're right."

She slammed her door so hard the china shook inside the highboys.

The day got even stranger as Hester went into Ypsilanti. She walked into Kate Bell's boarding house to purchase the latest copy of the *Liberator* only to have the women inside surround her excitedly.

Olympia asked, "Hester is it true you and Vachon are to be married?"

Kate called out from behind a customer's head. "It's always the quiet ones you have to watch. Congratulations, Hester. He's a fine-looking man!"

Hester found herself inundated with questions concerning wedding dates, wedding dresses, and offers to cater the affair. One woman even volunteered her daughter as the ceremony's soloist. Hester wanted to laugh at all the uproar but she was too appalled. "Quiet!" she shouted.

Everyone froze.

Hester said, "Thank you. Galen Vachon and I are not marrying as far as I know. Who says I am?"

"Viola Welsh," someone confessed weakly.

"Viola Welsh?" Hester exclaimed. "Everyone in here knows that woman can't be trusted. Who'd she hear this from, did she say?"

No one knew.

"But we saw Vachon watching you the night of the party!"

A chorus of female voices supported that position.

"That doesn't mean we are going to marry."

"If he looked at me in that fashion I'd marry him before the sun set," someone piped up.

Laughter rang out, followed by another chorus of agreement.

Hester shook her head.

Kate said with disappointment, "We thought you were going to give us something to talk about all summer, Hester. Guess not, huh?"

"Nope, Kate, sorry."

A chorus of groans went up.

Hester laughed, purchased her paper, and left.

But by the time Hester returned to her home late that afternoon, she found no humor in the visit she'd received from Foster. Did he actually believe she would let anyone turn her into a whore? Galen had never treated her with anything other than tender respect. If he were ever to trample on her dignity she doubted she would ever see him again. Yet, Foster apparently believed his wife's falsehoods just as Galen predicted. And how did Viola Welsh enter into this? The gossip lacked the viciousness which might point to Jenine as Viola's original source. So who had it been? Foster? She doubted that too. He and Viola had never gotten along. She tossed the problem over in her mind again and again but came away with nothing except these facts: Foster had termed her Galen's whore and her neighbors were hoping she'd become his wife.

Bea stopped by that evening to bring over some eggs and to share a few words of advice. "You've heard the rumors about you and Vachon?"

Hester replied sarcastically. "Which rumor? The one which claims I'm a whore, or the one which claims I'm to marry?"

"So you have heard them?"

"Yes."

Bea asked, "Is Vachon the reason you had all the questions the other morning?"

Hester nodded tightly.

Bea sighed. "Hester I've known you since you first came north and now with Katherine gone I feel responsible for you. I hope you haven't set your cap for Vachon. A man like him doesn't marry women like you and me."

Hester didn't tell Bea that she harbored the same feelings. "I know, Bea. I'm not foolish enough to chase smoke."

Bea smiled. "Good girl. Now don't let the gossips worry you. It will all die down soon enough."

As Bea headed out to her wagon, Hester wanted to stop her to talk about Lem, but decided she wouldn't; there was already enough intrigue swirling around Whittaker. Hester didn't want to add to it.

The following day, Andre Renaud stopped by to deliver a note from his employer. Galen wrote that he was leaving town on Black Daniel business and would return in a few days. He signed it *Love, Galen.*

That he had taken the time to write her of his plans made her heart sing, however, she began to miss him almost immediately.

Three days passed without further word. She did not know he had returned until Raymond LeVeq knocked at her door one morning.

The sight of LeVeq made Hester wonder if something had happened to Galen. "Is he hurt?"

Raymond chuckled, "No, I've come to take you to him. Maxi won't let him leave the house."

"Why not, is he ill?"

"No, he's angry."

"At whom? Not me, I hope."

"No, never you. Foster Quint."

Hester sighed. "What has Foster done now?"

"I'll leave that for Galeno to explain. Come, we must hurry before the dragon's fiery roar burns down the house."

It seemed Foster had confronted Galen about the alleged threats against Jenine. Galen tried to calm Foster down, but when Foster refused to see reason, Galen had not minced words. He told Foster just why he'd threatened Jenine and who had really been fornicating in the schoolhouse. Foster became so outraged he demanded satisfaction and instructed Galen to call his seconds. Galen, of course, laughed, which only enraged Foster more, but when Foster began to accuse Galen of dragging Hester's reputation into the street, and vowing to tell the whole county about the scandalous goings on, Galen had Raymond put him out before he became violent.

Hester, sitting in Galen's study hearing this, asked, "Foster challenged you to a duel?"

"Yes, he did. Does he know I could kill him with my eyes blindfolded? I will not let anyone brand you a whore and live. Marry me, Hester."

For a moment she almost said yes, but then she remembered the talk she'd had with Bea, and Bea's voice echoed in her head . . . *Men like him don't marry women like you and me. . . .*

Hester slowly shook her head.

Galen told her. "You are carrying my child—"

"You don't know that for sure."

Galen held onto his temper. "You are the contrariest woman I have ever met, Hester Wyatt. I will not have my child raised without a father."

"What if I marry you and there is no child? What then? What happens when you are bound for life to a purple-handed ex–slave woman you can't even present in public?"

"Would you stop using that as an excuse? You're afraid, Hester. Afraid that loving me is going to turn you into a woman who won't know her own mind."

She looked away, but he kept on, "You're afraid you're going to end up like your father, but think how deeply your father must have loved your mother to give over his very existence. He loved her enough not to care that he had no freedom. Loved her enough to turn his back on the world and all he owned. That took strength, Hester Wyatt, a strength you'll never know, all because you're afraid to trust your heart."

Hester raised her chin but said nothing.

"This is how much I love you, Indigo. By next week this time, you are going to be my wife, whether you care to be or not."

"You can't force me to marry you Galen."

Galen didn't argue. "Will you be in church on Sunday?"

She nodded.

"Good. So will I."

Hester stood. His eyes were sparkling with a determination that made her weak.

"You will be mine . . . " he whispered. "And the saints help us both."

That night, Hester lay in bed wondering how on earth Galen planned on gaining her hand. She could not fathom how he would accomplish it without her consent, but the prospects that he might indeed get his way made her toss and turn all night. In the morning, she awakened restless, tired, and still unable to glean Galen's scheme.

At church on Sunday, two days later, Hester parked her mule and wagon in the field amongst the vehicles and animals of the other parishioners. She noticed that some folks who usually greeted her with a smile and a friendly wave purposefully avoided her eyes. She could only assume that Foster had carried through with his threats. Stung by the cuts, she swallowed the humiliation and went on as if she hadn't been affected.

Hester went to a pew and sat. She tried not to show her upset feelings to the rest of the congregation, but it was hard to do when she could hear all the whispering going on behind her back and in the pews around her.

Foster entered the church with Jenine a few moments later, and the whispers became louder. It was the first time Hester had seen Jenine since the day at the school. Jenine pointedly avoided Hester's eyes. Foster, on the

other hand, offered Hester a angry nod, then took his
seat beside Jenine in a pew up front.

Hester was glad to see Bea come in and take a seat at
her side. They were soon joined by Kate Bell and her
husband, Harold, and Olympia and her aged mother,
Augusta.

No sooner had they all settled in when Galen Vachon
entered the sanctuary alone. The whispers became fast
and furious and everyone in the church turned to stare,
including Hester. He didn't acknowledge any of the
curious parishoners. He simply took a seat across the
aisle from where Hester sat with her friends.

Bea and the others sent Hester questioning looks but
she took her cue from Galen and refused to acknowledge
them. As the organist began the play, she stood with the
rest of the congregation and began to sing the processional.

Hester noted that Galen was as impeccably dressed as
always. In his all-black attire, he was by far the hand-
somest man in the county. Even though she and Galen
had not parted amicably the last time they were together, she couldn't keep her eyes from straying to his golden
good looks, and neither could any of the other female
churchgoers. Not even Jenine appeared immune. She
kept turning around to view him until Foster's increasingly hostile glares made her train her eyes on the front
of the church. As the last notes of the processional faded
away, everyone sat back down.

The reverend had always been a good friend to the
cause of freedom and to the people in the community,
but he viewed life with a strict morality dictated by the
times and by his own interpretation of the Word. He
stepped up to the pulpit and proceeded to give a rafter-
rattling sermon denouncing the sins of the flesh. He
spoke of deception and Satan, temptation and Adam
and Eve. He invoked the names of biblical whores and
preached on how they all got their just rewards. Hester
sat still as a post, caught between humiliation and fury.
Foster, on the other hand, kept making an obvious show

of turning around and looking Hester's way to judge her reaction. She met his eyes stonily.

Galen had had enough. He looked around the church, furious that these provincials dared to vilify the woman he loved. He wouldn't allow her to be dragged through the mud simply because she'd become his life. His vast wealth and influence would shield her from the consequences of the gossip that would result from what he was about to do. He just hoped she would see the right in his actions and eventually forgive him someday.

When Galen stood up in the middle of Reverend Adams's sermon, the reverend's voice faltered and then silenced. Hester's heart began to pound and she took in a deep breath to steady herself. The church was absolutely still.

Galen spoke into the charged silence. "Reverend, since we all know for whom this fire and brimstone is intended, why don't you just prepare to conduct a wedding?"

Shock widened Hester's eyes and the congregation began to buzz excitedly.

Galen turned to Hester, then back to the reverend, who looked as stunned as everyone else. "There are rumors that Hester Wyatt is my whore. You are wrong. It is my wife I wish for her to be."

Over the audible shock that greeted his declaration, he directed his blazing gaze at Foster, who had the sense to turn back around.

"Hester Wyatt is my love . . . my heart."

He then turned to Hester. With his eyes firmly fixed on her own he began to recite in a low, rich voice, "Thou hast ravished my heart, my sister, my spouse . . . thou hast ravished my heart . . . Until the day break, and the shadows flee away, I will get me to the mountain of myrrh, and to the hill of frankincense . . ."

Hester could hear soft gasps behind her but she could not move.

"Thy lips, O my spouse, drop as the honeycomb: honey and milk are under thy tongue . . . Thy navel is like a round goblet which wanteth not liquor . . . The joints of your thighs are like jewels . . ."

Each and every word had been filled with heat and passion. Hester's eyes slid closed. Such recitations did not belong in church, even if Galen was quoting chapters four and seven of the Song of Solomon. Hester's senses felt stroked, caressed. She wondered if the great African queen Sheba had been as moved when Solomon spoke these words declaring his love?

Galen appeared to be waiting for her to make some type of response, but Hester couldn't even breathe; she'd never been involved in anything as remotely unbelievable as this, and neither had anyone else in the church.

The reverend heightened the tension when he called, "Hester Wyatt, step up to the altar please."

She had no doubts what the gossips would say if she turned him down, their tongues would tear her to shreds. Even if she said yes, today's events would still be told up and down the Road from Whittaker to Chicago and back.

The Reverend Adams called her again. She had no other recourse but to stand. Forcing herself to ignore everything and everyone around her, Hester moved on shaky legs out into the aisle.

Up at the altar, Galen turned to her and smiled and, unable to help herself, she smiled in reply. She crooked a finger and beckoned him down so she could speak into his ear. She whispered, "I'm going to get you for this . . ."

He grinned.

Hester stood next to Galen and let herself be made his wife. When the brief ceremony ended, everyone applauded. Galen kissed her lightly on her brow to seal the union, then took her hand and led her from the church.

Inside his carriage, Hester sat silently. Galen had given the gossips something to talk about for decades to come. She could still feel his words vibrating over her senses as he recited the words of Solomon.

She had to admit a part of her was fairly ecstatic over

the union; she did love Galen after all, but she found great fault with his method. How dare he force this upon her. He'd gotten his way again, and whether he thought her afraid to love him or not, she still had nothing to offer a man like himself, no wealth, no status. She brought only her slave past and a fervor to end slavery. She doubted his social set would consider either sterling attributes.

She glanced his way and found his gaze waiting. "I doubt the reverend will ever use that passage again."

Galen chuckled. "I thought he was going to swallow his tongue."

Hester held his smiling gaze, then quietly confessed, "I have never been so moved."

He inclined his head, feeling the emotions he had for her grow even stronger. He whispered, "You are my heart."

His response made her soar, but she felt compelled to ask, "But couldn't you have declared it in a less dramatic fashion?"

He shrugged his wide shoulders. "You know I never do anything by half, it isn't in my nature, besides, you kept saying no."

"An answer you've never been able to accept."

"No, not when it's something I desire."

In his eyes she saw shimmering passion and her senses flared to its call.

He added easily, "If I had waited for you to agree, the child you may be carrying would be married and have a child of its own."

She shook her head upon hearing his teasing logic.

He asked then, "So, do you hate me?"

She met his brilliant gaze. "I should, but I can't."

"I'm sorry," he told her genuinely.

"If I am carrying, will you take a mistress?"

Galen searched her diamond-black eyes. "It was not something I had considered, no. Why do you ask?"

"I—thought that was what men of your class did. Take mistresses I mean."

Galen realized she was very serious. "I already have a mistress, Indigo. You."

"Galen, I'm your wife. Mistresses are for—" she hesitated.

He coaxed her to finish the phrase. "What? Pleasure?"

She nodded yes.

"You're correct, they are for pleasure, and because they are they're gifted with gowns and very extravagant jewelry. They are taken on trips to exotic lands and introduced to exotic sights and sounds—all the things I plan on doing for you."

At the end of the short ride, the coach drew to a stop in front of the Folly. As Hester took his hand to step down, she asked, "Is this where we are to live?"

"I don't know, I came here out of habit. If you wish for us to live at your home, we can."

"I suppose that's something we can discuss later."

He agreed. As she stood before him Galen reached out and stroked the wing of her dark eyebrow. "Will you do me a favor?"

"If I can."

"When we get in the house will you tell Maxi you don't hate me for doing what I did to you today. She was very angry when she found out my plans."

"How angry?"

"So angry she let Raymond eat my dessert last evening."

Hester chuckled. "That angry? I should let you suffer, you know."

"But because you love me, you won't."

She did love him, with all her heart and soul. "Yes. Because I love you I won't."

He kissed her mouth. "You are the perfect wife."

"And you are incorrigible."

Inside, Maxi had all the help lined up to make her acquaintance. Hester met the gardener, the stable hands, the two upstairs maids, and the coachmen. They were all dressed their best and Hester had never been so uncomfortable in her life. How in the world would she become accustomed to having servants? In spite of her unease, she greeted everyone with a smile then let herself be shown upstairs by her new husband.

Hester stood in Galen's large bedroom assailed by the memories of the last time she'd been here. Knowing that some couples slept in separate beds, she asked, "Where will I sleep?"

Galen gently lifted her chin. Looking down into her eyes he said, "Mistresses always sleep with their lovers, *petite*."

Hester's heart began to race. "Then I suppose I'll be in here with you."

"I can hardly give you pleasure if you're in another wing, now can I?"

Her heart pounded faster. "No—you can't."

He kissed her and said, "Come, I've something to show you."

He took her hand and led her through a door which connected Galen's bedroom to a smaller adjoining room. It was a beautifully furnished sitting room, but the furniture lay hidden beneath mounds and mounds of some unknown female's clothing. Hester wondered if it all belonged to his aunt Racine. There were cloaks, day dresses and ball gowns, traveling suits and handbags. One corner of the room held nothing but shoes, all in a multitude of shades and styles. Hat boxes were stacked against a wall in a column high as her head. There was not a space in the room unused. Every inch was crammed with female clothing. The place resembled a dress shop.

Hester couldn't fathom one person owning so much, but she supposed this was commonplace for women of Galen's class.

"Do these things belong to your aunt?"

"No, they belong to you."

Hester froze. "Me?!"

He nodded. "I told you a long time ago, I wanted to drape you in silks, so—?" He ended with a shrug as if that were explanation enough.

Hester could only stare around. She was so outdone she didn't know what to say.

Being careful not to step on anything, Hester took a slow stroll around the room. She saw fur-lined capes for winter, riding boots, and gossamer thin night wear. There were evening gloves, lisle stockings, and blouses made of silk. She found summer stoles, more shoes, and soft, velvet robes. Amazed at the sheer volume of apparel, she looked back over at Galen and she still had no idea what to say.

He smiled a half smile. "I suppose you think I went a bit over the top."

She nodded. "A bit, yes." Then she asked, "Where in heaven am I going to wear all of this? There is enough here to clothe every woman in the nation."

He seemed content to simply watch her.

Hester turned her eyes on the sumptuous ball gowns. "No one took my measurements. How do you know this will all fit?"

"Ah, you forget, I have taken your measurements, in my own fashion. I know that your waist fits between my hands. I can close my eyes and remember how long it takes me to caress you from hips to toes. I know that your breasts fill my hands like—"

Hester threw up a hand to halt his recitation. "My pardon for doubting you."

He grinned the smile of the consummate male.

Hester shook her head. "You really need someone to curb your extravagance, Galen."

"That's why I have you, *petite.*"

He watched her resume her slow walk around the room. She paused to pick up a pair of fine kid gloves. She scanned them, then gently placed them back alongside the other fifteen or twenty pair he'd purchased. He wondered what she would say if he told her he'd been shopping for her since leaving Whittaker last October. He was glad to finally be able to gift her with all the lovely things he'd been accumulating in anticipation of making her his own. Granted, he'd thought of her more as a mistress back then, but as time passed and his ardor deepened he knew he wanted her to be a permanent part of his life, in spite of her fears of his being ostracized by his peers. The opinions of others meant little when compared to seeing her smile or hearing her purr sweetly in response to his loving. Hester was his wife and the world be damned.

"So?" he asked. "What do you wish to wear to dinner with me this evening?"

Hester looked around the room. The idea of having to choose something from the extravagant cornucopia of garments was a bit daunting. "I've no idea."

"Will you let me guide you?"

She gave him a tiny nod.

Galen walked over and chose a beautiful gown of sapphire-blue silk. He handed it to her. "This."

A nervous Hester took the rustling silk. It was easily the most expensive gown she'd ever held. "Are we dining someplace special?"

"Yes, here."

Hester's eyes flew to his. The heat reflected in his gaze made her shake.

"Maxi has insisted upon making a special wedding dinner tonight. If you'd prefer not to, it can be postponed."

Hester shook her head. "I'm certain Maxi has gone to a lot of trouble preparing the meal. I wouldn't want to offend her my first day here."

Galen smiled warmly in response to her kind nature. "Good. I have some business to attend to this afternoon, but I'll return in time for dinner. Maxi will come up and put all this away. If you'd like to rest up, the bed is at your disposal."

Hester was a bit overcome by all this, but she had to speak what she felt inside. "I'm still uncertain how I feel about being married to you, Galen."

Galen looked down into her truth-filled eyes and replied, "I understand, *petite*. We'll go slow, I promise. If in the end you find it unbearable, well, we'll discuss that when the time comes. Agreed?"

"Agreed," she said softly.

Galen wanted to pull her into his arms and kiss her fears away, but he held himself in check. He had promised her he would go slow.

After Galen departed, Hester spent a moment looking around at all the beautiful clothes he'd purchased.

Maxi entered to bring Hester a light luncheon. She too took a moment to stare around at the wealth of garments. "Unbelievable," the servant said.

Hester replied. "I feel the same way."

"I want you to know, I was very upset when he told me what he planned to do today at the church. Not even Raymond could talk him out of it."

"Galen doesn't impress me as being swayable once he has set a path."

Maxi nodded. "But I am happy you are in his life. I was there with his mother the day he was born. He has always been special to me. Though I find fault with his methods today, I applaud his choice."

"Thank you, Maxi."

Hester wanted to discuss her fears, but she didn't know Maxi well enough to burden her with her problems. She asked instead, "I've heard you and Racine refer to Galen as 'dragon,' why is that?"

Maxi smiled, "Galeno was such an ugly little thing when he was born. His tiny face was all compressed and pointed. His mother took one look at him and cooed that he was ugly as a dragonlet. It became her pet name for him, and it stuck to him as he grew older."

Hester smiled softly in response to her story. She could hardly believe he was ever anything but handsome.

Maxi voice interrupted her thoughts. "Galeno said you might wish to rest after such an incredible day, and I agree. I will have a bath sent up later and the girls will come to help you dress."

"Maxi, I don't really need help dressing and I can haul my own water."

Maxi simply shook her head. "I suppose I should pay the maids for doing nothing?"

"Well, no—but—"

"No buts. This is how they make their living. You are Galeno's wife. Let us take care of you, *chiquita.*"

The look on Maxi's face forbade any further arguments, so Hester acquiesced with a nod.

Hester ate her meal alone in Galen's sumptuous room. Done, she stripped down to her slips, climbed into the big bed, and promptly fell asleep.

When she awakened a few hours later, Maxi and the two maids were quietly moving around the room. A large bathing tub now dominated the center of the room and the maids were filling it from large buckets. Maxi, seeing Hester awake, smiled, then shooed the two young women out.

Hester saw Maxi was about to add a handful of powders to the tub's water. "What is that?"

"Salts."

"Maxi, I don't use—"

Maxi dropped the salts into the water. Moments later, the air took on an evocative scent as the powders dissolved and released their aromas.

"As my mistress you will indulge yourself in all the luxury my Galeno can afford. I'll be back to look in on you later. There is soap and towels on the table there."

She exited.

Hester sighed. She wondered if all servants were so single-minded? Hester poured the remaining bucket of hot water into the tub, shed her clothes, then stepped in. The tub's large size rivaled her grandfather's tub at home. The water surrounded her like the warm arms of a lover. The salts made the water so soft she felt as if she were soaking in liquid silk. She ran a slow hand over the surface and then picked up a handful of water and dribbled it over her shoulder and neck. The water rinsed

away the clinging dampness brought on by her short
sleep. She leaned back against the edge of the tub and let
the heat steep away the day. And what a day it had been.
When she left home for church this morning, she'd no
idea she'd end the day by becoming Mrs. Galen Vachon.
She could almost hear the gossips. The Song of Solomon
would take on new meaning as a result of today.

Hester decided she should finish washing. It wouldn't
do for her to become accustomed to lounging around in
tubs, regardless of Maxi's mandates.

Galen quietly eased open the door of the sitting room
so he could check on Hester. He hadn't seen Maxi since
his return home a few moments ago and he assumed
Hester would be still asleep. Instead he stood frozen by
the sight of her standing nude in his tub. A gentleman
would have eased the door closed again, but Galen had
no intentions of passing up this opportunity for a quiet,
unhurried look at his lovely little wife. He found her
perfect in every way. Her dark breasts, flaring hips, and
lean legs were lush for a woman of such small stature. He
could spend the rest of his life undressing her so he could
feast his eyes and touch on her ebony beauty.

He watched her cascade water down her arms and legs
as she rinsed away the soap. Droplets clung to her throat
and hips. Thin rivulets came to rest in the valley of her
hair and his manhood swelled in response. As she bent
to bring up more water, she innocently offered him a
very a provocative look at her backside. Finding it
suddenly hard to breathe, he silently closed the door and
leaned back against it. Going slow was going to be
harder than he'd imagined. And this was only the first
day, he reminded himself.

Downstairs in his study Galen stared out of the
window, musing upon his wife. In truth, being tor-
mented by the sweet sight of her was really no more than
he deserved. He'd embarrassed her today, compromised
her in front of her reverend, her friends. Maxi had tried
to talk him out of interjecting himself into Hester's life

without her consent, as had Raymond, all to no avail. He'd had one selfish thought in mind, to make her his own and he'd gone after Hester like a conquistador after gold. It hadn't mattered that she might find fault with his methods. He wanted her, loved her.

Raymond's voice intruded upon his reflecting. "So, is she angry?"

Galen glanced over at his friend standing in the doorway, and replied, "No."

"Your vaunted luck holds." Raymond came in and sat down. "I was looking forward to eating your dessert."

Galen shook his head. "Are you here for a reason, or just to torment me?"

"I came to let you know that Racine has sent word that she will return in a few days. Your grandmother is a bit unwell."

Racine had left to visit Vada last week. She'd originally planned on returning today. Raymond had gone down to bring her back to Whittaker. "I suppose you told her everything about Hester and me."

"Just about. She said she will speak to you when she returns."

Galen sighed once more. It was all he needed, another person telling him how he'd wronged Hester. "Thank you, Raymond," he cracked sarcastically.

Raymond nodded in acceptance. "Well, I'm sure you would do the same for me."

Galen chuckled, "I cannot wait until a woman decides to stomp around inside your heart. Your squeals will be music to my ears."

Raymond's eyes twinkled with his amusement as he stood. "Take faith, *mon ami,* regardless of how I tease you, I am glad things are straightened out between you and La Indigo. It pained me to see you so unhappy."

Galen's eyes reflected the strong friendship they'd held over a lifetime. "Thank you, *mon frere.*"

Raymond inclined his head. "Well I'm off to Amherstburg for a few days. I have an assignation with a lovely, brown-skinned subject of Queen Victoria."

Galen gave him a wave of his hand and a smile. "Good luck."

Raymond replied, "Unlike the House of Vachon, we LeVeqs do not need luck."

"Out!" Galen told him with a grin. "May she have a husband who is seven feet tall."

Upstairs, Hester hardly recognized the woman in the beautiful sapphire gown staring back from the glass as herself. She had always carried herself with an air of confidence, but this dress, like the dress she'd worn to Galen's party, added an elegance to her persona.

The maids had departed only a while ago, but true to Maxi's dictates they'd overridden her objections to their help and assisted her with not only her dress but her underwear and her hair as well. She'd refused to let them restyle her signature knot, but had allowed them to use the curling iron to fashion a trailing, wispy curl at each temple. The two young women had oohed and aahed over their handiwork and even Hester had to admit the curls added a distinct softness to her face.

Still, she found the woman in the mirror difficult to recognize. The slippers on her feet would never last a moment in the garden or on the Road, but she supposed they were not fashioned for such tasks. They were soft and delicate and appeared to be more costly than any pair of shoes she'd ever owned. It would not do to get accustomed to this, she told herself. In spite of Galen's fervent denials, she couldn't see him being comfortable with this marriage for very long.

Chapter 17

D usk had fallen as Hester crossed back into the bedroom. In her absence an unknown hand had lit a few candles to lighten the shadows, and the bathing tub had been removed.

On the far side of the expansive suite, two French doors opened to the evening air. A quiet breeze wafted in, ruffling the drapes the doors had hidden behind.

The open doors led outside to a terrace. Intrigued, Hester started forward to take in the view, but stopped when she saw the first box. It lay on the floor in the spot where the tub had been. The box was small, square, and wrapped in indigo-colored paper. A bow fashioned from gold ribbon graced the top. Hester stooped to pick it up, and as she did she spied another box on the floor a few feet away, and then another. They were lined up in a path that led her out onto the terrace. Outside she found another. She looked around for more and stared right into the eyes of Galen Vachon.

The sight of him stole her breath away. He was elegantly attired in formal evening wear, and stood across the terrace leaning casually against the intricate ironwork of the waist-high terrace walls. Beside him was a white-draped table set with candles, gleaming china, and sparkling crystal.

Galen ran his eyes over his wife. Even though he had been lying in wait, he found himself mesmerized all the same. He'd known she would look exquisite in the sapphire gown but he'd not expected to be rendered paralyzed. She was, without a doubt, the most beautiful woman he'd ever known. With the way she looked tonight, she could easily wind up as the evening's dessert. "You look very lovely, wife."

Hester was still trying to regain the composure lost upon finding him waiting.

"I see you found the boxes."

She nodded.

"You didn't open them."

"No. I—didn't know if they were for me."

Galen simply shook his head, amused by her innocence. Any other woman would have ripped the wrapping away without a thought—but not his Indigo. "They are for you, *ma coeur* . . ."

Hester knew she would not survive this evening if he continued to address her as his heart. The husky sound of the endearment always made her blood rush. "Is this more of your extravagance?"

"I'm afraid so."

She said softly, "Galen, you must stop giving me gifts."

"Do they make you uncomfortable?"

She answered truthfully. "In a way, yes. You've given me more gifts in the past few months than most women receive in a lifetime."

"You aren't most women, Indigo." When she didn't answer he told her gently. "Indulge me. Open them— that one first."

Hester opened the first one and found an orange. She couldn't hide her smile.

Galen's once-jaded heart soared.

The second box, a bit longer and thinner than the others, held two tickets to a concert performance by songstress Elizabeth Taylor Greenfield, known to the race as the Black Swan. Hester had always wanted to hear the celebrated performer. She wondered suddenly when Galen had developed a sense for choosing the things she would value most.

He pointed out the next box to open, saying, "Be careful, the bottle inside is fragile."

Following his advice, she opened the box with care and extracted a beautiful crystal bottle that barely filled her palm. She undid the stopper, sniffed the delicate aroma, and asked quizzically, "Vanilla?"

"Pure extract from Madagascar."

"Madagascar?! Galen, you're jesting me."

"No. I had one of my ships bring some back about a month ago."

"Why Madagascar?"

"They grow the choicest beans."

Still awestruck by this last revelation, Hester opened the last box, which held an expensive pair of diamond-edged sapphire ear bobs that sparkled like something plucked from the heavens.

"Do you like them?"

"Why, yes, of course, but Galen—"

"No protesting allowed."

"Galen these are far too costly for a woman like me."

"You aren't listening to me, Mrs. Vachon."

Hester set the box with the others, unable to fathom any of this.

"Would you care for a brandy?"

She shook her head, no.

He accepted her reply with a polite nod, then asked, "Are you ready to dine?"

"Yes," she answered.

She took her seat, trying to calm the tiny tremors coursing through her as he helped her with her chair. She relaxed somewhat when he withdrew and took his spot at the opposite end of the table.

She picked up the soft linen napkin and placed it across her lap. When she raised her eyes he was watching her with a look so filled with contented pleasure, one could actually believe he did view her as his mistress.

"Did I tell you how lovely you look tonight?"

Hester nodded a bit self-consciously. "Yes, you did."

"Indulge me a moment more and come stand beside me. Bring the vanilla."

Hester swallowed nervously. His voice was as softly seductive as his manner. She picked up the small crystal container, then walked the short distance to his side. She handed it to him and watched as he set it on the table beside his plate.

"Give me your hands."

Hester held them out. He slowly stripped away her gloves, then softly kissed her knuckles. "I don't mind the gloves when we are out, but here at home there is no need to hide them from me. Agreed?" he asked softly.

"Agreed," she answered. She usually wore the gloves to forestall rude questions about her past. She'd learned at a young age that there were many unkind and ignorant people both inside and outside the race who would judge her not on who she had become, but on whom she'd once been.

But her attention returned to her husband when he gently eased open the crystal bottle of vanilla extracts. Holding her eyes captive with a gaze that burned bright as the candle flame, he picked up her hand and very lightly drew the stopper across the inside of her wrist. Then he gently kissed the scented skin in tribute. As he repeated the intimacy on the other wrist, her knees went so weak, she had trouble standing. Next he dabbed the tender inside of her elbows and then the satin tops of her breasts above the sapphire-blue gown. The feel of the damp stopper sliding so sensually against the curves and then valley between her breasts made her breath snag in her throat. Just when she thought she'd melt, the stopper was withdrawn and repositioned in its bottle.

Hester remembered very little of the dinner which followed. She knew the food was excellently prepared but she could not recall any specific dishes.

Galen's desire for his wife glowed like the candles set on the table. He'd had to force himself to replace the top to the vanilla to keep from shocking her by touching the

scent to the warm hidden skin beneath her gown.
Granted, she was no longer a virgin, but she was still
very much an innocent. She'd been a partner to his
loving only a few times and still had much to learn. If the
fates were kind, he envisioned spending the rest of their
married life teaching her the erotic pleasures found in
uninhibited passion.

But for now, he ran his eyes over her dark beauty and
thought she made an elegant addition to his table. Her
bare ebony shoulders looked soft as the August night, her
neck fashioned for his kiss. He'd felt her trembling when
he scented her with the vanilla. The night of love they'd
shared proved her sensuality ran deep. He wanted to
explore those depths fully and without restraint.

When they were both done eating, Galen pushed his
chair back and extracted a small jeweler's box from the
inside pocket of his black dinner coat.

Under the candlelight, she undid the paper wrapping
and opened the small hinged box. The ring inside
sparkled in the flame's glow.

"Your betrothal ring."

Hester was once again struck dumb by his generosity.
The diamonds and sapphire ring was delicately made. It
was the most exquisite piece of jewelry she'd ever seen.

"Sapphires are as close as I could come to an indigo
stone."

"Galen, this is beautiful."

"Ah, you're getting better at this."

"What do you mean?"

"Accepting my gifts."

Their eyes held until Hester, overcome, looked away.

"I'll be afraid I will lose it."

He shrugged. "I doubt you will, but should it occur,
I'll simply buy you another."

He made the statement as if the expense of having to
replace such a gift meant nothing. Once again she
wondered just how much wealth he possessed.

Galen stood up and came over to where she sat. He
offered his hand and silently Hester let him help her to

her feet. He held onto her hand while he reached down and picked up the ring box. He touched his lips to the finger the ring would encircle, then slowly slid the gem in place.

The ring seemed charged with a power all its own. She felt claimed. His.

Galen pledged softly, "I will do everything in my power to make you happy, *petite* . . ."

Hester was so wrought with emotion, she could not speak.

"And whether you believe my claim or not—I will love you for life."

Hester had to look away as tears of joy stung her eyes.

"Aw, hell, *petite,* don't cry, you know what that does to me."

She dashed away the moisture. "I'm sorry. It's just all so wonderful. I can't believe it's real."

"It is."

"But will it last?"

His eyes were serious. "If you wish for it to."

She looked up at him. "Can you understand how overwhelming this has all been?"

He nodded. "I can, but trust that it will be fine, and it will be. I promise."

"I love you, Galen, very much, but—what if there is no child?"

He kissed her hand again and said huskily, "Then we will have the pleasure of trying to make another."

Hester trembled under the force of his words and eyes. She asked, "Why did you become the Black Daniel when you could have spent your life in leisure?"

"An apt question, I suppose. Come sit on the divan with me and I'll tell you a story."

The deep green brocaded divan occupied a place in the corner of the large terrace near the table. The candles had burned very low, but still offered a soft light.

"I became the Daniel as a lark in the beginning. I had a friend named Burton Lee whose sister, Edna, had been

sold to the pens in Alexandria by the wife of her new
master."

Slave pens were all over the South. Due to the
decades-long ban against further importation of Africans, those who bought and sold healthy slaves were
guaranteed a fat profit. Many pens also took the feeble
and the dying. Hester had heard many horror stories
from fugitives lucky enough to escape the desperate
conditions found there.

"Was your friend Burton a slave also?"

"No. He'd been freed by his master father at the age of
eighteen, as had his older brothers before him. The
females his father sired were not. When the master died
in a carriage accident, his brother took over the place.
The new mistress sold Burton's sister to the pens less
than a week after."

"Why?"

"Because of Edna's beauty. Even though Edna was the
new master's niece, the wife viewed her as a potential
threat to her marriage."

As Hester listened, Galen told her how he'd first met
Burton at Oxford. They'd both been students and good
friends. After gaining their certificates, Galen went on to
Paris where he had relatives and Burton returned to
Virginia where he and his family, both slave and free,
resided. Galen lost touch with Burton Lee for three or
four years, but they discovered one another again one
afternoon in a tavern near the Maryland docks. Galen
was on his way back to France after attending a family
funeral in New Orleans. Burton was there on business.
They renewed their friendship over dinner and that is
when Galen first heard of Edna's plight in the pens.

"I was unaware Burton had captives in his family. He
was devastated by what had happened to his sister. Edna
was a slave and had been the personal maid of their half
sister, Beatrice, one of the legitimate daughters of Edna
and Burton's father. Edna was educated, spoke three
different languages, and accompanied Beatrice on a tour
of the continent. After the new mistress sold her to the

pens, the pen owners took one look at her beauty and arranged for her to be sold sight unseen to a procurer from the New Orleans fancy girl market."

Hester knew about the markets. Light-skinned slave women were sold there as mistresses to wealthy businessmen and planters.

"All the arrangements for Edna's sale had been done by post. Since the owners of the pen hadn't actually met the New Orleans procurer, I impersonated him."

Hester turned to him in surprise. "And you chastised me for impersonating Fanny Blackburn?"

He grinned and continued. "Because of my ancestry, impersonating a French Creole from New Orleans was a fairly easy task. Back then I passed myself off as foreign every time I stepped on American soil. It was my way of ridiculing the Black Code restrictions on travel and accommodations. You'd be surprised how many people are impressed when you claim to be a Brazilian ambassador or a crown prince of Portugal, especially when you can speak the language and they can speak nothing but a backwater drawl. I even posed as an Italian-speaking Haitian count one evening to dazzle the registration clerk at one of Baltimore's finest hotels. They strictly prohibited guests who looked like you and me. The clerk behind the desk hadn't an inkling of what I was saying, but once he finished bowing and scraping, he gave me the best room in the establishment. People oftimes see what you want them to see."

"So what happened when you impersonated the Creole at the pen, were you successful?"

"Very much so. I claimed to be the Creole's representative and Edna was turned over to me almost at once. Burton and I dressed her in widow's weeds, placed her on a train, and sent her north to my aunt Racine in Detroit. She and Gail Grayson took over from there and arranged for Edna to live in Grayson's Grove, over near Niles."

"I'll bet the real procurer threw a fit when he showed up and found his property gone."

"I'm certain he did. Both Burton and I knew we would be wanted for slave stealing as a result, so he headed for Canada and I headed back to France. I received a letter from Edna a few months later thanking me and asking if I could help the son of one of her Grove neighbors escape from a place down near Nashville. I'd become fairly jaded living in France. I agreed to help mainly for the excitement."

"Really?"

"Yes. Slavery and the Black Codes placed restrictions on me as a man of color, but it never kept our segment of the race from founding our own schools, owning our own businesses, or from printing our own English and French newspapers. Most of the adults of my class were very adamant about the abolition of slavery, but like a good portion of the sons, I was more concerned with owning the most prized horseflesh, attending the balls, and pursuing beautiful women. Although my family had come to America as French slaves in the early seventeen hundreds, they'd been free for nearly three-quarters of a century by the time my mother gave me life. The block did not become a reality to me until I became involved with stealing slaves. As the years passed and I aided more and more fugitives, I witnessed the true abominations of slavery, the despair and the filth of the pens, the anguish in the eyes of one fugitive mother who'd had to leave her child behind. It changed me. I went from being a jaded rake who slept in fine featherbeds, to a slave stealer who spends eight months out of the year sleeping in cold barns and on the damp ground."

Hester turned to him and although they were seated in the moonlit dark, she had no problem seeing the serious set of his face. "Your work is very valued, Galen."

"I know, petite."

"Will you continue?"

"Until slavery dies the ignoble death it deserves."

Hester thought about all he'd said. He had a depth to him one would never suspect. His commitment more than surpassed his wealth. Galen Vachon and the Black

Daniel were both good men. "I never knew how you came to be called the Black Daniel."

"The moniker was given to me by Edna Lee. In one of her early letters she likened me to the biblical Daniel and saw my lions' den as slavery."

"So you became the Black Daniel."

"I thought the name pretty dashing in the beginning."

"And now?"

"Now, it is simply how I am known. There is no swashbuckling glory in any of it, just fear and cold and fiercely determined men and women counting on me to lead them into freedom." He turned to her and said, "So you know."

Their faces were close enough for each of them to feel the other's heat. Galen reached up to stroke her soft cheek. "I told myself I would let you set the pace in this, but I lied. I want you tonight . . ."

He kissed her with all the passion and love he possessed, then picked her up and carried her to his bed. He removed her dress and underclothing with a wanton and slow expertise. Only after she'd been rendered breathless and made lusciously ready did Galen partake of the dessert he craved most.

The following morning, the dilemma over the child became moot. Hester's bleeding had begun sometime during the night. She admitted to herself how sad she felt that she was not carrying Galen's child.

Maxi brought in her breakfast and was concerned as to how unwell her new mistress looked. When Hester explained her state, Maxi took the situation in hand. She brought rags and a hot tea to ease the slight cramping.

Galen came in later after Maxi had Hester cozily ensconced in the big bed.

"Good morning, *petite*. Maxi says you're a bit ill."

Hester was embarrassed. Men weren't supposed to share this part of a woman's life. However, he wanted her to be his mistress as well as his wife, and although Hester had never met a mistress in the flesh, she had the

distinct impression that they were far less constricted
than traditional wives. A mistress would probably discuss matters such as this with her lover. "Good morning,
Galen. It is my monthly."

"Ah."

Women's functions were well known to Galen, but it
surprised, and pleased him that she would offer up the
information. He had not expected such intimate frankness from La Petite Indigo.

She asked, "It is impolite for me to reveal such things
to you?"

He came over and sat on the bed. She looked small in
the large space, small and virginal in the light cotton,
high-necked gown. He could see the slight discomfort
playing across her face. "No, it is not. I need to be aware
of what goes on with you."

"Maxi made me some tea. She says it will help, and it
has. It's made me terribly woozy, however. I feel sort of
the way I felt last year at the apple brandy competition."

"The apple brandy competition?"

"Yes. I was a judge."

Galen grinned. "What in the world were you doing
judging brandy?"

"Bea refused to let any of the men do it because the
previous year all the judges became drunk and began
fighting over which brandy was the finest. The contest
disintegrated into a terrible brawl. Took Sheriff Lawson
quite some time to settle things down again. They never
did declare a winner."

Galen picked up the tea and sniffed the contents. He
was amused to smell tea as well as rum. Maxi had been
born in the Carribean and firmly believed rum, in the
correct proportions and combined with the right herbs,
could cure anything. He had to admit she'd kept him
healthy most of his life with her concoctions. He doubted
she'd given Hester more than a thimbleful, but it appeared to have been enough to make her slightly tipsy.

"There's rum in this tea. Did you know?"

"Yes, Maxi explained when she brought it in. That probably accounts for this wooziness."

Galen smiled. "You didn't finish the story about your brandy judging."

"Oh, there wasn't much more to it. Before the final evaluations could be done, I was removed."

Galen chuckled. "Why?"

"Bea said I was quite drunk. She said I was grinning like an idiot when they took me home. I didn't remember any of it, just the wretched sickness the morning after. I swore I'd never touch any type of spirits again. However, Maxi's tea has done the trick."

Galen couldn't be more pleased with having her as his wife. He would hate having to leave her. "I came up to tell you I'm going away for a while, maybe as long as a fortnight."

Hester raised up. "Why?"

"Road business. Raymond has met a woman in Amherstburg who had to leave her infant son behind when she came north last month. We're going down to Kentucky and try and steal him. You won't mind me leaving you here to fend for yourself, will you?"

"You know I will not. Go, with godspeed."

He leaned down and kissed her brow. "I'll return as soon as I can."

"When will you depart?"

"As soon as I finish saying goodbye to my wife."

Hester's smile brightened her eyes. "Then go. Time is of the essence. We'll simply have to spend a longer time saying hello when you return," she quipped softly.

Galen cocked his head at her questioningly as if trying to decode her words, then said, "Agreed."

Hester wanted to say something else before he departed. "My monthly means there is no babe."

Galen looked down into her serious face and said, "I know, *petite*. But as I told you before, it only means we'll have the pleasure of trying again."

He stroked her soft cheek in departure, then stood and

walked to the door. He looked back. "If you need anything, go to Maxi."

"I will."

"Au revoir, Mrs. Vachon."

"Stay safe, Galen."

He bowed and was gone.

Several days later Hester awakened still no more accustomed to her new status than she'd been the day they married. She still found it silly having someone setting out her clothing each day and bringing her meals. Her protests on the first day after Galen's leaving fell on Maxi's deaf ears. Maxi insisted that this was they way things would be, and that was that. The servant's stubborness rivaled her employer's, Hester thought at the time.

So, Hester gave in and let herself be pampered by Maxi and her solicitous staff. She wasn't any more comfortable with the idea of being catered to, but since they didn't seem to care about her views, she simply ceased voicing her objections.

However, Hester did put her foot down when it came to the choice of clothing each morning. She absolutely refused to wear the costly day dresses which filled her wardrobe, opting instead for lightweight, Egyptian cotton blouses and soft, full skirts. She thought the dresses far too expensive to warrant casual wear. When one of the maids explained that some of the women in Galen's set went through four and five changes of dress daily, Hester couldn't keep the astonishment from her face. She couldn't fathom such a thing. Hester let it be known then and there that she had no intentions of assuming such wasteful habits.

All in all, Hester's first few days as Mrs. Vachon went fairly well. Even though there had been a slight clashing of cultures, Hester found no fault with her new status or in the way she was treated.

On Sunday, Hester went to church accompanied by Andre Renaud. It was her first appearance outside the

Folly since becoming Galen's wife. She'd almost opted not to attend the service rather than be subjected to all the talk and speculation, but she knew she'd have to face her neighbors eventually or the talk would never stop.

Her entrance did cause whispers, but Bea greeted her with a smile, as did Branton Hubble and many others. Hester took her seat next to Bea but Renaud stopped her by politely clearing his throat.

"This way please, Mrs. Vachon."

Hester shrugged in ignorance to Bea, then followed Renaud to the pews up front. He directed her to the very first pew, one Hester had never seen before.

Renaud explained in a quiet voice. "This is the family pew, Mrs. Vachon. Mr. Vachon had it installed last week. It once belonged to his mother."

Hester knew every eye in the church was directed her way but she could not keep the wonder from her face. *Galen's mother?!* The beautiful pew had been hewn from very dark wood and it appeared to be very old. The carvings on it reminded Hester of the wildflower workings on the chest of gowns she'd received from Galen, only these carvings were of angels and cherubs and crosses. The new Vachon family pew outshone every other piece of wood in the small church.

Hester sat down, stunned.

After the service, the Reverend Adams made a point of thanking Hester for her husband's generous donation to the building fund. Since Hester knew nothing about the donation, she simply smiled politely.

Hester left the reverend to visit with Bea and Branton, who stood talking in the churchyard. Afterwards, she and Renaud stepped up into the coach for the ride back to the Folly.

Inside, Hester asked, "How long have you been in Galen's employ?"

"Since I received my certificate from Oxford five years ago, but I've known him all my life."

Renaud was considerably younger than Galen and Raymond.

↑"You admire him greatly don't you?" Hester asked.

"He stole me out of a brothel when I was five, gave me a home, safety, and a first-class education. I don't admire the man, I owe him my life."

Back at the house, Hester changed out of her church clothes then went down to the kitchen, where she planned on forcing Maxi to let her help make the bread for the evening's dinner.

Since Maxi would not agree, Hester had to ask, "Am I not the mistress here?"

"Yes you are, *chiquita,* but, this is my domain."

"And as the mistress, can I do anything I desire?"

Maxi smiled. "Yes."

"Well, the mistress wants to make bread."

They studied each other silently for a moment.

Hester very nearly pleaded, "Maxi, I'm not accustomed to sitting on my bustle all day."

"Then find some way to occupy your time."

"How?"

"Civic works. Isn't there someone in need of all the money you now possess? Do you have a favorite cause you can assist?"

"Of course, there are many, but—"

"Then do something. Organize a fair. Your life has changed, *chiquita,* and being wealthy is far more joyous than being poor. I know, for I've been both."

"Well if I promise to organize a fair, will you let me make the bread, occasionally?"

"Today you may. In the future, we will see."

Hester graciously nodded her thanks.

After dinner as Hester sat in Galen's suite reading the latest installment of the *Liberator,* she eased the paper down and thought back on Maxi's suggestion. Maxi was right, there were many ways she could help the Cause now that she'd become the wife of a wealthy man. The choices were endless, from benevolent societies to fugitive relief, to aiding parentless children. Hester had only to pick one. She wondered if Galen would approve? She didn't see him denying her the use of the grounds for a fair, and she doubted she would need much financial help because she would use her own funds to support most of her plans. She decided she would ask his opinion when he returned, if he ever did.

She missed him terribly.

Chapter 18

$\sim\!\!O\!\!D\!\!\sim$

Hester's plans for a fair were quickly set aside the next morning when Bea brought over terrible news. A band of Shoe's men had kidnapped Bea's neighbor, Samuel Creighton, and his son, Peter. There'd been no writ, and no hearing before Sheriff Lawson. The kidnappers simply overran the small farm in the middle of the night and took them away.

The Creightons had only recently moved to Whittaker after living the past three years in Canada. They'd fled there along with tens of thousands of other members of the race to escape the potential kidnapping made legal by the passage of the 1850 Fugitive Slave Law. From what little Hester knew of them, Mr. Creighton was a carpenter, his son Peter, only twelve.

"Was his wife Emma harmed?"

"She was beaten very badly, but not taken south."

Hester could well imagine Emma's fear for her husband and son and her heart ached for the woman. "Did anyone go after them?"

"Branton and a few others, but Shoe's men are at least four or five hours ahead. I doubt they'll be able to bring them back."

Bea had tears in her aging eyes as she raged, "This has to stop, we shouldn't have to live this way. No one is safe, Hester, no one."

She went over and placed her arms around the older

woman. "We must stay strong, Bea. We must stay strong."

Later that evening, Hester, along with a large portion of the community, kept vigil at the church in hopes that Branton and his men would be successful. It was not to be. The men returned tired and disheartened. They'd been ambushed outside of Monroe by locals employed by the slave hunter Porter Greer, undoubtedly to slow their progress. In the ensuing gun battle, Branton Hubble had received a wound to the chest and hadn't survived.

Hester ran from the church, her heart screaming. She did not want it to be true. She stood out in the silent night, shaking, filled with grief. All Branton wanted was to be free. He spent his whole life pursuing freedom, only to be cut down by brigands already destined for hell. The tears ran freely down her cheeks. She stood there crying silently for what seemed an eternity. Renaud eventually found her, eased her to the coach, and took her home.

The community went into mourning. Women wore black, men wore black, and many of the businesses in Whittaker and Ypsilanti draped their storefronts with black wreaths. Branton Hubble had touched many people in the area and everyone grieved at his passing. The funeral scheduled for two days hence was planned by Hester and the women of her circle because Branton had no other family in the North.

The day before the funeral, Hester had Renaud escort her over to her old home so she could retrieve some platters needed to hold food for the after-burial dinner. While she went on inside, Renaud and the driver took a slow walk around the grounds to make certain things were in order. Everything appeared fine except for the two male runaways hiding in the loft of the barn.

When Renaud came into the kitchen and related his find, Hester stared a moment, then quickly went to see.

Sure enough, there were two men in the loft. One of them asked, "Are you Hester Wyatt?"

She nodded. "And you are?"

"William Madison. This is my cousin, Claude St. Clair."

"How long have you been here?"

"Almost five days. A friend in Ann Arbor said you would help us."

Hester looked the men over. There had been cases of Blacks being in cahoots with slave hunters. They'd oftimes pass themselves off as fugitives in order to gain the confidence of the residents of the community. Hester didn't believe these men were out to dupe her; she had a strong sense that they were who they claimed. "I apologize for not being available when you arrived, but I've recently married and now reside elsewhere. Have you eaten?"

"Not for a few days."

They both looked tired, but they appeared healthy. The conversation was abruptly interrupted by the coach driver running into the barn. "Shoe and his devils are coming up the road."

Hester didn't waste a breath. "William, you and Claude back up under the bales. Quickly! Slave hunters!"

The men hustled to hide themselves once more. Hester and Renaud ran behind the barn and pretended to be observing the progress of the fruit that would soon appear on the apple trees in her father's wild orchard. When Shoe rode up, he tipped his hat. "Howdy, gal. Sorry to hear about Hubble. Guess he's learned his lesson about poking around in the business of his betters."

Seeing his glee, Hester's anger rose, but she held her tongue.

He turned his evil grin on Renaud and gave him a slow look over. "You one of them Creoles from that fancy house up on the point?"

Renaud nodded faintly.

"You got papers, boy?"

Renaud replied blandly, "I don't need papers. I'm a

French citizen. In France we don't pedigree and paper the populace as if they were horses or dogs."

"You're pretty uppity."

"Thank you," Renaud said with a bow. He then asked coolly, "Now, what business do you have here?"

One of Shoe's riders spat. "Mighty uppity."

Renaud inclined his head at the man.

Shoe ignored them, continuing to hold Hester's stare. He said smoothly, "I just want her to know I've heard some real interesting things about her. Real interesting."

Hester's eyes were cold. "Such as?"

"You're free, but you wasn't born in the North."

"No, I was not. Last I knew that was not against the law."

"Maybe not, but then again, one never knows. I got somebody looking into it though."

Renaud asked frostily, "Looking into what?"

"Just how free that gal really is."

Hester felt the hair rise up on her neck. Shoe leaned down and said, "I can always smell a runaway, and you stink to high heaven, missy."

Hester didn't flinch. "Is there anything else?"

"Nope. At least not now. Just remember me and the boys got our eyes on you."

With a black-toothed grin and a mocking tip of his sweat-stained hat, Shoe wheeled his animal around, then he and his men rode off down the road.

Hester let out her breath. "I say we move William and Claude now, while Shoe's moving in the opposite direction."

"I agree. So much for his celebrated nose."

Hester quipped, "The only way he could smell a fugitive would be if the fugitive handed him soap and water beforehand."

While Claude and William made their way down from the loft, Hester questioned the coachman about the number of men in Shoe's party when he first spotted them coming up the road. She wanted to make certain Shoe had not left a scout amongst the trees to spy upon them. By the coachman's count he had not; Shoe had ridden up with six men and rode away with the same number.

Satisfied, Hester and Renaud hustled the barn's fugitives into the coach for the ride back to the Folly.

She turned the two men over to Maxi who fed them, showed them where to wash up, and put them to bed. In the meantime she and Hester rounded up clothes they thought would fit. The fugitives slept until late evening, after which they sat with Hester and Andre to discuss where they wished to go next.

"Canada," they said in unison. Both men had family and friends already in residence there. They'd escaped Tennessee with a forged pass saying they were needed in Chicago by their master, who'd suddenly become ill. The pass indicated the men were to escort the sick master back to his family in Nashville.

William, the taller of the two, explained, "We wrote the pass ourselves. The part about Master Day being in Chicago is true. When he departed, so did we."

Hester smiled at their cleverness.

Claude added, "I'm certain the news that we've run will ruin his trip. He was counting on us to keep his tables going."

Andre's face mirrored his confusion. "Tables?"

"Master Day owns a bordello in Nashville. William and I run the faro tables. We also keep the books. When we walked away, we took a week's worth of take, purchased two train tickets, and left his business in the hands of his wastrel brother-in-law, whose passion for drink far outpaces his business sense. If Master Day isn't in the poor house by now, he will be very soon."

Everyone laughed.

That night as she lay in Galen's large bed, Hester mulled over how best to aid William and Claude in going to Canada. She knew many people would be attending tomorrow's funeral and decided it would be the perfect opportunity for the men to move on. She doubted Branton would mind if a few fugitives were added to his funeral procession; in fact she was certain he would be honored to help move freight this one last time.

However, she'd no intentions of bringing anyone outside the house in on the plan. Shoe had frightened her this afternoon with his talk of looking into her past. He'd said someone had given him information on her and she hadn't an inkling as to who it might be. She wondered if this could be tied to Galen's mysterious traitor? As Galen had pointed out, the traitor could be anyone, so the fewer who knew of William and Claude's true identity, the safer the men would be.

She thought about Shoe then and his ugly face resurfaced in her mind. He'd reeked of confidence today and that added to her wariness. How much did he actually know about her journey north? She hoped the fates would not be so unkind as to fling her back into the hated arms of slavery, not after all this time. She hoped . . . but in times like these she knew nothing was certain.

The day of the funeral it poured rain. There were so many people, the little church could not hold the crowd, so the Reverend Adams moved everything outside. The fugitives William and Claude were hidden amongst the mourners from a church group in Sarnia. Once the service ended and everyone made the silent walk to the cemetery, William and Claude would depart with the group.

Throughout the solemn event, Andre Renaud held an umbrella above her head to keep her from being drenched, but it offered no protection from the grief and pain she felt inside. Branton Hubble had been a good, decent man. When she first came north, he'd been one of the many people who'd helped her with her lessons. She remembered with fondness how patient he'd always been with her. With his death the circle of those who'd helped her cross the bridge from slavery to freedom tightened, as did her heart. Burying Branton also brought back the memories of burying her aunt

Katherine. Hester hoped now that the two, no longer
bound by earthly ties, would find peace together.

The walk to the cemetery was a tradition, and Hester
had made the trek in the rains of spring, the heat of
summer, and the blowing snow and cold of late fall.
Never had she witnessed a downpour such as this one
today, but not a soul complained. They'd come to pay
last respects to a man whose life had been devoted to
freedom; no one in the cortege would be so disrespectful
as to grumble about mud-covered shoes or sodden
clothing.

They buried Branton with his Bible and a copy of
Francis E. Watkins's famous poem, "Bury Me in a Free
Land."

As the bearers solemnly shoveled the dirt down onto
the simple wooden casket, Hester, standing in the rain,
surrounded by the crowd, read the poem aloud in a
steady, clear voice.

> *"Make me a grave where'er you will,*
> *In a lowly plain or lofty hill;*
> *Make it among earth's humble graves,*
> *But not in a land where men are slaves.*
> *I could not rest, if around my grave*
> *I heard the steps of a trembling slave;*
> *His shadow above my silent tomb*
> *Would make it a place of fearful gloom. . . ."*

By the time Hester reached the eighth and final stanza,
her voice was choked with tears.

> *"I ask no monument, proud and high,*
> *To arrest the gaze of the passers by,*
> *All that my yearning spirit craves*
> *Is—Bury me not in a land of slaves! . . ."*

In the days that followed, Shoe and his kidnappers
struck again and again, from Ypsilanti to Detroit to
Monroe, where he teamed up with Porter Greer and his

band of thugs. Alone they were menacing, together they invoked terror.

All over the county people were afraid to leave their homes. Women hung quilts on their wash lines to signal fugitives that the area was unsafe. Men sat up at night, shotguns at the ready in case it became necessary to defend their homes and their families. Sheriff Lawson was doing his best to enforce the Michigan law that forbade forced kidnapping, but Shoe continued to elude Lawson's very undermanned possee. Hester had Renaud take her back over to the Wyatt house so she could transfer the small arsenal in her kitchen to Galen's stores. Hester still had an aversion to weapons, but she'd employ one if it became necessary.

As in the case of the Blackburns and the Creighton men, Shoe's kidnappings all involved lesser-known folks, people who were not connected in any way to the Road except for their fugitive status, people who stayed close to home and were rarely seen.

"It's as if someone is sacrificing lambs to Shoe," Hester told Renaud and Abigail Grayson over breakfast that morning. Gail had returned from Niles last night. She'd been very distressed by all the terrible happenings. Shoe's treacherous activities had even overshadowed the surprising news of Hester's marriage to Galen Vachon.

Gail agreed. "It is the oddest thing. Why would he concentrate on such helpless individuals?"

"Because they are helpless and he's a coward," Renaud pointed out.

Maxi interrupted them a moment to inform Hester that Foster Quint was here to see her. Puzzled, Hester excused herself from the table, then followed Maxi to the parlor.

Hester walked in determined to be polite, but nothing more. He'd dragged her name through mud; surely he didn't expect her to be warm. "Have a seat, Foster. How may I help you?"

He took a seat and smiled. "So formal, Hester. One would never believe we were to be wed."

Hester waited.

He appeared a bit uncomfortable with her manner but said, "I've come to ask you to sell me the Wyatt land."

Hester searched his face. "The land's not for sale."

"Why not?"

"Because it isn't, Foster. That land will belong to any children Galen and I have."

He chuckled bitterly. "Was it his money? Is that why you gave yourself to him?"

"I believe you are here to discuss land, nothing more."

"Yes, I'm here to discuss land. So how much?"

"It isn't for sale."

"Why not? My God Hester, you and Vachon already own this whole corner of the county. Why can't you part with a parcel of it?"

"Foster you held me up to ridicule from here to the Ohio border with your lies. Even if the Wyatt land were for sale, I'd give it away before I sold it to you."

"You owe me," he remarked angrily.

"For what, branding me a whore? I owe you nothing Foster, ever." She stood. "If there's nothing else I will send Maxi to escort you out. Good day."

Hester paid no attention to his malevolent eyes as she made her exit from the room.

She thought about Foster that evening as she lay in bed. How he had the audacity to believe she would sell him her ancestral lands after his slandering was beyond her comprehension. She put him out of her mind and went to sleep dreaming of her husband.

In the seven days since the burial of Branton Hubble, it had poured seemingly nonstop. It was now mid-August and Hester had spent the day delivering copies of Mr. Garrison's *Liberator*. Bea was the area agent, but she'd gone over to Marshall to visit an old friend. Had Hester known the deliveries would have to be made in a deluge, she might not have agreed to be Bea's substitute, but the *Liberator* was still widely read. Folks all over the county were waiting for this latest edition despite the feud Garrison was having with most of the east's Black

leaders over their confrontational approach to abolitionism.

When Hester returned home later that evening, Maxi
took one look at her drenched and shivering mistress
and immediately called for a hot bath. Hester tried to
protest, saying once she donned dry clothes all would be
well, but Maxi simply rolled her eyes and hustled her
upstairs. While the tub was readied, Hester stripped off
her sodden clothing and put on the flannel robe Maxi set
out. She tried not to let Maxi see her shivering but it
proved impossible to mask.

Maxi said, "Do you have any idea how Galeno will
yell at me if he comes home to find his wife sick?"

"Maxi, it isn't your fault I am soaked."

"I know it isn't. You know it isn't, and he will know
too, but he will still yell."

So to keep Maxi and everyone else from the dragon's
fire, Hester stepped into the warm water of the tub and
sighed pleasurably as the heat took the cold chill from
her flesh. She could certainly become spoiled by such
care, she thought contentedly. She continued to be
uncomfortable with the idea of servants, but luxuries
such as a hot tub on a cold, rainy day were too wonderful
to deny.

She had no idea how long she'd been in the water, but
when she heard a soft knock, she remembered Maxi
promising to return with something hot for her to eat.
Without opening her eyes, Hester called for her to enter.
She was so lulled by the water she paid no attention to
the footsteps or the sound of the door closing again so
quietly. Her only thoughts were ones of thanks to Maxi
for entering and not breaking her reverie.

"Good evening, *petite*."

The low voice made her eyes snap open. She spun her
head and saw Galen smiling at her. He came further into
the room and looked down on her with a heat-filled gaze.
"You make a delicious homecoming present, Mrs.
Vachon." Then he reached down and lightly teased one
dark, puckered bud. "A delicious sight."

He walked away and over to the fire Maxi had lit earlier in the evening. He was as dirty as Hester had ever seen him. His clothes and boots were covered with trail mud and soil. His beard had began to grow in again, giving him the look of a buccaneer.

He looked back over his shoulder at her and Hester's heart began to race. She sought to dampen the effect by saying, "I'll be done with your tub in moments."

His sudden appearance had taken her totally by surprise and she wasn't certain what her reaction should be. On one hand she found the idea of playing the role of his wife-mistress terribly intriguing, but on the other she remained the staid, conventional Hester Wyatt who was a bit embarrassed to be caught nude in a tub by a man— even if the man was her husband.

He answered by saying, "There is no rush. Take all the time you need. In fact, why don't I place your drying sheet closer to the fire so it will be warmed when you are done there?"

He placed the towel on a chair near the fire. Hester had not an inkling of what to do. His back to her, he stood against the fireplace mantel and scanned the edition of the *Liberator* she'd been reading earlier in the week. She asked quietly, "Was the quest successful?"

"Yes, we brought back the child, and took it on to Amherstburg straight away. Andre says Whittaker has been fairly lively in my absence. I am sorry to hear about Branton Hubble's death. I know how much he meant to you."

She nodded her thanks and replied, "He was a good man. Too good to die at the hands of Porter Greer's thugs."

"So, tell me all that has happened."

Hester spent a few moments relating Shoe's recent reign of terror. She also related Shoe's boast of looking into her past.

Galen's manner went cold. "I hope he knows I will shoot him like a rabid dog should he even think to harm you."

"Galen—"

"I swear on my mother's saints that I will personally send him to hell."

His direct speech made her almost wish she had not been so forthcoming about Shoe's interest in her past. Beneath the cultured veneer lurked the deadly fire of the dragon, a man Hester was less familiar with, but a man she knew would give his life to keep her safe.

She waited to see if the anger at Shoe would subside. She assumed it had when he said, "That water has to be cooling, *petite*. Come out before you shrivel away."

The water had indeed cooled to the point where if she stayed much longer she would begin shivering again.

Galen coaxed in a soft voice, "Wouldn't you enjoy being wrapped in this warm sheet?"

To Hester it did look inviting, almost as inviting as Galen. So, she stood.

He came over, gently wrapped her within the warmed folds of the sheet, and she could do nothing but purr as he picked her up and carried her to the rug by the fire. "I'm too dirty to sit on the furniture. Maxi will have me for breakfast, so let's sit here."

He eased her to her feet, then took a seat on the rug. He tugged her down onto his lap, then folded her in against his dirty chest.

She whispered, "I'm going to need another bath because of you, my filthy husband."

"That was a given, Indigo."

Hester's eyes widened as heat flushed her face. "So incorrigible."

"I'm still waiting for this long hello I was promised."

Hester smiled shyly. He was impossible to resist, even if he did smell like a goat. "You stink, do you know that?"

He grinned. "Raymond said the same thing, but he smells no better."

"Then I suppose I should be thankful both of you didn't come in and say hello."

He pinched her on the rear and she squealed with a

giggle. He looked down at her with a playful sternness and commanded, "Disrespectful female, I want my hello, now!"

Grinning, Hester leaned up intending to place a quick kiss on his lips, but the moment her mouth touched his, she was lost. All the longing she felt for him the last few days flowed over her heart and out of her soul and lit a fire that had long been cold. Her arms went around him in the same moment that he pulled her close. They both shared their hellos until they were panting with passion.

When he broke the seal of their lips, his eyes were glittering with a need that reflected her own. "I think I should have a bath prepared. Care to join me?"

She smiled saucily and whispered, "Yes."

His eyebrow raised at her willingness.

She quipped, "Is that not what a mistress would say?"

The brow rose once more. "I think this is going to be a most memorable homecoming."

She agreed. "I believe you may be right."

The servants brought up food and readied the tub for the dragon's bath while she and Galen ate dinner outside on the veranda's table. The rain had stopped sometime during the evening. The heat of August had returned, leaving the night air warm and damp.

"It is good to have you home," she said to him.

"It is good to be back. I missed you greatly."

"I missed you, too," she admitted. The house and her life had seemed emptier, less joyous without him near. She'd needed his arms to salve her grief over Branton's dying, but at the time she'd buried the selfish desire because her needs were secondary to the child he'd gone to steal away. During his absence there were many times when she would have liked to share a thought with him, or ask his opinion on some matter. They had not been man and wife for very long at all, but he'd always been willing to listen and very easy to converse with almost since the beginning of their relationship, though those first few days in her basement last October proved him to be stubborn, rude, and so filled with faults she found it hard to believe he was the same man.

"What are you thinking, *petite?*"

"I was reminiscing on our first few days together and how very awful you were to me."

He gave her a small smile. "But you nursed me back to health in spite of my manners."

"Lucky for you," she quipped.

"I am thankful every day, believe me."

Their eyes held under the flame of the candles on the table. Hester had donned a thin summer robe while he removed his coat but still wore the soiled clothing. He ran his eyes over her body so temptingly displayed beneath the gauzy gown. Her dark nipples were like veiled jewels. "I'm going to go make quick use of the tub to loosen this grime. When I'm done, we'll refill it for our bath."

Hester shivered in sensual anticipation as he disappeared inside the room.

He called her in a short time later. She'd spent the time alone remembering the other times he'd pleasured her and how overwhelming it had been. When she reentered the room, she was already pulsing with need. Her nipples had puckered, her skin tingling from his imagined touch, and her core had begun to blossom just from the thought of the sensual delights he would bestow.

He awaited her inside the candlelit room, tall, nude, and lushly ready. The sight of his strong desire for her gave her pause.

"It's much harder for a man to mask his need than a woman."

"So I see," she replied lightly.

He threw back his dark head and laughed, "You're learning your mistress lines well, *ma coeur.*"

"Thank you."

"Now come sit in the tub with me so I can soak away the many hours on horseback."

Hester fought her shyness and crossed the room buoyed by her own spiraling desire. In the tub she leaned back against his chest and let herself be enfolded by his arms and warm, hard thighs. She could feel his manhood pressing solidly against her back. The tub was large enough for them to be quite comfortable. She cuddled closer. "Is everything you own so large?"

He rubbed himself against her gently. "What do you think?" he asked slyly.

She couldn't suppress her chuckle. "You are such an arrogant, audacious man. I was speaking of the tub, not your—endowment. Do you even know the definition of humility?"

"There's not much call for that where I hail from."

"Now that I believe. I was referring to your possessions: your bed, carriage, home. Everything about you is grand."

"I'm a grand man."

He nudged her again meaningfully and she playfully smacked him across the arm. "Behave," she scolded.

He brushed his mouth against her collarbone and whispered against her skin, "If I behave you'll miss this . . ."

He touched his fingers to the already ripe buds of her breasts and worried them slowly. She arched in response.

". . . and, this . . ."

The hands slid down over her wet torso and waist. Once they journeyed below the water they dallied over the treasure between her thighs. He repeated the lazy, lingering caresses again and again, up and down. Her hips were rising temptingly in response to the uninhibited erotic play until she finally succumbed to a shuddering release.

Galen's need to love her fully overrode his need to soak away the muscle aches brought on by his long, arduous journey. He'd thought of nothing but her during the entire time he'd been away.

He paid scant attention to the water that cascaded

onto the floor as he carried her from the tub to his bed. He placed her on her back atop the mattress and used the trailing edges of the sheet to dry her neck and the upper planes of her breasts. He performed his task gently, lingering over the dewy nipples and the damp hair crowning her thighs.

Hester warmed and preened in response to his ministrations. When she was dried to his satisfaction, he eased her onto her stomach. He spent an inordinate time moving the sheet over her spine and shoulders, then down over her hips. He teased her, stroked her, cajoled her, until her thighs parted just enough. The expert touch of his caressing hand replaced the sheet and heat flared from Hester's head to her toes. He prepared her well; so well, she was fairly burning for him by the time he eased her onto her back and filled her without a sound. He rode her slowly at first, savoring her warmth and the look in her eyes, but soon, slow was not enough. Wave after wave of sensual pleasure rolled him on a rollicking passion-tossed sea, making his strokes longer, fuller, making him grip her hips as she met him measure for measure. He wanted to stay inside her like this for an eternity. As the orgasm exploded, he dropped his head back and roared out his release.

Later, much later, as the first rosy tendrils of dawn began to creep into the sky, the sated lovers lay entwined and tangled in the bedding, still touching, still stealing long, lush kisses, but too tired to accomplish much more.

"So, you will be my mistress?" he asked softly, slowly tracing her kiss-swollen lips.

Hester sensually flicked her tongue across his fingertip. "Yes. I would be inconsolable if you shared your grandness with another."

He chuckled and raised an eyebrow. "A jealous mistress?"

"Extremely, so be warned."

He kissed her fully, unable to get enough of her softness, and pledged, "Don't fret. If we are discreet, my wife will never suspect."

She stared at him with wide, laughing eyes. "Beast!" she accused and punched him on the shoulder. "You'd better pray your wife doesn't find out. I know her—she'll feed you arsenic if you so much as contemplate having another woman."

"Then I am thankful both mistress and wife are one and the same."

Hester kissed him again. "So am I."

Hester cuddled close and he enfolded her with his warmth. He kissed the top of her head. "We're going to do well together, you and I."

"I believe you may be right," came her whispered reply.

A few ticks of the clock later, they were both asleep.

Chapter 19

⟡

Hester awakened the next morning to the sounds of Maxi setting out her breakfast, and asked groggily, "What time is it?"

Maxi pointed over to the small decorative clock on the stand beside the bed. Hester raised up to peer at it and blinked in astonishment. In two hours it would be noon! "Why did you let me sleep so late?" she asked, rolling from the bed.

"Galeno said you needed the rest."

"But heavens, look at the time."

"In New Orleans this is considered early morning for a woman of the class."

"We aren't in New Orleans, Maxi. This is god-fearing, early-rising Michigan. Galen must think I'm the laziest woman in creation."

After Maxi's departure, Hester washed up in the small hip bath, then hastily got dressed. She couldn't remember ever being so late in rising, and vowed never to be caught this way again; such lying about had to be detrimental to the soul.

Hester made quick work of the buttons on her thin white blouse. Her intent this morning had been to approach Galen with her idea for a fund-raising fair to be held on the Folly grounds. With her luck something had come up and he'd been called away on another

Black Daniel quest. She wolfed down her breakfast, then quickly left the suite to search out her husband.

She ran across Andre Renaud on his way to a business appointment in town. He informed her that Galen could be found in the study.

Hester knocked tentatively upon the closed study door because she'd no idea whether Galen entertained interruptions when he worked.

Evidently he didn't mind because he bid her to enter and greeted her appearance with a smile. "Good morning, wife," he said, eyes glowing. "I didn't want to disturb you when I awakened earlier. How was your sleep?"

The passion of last night flashed across her memory. "My sleep was brief, as you are undoubtedly aware."

"How may I be of service?"

"I'd like to speak with you."

Galen's handsome face took on a look of mock disappointment. "Only talk? I had in mind a service far more stimulating."

Hester chuckled even as his words touched her senses. "I know, but contain yourself, if you can."

"And suppose I cannot . . . ?"

She smiled a smile as ancient as Eve. "Then I suppose I'll have to be shown what happens to a mistress who interrupts her lover in his study."

Galen blinked. His arousal rose hard and true in response to her heated challenge. She played the mistress well, he thought to himself, very well. "Lock the door and step over here, shameless indigo woman."

Hester complied and took a slow walk over to where he stood waiting. The initial kisses relit last night's still smoldering embers, and before long they were both plunged back into the storm. Neither suffered any guilt from the papers and inkwells and pens that went crashing to the floor as he laid her atop his desk. Hester was too busy swooning from having her drawers stripped down her legs and Galen was too intent upon turning her swoons into soft, breathless gasps.

Hester knew her passionate keening could probably be heard outside the locked door, but mistresses weren't supposed to care about things like that, so she didn't either. All she cared about was his passionate teasing and how lush and open she became as a result.

Galen slid himself into paradise and knew he'd never be able to work at this desk again, without remembering their lovemaking. He'd see her beautiful face tightened with passion, her breasts bared by the undone blouse, and want her beneath him just as he had her now, stroking her splendidly.

It had been a swift, carnal interlude that left Hester absolutely breathless. She raised up from the desk, pulsing, clothes twisted. He stood above her smiling, eyes glittering with dragon fire at the sight of her leaning back on her arms with her skirts raised above her slightly parted thighs and her nipples tempting him from within her gaping blouse.

She whispered softly, "You are entirely too outrageous for your own good, Galen Vachon."

When he recommenced dallying delicately with the damp, swollen place between her thighs, her head dropped back and she forgot whatever else she'd been about to say.

His voice was as gentle as his touch. "You were the one tossing about saucy challenges . . . mistress mine."

The heat began to spread again, soft and warm.

"Look at me, *petite* . . ."

Hester fought to focus through the luscious haze.

"Now . . . what did you wish to talk about . . . ?"

Hester wondered if he really expected her to answer. When next he raised his damp fingers to her breasts she once again lost the power of speech. When his warm mouth closed around the closest bud, she drew in a trembling breath, then crooned as the caresses lingered. He broke the seal of his lips, and raised his head, leaving the nipple glistening and as jewel hard as his gaze. "I thought you wished to speak with me about something . . ."

He eased her back down and she shuddered with pleasure as he slowly filled her once more. This time they went slower but the end result proved as blissfully explosive and earth-shattering as before.

Hester did finally get her chance to discuss the fair with her husband about an hour after her initial entrance. He thought it a great way to end the summer season, and agreed that the people in the area deserved a light-hearted gathering after suffering through Shoe's campaign of terror.

The fair was set for the last week in August. She and Gail posted handbills and placed notices in the local newspapers from Detroit to Amherstburg, Ontario, to Toledo, Ohio. Fundraising fairs were a tradition amongst Black women of the North. They used them to fund newspapers such as the *Liberator* and Mr. Douglass's *North Star,* to help political figures and fugitives such as William and Ellen Craft, and to benefit local and national benevolent organizations like New York's Colored Orphan Asylum, which housed more than a thousand children.

Hester planned on raising funds that would apply closer to home. A good portion would be sent to Mary Shadd in Canada to aid the refugee situation there, and the rest would be given to the Women's Society at the church to help fund their sewing projects for the poor children in the area.

The day of the fair dawned bright and sunny. The staff and the Men's Club from the church helped construct and set up the many booths. All in all, Hester had heard back from over fifty vendors of everything from pound cakes, to hand work, to well digging. Each seller had agreed to give a portion of their profits to the cause.

Hester walked the expansive Folly grounds to check on things before the arrival of the anticipated throng. There were fifteen hostesses for the event, all dressed in the same gaily-striped dresses. Their jobs would be to oversee some of the booths, give directions to certain special events, and generally be Hester's eyes because it would be impossible for her to be everywhere at once. They'd arrived earlier in the morning and were now milling about helping with the setup of things.

Galen had volunteered to provide the children's entertainment. Hester hadn't an inkling as to what he'd planned, but he kept promising she would be pleased and she held him to his word.

The affair proved to be a tremendous success. The mixed-race crowd filled the grounds throughout the day. Folks bought ice cream, played checkers, had their likenesses taken by an itinerant photographer, and a few even contracted to have new wells dug. There were vendors from as far away as Marshall and there was music and fiery abolitionist speeches. Hester saw children playing hide and seek, and she stood watching other small faces smile with glee at the antics of the dancing bear, trained monkey, and gaily-clad jugglers all hired by Galen. She made a mental note to reward him later for keeping his word so splendidly.

The only crimp in the affair was the sight of Foster squiring Jenine around, but Hester reasoned all coin was good coin, and if Foster and Jenine had paid the price of admission, she couldn't ask them to leave.

Later that evening, after everyone had departed, Hester thanked her hostesses for their help, then went inside and collapsed into the closest chair. She was so tired she didn't think she had strength to even climb the stairs to her bed. One of Maxi's baths would be dearly appreciated right now, she told herself wistfully. She wondered if her husband would enjoy sharing the tub? She enjoyed being his passion mate. Were other couples as bent upon having fun in their marriages as she and Galen? she wondered.

Hester struggled up. Maxi and the staff were out cleaning up the grounds. She had no intentions of lying around while others worked. She was very tired but not too tired to act as if she were now too privileged to lend a hand.

She found her husband outside talking to Raymond LeVeq. Seriousness etched the features of both men. At her approach they both looked up.

"Galen, has something happened?"

He nodded. "I've just received word of my grandmother's death."

Hester placed her hand gently on his arm. "I'm sorry."

He looked down at her with emotionless eyes. "Would you be willing to attend the burial service with me?"

She nodded that she would.

He took her gloved hand and raised it to his lips. "Thank you," he said quietly. "I'll have Maxi help you pack. We leave in an hour."

Hester's tiredness became a secondary consideration as she helped Maxi and the maids ready her for the journey.

"I want you to stay by Galen's side, *chiquita*. Some of his set will do their best to reduce you to tears."

Hester, deciding over her nightwear, paused and looked back across the room. "Why? Outside of the obvious I mean."

"Obviously because you are outside his class, but mainly because you are his wife and they are not. There will be those who will hate your very step."

"He is that much of a prize?"

Maxi chuckled, "Maybe you and I know better, but they have been after him since the day he was born. When he was seven years old, his grandmother Vada signed documents arranging his marriage to the newborn granddaughter of a prominent New Orleans family."

"Newborn?"

"Yes, Ginette, his intended, was born six years after Galeno."

"Ginette?"

"Galeno has not told you of Ginette?"

Hester shook her head.

"Well, don't fret. It is probably because he has not deemed the subject worthy of discussion."

"Was he engaged to this Ginette when we married?"

"As far as Vada was concerned, yes. Galeno, no."

Maxi's confident reply wiped away any misgivings Hester may have had over this surprising news. "How long have you been with Galen, Maxi?"

"Since the day he was born. I was brought to this country by Galeno's grandfather. He came into my restaurant in Brazil one day, enjoyed my food so much he asked if I would come to New Orleans and oversee his kitchens."

"I was under the impression that you were from the islands."

"I am originally. I was owned by a Spanish family there. They lost their cane plantation to a storm one year and were forced to move back to Brazil to live with the mistress's family. The wife's family did not believe in slavery so the master was forced to free me and the five others who'd worked in his house or find lodgings elsewhere. Free, I worked in kitchens all over Brazil, saved my coin and opened a small tavern in Bahia. When Galeno's grandfather came in and made me his offer, I agreed and never looked back."

"What was Galen like as a child?"

"Fiercely angry."

"Why?"

"Because after his parents died he went from being a dearly loved child to a thing beneath his grandmother Vada's feet. She hated him and he hated her in turn."

"Why would a grandmother hate her grandchild?"

"Because her daughter, Ruth, married a man who was not only outside their social circle, but had dark skin and worked with his hands. He was a shipbuilder."

"That's a very honorable profession."

"To many it is, however to those with inherited wealth like Vada, he may as well have been a street sweeper."

One of the maids entered, saying the coachmen were awaiting Hester's trunks so Hester had to set aside any other questions concerning her husband's past.

During the ride, Galen didn't have much to say and Hester respected his silence. The long day had caught up with her and it soon became increasingly difficult to stay awake. She felt herself dozing off once more when Galen startled her back into full alertness by easing her onto his lap. Without a word he gently positioned her head against his wide chest, then kissed her softly on her brow. She cuddled close as he whispered in the dark coach, "Get some sleep. I'll awaken you when we arrive."

Galen held his sleeping wife against his heart. She was the most precious addition to his life. Without her he would have continued on his solitary path never feeling the fresh air of her love blowing across his world-weary soul. He harbored no guilt, admitting he was in many ways glad Vada's bitter presence no longer walked the earth. She would not have been kind to his Indigo. She would have found fault with everything about Hester and would have encouraged her venerable friends to take up the same posture. Granted he had friends who would not care about Hester's past, her ebony color, or her indigo hands, but many in Vada's set would—to gain Vada's favor many would savage their own kin, so he could well imagine how they would pounce on an innocent like his wife.

But Vada was dead, undoubtedly suffocated by her own evil heart. Never again would he have to look upon her and remember the beatings and the foul treatment, or hear her brand his mother a whore and himself a whore's bastard. When they buried her a few days hence, he would pay his respects and then move on with his life.

They reached Detroit at daybreak. Hester came awake still held in her husband's arms as he walked her into the doorway of a small cottage. She peered around like a sleepy child at the unfamiliar but well furnished surroundings. When her eyes brushed Racine's and then the smiling faces of a few other men and women she'd not met before, Hester came fully awake. Embarrassed, she quickly turned her face back into his chest and hissed, "Put me down."

Instead, he said in a formal voice, "Everyone, my wife. Racine, you have my rooms prepared?"

Hester could not see the reactions on anyone's face, but she heard Racine say, "Certainly, Galeno. Bring your lovely bride this way, please."

Galen, his arms filled with his mortified wife, followed Racine to his rooms.

Once they were inside, Racine remarked, "You may put her down now, *neveu*. No one is going to steal her from you."

He did so reluctantly.

Racine, dressed in a simple black gown, approached Hester slowly. "Hello, Hester. Let me say how pleased I am to be able to call you niece."

"Thank you."

"The others are eager to meet you, but I think we should let you rest for the time being. We will speak again later in the day." She took Hester's hands in hers and squeezed them with affection. "Welcome to the family, La Petite Indigo. The dragon chose a most worthy mate."

She blessed her tall nephew with a smile, then left the room.

Galen put Hester to bed, promising to check in on her later. Hester wanted to ask him when he intended to sleep himself, but she was asleep again before he reached the door.

Downstairs, Galen joined his aunt for what he hoped would be a short discussion. He, too, needed sleep.

She was in the study surrounded by stacks and stacks of ledgers and documents. He stared around at the crates occupying the chairs and most of the floor. "What is all this?"

"Vada's business dealings. This is only a portion. The rest is being scrutinized by your uncle."

"Can he be trusted to give a true account?"

"With that money-grabbing wife of his? Of course not. I had everything that appeared to be of any importance brought here. I gave him the rest. All of the figures and legal Latin will bore him soon enough."

Galen grinned tiredly. He loved her dearly. He could not imagine what type of life he would have had if this strong, beautiful sister of his mother had not come to his aid. Many times, Racine had stepped in to bear his punishments, taking his canings across her own back rather than let him suffer more. In many ways he owed her his life. Maybe now with Vada's death, his beloved *tante* could live freely. "So have you found anything of import?"

"I've only been at this a few days, but it appears that although Mama had a horrid way with people, she had a flair for business. She more than quadrupled the money she received when Papa passed."

Galen stared, impressed.

"But much of it was accumulated in ways that are appalling. She brokered slaves, blackmailed friends and family, and charged a sinful amount of interest on loans she made to people in New Orleans. Those who weren't able to repay lost business, land, jewels. That box by your feet holds nothing but deeds to properties and shops signed over to her over the years. This one here on the desk is filled with ledgers containing the misdeeds and stumbles of everyone we know. Galen, this woman sat around controlling people like marionettes. There are payments here to midwives who kept her informed on illegitimate births. She has them organized by parish, for heaven's sake! She would then demand a payment from the woman's family in exchange for either her silence or help in finding a suitable man for the husband-less woman."

"Are you certain?"

"Yesterday, I made a few discreet enquiries using some of the information found inside these ledgers and yes, her heart was as evil as is painted here. I was told stories that curled my hair and some that turned my stomach. She will burn in hell, *neveu,* truly and eternally burn."

"So what are you going to do with it all?"

"Invite the most injured people on these lists, the ones she still held on strings until her death. One by one, I will invite them into the parlor and let them burn the paper which she held over their lives. Then I will see if the properties and shops can be restored to the rightful heirs."

"No doubt, she's spinning in her casket just hearing you contemplate such actions."

"Well, the more she spins, the more evenly she will roast."

Racine said the words with such a straight face, Galen threw back his head and roared with laughter.

Hester was surprised to see Maxi in the room when she awakened. "Maxi, what on earth are you doing here? When did you arrive?"

"Oh, an hour or so ago. I came down with most of the staff in the carriage which departed a few hours after you and Galeno left. Since Racine has fired the woman masquerading as a cook in her mother's kitchens, I am here to help, but mainly I am here to see with my own eyes that Vada Rousseau is truly dead."

"Well, I am glad to see you. Whose home is this?"

"Galeno leased this place after he left you last fall. Andre made the arrangements once we all came north in answer to the message you posted for Galeno."

Hester remembered the message; she'd assumed it had been coded.

"So, *chiquita,* I have your breakfast. Your husband appears as if he has not slept at all, but he awaits you when you are ready."

"Thank you, Maxi. I'm glad you are here."

"Let me know if you are in need of anything else."

Hester nodded, and Maxi left, quietly closing the door.

Hester found Galen in the small study poring over

papers from behind a desk filled with ledgers and documents. True to Maxi's description, he appeared dead on his feet. "Have you slept?" Hester asked.

"No, but you're the prettiest thing I've seen all day. Come give your tired husband a kiss."

Hester walked into the room and complied. When they drew away from one another, she asked softly, "How was that?"

Galen growled like a contented dragon as he held her in the circle of his arms. "So good, I'd like another . . ."

She complied yet again.

When they parted this time, she reached up and stroked the lines etching his face. "You need to sleep, Galen Vachon; not even you can survive without it."

"I know, *petite,* but I need to go through ás much of this as I can."

"What is it?"

"My grandmother's papers. It appears as if she has blackmailed every person in the city of New Orleans."

"What?!"

"Well, maybe not everyone, but a fairly large percentage. Her poisonous tentacles reached everywhere, I'm finding."

Hester didn't know what to say.

Evidently Galen read her face and said, "It's my worry, not yours. I'm going to finish up here and get some sleep. I'll join you later."

Hester looked up at her golden, moustached dragon and said, "I will only leave if you promise to get some sleep within the hour."

He raised her gloved hand to his lips. "You have my word."

Hester left him then, and went off in search of a familiar face. The house was much smaller than the sprawling Folly. Here all of the rooms were on one floor. She entered the parlor and found Racine talking quietly with a blindingly beautiful woman. Both were dressed in mourning black. They greeted her entrance with a smile.

Racine stood. "Ah, niece, come in. How was your rest?"

"Fine, Racine."

Racine invited Hester to join them. "Hester Vachon, this is a dear family friend, Ginette Dupree. Ginette, this is Galen's wife."

Ginette's smiling cinnamon eyes appeared sincere as she said, "You've no idea how pleased I am to finally make your acquaintance."

Hester was a bit taken aback by the woman's warmth. As Galen's contracted intended, Hester assumed the woman would be chilly at best.

Ginette must have sensed Hester's thoughts because she said, "I assume someone has already informed you of my position in Galeno's life."

"Yes. Maxi has."

"Well, rest assured, I couldn't be happier that you are his wife."

Racine stood and said, "I must meet with the priest this morning about the arrangements for the burial. You two stay and get acquainted. I'll return later this afternoon."

So there Hester sat, alone with this stunningly beautiful woman who claimed to be happy over losing her intended.

Ginette explained, "Galeno and I would never have suited as man and wife. I love him very much, but he's like a brother to me. He taught me to ride my first horse, and escorted me to my first ball. I thought him the bravest, smartest, strongest boy on earth. I still do. But I've loved him long enough to know he needs a woman just as brave and just as strong as he. Someone who will stand up to him as Raymond says you have done, someone he can converse with. I haven't had a lot of schooling, Hester, and he gets impatient with me when he wants to discuss issues I know nothing about."

Hester told her softly, "Reading a newspaper can solve that problem, Ginette."

"But I don't care about politics or talk of war or Mr. Douglass's position. Galeno sometimes teases me by saying my parents raised me with wool over my eyes and cotton between my ears, and he is correct. Galeno doesn't need a woman who can only discuss hemlines. Had he married me he would've wound up hating me. I couldn't bear that."

Her face was set with such seriousness Hester could feel the truthfulness of the words.

Ginette then asked, "Do you know where Galeno goes when he disappears for months on end each year?"

Hester kept her face void of any response but Ginette took her silence as confirmation.

"You do know, don't you? See, he would never trust me with his secrets, but he has you. Not even Vada knew, and even though she would roar at him, he never told her a word."

Hester found this to be one of the oddest encounters she'd ever experienced.

"So, shall we agree to be friends?"

Hester, taken aback once more, nodded yes. "I would like that."

"Then good. Now, tell me what you're wearing to the ball?"

"Ball?"

"Yes, Vada's burial ball. Her will states that a ball is to be given on the day of her burial or none of her relatives will get her money. Racine refused to plan it, so Galeno's uncle Reginald and his wife have instead. Reginald's wife, Mavis, is not known for her taste, but"—she shrugged—"we go and pay our respects, drink from Vada's celebrated cellars, and thank the heavens for removing her from our lives."

Hester stared. She dearly hoped her friends and relations would not sit around savaging her name when she passed on, but then again, Vada appeared to have been a detestable woman; maybe she was only reaping what she'd sown.

"Will this ball be a solemn event?"

"Heavens no. Vada might have viewed it as some grand tribute to all she stood for, but everyone else, especially Mavis, views it as a celebration. The women will be wearing their best gowns and jewels. Did Maxi pack some of your jewelry?"

"Maxi and I brought along gowns, but I don't have many jewels. I lead a very simple life, Ginette."

Ginette's eyes widened. "Galeno should be ashamed of himself. His wife should have chests of jewels."

"I don't need jewels."

Her eyes widened with astonishment. "Hester, never ever speak such blasphemy, especially not within earshot of any male. Just wait until I see that Galeno."

Hester shook her head. Her amusement could not be hidden. She found she did like Ginette, even if the woman's priorities in life contrasted sharply with her own. "As my friend, you must promise you will not speak to Galen about my lack of stones."

"But Hester, people will talk—"

"Ginette, you've no idea of the talk I've endured lately. To have someone denigrate me for not having jewels is something I can survive."

Ginette searched Hester's face. "Are you certain?"

"Positive."

Ginette sighed audibly in frustration. "I'll not speak to Galeno. I promise."

"Thank you, Ginette."

They spent a few more moments talking idly about the ball and the people who would attend. Ginette explained that only local members of Vada's family and friends would be at the burial. Racine had received a wire saying no one in Louisiana would be attending.

Hester asked, "Are there many family members in Louisiana?"

"Very many, but none wanted to go to the expense of coming all this way just to bury Vada. She was as mean as a croc, and didn't care that people knew. In fact, it seemed she went out of her way sometimes just to keep her legendary evil alive in people's minds. Poor Mavis and Reginald were reminded every day that they were eating her food and living in her house. The poor servants never stayed more than a season."

"But why did she treat people this way?"

"Bitterness. Her husband, Galeno's *grandpère* kept a dark-skinned mistress in the quarter. Vada was humiliated and appalled by her husband's choice. She used her influence to have the woman implicated in a slave insurrection and nearly succeeded in having the mistress sold into slavery. Galeno's *grandpère* was outraged. He used his own formidable influence to save the woman from the block, then publicly denounced Vada. He vowed never to live with her again, and he never did. He escorted his mistress to balls, the theater, the races, and didn't give a cat's tail about what people thought. He was happy. Vada had much thinner skin. The whispers and scandal drove her here to Michigan where her side of the family still owned land given to them by the French. According to my parents, she'd always been a manipulative person, even as a child. After her husband's denunciation, the bitterness and the thirst for revenge apparently consumed her. It seemed as if she weren't happy unless someone else was miserable."

Hester shook her head at the sad tale.

"Did she love her husband?"

"No. The marriage had been arranged. It was touted as the coming together of two very wealthy and powerful New Orleans families, but she treated him just as she did everyone else—as if he were mud beneath her feet. My mama says Vada would shriek at him at parties, hired men to shadow his movements every moment of the day. My papa says Galeno's *grandpère* showed much restraint by not having her visited by a paid assassin. She was simply awful."

She sounded simply awful to Hester as well. On the surface, one could hardly fault her husband for seeking peace in the arms of a lover, but what fate did Racine and Galen's mother suffer as a result?

"How did the children fare in the face of the scandal?"

"Vada brought Racine, Ruth, and their younger brother Reginald here. They lived with her during the winter months and spent summers in Louisiana. They grew to adolescence listening to her berate their father and his whore, as she always termed the mistress."

"It must have been a very unhappy life for them."

Ginette agreed. "Yes. Reginald grew up without any direction at all, Racine turned to her faith, but Ruth was headstrong and rebelled. Her choice of a dark-skinned man as her husband led Vada to banish her. Ruth went willingly. No one learned her fate until seven years later when Maxi brought the orphaned Galeno to Vada. Maxi had been the cook in the house down in New Orleans. When Vada came north, Maxi stayed to serve the *grandpère*. Galeno's parents were killed on a sea voyage and when the *grandpère* died a year later, Maxi had no choice but to bring him to Vada. His father James had no other family able to take in an orphaned boy. Maxi said at that time she thought about raising him as her own, but she felt his *grandmère* had more of a right to him, even though Maxi knew Vada's true character. Vada agreed to house Galen only if Maxi would stay and cook for the household. The two never got along well down in Louisiana, but for Galen's sake Maxi stayed."

Ginette's voice softened with emotion as she continued, "Vada used her own grandson as a slave. He slept in an unheated room with the servants, and spent every waking hour doing chores. He was a seven-year-old boy but he cut wood, polished furniture, silver, emptied the slop jars, helped the yardmen. There were beatings, punishments for the smallest offenses. She never forgave Ruth for not honoring the marriage arrangements she'd made and for loving a man whose color, as far as Vada was concerned, qualified him to do nothing but make deliveries to Vada's back door. Maxi was outraged, but she was powerless to change Galeno's fate alone, so she wrote to Racine in France and his aunt returned home immediately."

"Did Racine know of Galen's birth?"

"Yes, she'd been in New Orleans when he was born,
but Racine had joined an order in the years following
and so had no idea her *neveu* was suffering at the hands
of her mother. She'd been notified of her father's death
by his solicitor, but no one other than Maxi had written
her of her sister's death or of Galeno's fate."

"She left her order?"

"Yes, she said the Lord obviously had other work for
her to accomplish. She will tell you that she never
questioned that decision. Galeno needed her."

And he had, Hester thought as she tried to digest the
tragic story. Galen had every reason to be the fiercely
angry child Maxi had described.

"When Galeno reached his majority, he came into the
inheritance left by his mother, *grandpère,* and his
father's estates. It made him a very wealthy man. He
took Maxi from Vada's home the next day and he has
never looked back."

The burial service took place early the next morning.
As a member of the family, Hester took her seat in the
front pew of the Catholic church, and tried not to notice
the speculative stares and whispers of the congregation
seated behind her. Maxi had been correct, she'd endured
more than a few hostile stares from some of the women
present, but she didn't flinch from the venomous eyes or
turn away.

The ride to the cemetery took nearly an hour. Even
though Vada had spent her entire life disdaining the few
drops of African blood in her veins, in death she had no
say. Those few drops rendered her as Black as any other
member of the race, and because they did, she could not
be buried in a White cemetery. Galen thought it only
fitting that Vada spend eternity turning in her grave,
unable to deny her true ancestry; as Racine quipped the
other day, the more Vada turned, the more evenly she
would roast.

Chapter 20

After a buffet luncheon Hester was glad when she and Galen rode back to his leased house on the river while most of the guests were staying at the expansive old mansion ruled by Vada for over sixty years. All day, she'd been stared at and whispered about. She didn't know if Galen had noticed the hostile looks or the cool greetings, but it confirmed what she'd told him all along; his set was not prepared to accept her. Not that it mattered, she had no plans to live amongst them, and even if that weren't the case, they'd be nothing more than nodding acquaintances; her world encompassed more than gowns, hemlines, and hair dressing.

In the room she and Galen shared, Hester dropped down into an upholstered chair. She was tired and not looking forward to Vada's memorial ball.

Galen glanced over at his black-clad wife, and said, "You did well today."

"With all the cold looks I received it's a wonder I haven't been turned to stone."

"I noticed the stares. They are from women I wouldn't have married even had we not met, so don't let them upset you."

"Will we have to attend the ball?" She didn't know if she could endure many more stares without putting someone in her place.

"I asked Racine the very same question."

"And her reply?"

"Yes, if only for a short while."

Hester pouted like a disappointed child.

He couldn't contain his chuckle. "My sentiments exactly, *petite,* but—" He shrugged.

While she brooded he came over and stood before her. "How's this for a compromise. Suppose we head for home as soon as the ball ends?"

Hester's eyes shone. "Are you sincere?"

"I want to go home."

She got to her feet and rewarded him with a kiss. She wished to go home, too.

An hour before the ball, the maids came to help Hester dress, so Galen excused himself. He would don his attire in the room shared by Raymond and Andre.

When the maids uncovered the gown for the evening, Hester's eyes widened at its beauty. She'd never seen this gown before.

"It's a surprise. Mr. Vachon had it special made," one of the young women told Hester, who stood transfixed by the dark green silk gown. The color was so deep it reminded her of the green of a dark forest. The capped sleeves were softly pleated and would leave her arms bare below the crown of her shoulders. Even on the hanger, the decolletage was daring, while the rest of it flowed like a silk cloud to the floor. The maids produced little heeled slippers to match the green gown, and a pair of long gloves to complete the ensemble.

Dressed, and with her hair coiled up, Hester stared at herself in the long cheval glass. It amazed her how Galen's choice of clothing could transform her from simple Hester Wyatt into La Petite Indigo Vachon. In the beautiful dress she looked as if she truly did belong at his side.

He entered the room at that moment and she smiled at the handsome sight he made in his formal all-white attire. The only spot of color came from the dark rose in his lapel. The flower bore the same rich color as the one he'd left beneath her pillow on that night months ago. He appeared taller, and even more handsome, if that were possible. She'd be the envy of every woman in attendance tonight.

"You look ravishing," he said.

"And you are going to have your wife turned to stone with your handsomeness."

Galen stilled. It was the first time she'd referred to herself as his wife and the sound of it on her lips pleased him very much.

"Is something the matter?"

"No. I'm just enjoying the sight and sounds of you."

Hester didn't know what to make of the reply, but the pleasure in his tone made her suddenly shy. "Is it time to depart?"

"In a moment. We have to remedy a few things first."

"Such as?"

He withdrew a slim box from within his coat. "Close your eyes."

Hester viewed him suspiciously.

"Close your eyes."

She complied.

A few moments of silence passed, then she sensed him at her back. She jumped a bit at the feel of a necklace being draped against her throat. With eyes still closed, she raised her hand and gently passed her fingers over the jewelry while he closed the clasp.

"You may open your eyes now," he told her.

In the mirror, Hester stared at the beautiful strand of linked emeralds. They were surrounded by diamonds that made each green stone appear to be a sparkling, emerald-centered snowflake. Before she could get over the wonder of the gift, he held out earrings to match. She placed them in her ears with shaking fingers. She surveyed the effect in the mirror and had to admit the emeralds were the crowning touch.

Galen thought so, too. Too bad they had to attend Vada's gala. He didn't want her beauty viewed by any eyes but his own this evening.

"Now . . . one final touch."

When she saw him reach into his pocket and extract the small flask of vanilla he'd presented her with that night on the veranda, her heart began to race. It beat faster still as he reached up and slowly traced the stopper behind each of her ears. Next came a gentle touch on the back of her neck, then a deliciously lazy slide over the soft trembling tops of each breast. He placed a fleeting kiss there and she swayed, eyes closed.

"Lift your dress . . ."

Hester, having not an inkling as to what he would do next, modestly raised her dress to just below her knees.

"Higher, Indigo . . ."

Holding his eyes, she slowly revealed the tops of her silk stockings and the lovely little garters which anchored them.

Galen's eyes glowed. He touched his mouth to her lips—a reward for being so agreeable.

The reward intensified as he bent and trailed a whisper of scent across the bare skin above the tops of her stockings.

"Turn for me . . ."

She was a prisoner of his spell and so complied without thought.

"This is all I want you to think of tonight . . ." Galen whispered as he languidly grazed the stopper over the back of each thigh. He drew a lingering line just below the soft undercurve of her silk-drawered bottom, then as she trembled, drew it up the inner edge of one thigh, and seductively down the other.

"Don't think about the harpies you'll meet tonight or the gossip you will hear . . . only of me seeking out these hidden scents later . . . when we are alone."

Hester drew in a ragged breath.

"Now you can let down your gown . . ." he instructed gently.

The haze of rising desire muddled her vision and thinking. The gown rustled softly back to the floor.

He raised an eyebrow and smiled. "Are you ready?"
She somehow managed to say, "Yes."
He kissed her softly, then drew away reluctantly.

At the ball some of the people Hester met were surprisingly friendly while others were January cold. Hester paid them no mind whatsoever. All she had to do was catch her husband's eye, feel the heat reflected there, and be warmed by his shielding love.

But after a while she sought solitude and fresh air out on the veranda. There were so many people inside, the crush and heat became too much to bear. She saw quite a few others outside taking advantage of the late August evening. As it had been since her arrival, some of the guests acknowledged her polite nods, while others did not.

"I thought I'd find you out here."

Hester turned to see Ginette at her side. "Hello, Ginette, are you enjoying yourself?"

Ginette was dressed in a beautiful creme-colored gown, set off by the sapphires around her neck and golden hoops in her ears. Ginette smiled. "Yes, and you?"

"I suppose. Some of the people have been very nice while others—" Hester shrugged.

"Well, I shouldn't say this, but had Galeno ever looked at me the way he has been looking at you all evening, I would have married him, and gladly. You and he are all people are talking about inside."

Hester didn't really care to know that. "Lately, it seems as if I fuel gossip wherever I go."

"The gossips may say whatever they like, but Galeno's love for you is very apparent."

The statement cheered Hester.

"And do not worry about the gossips. Galeno will kill the first person to insult you, and with the saint's blessing the first to die will be this woman approaching us now."

Hester stared at Ginette, then looked at the man and woman crossing the veranda. Under the light of the torches set around, the woman seemed to be smiling genuinely as she approached.

Ginette said, "She has the smile of a croc, *n'est ce pas?* Someday, I hope she will be skinned and turned into a lampshade."

"Ginette?!" Hester laughed.

"Shhh. Here they come."

The man introduced himself as Leland Winters. The woman on his arm, Belle Monet, looked to be near Racine's age. Her pale face had probably been very beautiful in her youth, but the heavy powder atop it now appeared to age her well past the years she had meant to conceal. She was tall and junoesque. Her gown was so sheer Hester had to force herself not to stare in shock at the rouge so obviously applied to her nipples!

Belle's French-inflected words brought Hester's eyes back to her face. "So, you are Galeno's little Hester. Tiny thing, isn't she Leland?"

Leland, dressed as formally as the other men in attendance, was light-skinned, curly-haired, and handsome. He was grinning at Hester as if he were planning to buy her. *"Mais, oui."*

Belle then turned to Ginette and said, "And here is the poor Ginette. Surely Galeno's marriage broke your heart."

Ginette didn't rise to the bait. She said sweetly, "I am fine, Belle. However, I was a bit worried when I heard from the servants about *your* rage when you received the announcement that Hester and Galeno were wed. Is it true you took to your bed for three days?"

Hester watched the smile drop from Belle's face. Her dark eyes were cold when she said, "Galeno and I ended our association many years ago."

Ginette said easily, *"Many* years ago, if my memory serves correct."

It was a barely veiled slap at Belle's age and Hester

now understood why Galen said he'd been raised amongst vipers.

Belle, her croc's grin once again in place, turned from Ginette to Hester. "Is it true you are a former slave?"

"Yes."

Belle seemed a bit taken aback by Hester's blunt response. She looked her over as if she could somehow see Hester's past in her manner. "How ever did you meet someone like Galeno Vachon?"

Hester answered truthfully. "Through mutual friends."

"Mutual friends?" Belle skeptically echoed.

Hester didn't elaborate, she merely stood and awaited the next rude question.

It did not take long. Leland Winters asked drolly, "Word has it you have indigo-stained hands. Belle and I thought we'd come and see if it were true."

By the look in his eyes Hester realized he actually believed she would honor such a request.

Before Hester or Ginette could give him the set down he so richly deserved, Galen appeared at her side. "My wife only removes her gloves for me, Winters."

To emphasize the point, Galen raised her gloved hands to his lips and kissed them. Ignoring Hester's tormentors, he asked, "May I escort you two lovely ladies back inside. Racine wishes to speak with you."

He didn't even acknowledge Winters or Belle as he ushered Hester and Ginette away.

When they were out of earshot, Hester looked up at her golden knight and asked, "Did you really have an arrangement with that Monet woman?"

Galen smiled. "Unfortunately, yes, but chalk it up to the insanity of youth."

"How old were you?"

"Seventeen."

"Seventeen! How old was she?"

"Twenty-eight."

Hester stared, too shocked to ask anything more.

She and Galen set out for home a short while later. In the shadow-filled coach she felt herself relax for what seemed the first time in days. She hoped she would not have to visit Galen's world again anytime in the near future. So much venom had to be detrimental to the soul.

Galen was seated on the velvet seat across from her. His voice came at her out of the shadows, "Did Belle and Winters say anything to offend you?"

She shook her head. "No, not really. They reminded me of the children who taunted me my first year in school. I've learned since then not to let the ignorance of others touch me."

"I promise you, we won't travel in those circles any more than is absolutely necessary."

"I plan on holding you to your word," she said, happy he knew how she felt. "I did enjoy Ginette's company, however. She's rather nice."

"She's grown into a surprisingly competent woman. Maybe now that you and I are wed, her parents will let her marry the man she really loves."

"And who would that be?"

"Raymond's youngest brother, Gerrold."

"Raymond has a younger brother?"

"Raymond has five younger brothers. Though you didn't meet them, they were the men who accompanied Raymond the night he came to take me home."

The memory of that steamy October encounter was still vivid. What a night that had been. "Does Raymond have a love?"

"Raymond?!" Galen echoed skeptically. "He boasts an inborn immunity to Cupid's sting. But if it can happen to me, his time is surely running out. I can't wait until he meets her."

"You two tease each other mightily."

"We've known each other our whole lives. He lived up the road from my *grandpère*. When my parents' death forced me to come north, we lost touch for a while, but once Maxi and I moved back to New Orleans after I gained my majority, he and I resumed our friendship. We've been inseparable ever since—until I met you . . ."

His words touched Hester like a caressing hand as his dark eyes held hers through the moving shadows that played over the interior of the rolling coach. The air had become thick with anticipation and unspoken desire. Hester's lips parted of their own accord and her nipples rose as if they'd already received his touch. As she'd been instructed, all evening she'd thought of nothing but his scenting of her, and his promise to seek them out later when they were alone.

Galen ran his eyes over his seductive little mistress-wife and knew that hidden beneath the voluminous emerald cloak lay ebony skin that had been scented by his own hand. He'd been fighting his arousal all night, but now that they were alone, he could have his way with her. "Since that day in Detroit, I've wanted to make love to you in this coach."

His soft declaration made her tremble, because he'd voiced her own secret desire.

"I want to open your cloak and kiss the tops of your breasts. I want to place you atop my lap, then watch your eyes when I fill you . . ."

She couldn't speak. His heated words touched her in all the places he'd attuned to passion. The gates he'd opened were ones she could no longer close. His presence streamed over her like the annual spring flooding of the Nile, leaving her rich and full as a delta.

"Come sit beside me," he invited.

When she was by his side, Galen slowly opened the frogs of her cloak, then parted the halves to reveal her beauty. He leaned down to kiss the ebony throat above the necklace, then the fragrant sweetness below. His hand slid up her back, and with a touch made her arch to bring herself closer. The scent of the vanilla had been warmed by the heat of her skin over the course of the evening and had mellowed to a deep, full richness. It clung to her shoulders, her jaw, the smooth plane beneath her ears. How such a simple vanilla bean could invoke such an erotic aroma was a question he had no time to ponder; her pleasuring and the heights he'd take her to this night were his only concern.

He surrendered to the temptation of her parted lips and kissed her mouth. She met him willingly, enticing him with tiny bites on his lips, and sultry licks of her tongue. He pressed her back against the seat, then kissed her possessively.

It evolved into a lingering, seductive encounter; her bodice was eased down, her gown was rucked up. As promised, he sought out the scents he had hidden earlier, kissing, exploring, shocking. Until finally, just when Hester thought she might melt from the heat, he eased her atop his lap. He filled her with his desire and held her eyes as he taught her the glory of making love astride.

The coach rolled on.

Dawn had just pinkened the sky when the coach pulled onto the road leading to Whittaker. Hester wanted to stop by the Wyatt house before going on to the Folly. Although she and Galen had only been gone a few days, she needed to make certain no runaways were awaiting her return.

As the coach halted, Galen said, "You're going to have to put down your gown . . ."

It had been a heated, erotic ride, and throughout it all she hadn't known who'd been the more demanding, Galen or herself. She could make love to him for an eternity.

In contrast to his words however, his hands continued to explore the dewy offerings beneath her skirts.

"You'll have to stop, Galen." The bliss pounded between her thighs like a heartbeat.

"You'll have to lower your dress. There isn't a man alive who could stop touching you, posed as you are."

She was seated crossways across his lap, her head

resting on his shoulder, her skirts in scandalous disarray about her dark thighs.

"Lower your gown, *petite,* otherwise we'll have to begin again."

She leaned up and kissed him warmly, "Is that a promise?"

Galen raised an eyebrow, then drew away. "I may change your name to 'Insatiable' if you're not careful."

She smiled the smile of a thoroughly loved woman and said, "That wouldn't be a bad thing. I could be the Insatiable Indigo—Mistress and Wife of the Dragon Vachon."

Galen felt his manhood harden sharply beneath her soft hips. "Up, shameless woman. Lower your gown and fix your clothing before you really rouse the dragon."

Hester gave him a mock pout of disappointment but slid from his lap.

"Shameless," Galen echoed.

Grinning Hester adjusted her gown. When they were both ready, she let him help her down from the coach. Her steps faltered upon seeing the door of the house ajar.

"Galen, I don't remember leaving the door open."

Galen ran his eyes over the door, the house, the grounds. He then glanced up at the coachman and nodded.

"Hester, stay here. James and I will enter first. I'll call to you if it's safe."

"Galen—"

"We'll only be a moment."

Hester stood by the coach.

However, they were gone for so long she disobeyed Galen's instructions and went inside. The destruction which greeted her made her gasp and put her hands to her mouth. Every piece of furniture—tables, sideboards, highboys, had been broken and turned over. There were shards of shattered crockery and china littering the floor. Her dry goods from the kitchen had been scattered everywhere. Lamps lay smashed, their oil seeping into the floor like life's blood. Curtains were shredded and partially ripped from their rods. The vandals had taken a sledgehammer to the walls that had first been smeared with syrup and lamp oil, and they were honeycombed with gaping holes and cracks. The damage was so extensive she couldn't breathe.

Galen's sad voice caught her attention. "I thought I asked you to wait."

He stood on stairs, where the railing had been splintered and torn apart.

"Who did this?"

She ran to the steps intending to see how the upper levels had fared but he stopped her with a gentle hold. "You don't want to see."

Hester stared, her eyes wide with shock and disbelief.

"The dogs were let loose up there. They've fouled everything—your bedding, your clothing."

"Dogs?!"

"It was Shoe."

Hester couldn't believe any of this was happening.

Galen debated whether to show her the note, then decided he would. She was his wife, she trusted him to be honest.

Hester's hands were shaking as she took the small piece of paper. *Since you're going to be returning south, me and the boys decided to throw you a going-away party. Too bad you missed it. See you soon.*

Chilled, Hester looked up at her husband.

"Don't worry, the only person going south is Shoe. South straight to hell."

Hester's next thought froze her with fear. "Oh, lord, Galen. My papers!"

Hester ran past him and up the steps.

The stench in her room arrested her steps a moment but she went on inside. There were tears in her eyes as she took in the fouled room and the hateful words smeared over the walls in excrement. The big wardrobe which sat in front of the wall near her bed had been turned over and smashed. Its back had been splintered. Hester knew without even looking inside that the papers were gone. They'd been in the false back of the wardrobe since her arrival north. She walked over to the wardrobe, and discovered that, indeed, they had been stolen.

Galen asked "Who else would have known the papers were hid there?"

She sat on the floor overwhelmed by all she'd seen. "The officers of the Vigilance Committee: Reverend Adams, Bea, Lovejoy, Branton Hubble, of course, but no one else."

"Are you certain?"

She replied in a distant voice. "Fairly certain, yes."

Hester looked around the room she'd loved so much and felt her stomach roll in reaction. She'd die before she'd let Shoe take her south again.

Galen's heart twisted with pain seeing the devastation on her face. "You once told me your aunt filed a set of your papers with the local sheriff when you arrived north."

Hester nodded tightly. "There should be a duplicate in Sheriff Lawson's office."

"I'll send Andre over to check on that as soon as he and Raymond and Maxi return."

Galen wanted to hold her in his arms and reassure her that all would be well, but until Shoe could be found and stopped she was in danger. "We should go home, *petite*. There's nothing we can do here at this point. We can return later in the day or tomorrow and begin cleaning if you'd like."

She nodded and let him lead her out.

Hester watched the house through the coach's small portal as they pulled away. She wondered if it would ever be restored so her ancestors could resume their nightly walks. The house had stood as a monument to their freedom and pride for over a half century. Now it lay in shambles, destroyed by hate.

For the rest of the day, Hester was numb. Gail, who'd

stayed at the Folly while they were away, blamed herself when she heard the news, saying she should have gone by and checked on the house while Hester and Galen were in Detroit. Hester reassured her that she was not to blame, but Gail's sadness showed plainly in her face.

Maxi and the rest of the household arrived at the Folly a few hours later. Everyone was appalled by the news of the destruction. Galen sent Andre straight into town to check on Hester's papers. Raymond LeVeq wanted to hunt Shoe down immediately. Galen was of a like mind, but wanted to wait for Andre's return before formulating a plan.

Andre returned and confirmed that Hester's papers were still on file with Lawson. The sheriff vowed to bring Shoe in for the vandalism.

Galen did not relax. By law, the special commissioners who tried runaway cases were given ten dollars if they ruled the fugitive had to be returned but only five if the claim by slaveowners proved false. In the years following the law's implementation, more than two hundred alleged fugitives had been brought to court, but less than two dozen were ruled not to be property. Should Shoe successfully have Hester arrested, her chances of returning to life as his wife were not good. Frederick Douglass had once said, "The only way to make the Fugitive Slave Law a dead law is to make a half dozen or more dead kidnappers," and Galen wholeheartedly agreed.

The next morning, Hester, Gail, Galen, and some of the house staff went over to the Wyatt house to begin the cleanup. Maxi swore in Portuguese upon seeing the destruction. Hester simply closed her heart and mind to the hurt and went to work.

Throughout the day many neighbors stopped by to lend a hand after hearing the terrible news. By mid-afternoon, there was a small army at work, hauling out debris, burning fouled bedding and garments, and sweeping up the glass and dry goods. Bea didn't come over until late in the day, and when she stepped into the house and saw the holes in the walls and the splintered handrail of the stairs, she broke into sobs and hurried back outdoors. Hester set aside her broom and went out to console her.

Bea, standing on the porch, turned to Hester with red-rimmed eyes, then turned away, her face distant. "This is all my fault."

Hester hugged her tightly. "It's no one's fault but Shoe's, Bea. Gail said much the same thing. She blames herself for not going over to check the place while I was away, but it isn't her fault either."

Bea slowly disentangled herself from Hester's embrace, and said softly, "Yes, Hester it is my fault."

Something in Bea's eyes and voice sent a chill up Hester's spine. "What are you saying?"

"I'm saying this is my fault. Had it not been for me—" Her voice trailed off. "Go inside and get your man, and I'll try and explain."

Hester returned with Galen and Raymond.

Bea nodded tightly at the two men, then turned away. "I'm a stupid old woman, Hester. The traitor we've been looking for is me. I'm the traitor."

Hester stared in shock. Galen and Raymond looked grim.

Bea spoke in a low monotone. "When I left Tennessee thirty years ago, I left three children behind, two boys and a girl. I wrote the master after I began my life here. I wanted to see if he would let me buy their freedom. He wrote me back and said not only would he not allow me to buy their freedom, he planned to sell them deep south to punish me for running."

Bea's eyes were filled with pain and loss. "I wrote him back, begging him not to, but he didn't respond. I never heard from any of my children again, until Lem showed up. He's my oldest boy, he was six when I ran. Smart as a whip he was. I was so happy to see him Hester. So glad I didn't realize he was a snake until it was too late." Bea wiped at the tears in her eyes. "He kept telling me he didn't know what had happened to my other two children, said they'd been sold separately after I ran, but he was lying."

"How do you know?"

"He told me so himself, the day Ezra Shoe came to visit."

Galen asked, "When did this happen?"

"About two weeks before you first came to us as the Black Daniel."

Galen stared, surprised that she had known of his alterego all along.

"Yes. I know who you are. I've doctored a lot of folks in my time, seen them beat up, seen them healed, and I never forget a face."

"So where are your other children?" Raymond asked.

"Dead. Both dead."

There was a silence before Bea's emotionless voice continued. "My daughter died in childbirth, my other son of snakebite in Texas."

"Why did Shoe visit you?"

"He and my Lem are half brothers."

Hester heart stopped. "Brothers."

"Yes, they have the same father, my master. Shoe's mother was the wife of the overseer and the master used her too."

"Good lord," Hester whispered.

"Shoe and Lem are mercenary slavecatchers. They've ridden with some of the most brazen kidnappers in the country: the Gag Gang, Patty Cannon's Gang."

Patty Cannon was well known to those working the Road. Whereas people like Hester and Galen helped fugitives out of the South, Lucretia (Patty) Cannon worked to send fugitives back to slavery. She and her gang of East Coast kidnappers employed both Black and White conductors, used secret houses as stations, and sent messages by code. The abduction of twenty children from the Philadelphia area was said to have been the work of her gang. She was both feared and hated.

Hester shook her head sadly. "Why would your son work for kidnappers?"

"Because it is what he does. He said it is an easy way for him to earn a wage."

"Duping your own people?"

"Yes, duping his own people. He isn't the first to have no loyalty to the race."

Hester knew Bea was correct. The Black press and antislavery journals made it a point to inform their readers of Blacks who preyed upon the race by publishing the traitor's descriptions and last known whereabouts. Such vigilance kept the number of betrayers low, as did the physical violence oftimes meted out by members of the community upon such individuals. In Cincinnati last year, a man named Robert Russell was tarred and feathered after it became known he'd been paid ten dollars for his assistance in helping kidnappers seize a fugitive. In another Cincinnati incident, a Black man named John Brodie was beaten so badly by members of the community for his aiding role in a kidnapping, he delivered himself to the county jail in fear for his life.

So, while it was always shocking to learn of a Black man aiding someone like Shoe, it was not uncommon.

But for such a man to be Bea's son was heartbreaking.

And Bea appeared as if her heart had broken. "He and Shoe were hiding in the house the night the Wesleyites saved the Daniel from that other group of kidnappers. After the Wesleyites delivered the Daniel to Mr. Wood they rode on to Detroit but stopped by my place for food. They did it often, but I knew Shoe and Lem were in the house so I hustled the old man and his sons out as quickly as possible, but not before Wesley told the tale of saving the Black Daniel."

"So that's why he began searching everyone's homes."

"Yes and later that night, you sent for me, Hester."

"Did they know where you were going?"

"No. They knew how much the bounty was on the

Daniel's head so as soon as the Wesleyites left, they hightailed out to the road hoping to find the Daniel."

"Did they know Galen was here in Whittaker?"

"No, Wesley said he thought the Daniel would be taken to a safe place somewhere in the county, but he didn't know exactly where. His only concern was that the Daniel was safe."

Galen interrupted, "But what about the slavecatchers who tried to kill me? How did they know I was on my way to Detroit?"

"Once again, it was my doing. And Branton's, rest his soul."

Hester's confusion claimed her face. "Branton?"

"Yes. Did you know Branton was a member of the Order?"

Hester's eyes widened. "No." She'd no idea he was a member of the Secret Society of Conductors in Detroit.

"Well he was, and as a member, he knew about the Daniel's coming. He told me about the visit at my kitchen table one morning. Unfortunately, Lem was there also. At the time I was still under the impression that he was the runaway he'd claimed to be. Branton and I saw no harm in talking about the Daniel with him in the room, but I know now that our carelessness nearly cost your life, Galen."

"And Lem gave the information to Shoe?"

"Yes, Shoe was down in Monroe with Porter Greer. It was Greer who alerted the other kidnappers, but because Branton hadn't known the exact date of the Daniel's arrival, they'd been patrolling the Ohio border every night for two weeks. The ones who eventually found him were simply lucky that night."

Hester didn't know what to say to the tragic tale.

"So," Raymond asked. "Where is your son now?"

"More than likely down in Monroe, waiting for me to throw them another sacrificial lamb."

Bea saw the questions in Hester's eyes. "I gave them the Blackburns, the Creightons, and everyone else."

"Why?"

"Initially to learn the fate of my children. That was the original bargain."

"You traded the freedom of your neighbors for information on your children?" Raymond asked angrily.

Bea's voice was cold. "Yes, and until you have children of your own, do not be so quick to judge me. I may be a stupid old woman, but leaving my children behind choked my heart everyday for thirty years. I needed to know what had happened to them. Lem told me they were alive but wouldn't say where until I aided him."

Her voice softened. "So, I did."

"But you helped free Fanny Blackburn."

"Yes, I did. I told them afterwards you would've been suspicious if I hadn't. Shoe was furious that you deluded him. He wanted to know everything about you after that."

"He has my papers, Bea. Did you tell him about the wardrobe?"

"Heavens, no, Hester! Is that why the house was ravaged so, because they were looking for your free papers?"

"We aren't certain, but the papers are gone."

"Shoe pressed and pressed for information on you, but I refused to give it. They threatened to expose me to the community as a traitor, but by then I knew my children were both dead and I didn't care what they did to me. I loved your aunt like a sister. I'd've killed myself before sacrificing *you*."

Hester pulled Bea into her arms and both women cried.

"I'm so, so sorry," Bea whispered. "So sorry."

Back at the Folly, later that evening, Raymond, Galen, and Andre were huddled in Galen's study, discussing Bea's story and Shoe's part in it.

Raymond asked, "So what do you propose we do, *mon frere?*"

"If necessary, find Shoe and shoot him down like the jackal he is," Galen pronounced coldly. "I will not let this hang over my wife's head."

"I agree," Raymond said. "Shall I contact my brothers?"

"Yes. How long do you think it will take them to arrive?"

"Less than a week's time. They were going on to Toronto after they helped us bring back the Amherstburg child. It shouldn't be very hard to get word to them."

"Then go ahead. Their presence will even the odds."

Tired, Galen went up to bed a while later. He thought Hester would be asleep, but she was standing out on the veranda in her nightgown gazing out over the dark river below. At the sound of his footsteps she turned and gave him a small smile. "Are you men finished with your plans to save me from Shoe?"

"I will not let anything happen to you, *petite,* I promise."

"I know Galen, but sometimes promises made by people like you and me are nearly impossible to keep."

She went to him and he wrapped her into his arms. "What you say is true, but not in this case. Are you prepared to leave here should it become necessary for us to run?"

She hadn't thought about having to leave the country before, but she was prepared to join him wherever the future led. "Yes."

He kissed her brow. "Good, because the only way to stop Shoe may be to kill him."

Hester went still. She looked up into the eyes of the man she'd come to love as much as life, then placed her head against his chest. He held her tight. "I hope it won't come to that," she said quietly.

"I hope it won't either," he told her. "But it may."

Chapter 21

I t took nearly a week to remove all the debris from the interior of the Wyatt home, and Hester was there each day, overseeing the task. Racine joined the cleaning team after returning to Whittaker about midweek, bringing with her the lovely Ginette, who took one look at all the physical labor involved and opted to help Maxi with the meals for the crew instead. Hester did not fault her, although Gail had a few choice things to say, until reminded that Ginette came from a world of privilege and servants, she knew absolutely nothing about cleaning. More than likely she would just have been in the way.

As the days of August gave over to the cooler days of September someone began waging a shadowy guerilla campaign against Greer and Shoe's forces down in Monroe. It began with Greer's stables and livery burning to the ground. When Hester questioned Galen about it, he shrugged. Raymond, on the other hand, simply smiled a knowing smile and winked when asked about the fire. A few days after the fire, all of the dogs belonging to Shoe and Greer were fed hushpuppies by an unknown source, and as a consequence would never again track another fugitive. A well-known Road conductor, Deacon Theron Trowbridge of the Congregational Church of Denmark, Iowa, invented the

hushpuppies. The deacon would heavily spice corn
dodgers with strychnine and then feed them to the
bloodhounds of slave catchers who tracked fugitives to
his station. He was known to say that the only good
bloodhound was a dead one.

Gail made arrangements for Bea to go the Grove for a
respite from the intrigue and to place her out of harm's
way. Gail's brother Absalom, and his friend Adam
Crowley would keep her safe or die in the effort. All in
all it gave everyone one less thing to worry about.

Bea's son Lem also became one less worry. His dead
body was found floating in the Detroit River. His hands
were bound and the words traitor had been burned into
his chest with a brand. Some said the Order had taken
the matter into their own hands, but there was no proof.
The authorities were investigating, but held little hope of
finding those responsible because undoubtedly no one in
the community would aid them.

Galen and Hester enjoyed a guarded peace. They
made mud pies down at the river, made love, and spent
the days of September learning more about the special
magic they found in one another. By the end of the
month, the apples in her father's wild orchards were fat
and ripe and ready to be picked.

Hester was ripening in her own way. She was fairly
certain she was carrying Galen's child, but to be certain
she decided to hold off telling him for another few
weeks.

During the last week of September, Raymond's brothers arrived, much to everyone's delight. Hester found all
five as handsome and debonair as their older sibling.
Ginette was in heaven over the presence of her true love
Gerrold, but her enthusiasm was slightly dampened
when she realized Maxi and Racine planned on being
very strict chaperones.

Since the finding of Shoe's note, Hester had been
expressly forbidden by everyone to go anywhere unac-
companied. She did not quibble. She had no desire to be

kidnapped and taken south. As a consequence, someone was always with her, and today it was Gerrold as she worked cleaning up the last of the mess in Wyatt house.

When Foster and Jenine drove up to the house, Gerrold and Hester turned to each other with a concerned curiosity. Foster jumped down and ran up the walk yelling her name. Hester hurried out to meet him.

"Hester! Shoe has arrested your husband! Jenine just passed Sheriff Lawson on the road and he begs that you come to town, right now!"

Hester's insides went cold as ice.

She was already running to the wagon when Gerrold shouted, "I'll go back to the Folly and see what I can learn. I'll meet you in town!"

Hester could think of nothing but Galen. She hadn't even told him about the child. She prayed for him as she quickly followed Foster.

"Come on!" Jenine shouted. "Hurry!"

Hester scampered into the bed and Foster grabbed up the reins and slapped them hard.

They'd only gone a short distance when Jenine pulled a pistol from her handbag.

Hester said, "Good thinking, Jenine, we may need a weapon."

When Jenine began to laugh, Hester asked, "What's so funny?"

"The two of you," she replied smiling. "If you could see how deadly serious you both look."

Foster stared back in confusion, but kept the horses on pace.

Hester froze as a cool-eyed Jenine trained the weapon on her and called out, "Stop the wagon."

Foster stared in surprise at the gun and drew the horses to a stop.

The determination and firmness of Jenine's posture set Hester's heart to beating fast.

Foster barked, "Jenine, what are you doing?"

"Find a rope and tie her hands, Foster."

He stared a moment. "Have you lost your mind?!"

"Dammit, get a rope!"

"I demand an explanation."

Jenine snapped, "Find a rope or I'll shoot her right now!"

Foster looked about to argue further, but Hester told him quietly, "Do as she says, Foster."

Foster found a length of rope in the wagon bed and tied it around her wrists.

Jenine warned, "Tightly. I'd hate to have to shoot her in the back if she tries to run."

Foster appeared so very confused Hester's heart went out to him in spite of the recent problems that had undermined their friendship.

He asked, "What is this about, Jenine?"

"Get behind the reins and drive on."

Foster tried again for an explanation. "Jenine—"

"Drive," she told him coldly.

He drew in an impatient breath and did as he was told.

As they got under way, Hester said to Jenine, "Galen isn't really in danger, is he? You lied to Foster. You haven't seen Sheriff Lawson."

"No, I haven't, but I needed Foster to drive while I held the gun."

The answer gave Hester heart. As long as Galen was safe she felt up to any challenge Jenine might present.

Jenine looked around at the landscape as if judging her location, then told Foster, "Take the next fork, and head south."

"Where are we going?"

"You'll know soon enough."

Hester knew that Galen would move the sun itself to find her. She simply had to avoid being shot until then.

At the fork, Foster headed south. The road was rarely used, and because of the rain last night, it was a muddy mess. The going was slow, but Jenine didn't seem to mind. She appeared deadly confident.

After about a two-mile drive, Jenine gave the order to

stop. "Now get down slowly, Hester, and don't think I won't shoot."

Hester thought no such thing. She got down from the buggy, slowly, just as instructed. Hester could just about imagine the fear that Galen must be experiencing, and it weighed heavily on her heart. Her disappearance had to be causing him great pain. The knowledge made her more than a bit angry. However she swallowed it as Jenine motioned her and Foster to walk forward.

They took a skinny little path through the high brush and trees. After a few hundred feet, she stopped them in a small clearing that sheltered an abandoned and derelict shack. She motioned Hester to a seat on a nearby tree stump. "Now we wait," she declared.

"For what?" Foster demanded.

"An old friend of mine. Ezra Shoe."

Hester stiffened and glanced over into Foster's astonished eyes.

Foster stared at Jenine as if he'd never lain eyes on her before. In all reality he had not. As Galen had predicted, Jenine had finally shown Foster her true colors. He was devastated. "Why are you doing this?" he asked.

"Money. Shoe promised me enough to make my way west."

"Money?! You would let her be sold south for money?"

"Yes," she said without guilt.

"But she is of your own race."

Jenine scoffed, "The race. What has being in the race ever done for me? Being born Black is a curse, a stone around my neck, but the more money I have, the less the stone will weigh."

Hester interrupted, "Jenine, my husband is a very wealthy man, if it is only money you seek, he will beggar himself for my return."

"If it were that simple, I'd consider it but all the money in the world won't bring Lem back."

"You're doing this for revenge? Lem was a traitor."

"Yes, he was. But he was also my lover."

Hester watched Foster's face pale and his shoulders slump. For a moment, his eyes held a bleakness that tore at Hester's heart.

He asked, "So you never loved me?"

She gave him a mocking, sad smile. "You were simply the Gallahad I needed."

"What were you doing in England?"

"A very wealthy man took me there. I was his mistress. He was killed in a brawl and I was left penniless. When you came across me in the hold, I was on my way home because my money had run out."

"Yet you pretended to love me. Why?"

"Because I knew you'd get me to Michigan. My other candidate was that student from Cleveland we met aboard ship. Residing in Ohio would have been amenable because of its proximity to this state. I picked you because you said you were from Whittaker. I knew Lem was here because he'd written me after finding his mother."

Hester said pointedly, "The mother whose heart he broke."

"Just as she broke his when she left him behind and never returned. He hated her, which is why he harbored no guilt in using her the way he did."

"Where is your family?" Foster asked.

"I had no other family. I was sold as a babe and never knew of any kin."

Hester realized she and Jenine had similar beginnings, and mused over how her own life changed for the better after being found and spirited north. Where would Hester be had there not been a Katherine Wyatt? Would she be duping and kidnapping her neighbors? She doubted it, but knew there was no guarantee. "Where are my papers, Jenine?"

"Shoe has them. He's been wanting to get his hands on you for some time."

"Were you there when they savaged my house?"

"No, I was at home at the time. I heard the damage was rather extensive though," she said with a nasty little smile. Then she added, "Ezra figured you had them in the house somewhere. All you fugitives think alike it seems. The false backs of highboys and wardrobes are a fairly common hiding spot."

Hester was relieved to know no one had betrayed her, but she made a point to inform folks of the need to be more imaginative when hiding their papers once this ordeal ended. And it would end because she knew Galen would find her. She asked Jenine, "Do you have any idea what my husband and his friends have in store for you once they learn of your involvement with Shoe?"

Jenine smiled coolly. "Once Ezra pays me my share, that fancy mulatto of yours will never find me."

Hester replied easily, "For your sake I hope not."

Foster who seemed to have just recomposed himself after hearing Jenine's startling tale, told Jenine softly, "I can't let you do this, Jenine."

"I'm terrified. Now, get over to that stump and sit. We shouldn't have too long to wait."

Although Hester presented a brave front she viewed the impending appearance of Shoe with increasing unease. If, against all odds, he succeeded in taking her south, both she and her unborn child would become slaves, subject to the whims and desires of whomever owned them. Her child could be sold away from her, as it had happened to her and her mother. She shook off the grim scenario because of her faith in her husband.

Foster looked over at Hester and said sadly, "I've been a fool."

Hester shook her head. "No. She played on your most vulnerable possession, your heart."

He echoed himself, "A silly, blind fool." He then asked Hester bluntly, "She didn't find you and Vachon in the school, did she?"

Hester shook her head no.

He turned a cold gaze on Jenine. "Was it the other way around? Was it you in the school that day?"

Jenine said quite simply, "Yes."

He face twisted into a snarl. "With whom?"

"Lem."

"And you called Hester a whore," he responded through gritted teeth. "You let me believe you were too shy to share my bed. Yet you were cuckolding me for all the world to see?!"

He made a mad dash at her and she very calmly shot him. Foster fell to the ground rolling in pain and holding his injured arm.

Hester ran to his side. With her hands bound she could do nothing more than bend over him to see how he fared. He slowly turned over and struggled up to a sitting position so he could brace his back against a tree. He was breathing harshly. Blood flowed from between the fingers clamped to his wounded shoulder. The gunshot was not fatal, but he desperately needed a doctor.

Hester gave Jenine a malevolent look.

Jenine replied, "Why do men believe an armed woman will not shoot?"

Hester snapped, "I think he was motivated by his emotions, Jenine, not logic."

Jenine then spoke to the man she'd called her husband. "Foster, I can hit a fly on a barn at one hundred paces. If I had wanted to kill you I would have. Don't test me again."

Hester felt useless kneeling beside Foster. He was having trouble stuffing his handkerchief into the shoulder of his coat to slow the bleeding. He managed however, and when he finished he leaned back to catch his breath.

Shoe and his men rode into the clearing less than an hour later.

When he saw Hester poised upon the tree stump, his ugly face widened into a smile. He dismounted, but the other six men did not. "You did a good job, Jenine."

Jenine beamed. "Do you have the money?"

"Of course. You and I had an agreement."

Shoe ignored Foster and came over to stand before Hester. "Well, gal. We meet again. You ready to resume your natural place in life?"

"There is nothing natural about slavery, Shoe."

He chuckled. "Still feisty even though the jig is up. I like that."

He reached out to touch Hester's cheek, but she drew away.

Shoe called out, "I don't think she likes me boys."

His men laughed. One of them remarked, "She's going to like you soon enough, Ezra."

Another added, "She's going to like us all soon enough."

The remark brought on more laughter. Hester steeled herself against their feral eyes.

Shoe said, "Yes she will."

He then brought out some documents from his soiled coat. "These are your free papers and this here is a warrant for your arrest. Remember when I said I had someone looking into your past? Well, he's a lawyer friend, and he was able to trace you back to Charleston. He couldn't find the speculator who took you out of Carolina, but he did find everyone else who helped, and you know what, they were all property-thieving abolitionists. None claimed any involvement of course, except one old woman. She remembered you as a gal her husband and daughter took on a train to Philadelphia. She used to be a friend of your kind, but she ain't anymore. Her husband had the bad taste to fall in love with one of you and he left his wife and children. She was real eager to help."

"You've no way to verify if that girl was me or not."

"There is if you've got purple hands."

Hester fought down the bile rising in her throat while Shoe cut the rope tying her hands.

"Take off the gloves."

Hester didn't move.

"Take 'em off, or one of the boys will be happy to do it for you."

Hester slowly peeled off her gloves. When her hands were revealed, Shoe grinned. "Well, well, well. Look at that boys. Ever seen hands like them?"

"Guess she got to come with us," one said.

"Guess she does," Shoe echoed.

Jenine interrupted. "My payment, Shoe?"

"Ah, yes. Here you are," he said as he handed her some bills.

Jenine stared in surprise. "This is only ten dollars. Where is the rest?"

"There is no rest."

"You promised me enough to buy my way west. You gave me your word."

"I don't give my word to someone like you. What do you think I am, an abolitionist? Lem was my kin, that's the only reason you get anything."

"Damn you, you promised!"

Hester enjoyed a moment of satisfaction seeing Jenine's angry face.

Shoe pushed Hester in the direction of one of the riderless horses being trailed behind the main pack. "Mount up!"

Jenine snarled, "You're not going to get away with this."

The mounted Shoe looked down upon the irate Jenine and said, "If I were you, I'd take that money and buy a ticket for a place far away. Once word gets out how you helped me, your life won't be worth beans.

"Head out!"

The pack rode away, leaving behind the injured Foster and a very angry Jenine.

It took the kidnappers the balance of the day to make Monroe. They'd been pushing the horses hard, and so stopped to rest a bit along the banks of the Raisin River. One of the men went off into the trees to relieve himself. He was gone for so long, Shoe sent one of the others in after him. When he also failed to return, Shoe grabbed up his rifle with one hand, Hester's arm with the other, and peered around. He ordered two more men to go into the brush and look for their companions but when they returned they could only shrug in confusion. The men had vanished and could not be found. The silence was ominous; there was no wind, and no birdsongs. The air held an eerie quality that made the hair stand up on the back of the neck.

"What the hell happened to them?" Shoe barked.

"Don't know, Ezra. Maybe we should leave this place."

Shoe didn't look nearly as confident as he had previously. Before he could give any orders though, Galen, mounted on his stallion, appeared on the banks above, flanked by six black-dressed riders whose faces were covered by black hoods. At the beautiful sight, Hester's legs weakened with relief.

"Hello boys," Galen said. "Nice day for a ride."

Shoe's eyes widened in shock and fear. Because he was down two men, he was outnumbered four to six. He tried bravado first. "I got a legitimate warrant for her, Vachon. You're interfering in government business."

Galen smiled the smile of an assassin. "And you are interfering in my life. That is my wife you know." Galen looked down at Hester and inclined his head slightly. "Don't worry, *petite*. We'll be on the way soon."

He turned his eyes back on the kidnappers. He stuck out his hand and one of the riders at his side placed a small weighted velvet pouch into his palm. "Have you boys been paid?"

Shoe's men glanced at each other quizzically.

Galen explained, "I'm asking because I don't believe any of you want to be a part of this any longer. Fifty dollars in gold to each man who'll ride away."

Hester saw Shoe's face widen. "Don't listen to him, he ain't got that much coin."

"No?"

Galen turned the pouch upside down and a shower of gold coins rained down on the ground. "My offer won't hold for long."

The men seemed to hesitate a moment. They looked at each other, then at the gold lying on the ground, and then to Shoe.

Galen asked, "What's Shoe paying you, two, three dollars a piece? That will buy you a few drinks, a few cheap whores, but you boys are smarter than that. Think how much whiskey and women you could get if you had fifty dollars gold in your pocket."

Shoe snapped, "Don't listen to him!"

Hester could almost see the rusty wheels turning in their heads as they pondered Galen's words.

Finally, one of Shoe's men said, "Hell, y'all know we ain't never going to see that much gold at one time hauling ass, so I'm taking it."

The other mumbled agreement. They started up the bank.

"Stop dammit!" Shoe screamed, but they paid him no mind. They scrambled over the gold like dogs over a fugitive. Some came out of the fray with more than their share, but all were far richer when it ended than they had been when it began.

Shoe was furious, threatening to kill them all, but they were armed also, and outnumbered him. They pocketed their bounty and mounted up.

Up on the bank, Galen smiled down benevolently. "There's only one condition."

Shoe's men looked his way.

"Never, ever show your faces in this state again. If you do you will be shot on sight."

The men's eyes widened.

"Agreed?" Galen asked.

They nodded quickly.

"Have a good trip home, boys."

In departure, the men gave the red-faced Shoe a chorus of "See you Ezra," and galloped on down the riverbank. None looked back.

Galen smiled. "Well now. I guess they weren't as bent on slavecatching as you thought, eh, Ezra? Release my wife," he demanded coldly.

Shoe quickly put his gun to Hester's head. "The gal is leaving with me."

Hester heard Raymond laugh from behind his hood. "We should shoot him simply for being stupid."

"Yes we should," Galen said but there was no smile on his face. "Release her Shoe. I've grown weary of this now."

"No! I—"

The first shot hit his shoulder, the second hit the kneecap. The force spun him away from Hester. He lay on the ground screaming from the pain.

Hester did not hesitate. She ran up the bank to her husband and was snatched up into his arms. He pulled her close and held tight. "Oh God, *petite*. I was so worried."

Hester was crying and kissing him. She was overcome by her joy, and thanked heaven her prayers had been answered. "I knew you would come for me. I knew."

"I was scared to death."

The sound of Raymond clearing his throat interrupted the tearful reunion. "If you two don't mind, we still have some offal to dispose of."

Galen grinned. Now that he had his Indigo back in his arms, he didn't care what happened to Shoe. "Do whatever you like with him. La Indigo and I are heading home."

Raymond asked. "May I kill him?"

"No, *mon frere*. I'm certain you can come up with something far more creative than that."

So Galen and Hester left Raymond and his brothers to ponder their capacity for creativity.

Chapter 22

"So, what did you decide to do with our friend, Ezra?" Galen and Hester asked Raymond at the breakfast table the next morning. Hester's return last night had filled the household with joy. Raymond and his brothers celebrated into the wee hours of the morning, long after she and Galen had gone to bed.

"By now, Shoe's on his way south just as he would have liked."

"Except for the bound and gagged aspects of the journey," Gerrold added.

Hester glanced at Ginette, who appeared as confused as she.

Gail Grayson asked, "What do you mean?"

"We sent him to a friend of ours in Tripoli."

Galen laughed. "You had him shanghaied?"

Raymond nodded. "Our Tripoli friend is a prince, and is always in need of servants to muck out his barns. He's a horseman, you see. I figure by the time Shoe is done with the stables he will be an old man."

"But what if he tries to escape?"

Galen said, "The prince will have him killed. They frown very heavily on escaped slaves there."

Hester's eyes widened. "You sent Shoe to slavery?"

Raymond nodded without apology. "I thought it would be a nice tribute to all those he sent south. Maybe now he will recognize the value of freedom and understand how truly precious it is."

"So what about Jenine and Foster?"

Galen took over the conversation. "We found Foster first. Jenine had left him to his fate. He told us what had happened. After he assured us he was not too injured to ride, we put him on a spare horse and headed out after you. We ran across Jenine a short while later. The wagon had become mired in the muddy road. She was not pleased to see me. We freed the wagon, put her and Foster in it, and sent one of the brothers back to Whittaker with them. Foster will undoubtedly recover, but Jenine's fate lies with the men of the Order."

Hester stood out on the wrought iron veranda of the bedroom and watched the sun fade from the sky. She pulled her cloak closer around her shoulders to shield herself against the chill of the rising wind. It was now mid-October, nearly one year to the day since the night Mr. Wood brought the injured Black Daniel into her home. The year had been an eventful one. Had someone told her then that in a year's time she would be deeply in love and married to the cynical, rude man hidden in her cellar, she'd have asked if they been dipping in the applejack. But she had married him, and she was deeply in love. She was also carrying his child. She still hadn't told him, but she would tonight, now that the world seemed to have regained its equilibrium.

Hester heard him enter the room. She smiled as their eyes met, but the smile faded when she saw Galen's anxious face. She went to him asking, "What has happened?"

"John Brown has attacked the federal arsenal at Harper's Ferry, Virginia. The telegraph office in town is filled with people awaiting the news of the outcome."

"Has anyone been killed?"

"It is uncertain. The first wire indicated one man, a baggage master, has been killed, but there's been no further word."

Hester sank down into a chair. "Good heavens, what will this mean?"

"No one knows. There will be repercussions with either outcome. God, I admire that old man, but I wished he'd waited. Douglass tried to dissuade him when they met secretly this past August in the old quarry near Chambersburg, Pennsylvania. Douglass thought the place was a perfect steel trap. The heights around the arsenal make it indefensible against a counterattack. He told Brown he'd never get out alive, and I fear Douglass will be right."

Over the next few days more became known. Brown entered Harper's Ferry, on Sunday night, October 16, 1859. With him were twenty-one men of mixed races.

Three of Brown's men were left behind at the base of operations at the Kennedy farm in Maryland. Of the eighteen others in the band, five were Black: escaped slaves Shields Green and Dangerfield Newby; two Black men from Oberlin, Ohio, Lewis S. Leary and his nephew, John A. Copeland Jr.; and Osborne Perry Anderson. Of the remaining Whites, three were Brown's sons.

The armory was defended by a lone watchman and was quickly overrun. Brown had hoped the slaves in the area would mass and join him in this fight for their freedom, but no advance word had been sent to alert them of his plans. Nevertheless, he sent men out into the countryside to spread the word and to garner hostages. The patrol returned with only a few recruits and a few hostages, one of which was the great-grandnephew of George Washington. The baggage master alluded to in the first wire was a free Black named Heywood Shepherd. He was killed by some of Brown's men positioned on the bridge. He was supposedly shot when he walked out onto the trestle searching for the night watchman.

Some said Brown knew he couldn't win, that he'd given up before the raid began due to his perceived lack of support from men like Douglass and others who'd declined to join him. Others pointed out that it was simply a matter of the Old Man lacking the forces and the military strategy necessary to successfully carry out such a daring strike. Whatever the reason, the ironic death of Shepherd, a free Black man, seemed to symbolize the fiasco that followed.

After Shepherd's death, Brown stopped the eastern-bound midnight train and kept it sitting on the tracks for hours, then, and no one knows why, he let it proceed. The train's occupants quite naturally alerted the authorities.

When the morning of Monday, October 17, 1859 dawned, the residents of Harper's Ferry, very aware by now of Brown's presence, began a sniping campaign aimed at Brown's men. Marching quickly to the town's aid were the combined forces of the Virginia and Maryland militias. By afternoon, two of Brown's sons and six others of the band were killed, along with three townspeople. Seven of Brown's men deserted him and escaped. Two were later recaptured.

Taking his surviving men and his remaining hostages, Brown sought cover within the thick walls of the fire engine house. That night the U.S. Marines arrived, commanded by Colonel Robert E. Lee and Lieutenant Jeb Stuart. When the militias decided they didn't want to be the first ones in, Lee sent in the marines.

In all, the raid on Harper's Ferry lasted less than thirty-six hours. Brown lost ten men, including Newby and Leary. Copeland and Shields Green were amongst the seven captured. Osborne Perry Anderson and five others escaped.

Hester was one of the many Black women who wrote to Brown after his capture. Her letter joined those sent by the famous poet and lecturer, Francis Ellen Watkins, and those sent to Brown's wife. The race also extended a hand to Mrs. Leary, the widow of Lewis S. Leary, and her child. The other Black man who gave his life at the Ferry, escaped slave Dangerfield Newby, left behind a wife and seven children, all in bondage.

The verdict from the jury was swift. Virginia mobs were calling for Brown's blood. Their calls were answered. Brown was convicted of treason, murder, and of inciting insurrection on November 2, 1859. He was sentenced to hang one month later.

Only the happiness instilled by her pregnancy helped Hester through the sorrow following Brown's incarceration in Charleston. Galen and Raymond journeyed to Virginia for the trial, leaving Hester in the care of Maxi and Gail. Racine and Ginette had returned to Louisiana shortly after Brown's capture, but both pledged to come back in the spring to help spoil the baby. By Bea's calculations the babe would be born sometime in late June.

Galen returned the last week of November. Raymond went on to Amherstburg to check on his paramour. Galen and Hester were so glad to see one another the lovemaking began on the carriage ride from the train station. By the time they reached the Folly, Hester was dewy and pulsing, and Galen couldn't ever remember wanting one woman so very, very much. He carried her into the house and up the stairs. He'd just reached the top when Maxi appeared.

Galen said firmly, "For the next three days no one is to disturb us unless the house is afire or war is declared."

Maxi smiled at the happiness shining in Hester's eyes. "Yes, your highness."

Galen added, moving on toward his wing, "And that includes Raymond!"

Inside the room, Galen kicked the door closed with his booted foot, then set his wife gently atop the bed. He found he wanted to just look at her a moment, savor the beauty of her face, the curve of her smile, the sparkle in her gaze. He still found it hard to believe that they were headed for a long life in each other's arms. That she loved him made his heart sing songs it had never sung and made him awaken each day glad to have her by his side.

"Whatever is the matter?"

"Just enjoying the sight of you. I missed you truly."

"Then come here and show me just how much."

He grinned as his eyebrow raised. "Is this my mistress speaking or my wife?"

"Both," she purred.

Galen removed her saucy little felt hat and set it aside. "I'm not certain I can satisfy both of you, you're both insatiable." He leaned down and touched his lips to her mouth. "But I will dearly try . . ."

And his trying set Hester afire. He spent an inordinate amount of time removing her dress, then the silken undergarments beneath. He lingered over the removal of her stockings and garters, making her senses shimmer from the intensity of his touch. With kisses and caresses he showed her just how much he'd missed her and she shamelessly showed him the same.

They spent the next three days immersed in one another. He fed her grapes, shared her bath, and taught her to juggle. They teasingly argued over names for their firstborn and settled the issue with a rousing pillow fight. They played checkers, donned formal finery, and danced to music no one else could hear. They opened the door only to receive Maxi's magnificently prepared meals and to call for fresh water for the tub.

The days were glorious, but on the third day, Raymond knocked loudly.

"Go away!" Galen called from the bed. "I'm staying in here forever."

Raymond laughed. "The hell you are! I'm not letting the business go to rot just so you can continue to play Romeo. There's work to do Galeno. Do you want my future nephew to be born in the poor house?!"

"It's going to be a niece, Raymond!" Hester shouted at the door.

"No it isn't!" came his reply. "Galeno, you have until noon!"

They took the resulting silence to mean he'd gone.

Galen sighed and looked over at his nude wife sitting cross-legged beside him on the bed. "He's right you know. There is work to be done."

"I know, but I wish we could stay in here forever."

He leaned up and kissed her on the lips. "Noon is three hours away. How about we make the best of it?"

He waggled his eyebrows meaningfully.

Hester smiled. "And you call me insatiable."

On December 2, 1859, John Brown went to the gallows with quiet dignity and was hanged. Some in the South celebrated. Black abolitionists called the day Martyr Day. In northern cities all over America, the multiraced opponents of slavery paused to mourn his death. Black businesses were closed. Church bells were rung. Members of the race fasted, and wore black armbands to the many services and rallies held in his honor. Hester and Galen joined Detroit's Black citizens for the memorial held at Second Baptist Church. The Detroiters passed a resolution declaring John Brown "our temporal leader whose name will never die."

In New York, people met at Shiloh Church. In Philadelphia, public prayer meetings were held at both Shiloh and Union Baptist. In Cleveland, two thousand people of both races crammed into Melodeon Hall to hear the speeches given by judges, members of the Ohio legislature, and the presiding officer, Charles H. Langston. Outside the hall were another thousand people unable to get in.

The editor of the Lawrence, Kansas *Republican* declared in the day's edition, "the death of no man in America has ever produced so profound a sensation."

The pall of Brown's death lifted somewhat as the Christmas season approached. A week before the holiday, Gail left the Folly to go and spend the season with her family in Niles. After seeing her off, Hester and Maxi were in the kitchen making bread when Galen and Raymond came in. Galen sidled over to filch one of the small cakes Maxi had made earlier in the day for the children's party. When he reached, Maxi slapped her spoon across his knuckles.

He yelled, "Ow! That hurt. You're a vicious old crone, do you know that?"

Maxi cut him a look.

He quickly added, "Beautiful, though, very beautiful."

She couldn't resist him, no woman could. "You have the tongue of the devil, do you know that?"

Galen bowed, "One of my more stellar traits, wouldn't you say, wife?"

Hester turned and replied drolly, "And add to your already terribly inflated opinion of your charms? Certainly not."

Raymond roared.

Galen feigned a wounded look.

Maxi patted Hester on the back approvingly. "You're learning, *chiquita.*"

Maxi then asked the two men she'd helped raise to men, "What can I do for you? Surely you aren't hungry, luncheon was less than an hour ago."

Galen explained, "I came to have my wife answer a question for me. Raymond is just tagging along getting pointers on how to woo a beautiful woman."

Raymond said something in French that made Hester think she was glad she couldn't understand the language.

Maxi ignored the men, then asked meaningfully, "Is this a question a crone can hear or should I leave the room?"

Hester was so embarrassed she turned and said, "Maxi?!"

"Don't Maxi me. I can hear the two of you clear on the other side of the house. Your poor babe will never learn to sleep all night with parents so loud."

Galen confessed with a straight face, "It's mostly Hester, Maxi."

Hester's eyes widened. "Galen?!"

"Well it's true."

Raymond roared with laughter.

Hester used her wooden spoon to smack Raymond across the knuckles just like Maxi had done Galen, and the roar stopped. He looked surprised and wounded. He turned his puzzled face to Galen and said, "She's almost as good with that thing as Maxi."

"Terrifying thought, isn't it?" Galen replied, his eyes glowing at his determined little wife.

Hester narrowed her eyes. "Dammit, ask your question."

Raymond asked in wonder, "She curses too?"

Galen grinned. "In her own fashion. 'Dammit' is about the extent of her salty vocabulary, though."

Maxi was shaking her head and smiling. "Hester, these two are like two playful tiger cubs, and like cubs they will play with you whether you wish it or not."

Hester certainly had to agree. "Are you two finished?"

Both men stared back innocently.

She took a calming breath, then smiled at her moustached husband. "Now what did you want to ask?"

"When is your birthday?"

Hester turned back to the biscuit dough. "I—don't know."

Galen peered at her stiff back and felt his heart twist. He felt absolutely stupid inside. A thick, uncomfortable silence hung in the air. Maxi and Raymond exited quietly, correctly sensing the couple needed to be alone.

Galen came to stand behind her and said sincerely, "My apology. I wasn't aware you didn't know."

She replied softly. "Don't fret. There's nothing to apologize for. After all, it is a question a husband would ask his wife."

He wrapped his arm around her waist and she savored the strength and safety his embrace always seemed to imbue. "My aunt was never sure about the actual date, so instead every year we celebrated the day I came north, the fourteenth day of October." She leaned back into her husband's strong chest and the memories of that first day rose vividly. "I thought Michigan was the coldest place on earth. When my aunt explained that it was only autumn, and that the winter would be much worse, I thought she was fooling. She wasn't though."

Galen chuckled, then kissed the top of her hair. "How about we celebrate your birthday on Christmas Day?"

She turned in his arms and smiled. "Why that particular day?"

"So that I may give you double the amount of presents."

She shook her head. "What else in the world is there left for you to buy?"

"It doesn't have to be something purchased."

"I know that, but do you?"

His provocative moustache lifted with his smile. "Touché, *petite.*"

He kissed her on the forehead. "Do you think Maxi and Raymond will stay away long enough for me to make love to you?"

Hester's eyes widened. Then she grinned and whispered. "In here?! No. Take your insatiable self off before you embarrass us both."

But in exception to her words he was already undoing the tiny buttons of her blouse. "I'll just take a tiny boon then."

Her camisole was lowered, then he proceeded to slowly tease and suckle her breasts until she purred.

"I'll have the rest of you later," came his hot promise.

He raised his head. Seeing her passion-lidded eyes, his brilliant gaze sparkled.

In moments he had her buttoned up and proper again. Grinning he touched his mouth to her lips, and departed.

Christmas day dawned with a blowing snowstorm. Luckily there was no need to go outdoors.

Galen had purchased so many presents for his wife and unborn child, Raymond cracked they'd have to put a new wing on the Folly just to store the haul. Hester received jewelry and gowns, bath salts and a new crystal flagon of vanilla; there were juggling balls and a beautifully carved crib that put a sheen of happy tears in

Hester's eyes. Galen opened his gifts and smiled over the crystal dragon Hester had purchased for him as well as the new globe she'd given him for his study. Raymond's presents to Hester were a new set of wooden spoons and a delicately carved music box.

The meal was glorious: there was goose and turkey and pies, winter vegetables, gumbo, and Maxi's special jambalaya. Hester could barely stand when the last of the dishes were taken away. Galen ushered her into the parlor where they sat cuddled together before the fire.

Hester sat there basking in his nearness and wondered about the future. "You know, next Christmas there will be one more at the table."

"Yep, I can hardly wait to see this new little Vachon."

He reached over and gently caressed the small roundness that was his still forming child.

Hester placed her hand atop his and felt their combined love flow into the new life she harbored. "Will you still love me when I'm fat?"

"I'd love you if you grew as large as the Sphinx."

Hester cuddled closer, happy with the reply.

"Are you ready for birthday cake?" he asked.

The thought of more food almost made her groan. "Galen, neither I nor your child can eat another bite."

"Just one bite. For me?"

She turned her face up and said, "For you, anything."

He hopped up. "Good. Now close your eyes."

"Galen—"

"Contrary woman. Close your eyes."

She giggled and obeyed.

"And don't cheat. Keep them closed."

"Okay."

There was silence a moment, then came the rustling of feet.

From behind her hands she asked, "Galen, what are you doing?"

"Be patient, *petite,*" Galen called.

Galen looked around the room to make certain everyone in attendance was in place.

"Okay, *petite*. Open your eyes."

The first thing Hester noted was the tall, beautiful, white-iced cake being carried her way. Atop it were lit Chinese sparklers. She grinned around at Maxi and Raymond, then paused to stare quizzically at the unfamiliar woman bearing the cake. Hester was certain she'd never seen the woman before yet she experienced a very strange sense of familiarity.

The woman drew nearer. Hester noticed that although she was smiling, there were tears in the woman's eyes. Hester stood, seeking to help in some way, but the woman set the cake down without a word.

Terribly confused, Hester stared over at Galen, who answered with a shrug.

The woman began to speak in a voice thick and soft with tears. "Christmas Day really is your birthday . . ."

Hester went stock still. She ran her eyes slowly over the aging but still lovely face, saw the dark skin, the black eyes, and her heart began to pound. The only person in the whole world who could claim to know that date for certain would be—

Luckily for Hester she was standing by the settee because when she fainted dead away, it kept her from hitting the floor.

When her eyes flickered open again, she was lying down while everyone in the room stood above her. She heard Raymond say, "You didn't say she would faint, *mon frere.*"

Galen replied, "How was I supposed to know?"

"Well, tell her not to do it again. Scared me to death."

"How do you think I felt?"

Maxi gave them both a look, then she gently eased Hester up. "Are you all right, *chiquita?*"

Hester stared into the eyes of her mother and realized that this was not a dream. "Are you really Frances Wyatt?"

Nodding gently, her eyes watery, she said, "It is Wyatt Donaldson now, but yes, I am your mother."

The tears ran down Frances's face. She wordlessly held

out her arms and Hester let herself be enfolded. For endless moments they rocked one another and cried over the separation, the pain, the joy.

When they were able to turn each other loose, Hester held onto her mother's hand and looked over at her husband. "Since you are truly the most extravagant man on this earth, I will assume you are responsible for this so very precious gift."

He bowed. "It was purely by chance that I met her, believe me. It was on the trip Raymond and I took to Charleston for the John Brown trial."

Frances took up the tale. "I run a boardinghouse and diner in Charleston. Your man and his friend over there came in one day during the trial and ordered a meal. They kept staring at me as if they knew me. I ignored them, but noticed it went on during the whole time they were there. They didn't say anything that day, but when they returned the next day, Galen approached me. He told me I looked just like his wife, Hester. I told him I once had a daughter named Hester but she'd been sold away as a baby."

Galen continued at that point. "Then I asked her her name. When she told me her name was Frances, I didn't dare even think she might be Hester's mother for fear it would not be the true Frances."

"When he asked my full name and I responded, he went so still I began to fear he'd suffered some type of fit."

Galen replied with a smile, "I thought I had. My heart fairly froze in my chest when she told me her name was Frances Wyatt Donaldson."

Hester asked, "So do you have to return to Charleston?"

Frances glanced over at Galen, then back. "I really don't know. Thanks to your extravagant husband I am no longer in bondage. For the first time my life is my own."

Hester could not contain her tears as she met her husband's misty eyes.

Frances explained. "The Master Donaldson and I had an agreement. If I could make enough profit to buy the building, I could also buy my freedom. Of course, he set the price near the moon, but evidently your man buys items from the moon quite regularly. He met Donaldson's price, threw in a bit more as a sweetener, and what could the master say? He certainly wasn't going to turn down all that gold just so he could keep a middle-aged woman like me in slavery. He agreed. I woke up that morning a slave and by luncheon I was free. My head is still swimming."

Hester said, "Galen does have that effect, especially when he is shopping."

Her mother smiled.

"Please Mother, say you will stay and live with us. We've more than enough room."

Galen said, "I've already extended the same invitation, *petite.*"

"Did you agree, Mother?"

"Hester, I can't just barge back into your life after all these many years. Suppose we find we don't like each other?"

Raymond pointed out helpfully, "I don't like Galeno but he's allowed to live here."

Hester dropped her head and shook it slowly. Maxi did the same.

Galen was grinning.

Hester said, "My baby will need a grandmother. You must stay."

Frances's eyes widened. "What baby?"

"Galen didn't tell you we have a baby coming?"

Frances stared over at Galen with narrowed eyes. "No, he did not."

Galen raised an eyebrow and replied, "Merry Christmas."

Frances smiled a smile very reminiscent of her daughter's and said, "He is a devil, that one."

Hester agreed, "Yes he is, but as Raymond said, we allow him to live here anyway."

After the laughter faded, Frances turned to Maxi and asked, "You would be amenable to my coming to live here?"

Maxi smiled. "I have already raised one generation of Vachons. I am getting old. If the young one is anything like his sire, I will welcome all the help I can get."

Everyone laughed.

So it was agreed. Frances would stay.

Hester lay in bed that night the happiest woman in the world. She had a husband who loved her, her mother had been found, and her baby inside her continued to grow and thrive. What else could a woman like herself want from life? The end of slavery would make the picture complete, but until it occurred she would be thankful for life's smaller joys. She looked over at her husband sleeping at her side. Through him all blessings flowed. Who else would be so extravagant as to give someone their mother for Christmas? Only Galen Vachon, the Black Daniel, the dragon—her love. She leaned over and kissed him softly. He stirred.

"Something the matter?" he asked sleepily.

"No," she whispered. "I just love you. Go back to sleep."

He gently pulled her in against his body and promptly did just that.

Content, Hester cuddled closer, then closed her eyes to sleep safely in her husband's loving arms.

Author's Note

The Vachons were first introduced in my second Avon historical novel, *Vivid*, but there Galen's character was named Caleb. In the process of writing *Indigo*, I felt the name Caleb no longer fit. The character needed a name with more élan. I came across the name Galeno while trying to help my first fan, Rochelle Hardy, with names for her soon-to-be-born son. When I read that it was Spanish for "the light one," and that Galen was the English derivation, I knew I'd hit it. So to all the readers of *Vivid*, my apologies. I hope the name change didn't throw you too much.

The two letters in the *Indigo* prologue are products of my own imagination, but the account of a free man selling himself into slavery for love is based upon fact.

> *I knowed a man name Wyatt, who was free. He wanted to marry a slave girl name Carrie, and he gave himself to Carrie's master, to marry her. He was crazy to do that. That love is an awful thing. I tell you. I don't think I would give my freedom away to marry anybody.*

This quote from a former slave can be found in the book, *Bullwhip Days*, published by Avon Books in 1988. *Bullwhip Days* is a nonfictional compilation of the remembrances of former slaves. The Wyatt reference is one of the most startling pieces of information I have come across in my research, and it left me both fascinated and disturbed. (Can you imagine selling yourself into slavery for love?!) I knew I could not write a story about Wyatt and his Carrie. Being a woman of color, I feel that the harsh and painful realities of slavery have no place in the feel-good arena of mainstream romance—because there was nothing feel-good about it!

But I asked myself what if this couple had a daughter, and what if she were somehow able to escape slavery? Out of these questions grew *Indigo*.

The abolitionist period of American history has always fascinated me, and thanks to such celebrated historians as Benjamin Quarles and Charles Blockson, I now have a truer sense of the crucial role played by Black abolitionists in the fight for freedom. If you would like more information, please look for the books I've cited below in your bookstore or at your local library. Remember, knowledge is power, but shared knowledge empowers us all.

Blockson, Charles L. "Escape from Slavery: The Underground Railroad," *National Geographic,* July 1984, pp. 3–39.

Blockson, Charles L. *Hippocrene Guide to the Underground Railroad,* New York: Hippocrene Books, 1994.

Blockson, Charles L. *The Underground Railroad: Dramatic First-Hand Accounts of Daring Escapes to Freedom,* New York: Berkley/Simon & Schuster, 1989.

Bennett, Lerone Jr. *Before the Mayflower: A History of Black America,* New York: Penguin Books/Johnson Publishing, 1987.

Boyd, Melba Joyce. *Discarded Legacy: Politics and Power in the Life of Frances E. W. Harper, 1825–1911,* Detroit: Wayne State University Press, 1994.

Litwak, Leon. *North of Slavery: The Negro in the Free States. 1790–1860,* Chicago: University of Chicago Press, 1961.

Lumpkin, Katherine DuPre. "The General Plan Was

Freedom: A Negro Secret Order on the Underground Railroad," *Phylon* (Spring 1967), Atlanta: Atlanta University, pp. 63–76.

McPherson, James M. *Battle Cry of Freedom: The Civil War Era,* New York: Oxford University Press, 1988.

Quarles, Benjamin. *Black Abolitionists,* New York: Oxford University Press, 1972.

Sterling, Dorothy A. *We Are Your Sisters: Black Women in the Nineteenth-Century,* New York: Doubleday, 1976.

Still, William. *The Underground Railroad,* Chicago: Johnson Publishing, 1970. (This book was originally published in 1871 by Mr. Still, one of the most famous conductors on the Road. Hundreds of fugitives passed through his Philadelphia station. His book chronicles their stories. Anyone who is seriously interested in a true account of the fugitive experience will find these narratives fascinating. Kudos to Johnson Publishing for keeping this very valuable resource in print.)

In parting, let me say thanks to all the many fans who've written to me—your blessings, prayers, and words of encouragement keep me strong. Peace.

Avon Romances—
the best in exceptional authors and unforgettable novels!

WICKED AT HEART **Danelle Harmon**
78004-6/ $5.50 US/ $7.50 Can

SOMEONE LIKE YOU **Susan Sawyer**
78478-5/ $5.50 US/ $7.50 Can

MIDNIGHT BANDIT **Marlene Suson**
78429-7/ $5.50 US/ $7.50 Can

PROUD WOLF'S WOMAN **Karen Kay**
77997-8/ $5.50 US/ $7.50 Can

THE HEART AND THE HOLLY **Nancy Richards-Akers**
78002-X/ $5.50 US/ $7.50 Can

ALICE AND THE GUNFIGHTER **Ann Carberry**
77882-3/ $5.50 US/ $7.50 Can

THE MACKENZIES: LUKE **Ana Leigh**
78098-4/ $5.50 US/ $7.50 Can

FOREVER BELOVED **Joan Van Nuys**
78118-2/ $5.50 US/ $7.50 Can

INSIDE PARADISE **Elizabeth Turner**
77372-4/ $5.50 US/ $7.50 Can

CAPTIVATED **Colleen Corbet**
78027-5/ $5.50 US/ $7.50 Can